Lone Rider

Lauren Bach

WARNER BOOKS

An AOL Time Warner Company

WARNER BOOKS EDITION

Cover design by Diane Luger
Cover photography by Franco Accornero

Warner Books, Inc.
1271 Avenue of the Americas
New York, NY 10020

Visit our Web site at
www.twbookmark.com.

For information on Time Warner Trade Publishing's online publishing program, visit www.ipublish.com.

 An AOL Time Warner Company

Printed in the United States of America

First Printing: November 2001

10 9 8 7 6 5 4 3 2 1

HE SMELLED OF THE NIGHT, A POWERFUL MALE SCENT.

A small moan started low in her throat as desire mingled with arousal. Dear God, she had never been kissed like this. With heat, with passion. With promise. And she had never imagined anything this pleasurable.

Or this forbidden.

What was she doing letting this man kiss her? She shoved her hands against his chest. It was like pushing granite.

He moved closer still, forcing his legs between hers before catching her hands and lacing her fingers between his. Lifting her arms, he pulled her hands around his neck and held them tight. Then he deepened the kiss, using the full length of his body to pin her in place.

The motorcycles came to a stop, encircling them in a dusty halo of blinding headlights and reverberating engines.

Dallas made a low noise in her ear, as if warning Tess to remain quiet, then pressed his lips to her temple. "Trust me," he whispered.

"A gritty and very real tale, LONE RIDER is a five-star read complete with a mouthwatering hero, sizzling passion, and spine-tingling suspense that's sure to have readers on the edge of their seats." —*Rendezvous*

"Chilling danger and menacing treachery form the intense underpinnings of this thrilling debut novel. Ms. Bach is an invigorating new talent who will unquestionably catch the attention of romantic suspense readers everywhere."

—*Romantic Times*

So many to thank, so many I love . . .

Family . . .
Nolen, my husband, my best friend,
Michael, my son, my joy,
Mom and Dad, for believing,
and my tribe:
Karen, Kevin, Kris, Kurt, Kaye, and Kyle . . . we rule!

Friends and Fellow Writers . . .
Lori Harris, the angel on my shoulder,
Rogenna Brewer, who knows everything and shares.
Ladies . . . words are inadequate.

Secret Keepers . . .
Susan Cannon and Candace Kirby
for being there . . . you rock!

Lone Rider

Chapter One

Careful to keep her low-slung convertible on her side of the road, Tess Marsh stared up at the starry night sky. Spread out endlessly before her, the ebony heavens twinkled, flaunting their diamond-encrusted landscape.

Diamonds. Yes! Hundreds of them, very small, less than one point, perhaps even a half point, but still a girl's best friend.

Drawing a deep breath, she envisioned a diamond brooch replicating the free-form pattern of star constellations. It would be an eye-catcher, brilliant, with first-quality diamonds, set in platinum, with minute amounts of delicate, angel-breath, filigree.

And she'd call the line of jewelry Sky Fire.

"That's it!" Now she couldn't wait to find a motel room and start sketching the designs dancing in her head.

This new line would be fabulous.

Maybe even fabulous enough to quiet once and for all the critics who wondered aloud whether her jewelry-design work received praise on its own merit or because she was the daughter of John Winston Marsh III.

Well, they hadn't seen anything yet.

She was determined to succeed and knew exactly where

she was heading. Besides, she'd just hooked her wagon to a star!

Forcing her concentration back to the road, she shivered from excitement as well as the cool night air. She glanced at the digital clock on her dashboard. Holy crow, it was almost two! Where had the time gone? Three hours had disappeared in a creative fugue.

She had undoubtedly missed her turn. Slowing, she started looking in earnest for a place to turn around and double back.

The attendant at the last gas station warned her this was a desolate stretch of highway—the reason she'd chosen it. She did her most creative thinking behind the wheel. In fact, the majority of her top-selling jewelry designs had been conceived driving at night.

Of course, that driving had usually been done within a few hours of Boston, which she knew like the inside of her own closet, not half the country away, on a deserted highway in northeast Montana. She pressed down on the accelerator.

But instead of picking up speed her car sputtered and jerked, coughing itself to death as it slowed. Alarmed, Tess steered onto the shoulder. The car was only a few months old and had never given her trouble. She eased the car out of gear before trying to start it again. The ignition whirred, but the engine didn't turn over.

Her eyes drifted across the dash to the gas gauge and its blinking caution light. The one that warned you were almost *out . . . of . . . gas*. She sighed. How long had *it* been blinking?

She drew her jacket closer. All of a sudden she felt cold. Even though it was the first week of July, this far north the lows could drop into the forties. Reaching behind the seat for her backpack, she dug out her cellular phone and turned it on, her hand stopping in midair. The phone's LED message read "no signal."

Leaning forward, she banged her head against the steering wheel. Moments ago she soared on a jet stream of optimism. Now she'd crashed and burned.

Tess climbed out of her car and slammed the door. Then she started swearing. Now what?

She stared dubiously east, in the direction she'd been headed. How far to the next town? Or even a farmhouse? She squinted. For that matter, did the road even go any farther than this?

She stuck out her arm, unable to see anything beyond her hand. Now she realized why the stars seemed bigger than life tonight. There was no moon, no ambient light. Just lots and lots of dark. The really *black* kind.

As far as she could see.

The cold closed in. She zipped her jacket and crammed her hands in her pockets. She stepped back toward the car, her foot kicking up loose gravel. The noise seemed to intensify in the stillness. Then it grew quiet.

Very, very, quiet.

She swallowed, senses alert.

A different noise sounded on the far side of the road. A stick-broken-underfoot type of noise. Apprehension pressed a hand to her lower back. If she were stranded on a deserted road, in the middle of the night in Massachusetts, she might have worried about muggers. But here in Montana—God's country—the first thought that came to mind: *wild animal.*

Tess scrambled for her car and jumped back inside. Twisting the key to ON, she jabbed the power buttons to close the windows and raise the convertible top. Thankfully, the car had a strong battery.

When the top was secure and the doors locked, she leaned forward and listened. No noise reached her from outside.

What had caused the noise? A grizzly? She eyed the convertible top, realizing how little protection it offered. The claws of a strong bear could easily rip through the canvas exposing her like a can of sardines. She winced, imagining herself on a cracker.

She scanned the car's interior. Anything that qualified as a weapon was locked in the trunk. She'd even abandoned her key-chain pepper spray once she left Boston, lulled by the West's pervasive sense of small-town security.

She squirmed, watching the windows fog as ten minutes stretched to twenty. Finally, her curiosity got the better of her. Rubbing the moisture from the glass, she peered out at the dark highway.

And started laughing.

Two gigantic elk, one with an impressive rack of antlers, the other without, drifted in and out of the darkness in the middle of the road. They stared at her car, their steamy breath looking like smoke as it left their large nostrils.

She studied the unmoving animals, trying to recall what she'd heard about elk. Something about forest fires driving them from their normal habitat in search of food. That wasn't much.

Were they an aggressive species? Did they eat meat? She watched the big one shake his head furiously. She gulped, keeping an eye on the wide swath his antlers cut.

To her horror, the animal stepped closer, neck extended, and started scraping at the asphalt with a front hoof. She suddenly remembered that *other* thing she'd heard about elk, gruesome stories about rutting and aggression. Surely, the elk wouldn't . . . It wasn't even that time of year, was it?

The second elk moved in. She sank lower in her seat, spooked.

Their deliberate disregard eroded her relief—and dissolved what little bravery she'd mustered. So much for taking care of herself, like she promised her mother. Madeline would pass out if she knew of Tess's present predicament. But at least her mother would call out the cavalry before she fainted.

And even though Tess rarely agreed with her mother on anything, now *would* be a good time for the cavalry to come by and rescue her.

⌒

Engine wide open, the Harley-Davidson ate up the miles of deserted highway.

Dallas Haynes stared above the horizon, catching sight of a falling star. An omen, he thought. Good or bad? Of course, out here falling stars seemed commonplace. There was a reason this was called Big Sky Country. Nights like this proved it.

He shifted on his motorcycle, glancing at the odometer. Another thirty miles to go. Compared to the last eight hundred, it would be a piece of cake. He'd been riding for nearly twelve hours, crossing over from Canada at the Michigan border. He couldn't wait to pry this bike off his ass.

He glanced at the dark highway, ever watchful for deer and antelope grazing along the side of the road. They could wreak havoc on an unsuspecting driver.

It seemed strange to be riding alone. Bogen's men usually traveled in pairs. Or packs. However, this wasn't the usual trip. He was on a special mission, with a special message for Bogen from Sanchez. A message Sanchez wouldn't trust with just anyone. That trust acknowledged Dallas's status. He was one of Bogen's lead men, and Sanchez's action seeded him for the top position. Which was exactly the spot Dallas sought.

Reaching the crest of what he recognized as one of the

final hills before his turnoff, he sat forward, hand easing off the throttle. Below him, in the valley, on the opposite side of the road, he saw the blinking yellow flashers of a disabled vehicle. He slowed. Probably some damn farmer's kid had run out of gas while out driving and drinking on a Saturday night.

Well, he wasn't about to stop. The kid was probably long gone anyway, not wanting to get busted for DUI if a deputy cruised by. Gunning his engine, he picked up speed.

As he drew closer, a glimmer of movement on the highway caught his eye. A pair of elk bounded from around the vehicle!

Braking hard, he skidded. Tires screeched as he fought to hold the bike steady without laying it down. Acrid smoke billowed thickly in the night as he careened sideways to a stop, just beyond the car. The elk disappeared, leaving the highway clear.

Revving his engine, he looked over his shoulder at the car that had distracted him in the first place. To his surprise, the car's interior light came on as the door swung open. He started swearing as soon as he caught sight of the driver's slight frame. A woman. Of all the rotten luck. Turning his motorcycle around, he headed toward her.

Make that a gorgeous woman, he corrected as he pulled in behind her car, his headlight capturing her. That was even worse. She had apparently started to come after him, as if afraid he'd drive past without stopping. Now she hovered in the middle of the highway, reminding him of a doe caught in the lights. Or a damn elk!

He switched off his engine, leaving the headlight on and taking advantage of her temporary blindness. She was one neat package, he admitted begrudgingly. The wolf in him wanted to whistle at the long lines of her legs and the obvious curves beneath her jacket. Her eyes had been huge, making him curious to know their color. Blue? Green? A light breeze carried her scent. Roses. God, she even smelled alluring.

Several strands of windblown, light-colored hair had escaped the neat knot atop her head, framing a delicate oval face. He'd bet she'd been cruising with the top down. *Tourist style.*

She wasn't from around here. He'd known that even before he'd seen her out-of-state plates. Massachusetts. He would have guessed that. Or New York. She looked like old, East Coast money.

He sized up the situation: a beautiful woman, alone on the side of the highway with a brand-new, broken down BMW. Damn it! Did she have any idea how much trouble she could be in? He climbed off the motorcycle and strode toward her.

Tess stared at the dark silhouette of the lone rider as he dismounted. When she'd first spotted him and realized he was speeding up but hadn't seen the elk, she had scrambled to get out of the car and scare the animals. She hadn't been quick enough, but fortunately, he had still managed to avoid an accident.

The concern she felt for his safety evaporated as the man stepped out of the glare and strode toward her.

Every Hollywood stereotype of a motorcycle gang member came to mind. He wore boots, wickedly tight jeans, ripped at both knees, and a worn leather jacket—black of course. He wore no helmet, his dark hair pulled back in a ponytail. A Fu Manchu mustache and an abbreviated V-shaped goatee completed the bad-boy picture.

She started to wave him on, tell him she was okay, that help was on the way, but he was already in front of her. Self-conscious, she backed up toward the safety of her open car door. The man was tall, probably six-two, which gave him eight inches over her, and added to the menacing figure he cut.

When he stepped closer, into the narrow band of light spilling from the car, she gasped, the stereotype crumbling. The man was incredibly handsome. From his chiseled jaw to his bedroom eyes, his face was perfect. The day's stubble on his cheeks only enhanced his dark good looks.

If you liked that type, she amended quickly, which she didn't. He looked like trouble cruising for a place to land.

She backed up another step and bumped into her car, but still the man approached, crowding her, not stopping until he was almost on top of her. He stretched out an arm, resting his hand on the edge of the car's roof, mere inches from her head, and leaned in close, bowing his head slightly so he controlled the eye contact.

She held her breath and stared up at him, catching a glimpse of icy silver eyes. Unusual eyes. She opened her mouth to speak, but he cut her off.

"You got any idea how dangerous this is? Stuck in the middle of nowhere, on a deserted highway?"

A woman alone was implied.

"I—I ran out of gas," she grasped for an excuse. "Besides, I'm not alone." She looked up noticing that the elk were moving in once more, no longer frightened now that the motorcycle's engine had shut off. They were a big help.

"My . . . friend . . . is walking to the gas station and should return any moment."

The man pushed away from the car and backed up slightly. Just enough so she could breathe.

"Back that way?" He pointed in the direction from which Tess had come.

A lousy liar, she nodded. She couldn't very well say the direction *he'd* driven in from! She wrapped her arms across her chest in an effort to warm herself. And to bolster her courage.

He smiled, revealing white, even teeth. And a deep, sexy, dimple not quite hidden by his mustache. "Then you know there's no gas station in that direction for forty miles. And Jeb's won't open till seven."

She closed her eyes in disbelief, opening them again just as quickly. The man hadn't moved, watching her expectantly. What did she do now? Admit she lied and ask for his help? Or stick to her story?

She looked at him again, trying to size him up. He didn't seem nearly as threatening now that he'd backed off. The smile had helped. So had the dimple. Surely if he had meant her harm, he wouldn't have stepped away.

"You're not from around here, are you?" he asked, his tone softening. His voice was low, masculine.

She met his gaze, suppressing another shiver that had nothing to do with the cold. She'd bet he could ooze charisma. When he chose.

She angled her head, deciding to be forthright. Everyone she'd met out West thus far had been open and honest, expecting the same in return.

"I'm from Boston. I guess I got lost in thought."

He nodded. "You're lost all right. Look lady—"

"Tess." She held out her hand. "Tess Marsh. And you are?"

"Dallas." He stepped close once again, grasped her hand briefly, then released it, but didn't step away. "Look, *Tess*, here's your options. The closest gas station is twenty miles that way, in Jordan." He pointed in the direction from which he'd approached. "But it won't open till daybreak. There's a small motel in town. You—and your imaginary friend"—he winked, letting her know he knew—"can stay there and get help in the morning."

His words took a moment to sink in. "You're going to give me a ride?" She pointed to his Harley, fighting to keep the squeak from her voice. "On that?"

He chuckled. She wore indignation like a rose wore thorns. A ravishing rose. Little Miss Priss with a steel spine. In a different life he'd be all over this woman. "You've never been on a motorcycle?"

"Never."

He shrugged. "The choice is yours. Stay or go." He wasn't about to leave her out here alone, but he could sense her hesitation and hoped that by giving her an option she'd decide to go on her own free will. It was a hell of a lot easier than using force.

Stay or go, Tess thought. Both held risks. The thought of being left alone held little appeal. It grew colder by the minute, and it wouldn't be light for hours. And even then, who knew when another car would come by? Or worse, who would be in that car. . . .

She looked Dallas directly in the eyes, searching, considering, deciding. She'd never made a faulty evaluation when she judged someone by his or her eyes. And her instincts approved. She'd be safe with this man. His eyes were trustworthy. They were also sinfully sensual, but she decided not to hold that against him.

She sighed. Well, she'd wanted to have an adventurous summer, hadn't she? This would certainly be a start.

"I've got a duffel bag in the trunk. Can we strap it on the back?" She pointed to the vertical back bar on his motorcycle.

He grunted, doubtful. "How big is it?"

"See for yourself." Tess led the way to the rear of the vehicle.

Dallas whistled when he saw the contents of her trunk. It was crammed with boxes and tool cases. He pointed to a worn pickax. "Don't tell me. Your great-great-granddaddy left you a map to his gold mine and you're out here looking for the mother lode." His voice held a gentle ribbing quality.

She laughed. Maybe she'd been too quick to pigeonhole this man because of his appearance. There was definitely more to him than met the eye. Hadn't she recently read a magazine article about the increasing number of young professionals—lawyers, doctors, and bankers—who rode motorcycles, complete with the grunge look? Weekend warriors?

He had confidence. He had finesse. Yes, she could picture him in a three-piece suit, in a courtroom. But as her doctor . . . never! She glanced to where his hands rested on the car, taking in his long, thick fingers. The artist in her had a thing for strong hands. And his were definitely a ten.

She shoved the pickax to one side and scrambled to divert her line of thinking. "Actually, I design jewelry. I did a short internship at a mine in Idaho to get a firsthand look at gems and stones in their natural environment."

"Near Coeur d'Alene? Rough country." Dallas's eyes swept over her, trying to reconcile her polished fingertips and porcelain skin with the sweat and grime he knew it took to swing a pickax. His image of miners encompassed decrepit old men. Not dazzling blondes. Or stacked blondes. Or his favorite kind: adventurous blondes. His pulse stepped up.

His eyes flickered briefly over her hands. No rings adorned her fingers, engagement or wedding. He'd wager she was uninvolved. What man in his right mind would let a woman like her wander freely about the countryside? He damn sure wouldn't.

"So where are you headed now?"

"The Fort Peck Indian Reservation. Their big arts and crafts festival is this weekend, and there's two silversmiths I want to meet."

"Planning to intern with one of them?"

"No. Actually, I'm hoping to buy inventory for my store in Boston. I'll be following the summer craft show circuit for a few weeks, looking for new talent." A note of pride crept into her voice. "I can't keep up with demand by myself anymore. And my clients want variety."

Dallas frowned, thoughtful. "You must have trustworthy help to be able to leave for weeks at a time."

She shrugged. "The shop is closed from Memorial Day to Labor Day, which gives me time to build up stock for Christmas."

"And probably heightens demand." He studied the two necklaces she wore. One was an antique silver choker. Old and valuable. A family heirloom, he'd bet. The other piece looked newer and vaguely familiar.

Giving in to the temptation to touch, Dallas reached forward, picking up the small medallion nestled below the hollow of her throat. The delicate silver crescent was heavier than it looked.

"Did you design this? It reminds me of one of the symbols favored by the Cuna Indians."

Tess smiled, her skin tingling where the pads of his fingers had brushed. The Cuna Indians lived on islands in the San Blas archipelago off the Caribbean coast of Panama. They were a matriarchal society, rare in today's male-dominated world. Few people had ever heard of them, and even fewer were familiar with their art. Dallas was either well traveled or well educated. Perhaps both. Which hopefully explained the growing attraction she felt toward this man.

She relaxed, warmed by his genuine interest. "Yes, I designed it. In fact I have a whole line of jewelry inspired by the art of the Cuna tribe."

"You exploit indigenous people?"

Warmth flared. To fire. She tugged the medallion from his grasp. "Yes. And small children."

"I didn't mean—"

She cut him off. "You insulted them, not me. The tribal elders negotiated the deal. One of them has a law degree from Harvard. They're pretty savvy. A healthy portion of the sales goes back to the tribe in the form of royalties to help preserve their heritage."

Dallas laughed, throwing his hands up in mock surrender. The rose had thorns. Sharp ones. "Easy! I take it back. You obviously have talent *and* a sense of fair play. Plus your work is beautiful."

Tess glanced at him, embarrassed that she nearly lost her temper. She usually wasn't so easily riled. "Uh-huh. Trying to flatter me now?"

"Yeah. Is it working?"

Too well, she thought. Ignoring his question, she grabbed a compact nylon duffel bag and closed the trunk.

Dallas reached out, his fingers purposely skimming hers. One touch hadn't been enough after all. "This is it? You travel light."

"For a woman?"

"Touché." He could enjoy spending time with this lively lady. It had been too damn long since he'd been around someone like her.

Taking the bag, he quickly strapped it on the back of his bike, beside his own, then turned to ask if she was ready. A distant sound caught his ear. Low, rumbling; barely there.

Motorcycle engines. Heading this way. He knew instantly who the riders were. Shit! How much time had he wasted making small talk? Five minutes? A mistake he wouldn't make again.

Moving quickly, he started to rush her. "Lock 'er up and let's go."

Tess had climbed back in her car. "Just a minute," she called over her shoulder. "There's some stuff I've got to get out of the backseat. It'll only take a sec."

The engines grew louder. They'd clear the hill any moment. Grabbing the waistband of her jeans, he tugged her out of the car. "*Now!*"

Tess whirled about, dropping her backpack at his feet, shocked that he had pulled her out of the car. Knocking his hands free she tried to step away but found the way blocked. "What do you think you're doing?" she lashed out.

The roar of motorcycle engines caught her attention just then. She looked up as headlights began spilling over the hill. There must have been at least a dozen bikes. And they were all slowing down.

Her mouth went dry. She stared at Dallas as if seeing him for the first time. Gone was the easy smile that hinted at an educated humor. In its place was the steely-eyed look of a seasoned hoodlum. "What's happening?" she whispered hoarsely.

Dallas moved close, backing her up against the car, forcing her into his arms and against his chest. "Stay by me and you won't get hurt," he ordered. "I'm going to kiss you, Tess, and to make this look good, you need to kiss me back."

Then his mouth swooped down on hers, capturing her lips in a rough, forceful kiss. She felt his fingers slide through her hair, loosening it, drawing her closer as his tongue swept unexpectedly into her mouth.

It was like kissing fire.

His actions stunned her even as he branded her with his possession, robbing her senses, making her his. She melted against him, defenseless against such a fierce assault. His mustache felt silky smooth against her lip while in contrast his unshaved cheek chafed hers, sensitizing the tender skin.

Her pulse leapt beneath the blunt tips of his fingers as they skimmed down her neck.

He smelled of the night, a powerful male scent. A small moan started low in her throat as desire mingled with arousal. Dear God, she had never been kissed like this. With heat, with passion. With promise. And she had never imagined anything this pleasurable.

Or this forbidden.

What was she doing letting this man kiss her? All at once desperate to end the kiss, she shoved her hands against his chest. It was like pushing granite.

When he didn't budge she tried to kick his shin. He moved closer still, forcing his legs way too intimately between hers before catching her hands and lacing her fingers between his. Lifting her arms he pulled her hands around his neck and held them tight. Then he slanted his mouth and deepened the kiss, using the full length of his body to pin her in place.

To anyone observing them it probably looked like she was an active participant in a crude act. Too late she realized he had her neatly immobilized. She couldn't even knee him in the groin. She tried to shout, but his mouth effectively cut off all sound.

The motorcycles came to a stop, encircling them in a dusty halo of blinding headlights and reverberating engines.

Dallas drew back only slightly, breaking the kiss. The move brought his lower body into even closer contact with hers, emphasizing her vulnerability. He made a low, *ssshhh* noise in her ear, as if warning her to remain quiet, then pressed his lips to her temple, forcing her attention back to him. "Trust me."

The words were whispered so low Tess thought she had imagined them. Trust him? Why? She sensed danger. It hung thick in the air, noxious, choking her. Her fingers tightened over his knuckles.

She trembled, shifting indiscernibly closer, not knowing which was worse: the feeling that Dallas would protect her or the perception that she needed protection. The temptation to hide her face on his shoulder was strong. Except she knew that burying her head in the sand wouldn't get her out of the situation. She needed to stay alert.

Several of the men dismounted and walked up behind Dallas. Never taking his eyes from her, Dallas addressed one of them. "Get lost, Snake. I'm busy."

"Just waiting my turn, *amigo*." The man named Snake moved beside Dallas. Wearing an eye patch and sporting a mouthful of rotten teeth, Snake looked like he had stepped out of a B movie. As tall as Dallas, Snake had a soft, paunchy gut hanging over his jeans. Tess involuntarily leaned away. Though she'd never admit it aloud, she did feel safer with Dallas.

When Snake bent closer, inspecting her, Tess got a whiff of cheap bourbon. She tried once more to free her arms, but Dallas only tightened his grip, pulling her closer. Terrified, she ceased struggling and arched into Dallas, seeking to get as far from Snake as possible. Hadn't Dallas said she wouldn't be hurt if she stayed by him? Right now she desperately needed to believe that.

Snake reached out a finger, angling to catch her chin. "Here, kitty, kitty. Nice kitty." Raucous laughter echoed from the men with him.

Dallas's hand shot out, grasping Snake's wrist before he touched her. "I said, get lost." He nuzzled his chin against Tess's hair, gentling her. "You know I don't share."

Snake snatched his hand back and began laughing. "Fine. I'll wait and get her when we're back at camp." He leered at Tess. "I think she'll be worth waiting for."

Dallas bared his teeth, his voice a dangerous growl. "Who says I'm taking her back? You know the rules."

"No locals," Snake said, still grinning. "And she ain't local. The car tag says Massachusetts. Hell, she's got outsider written all over her. If you don't take her, I will."

Tess's mind reeled, her knees weakening. *Take her?* What did he mean? Kidnap? Or rape? She couldn't handle either. Bile rose in her throat. While the thought of being "taken" by anyone repulsed Tess, she'd rather die than have Snake touch her. She looked away, her mind refusing to contemplate the horrors Snake had in mind.

She stared up at Dallas, silently imploring his help. He obviously knew these men. He also had to know he was her only hope against them. She searched his face for a veiled reassurance, but his silver eyes revealed none of his thoughts. Or intentions. Could she really trust him?

"She's mine." Dallas addressed the crowd at large.

Tess opened her mouth to protest. Dallas's grip tightened painfully, drawing her eyes back to his. *Don't say a word*, his look commanded. He waited until the grumbling quieted before continuing. "Nobody touches her."

Snake spat on the ground before backing away. "Oh yeah?" he challenged. "We'll see what Bogen has to say about that."

Grabbing a beer from the closest rider, Snake drained the can and tossed it over his shoulder, sending the can ricocheting noisily into the brush. Stepping around Dallas, Snake ran his hand over the hood of her car, whistling. "A beemer. This'll bring in a nice piece of change, too."

"Only if you're a fish. The car's going for a swim," Dallas said.

Tess listened in cold trepidation as the conversation made grim sense. These men were going to sink her car—probably in a lake—after abducting her and doing God knew what. She felt her stomach lurch.

"No," she began softly, addressing Dallas. Her voice cracked as she fought not to cry, her throat wanting to close. "I've got money, jewelry. I can get more. Please don't do this."

"Please don't do this," Snake mimicked in a high-pitched voice. Several of the others laughed and hooted. Encouraged, Snake moved closer. "Let's see you beg, darlin'. Exactly what are you willing to do to earn your freedom?"

Ignoring Snake, Dallas reached down and snatched her backpack from where she'd dropped it at their feet. "Frankie, get some gas in this tank and take it up to Lake Summer. Then let's get out of here before someone comes along."

The laughter ceased immediately as two men dismounted and headed toward her car. Tess noticed no one questioned Dallas's authority, which increased her unease. They'd do anything he said.

Well, these men might be accustomed to taking orders from him, but *damn it*, she wasn't.

Burying her heels in the ground, she resisted when he pulled her toward his motorcycle. The thought of what these men had in mind for her was numbing. She would not go willingly, she would not make it easy for them. She'd fight to her last breath.

When Dallas yanked her arm, she held back, then lost her footing and stumbled forward. He caught her, hauling her up against his chest once more to steady her.

She tried to move away and was reminded immediately who had the superior physical strength. As if there'd been any doubt.

He pulled her the last few steps to his motorcycle, then abruptly released her. "Climb on," he ordered as he fastened her backpack alongside her duffel bag.

Behind them two men used a small section of rubber hose to siphon gas into her car. There were several thousand dollars' worth of tools and jewels in the car, besides the value of the car itself. And these men were going to sink it. Obviously they cared little for money.

Which meant they'd probably care even less about her life. She thought of her family and friends, a sharp pain erupting in her chest at the thought of never seeing them again. She couldn't—wouldn't—let that happen.

She bolted toward the road, frantic, twisting to dodge past Dallas. Her escape was short-lived. He came up behind her quickly and easily, locking his arms over her chest and swinging her back to stand beside his motorcycle. She screamed. Catcalls arose from Snake and the others.

"Get on." Dallas's voice was clipped, low. Deadly.

"No." Tess stepped back, ignoring the feral gleam in his eyes. "I am not going anywhere with you. You can't do this! It's illegal. It's kidnapping."

Dallas knew Snake was watching, waiting, wanting. And listening. He grasped her shoulders, overpowering her, his fingers biting into soft flesh as he shook her harshly, getting her full attention.

"It's over, Tess, and you're making this harder then it has to be. You can climb on yourself, or I'll get Snake to help. Your choice." Dallas disliked using her fears to force compliance, but he wasn't in the mood to argue.

His threat and rough handling deflated her ire. In spite of what he'd just said, there was no choice. She was ridiculously outnumbered. Once again fear swamped her, leaving her cowering pathetically in his arms as silent tears tracked down her cheeks.

At her nod, Dallas relaxed his punishing grip, releasing her. Biting her lip to keep from crying out, she started to turn toward his motorcycle only to stop when Dallas laid a hand on her shoulder.

He leaned close, whispering quickly in her ear. "I won't hurt you, Tess. Just climb on."

His words gave her a small amount of hope. Perhaps he did intend to help her.

Still, when she swung one leg over the leather seat and mounted the bike, she was careful to lean as far back as possible, away from him when he swung on in front of her. If she kept a wide enough space between them, she'd have a better opportunity to leap from the bike once they were under way.

Whether she believed Dallas would protect her or not was a moot point with this crowd. There was only one of him and how many of them?

Dallas started the engine, gunned it to life. "Wrap your arms around me," he yelled over his shoulder.

"I'm fine like I am," she shouted in his ear.

"You don't listen, do you?"

To her consternation, Dallas leaned back and grabbed her wrists, pulling her forward. The move forced her closer, pressing her fully and intimately against his back, her thighs spread almost painfully to encompass his hips.

Tess began struggling, but he didn't release her. Damn him, he had no right—

Then she heard a ratcheting sound and felt cold metal snap around her wrists. Too late she realized he'd handcuffed her!

"No," she screamed. "Don't do this!" She tried to pull back but found her arms locked snugly around Dallas's waist.

Fresh tears crept into her eyes as a crippling paralysis settled into her limbs. He hadn't meant a word he'd said. In fact he'd taken advantage of her trust and used it against her. She was a fool.

As the sordid reality of her situation hit her, every imaginable depravity came to her mind. They'd kill her. Of that she had no doubt. But equally frightening was the thought of what came before that. Rape? Torture?

Snake pulled up beside them, revving his engine. "Boomer's gonna help Frankie ditch the car," Snake shouted. "Duke and Eddie are gonna follow you back to camp to make sure Bogen knows I consider this matter still open."

"Where are you going?" Dallas demanded.

"I've got some business in town." Snake winked at Tess and grinned. "Don't worry, darlin'. It ain't over between us. Bogen will see to that."

"Back off, Snake," Dallas warned. "Or we'll settle this here and now."

Snake stared at Dallas, coldly, like a rattlesnake, before wheeling his bike in a big circle and riding off into the night.

Their posturing left Tess feeling like she was no more than a bone for a couple of dogs to fight over. And the biggest, baddest dog won. How perfectly horrid.

Her throat burned, and she buried her face against the back of Dallas's jacket, unable to stop sobbing. She felt one of his hands close over hers, squeezing lightly.

"I meant what I said earlier," he whispered. "You're safe with me."

But his words gave her no comfort as they sped off into the night.

Chapter Two

Tucked in behind Dallas on the motorcycle, Tess yearned for warmth yet sorely resented the fact she needed his body to shelter her from the whipping winds. The bastard. If he hadn't kidnapped her in the first place . . .

Kidnapped. It seemed incomprehensible; a nightmare. Except it was real. Too real, she amended.

The metal handcuffs cut into her exposed wrists, the pain warring with that of her frozen skin. Once again she felt Dallas's hand cover hers, offering limited warmth. Too miserable at the moment to sustain her contempt, she accepted his touch, even let herself imagine that he offered a bit of silent reassurance. Then just as quickly he withdrew his hand, abandoning her once more to the elements.

By the time they stopped again, Tess felt numb. She shook with cold—and dread—as Dallas released the handcuffs and climbed free of the motorcycle. Wrapping her arms around herself, she huddled alone on the seat.

She watched the other men disappear along a wooded path. She already concluded Bogen was the leader of this motley crew, and if this was where he lived, they were probably in a hurry to get to him first and present Snake's side of the story. Her stomach flip-flopped, dreading what would happen next.

She felt Dallas's fingers brush her cheek as he smoothed the wind-tangled hair away from her face. She pulled back as if stung. His actions confused her. When no one could see, he treated her gently. Yet look what he'd done.

"Where are we?" she demanded, teeth chattering. "And what are you going to do to me?" She hated that her voice sounded watery, hated the choking lump of fear in her throat.

"I won't hurt you, Tess." His voice was low, barely above a whisper. "And I'll do my best to make sure no one else does either."

She stared at him, unable to reconcile his sincere tone with his deeds. Then the meaning behind his words hit, freezing the blood inside her veins. She was in danger here, danger he might not be able to protect her from. *I'll do my best.*

And if his best wasn't good enough?

Dallas reached up to touch her again, then stopped his hand midair. She looked stricken, but it made no sense to coddle her. Not now. The worst of it still lay ahead.

Unfortunately, the night had taken a different twist for both of them, and there was no turning back. His options had been severely limited the moment Snake pulled up. He didn't like it any more then she did. The trick would be remembering not to take it out on her, even though, damn it, it was partly her own fault. If she had paid a little more attention to her gas gauge . . .

"I know you're frightened," he continued. "But right now your well-being depends on how well you listen. You must do everything I tell you, without questioning it."

She scowled at him, temper flaring. "Go to hell! You have no right bringing me here. I'll see that you're arrested and prosecuted to the fullest extent of the law. All of you."

He looked away briefly, then pinned her with narrowed

eyes. "Seeing as there's no cop around, you'll forgive me for not quaking in my boots. Tess, whether you realize it or not, I'm your best hope of getting through this; the only protection you're likely to find. *Trust me.*"

There were those two words again. "Why should I trust you?"

Ignoring her question, Dallas lifted her off the motorcycle. Their bodies touched as he slid her down his length in a blatant show of masculine power. When her feet touched the ground she pushed away. He caught her arms, holding her tethered, closer than she wanted to be, silently daring her to test him.

She met his stare. "Let me go!"

"I'm afraid I can't do that."

Shifting his position only slightly, Dallas neatly spun her around so her back was to his chest. Too late she realized his intention as he grasped her wrists and pulled them behind her.

"No! You don't need to do this." She fought in earnest, struggling to prevent him from cuffing her hands again, twisting her head, trying to watch him. "I promise I won't cause any more trouble."

"It's for your own protection. So's this." Dallas stuffed a piece of cloth into her mouth and secured it with a bandanna.

Protection? She didn't need his brand of protection, she needed to get away from him. She bucked her shoulders, trying to break free, but Dallas held her fast, knotting the cloth tightly.

The gag stifled, and for a moment she thought she wouldn't be able to breathe. She felt his warm breath at her ear as he rubbed his hands briskly over her upper arms. "I know you're cold. I promise I'll get you warm as soon as this is over."

Over, she wanted to scream. When would it be over? She

tried to talk through the gag, but only indecipherable sounds came through. She tugged uselessly at the tight cuffs, scarcely able to move her arms. Angry, she kicked backwards, landing two solid blows to his shin.

Swearing, Dallas gripped her shoulders and snapped her body hard against his chest. It was like slamming against a brick wall. There wasn't an ounce of softness on his frame. She gritted her teeth in frustration.

"Give it up, Tess," he whispered harshly. "If I have to, I'll hog-tie you and carry you in."

Even though his leg smarted where she'd caught him off guard, he wasn't angry. Her show of spunk, however small, encouraged him. It would help her survive. He looked at her, taking in her bowed head, her muffled sobs. The lady didn't like people to see her cry. He respected that.

He shifted his weight from one foot to the other, giving her a moment to pull herself together. The part of him that wasn't royally pissed at her longed to comfort her, tell her everything would be okay.

Except it wasn't going to be. The best he could hope for was that Bogen would indeed let him keep her.

He had one ace up his sleeve: Bogen owed him a favor. If Bogen agreed, Dallas could offer her some protection. She'd be a prisoner for now, but it beat the hell out of the alternatives.

He stared at her, guilt knifing a dull blade through his stomach. He didn't like seeing her like this, scared, fragile. He recalled his first glimpse of her. A foolish blond angel stranded by the side of the road. Damn if she hadn't shaken his equilibrium. Kissing her hadn't helped. Even her resistance tasted sweet, soft. He'd wanted more but hadn't dared take it. He'd already violated several rules he'd normally never break.

And she was far from normal. Though she had tried to

hold herself back from him, he'd felt her firm curves as they rode. She had a fabulous body—which wouldn't go unnoticed by Bogen. He needed to be prepared to do some fast talking if Bogen decided he wanted to send her to Sanchez.

She stood warily in his arms, still shivering. Wrapping his arms around her, he pulled her unresisting form tight, dropping his voice. "I meant what I said earlier. It's very important you do everything I say. Your life depends on it."

She tried to argue, but her words were unintelligible with the gag.

"I know it's crazy to ask," Dallas continued, "but you've got to believe me."

He pulled her up the same path Duke and Eddie had used, deliberately slowing his pace to match hers. They reached a clearing before a ramshackle two-story farmhouse. Dim yellow light poured from the front windows.

A man stepped out from the shadows, armed with a nasty-looking assault rifle. The guard nodded to Dallas. "Bogen's expecting you."

As they passed, the guard scrutinized Tess intently. Too intently. The look on his face repulsed her. She inched closer to Dallas and felt the slight tightening of his hand on her forearm. Silently she admitted she did feel safer with Dallas than any of the others.

Dallas led her into the front room, where Duke and Eddie huddled around a desk, speaking in low tones. Behind the desk sat a large, dark-haired man. Even though it was night, the man in the chair wore sunglasses. Bogen?

She could feel his eyes dissecting her. She met his stare, trying unsuccessfully to see behind the glasses. Dismissing her, Bogen turned and listened once more to Eddie.

Tess quickly scanned the rest of the room, searching for avenues of escape, finding none. The other furniture in the room, a stained sofa and four ragtag recliners, circled around a large-screen television.

She glanced back at the desk, then quickly dropped her head to hide her excitement. On a scarred credenza behind the desk sat a *telefax machine.* If she could somehow get to it and use the phone!

Hoping to appear nonchalant, she looked at the adjacent room. Probably a dining room in another time, the room now held a pool table. The windows were boarded shut. There appeared to be nowhere to run in that direction. She glanced furtively back at the desk. The telephone on the fax machine was her best chance. The problem would be getting the opportunity to use it . . . before it was too late.

Would Dallas help her? If he could distract the others and buy her just a few moments alone with the phone—

The room grew quiet as Bogen suddenly pushed out of his chair and stood. An obese man, Tess wondered how he managed to move with such ease. Bogen's attention shifted back to her, cold and calculating, stripping her, assessing her, making her feel violated. Her mouth dried in revulsion, her senses screaming like an activated burglar alarm.

Bogen radiated hostility. And at the moment that hostility was directed at her. Her skin crawled in a new direction under his gaze. Snake seemed like a gentleman compared to Bogen.

She backed away until she ran into Dallas. His hand clamped over her shoulder, pinning her in place.

"Nice," Bogen said, nodding. He stepped forward and tugged her jacket apart, scrutinizing the thrust of her breasts. Tess held her breath, expecting to feel his hands grope.

"I see why she's caused such a stir. We need to talk. *Privately.*" Taking their cue, Duke and Eddie started for the door, but Bogen stopped them. "Lock her up, Duke."

Lock her up? Tess started to scramble away as they closed

in. She skittered to the right, but found herself tethered by Dallas's firm grip. Damn Dallas and his lies! Damn them all!

When Duke grabbed her and tugged, she swung out her leg and tried to kick him.

"Pop her," Bogen ordered.

Ceasing her struggles, Tess steeled herself for a blow, but none came. Instead Duke stepped away, toward the desk, leaving her to watch incredulously as he retrieved a small glass vial and a hypodermic needle from a drawer. Their intent became clear.

She shrank backwards, her eyes never leaving Duke. If they drugged her, they could do anything to her, with her. She'd be helpless. But what could she do to stop them? It was four against one and she was starting . . . to feel . . . faint.

She blinked rapidly, aware that she was hyperventilating, the gag impeding her breathing. She felt Dallas slide an arm around her waist.

"No needles," he said firmly.

Tess sagged against his arm.

"I'll give her six of these." Dallas held up a prescription bottle. "She won't give you any trouble after that. Eddie, get some water."

Turning her to face him, Dallas grasped Tess's chin, forcing her to meet his eyes. "If you don't swallow these, we'll use the other. Choose wisely."

Once again Tess faced an impossible choice. She'd seen the hypodermic Duke held. The needle wasn't even capped. It obviously wasn't sterile and had probably been used before. What ghastly disease would she get from it? And who knew what drug was in the vial?

She caught a glimpse of the bottle Dallas held. A tranquilizer. Or so the label read. Her mother had used them on more than one occasion. And while Tess had never taken it, she knew it was a common prescription. But six of them?

"I'll loosen your gag so you can swallow," Dallas continued. "Then it's going right back on. I don't want to hear one word."

She glared at him, but nodded. As soon as he freed her of the gag, she took a sip of water to wet her mouth. She heard the rattle of pills as Dallas opened the container, shook out pills, then held them close to her mouth. She shot him one more murderous look, then glanced at his palm.

Three pills.

She looked up, hoping for a sign, receiving none. Instead he shoved his hand even closer. Confused, she opened her mouth and took the small, bitter pills. She could have sworn he said he was giving her six pills. Had he practically shoved them down her throat so the others wouldn't see there were only three?

As soon as she swallowed, Duke moved up and replaced her gag. Just that quickly Duke pulled her away.

Dallas watched her leave, careful to keep any emotion from showing on his face. He knew she felt betrayed. He'd purposely tried to cultivate her trust and now this. She had to be out of her mind with fear, imagining the worst.

What she didn't know was how important it was for him to play along with the game. There were more lives at stake than just hers.

"I'm eager to hear your side of the story," Bogen began when they were alone. "Duke says you found her on Pitmann Highway and Snake's staking a claim on her. Seeing as you both know the rules, I'm curious why she's even here."

"She's not local. She ran out of gas, and I stopped to help her. She was demonstrating her gratitude when Snake crawled along. I had planned to roll her, then give her a lift to Jeb's, which would have been the end of the story. Except Snake had to horn in."

Bogen shook his head. "That jackass."

"He said he'd take her if I didn't. By then she had 9-1-1 written all over her face. I knew I couldn't let her go and risk the chance she'd call the sheriff."

Swearing, Bogen moved back toward his desk, the chair groaning loudly as he settled his bulk. "That damn sheriff's dying for a reason to come back out here. Where's her car? And where the hell is Snake?"

"The car's in Lake Summer. Snake said he had business in Jordan."

"Blast him!" Bogen slammed his fist on the desk, the sound echoing in the room.

The silence swelled for a moment, then Bogen cleared his throat. "Under the circumstances, you did the right thing. We'll ship her to Canada and let Sanchez handle it. I—"

"I'm keeping her, Bogen."

Dallas's statement stretched between the men like a taut rope in a game of mental tug-of-war.

Bogen fumbled in his pocket and pulled out a cigarette. Inhaling sharply, he blew out a geyser of smoke. "I'll be damned. I was beginning to wonder about you, Haynes. One of 'em finally got under your skin."

Dallas snorted. "She has me intrigued. That's all."

"You've never shown much interest in the women here."

"I don't share."

"So you'll want her for yourself?"

"Completely."

"That means you're responsible for her. She's a piece of high-class ass, which spells pure fucking trouble." Bogen leaned forward, propping his elbows on the desk. "We both know I owe you one. This would even the score."

Dallas nodded once.

"I'll think about it," Bogen said finally. "Grab a beer and let's hear the news from Sanchez."

Dallas made his way through the dining room and into the

kitchen, relieved that Bogen hadn't flat out denied his request. He eyed the heavy padlock on the pantry door as he opened the refrigerator and grabbed two long necks.

The pantry served as a makeshift prison. She was in there he knew. Asleep, he hoped. The drug he'd given her would be kicking in right about now. If it didn't knock her out, she'd be sleepy as hell. He would have liked to go to the door and offer reassurance. But he didn't. Too damn risky.

Instead he slammed the icebox door and hurried out of the kitchen. He hated this part of the job. Taking care of business whether he wanted to or not. In a perfect world he would have preferred to take Tess back to his cabin, try to soothe her fears privately. Hell, in a perfect world they would have met under different circumstances. But his world was far from perfect.

After handing Bogen a beer, Dallas recounted the details of his meeting with Sanchez. Bogen and Sanchez were both hard-core criminals, but Sanchez called the shots, monitoring Bogen's illicit activities in the Pacific Northwest. Sanchez, however, was not the top man. That man, the cartel's leader, operated out of South America.

Bogen listened as Dallas repeated the message, the only clue to his tension the white-knuckled grip he kept on the beer bottle.

"So Sanchez knows we've got a leak, but he's still not sure *where*?" Bogen laughed bitterly. "We've known that for months. How the hell does he intend to fix it?"

Dallas shrugged. "He didn't say. He said he needed additional time to flush the pipes and that he's holding off on future shipments until the problem is resolved."

"That sonofabitch! How long does he think that will take?"

"A few weeks at the most. He wants you to lie low until he contacts you again."

Bogen leaned back from the desk, his face a mottled crimson. "So now he thinks he can tell me how to run my operation. Bastard! Did you tell him where to shove it?"

Dallas shifted, hooking one leg over the arm of the couch. "I considered it, except I know you don't like anyone putting words in your mouth. I figure if you've got a message for Sanchez, you'll see that he gets it."

And Dallas hoped he'd be the one sent to deliver it. If Sanchez were going into hiding, Bogen would be the one man who'd know where. Dallas knew Sanchez would hide at the cartel's South American headquarters.

Draining his bottle, Bogen stood. "You're right, as usual, Haynes. But the girl stays here until I talk with Snake."

Dallas took a pull of his own beer. Disappointment soured the taste. "Just do me a favor and keep Snake away from her. That bastard's interfered in my life one time too many."

Knowing there was nothing more he could say, Dallas strode out of the house and into the night.

⌇

Tess had no idea how much time passed since she'd been locked in the pantry. Earlier she'd heard someone in the kitchen. Muffled voices had drifted from the living room, but she couldn't distinguish the words. Then the house grew quiet. Eerily so.

The pills she'd been forced to swallow were making her drowsy and once again she wondered exactly what drug she'd been given. It was difficult to focus. She struggled against the mental fog, afraid that if she drifted off, she'd never wake up. Or wake up in a worse predicament.

And certain scenarios were indeed worse than others. The thought of being gang-raped was abominable. Especially since she was a virgin. Such cruel irony to lose something brutally that she'd been saving for a nonexistent Mr. Right. The idea of Snake and his cronies touching her made her want to vomit. Death almost seemed preferable. Almost . . .

Dallas! If ever she needed to believe he might help her, it was now. He seemed her only hope of salvation, and the thought of not seeing him again was unbearable. She wouldn't survive if left at Bogen's mercy.

She shook off a wave of lethargy, fighting the effects of the drug, forcing herself to concentrate on her physical discomfort to stay awake. Her head throbbed where she'd slammed against the water heater when Duke shoved her inside the pantry. Her jaw hurt from the gag; it interfered with breathing, swallowing.

She shifted, trying to move her cramped arms to a more comfortable position. Drugged or not, she needed to be ready to bolt at the first opportunity, taking any avenue of escape.

A sound caught her ears and she strained to listen, pulse drumming. The sound repeated itself. It took a moment before she realized someone was coming in a door, probably the back door. When the kitchen light snapped on, thin lines of light shone through the louvered pantry door.

She drew her legs closer. Who was it? Were they coming for her? Oh God, what did she do now?

Heart hammering, she listened as new sounds, heavy footsteps on creaking boards, caught her ear. Someone approached the pantry.

"Don't touch that door." She recognized Bogen's voice.

"She's in there." The sound of Snake's voice made her stomach contract painfully.

Fighting vertigo, Tess managed to ease noiselessly to her knees and scoot closer to the door. Though the louvered door had been reinforced on the inside with steel braces, a large crack ran close to the bottom, where a slat was missing.

Bending low, she peered out. Snake and Bogen were on the opposite side of the kitchen standing nose to nose.

"The girl," Snake said. "What are you going to do with her?"

"I'm giving her to Haynes. For now at least."

Relief poured through Tess. Bogen would return her to Dallas!

"That's not fair. I want a piece of her."

"Not fair? I tell you what's not fair," Bogen ground out. "Sanchez has lost his nerve. He doesn't want any shipments until the rumors of a leak are gone. You got any idea what that will cost?"

"Screw Sanchez. We did fine without him."

"No, we didn't. We're making ten times the money and with a lot less bullshit."

"If I fix the problem with Sanchez, will you give me the girl?"

Tess shook her head at Snake's words, partly in denial, partly to clear it. She had no idea who Sanchez was or what they were discussing. She did know she didn't want to go anywhere with Snake.

Bogen snorted. "You? How?"

"That leak we talked about earlier. I'm plugging it tonight."

"What are you talking about?"

"Matt Michaels. I confronted the bastard in town. He put up a pretty good fight, but I nailed him. Now he's gonna pay."

"Christ! What have you done now? Where is he?"

Snake hiked his thumb over his shoulder. "Out by my bike."

"You stupid idiot! I ought to—" Bogen exploded. "Why the hell didn't you check with me first?"

"You weren't here. And I heard Michaels had an appointment with the sheriff in the morning. I knew we couldn't let that happen."

"Do you know *why* he had an appointment?"

Snake didn't answer.

"Imbecile!" Bogen snapped. "There could have been a hundred reasons for them to meet. Michaels does repairs on the sheriff department's motorcycles."

"He's also a prime suspect for ratting on us, and you know it," Snake shot back. "We never should have let him past the front gate."

"There are several people considered prime suspects. What are you going to do? Kill them all? The sheriff would have the goddamned FBI swarming this place. He's just looking for an excuse to harass us."

Bogen paced away. The refrigerator door opened and a bottle cap clinked as it hit the floor.

"He's the one," Snake insisted. "I know he's guilty."

"Whether he is or isn't doesn't really matter now, does it? Bring him in."

Tess watched as Snake stepped out the door and just as quickly returned, practically carrying the man she assumed to be Matt Michaels. He was medium height, with a slender build. Snake probably outweighed the man twice over.

She tried to see his face and immediately drew back. The man had been severely beaten, both eyes swollen and bruised. Blood oozed from a nasty-looking wound right above his kneecap. A gunshot?

Bogen's voice, deceptively low, caught her attention. "Talk to me, Michaels. Give me a reason to let you live."

"I . . . didn't . . . do . . . it." It was obvious Michaels was in a great deal of pain. His breathing seemed labored and loud.

She heard the solid *thud* of Snake's fist delivering a blow. Tess winced as if she'd been struck. Then she heard choking sounds. Helpless tears streamed down her cheeks. What could she do to help this man? To stop Bogen and Snake?

"Give me a name, and I'll let you go," Bogen promised. "Who's your accomplice?"

In a moment of clarity, Tess recognized that Matt Michaels was being accused of treason against the gang. They clearly didn't believe he was acting alone.

Was it true? Her hopes soared. Did someone else know what was going on here? Perhaps she had a better chance of rescue then she originally thought.

Tess watched Michaels straighten slowly. Give them a name, she begged silently. Any name, just to buy time and save yourself.

Any name except Dallas.

Because in that moment she knew that Bogen and Snake intended to kill whomever Matt Michaels named. And God help her, she didn't want it to be Dallas.

She battled a wave of dizziness, struggling against the wooziness the pills caused. Dallas. Good or bad, he was her guardian. She wouldn't survive this without him.

Michaels looked directly at Bogen now, and Tess held her breath, awaiting his reply.

"Go to hell."

She expected Bogen to fly into a rage, to strike the already injured man. Instead he simply folded his arms across his chest and nodded at Snake.

She saw a brief flash of steel as Snake drew a knife . . . and plunged it into Michaels's back, raising him off the ground with the force of the blow. It was the act of a coward. Michaels never saw it coming.

Snake stepped back, letting Michaels fall to the ground, his body convulsing, his life's blood discoloring the floor. It seemed to take forever, but finally he stopped moving.

Tess watched, unable to move, unable to think, paralyzed

by an appalling, drug-fogged torment. With awful certainty she knew he was dead and for the first time in her life, the prayers she'd learned by rote in Catholic grade school failed to come.

"You asshole! You could have done that outside!" Bogen shouted. "Take him up to Scab Point and dump him in the lake. Make sure you use plenty of concrete this time. And don't let anyone here see you. Then get back and find Haynes. We've got business to take care of."

Snake leaned over the body and withdrew his knife, drawing the blade across the knee of his own jeans before returning it to the sheath on his belt.

"What about our deal? I fixed the problem. Do I get the girl?"

"Hell no."

Snake started swearing.

"You don't get it, do you?" Bogen interrupted. "All you've done is create a new problem. If Michaels was the rat, I doubt he's working alone. Once he shows up missing, the heat could get unbearable."

"I can handle it."

"I'm starting to doubt that. You're getting careless. Don't let it be your downfall. Now get out. And find Haynes."

When Snake grabbed for Michaels's body, Tess closed her eyes, trying to inhale fresh air, fighting the urge to be ill. A man had been murdered right before her eyes, and his body was going to be tossed into a lake.

An icy sweat broke out across her forehead. Did that same fate await her? Would she be beaten and stabbed, too, or would they merely weight her down with concrete blocks and heave her into a lake? Since a childhood boating accident Tess had an unnatural fear of water. The thought of being trapped below the surface, dead or alive, was unthinkable.

Woozy, she moved as far away from the door as possible

and lowered her head to the floor. She no longer resisted the effects of the drug, letting her body shut down. The anesthetic blackness of unconsciousness beckoned, and this time she did nothing to fight it.

Then there were hands on her shoulders, shaking her. She blinked as light poured in the pantry and illuminated Bogen's menacing hulk. He slapped her hard, twice. "Wake up, bitch!"

Instinctively she drew back, filled with a new fear and loathing.

Bogen shoved her against the wall. Then he leaned back against the doorframe. "Can you hear me?"

She tried to nod, her whole body shaking.

"Against my better judgment, I'm giving you to Haynes. Just don't think you're on Easy Street. Haynes will tell you when to eat, drink, sleep, piss. And you'll do everything, *and everybody*, he says, whether you like it or not. You're his property to do with as he pleases. Unless you cause trouble."

Bogen kicked her foot, assuring he held her attention. "I can take you back if I decide you're a problem, and, believe me, you wouldn't like that. Do I make myself clear?"

Tess nodded, praying her relief wasn't too obvious. More than anything she wanted to see Dallas again. To leave this hellhole and try to forget the awful act she'd witnessed.

"Don't ever cross me, lady! You'll get burned. I know thousands of ways to make you hurt, make you wish you were dead." As if to drive home his point, Bogen bent over and leaned in close, removing his sunglasses to reveal a horrifying scar that extended above and below his right eye. "And in your case I could probably think up a few new ones."

If he meant to scare her, he'd succeeded. Tess had no doubt about his threats. She was crying now, more afraid then she'd ever been in her life. Bogen left, mumbling under his breath as he shut the door.

And this time she was grateful for the numbing dark—thankful he'd left her alone. And alive.

When Bogen signaled that their meeting was over, Dallas stood. Snake stormed out of the house, swearing to get even.

Dallas knew he'd have to be extra cautious with Tess where Snake was concerned. Even though Bogen had made it clear that Tess was Dallas's sole responsibility, he didn't trust Snake. If an opportunity arose . . .

Dallas made a fist. The ever-present tension between them had escalated with this incident. It would just be a matter of time to see who threw the first punch. Or drew first blood. He couldn't trust the man. With Snake you had to worry about a shot in the dark or a knife in the back. And now he had a woman to protect as well.

Bogen shuffled off to bed, leaving Dallas alone. Palming the key to the padlock, he hurried to the kitchen and unlocked the pantry door. He found Tess still handcuffed and gagged, huddled on her side on the dirty floor. It was cold as hell in the unheated pantry.

He knelt beside her as his eyes swept over her. She was covered with dust and old cobwebs. Her hair had come undone and spilled over one shoulder in a surprising golden tangle that nearly reached her waist.

The relief he felt at seeing her again warred with his guilt at forcing her to take the tranquilizers, which he quickly squashed. The alternative, after all, had been unacceptable. He knew the drug vial contained a strong and sometimes dangerous sedative, knew how easily she could have been given an overdose with the filthy syringe. He'd heard that had happened more than once. Better to control what he could.

Still, he thought her breathing seemed too shallow. Tugging the gag free, he pressed two fingers against her neck, concerned. People reacted differently to drugs. What barely fazed one person could kill the next.

Her pulse felt weak, but steady. Intent on carrying her out of the pantry, he bent to pick her up, but stopped when she started struggling.

"Tess! It's me, Dallas."

Her eyes fluttered open, wide and scared. And very dilated.

"You . . . you came back," she rasped.

His chest constricted. The past few hours must have been hell. "I came back."

He watched her strain as she tried to rise and moved to help. That's when he saw the cut near her temple.

"Who did this to you?" he demanded.

Squatting in front of her, he gently grasped her chin and turned her face up for a closer inspection. A quarter-sized lump had risen beneath the cut. Tear-streaked smudges of dirt marred her cheek but didn't disguise the bruise below her eye.

"I'll be right back." He retreated to the kitchen and returned with a dripping wad of paper towels. He carefully dabbed the dried blood around the cut.

"What happened?" he asked again, more quietly.

The wet towel stung where he touched it to her forehead. She scowled, pulling back, nearly toppling over from the rapid move. Dallas caught her arm, holding her upright.

She had to swallow several times before she could speak, her voice gruff. "When Duke shoved me in here I lost my balance." She nodded toward the rusted water heater. "I hit my head."

She started to tell Dallas about Bogen slapping her, but stopped, recalling Bogen's threats.

Dallas suspected there was more, but kept his thoughts private. He'd settle with Duke later. "Did the bastard even bother to check if you were okay?"

She shook her head, regretting the action as the closet-sized room spun. "You imply he'd care."

"Let's get out of here. Do you think you can stand?"

At her nod, Dallas helped her to her feet. She winced when he grasped her arm to steady her. Hell, her arms were probably numb from being cuffed behind her. She probably needed to use a bathroom, too. Not to mention food and sleep.

"There's a bathroom right around the corner. I'm going to unlock the cuffs. If I have to run you down, they'll go right back on." Moving behind her, he freed her arms.

Tess didn't know whether to laugh or cry at his remark. Putting one foot in front of the other and making it to the bathroom without falling would be a major accomplishment.

She rubbed her chafed wrists, grimacing as her muscles tingled with restored blood flow. She tried not to think of how wonderful it felt to have her arms free, and it was on the tip of her tongue to say thank you. But she didn't. She owed him no gratitude after what he'd done.

The small bathroom had a filthy toilet she'd normally refuse to use and an equally dirty sink that didn't work. She stared at her reflection in the broken mirror. Her lips were dry and cracked from the gag, her hair tangled and matted. The cut on her temple looked swollen and bruised. Dried blood and dirt were smeared on her cheek, a sobering reminder of her circumstances. But at least she was breathing, which meant she still had a chance. *Unlike Matt Michaels.*

Dallas was outside the door, holding a glass of water, when she came out. "Small sips," he cautioned.

Tess took the glass. Once again she refused to thank him. The water was icy cold. She pressed the damp glass against her forehead, the coolness a welcome balm.

"Headache?" Dallas's voice was low and oddly soothing.

She nodded, fighting a wave of weakness, then took another sip. She glanced at him over the rim of the glass.

A part of her felt overjoyed to see him. *He had come back for her.* After Bogen left she realized he could have been lying about returning her to Dallas. She had also worried that Snake might show up before Dallas.

Without a doubt, she did prefer Dallas's company. And right now he was the only person she could conceivably count on, the only person she might be able to trust. But what made her feel so drawn to this man? Her own weaknesses? Or his strength?

He led her back into the kitchen, pausing to place the glass on the counter. Tess's gaze drifted to the kitchen floor. The blood was gone, the dingy, cracked linoleum conspicuously lighter where someone had obviously performed a hurried cleanup job. Bogen had instructed Snake not to let anyone see him with Michaels's body. Did Dallas even know about Matt Michaels's murder? Did anyone?

A replay of the stabbing filled her mind. "No," she whispered hoarsely. The outer fringes of her vision started clouding, and she felt Dallas's hand close over hers as he slid an arm around her, catching her.

"Easy."

"Don't touch me!" she cried out, aware she was sinking to the ground but unable to stop it. The lack of control over her mind and body frightened and enraged her.

"You're hurt." Dallas scooped her up into his arms and headed out the door.

She struggled, but her actions had no impact. "Put me down. I prefer to walk."

Dallas's temper flared. "In case you didn't notice, you can't. And I'm not putting you down, so quit wiggling."

She hated that he was right. Her legs and arms felt disconnected from her body, and the struggle to stay awake exacted a heavy toll.

"What did you give me?" Her tongue felt thick and foreign in her mouth.

"A tranquilizer. A healthy dose. You'll feel it for a few more hours."

It was still dark, and Tess vaguely wondered how long she'd been out. Was it just before dawn, or just after dusk?

"Where are you taking me?"

"To my cabin." Dallas kept his tone to a rough whisper. "You'll be safe there. And you'll feel better after you've slept."

She wondered if she'd ever feel safe again. "I won't sleep."

"You will."

She started to argue, then stopped as another wave of uneasy lethargy rippled through her.

"Tess? Still with me?" Dallas's voice seemed to come at her from a distance. The drug kicked in again, and she had little strength to combat it.

"Promise you won't lock me up like that again," she whispered.

The anxiety in her voice was tangible, and Dallas wished he could give her the reassurance she sought.

He couldn't.

Chapter Three

*D*allas watched Tess sleep, finding solace in the slight rise and fall of her chest. Except for an agitated nightmare earlier, she hadn't moved since he laid her on the couch two hours ago. Which was probably just as well. Sleep would help clear the drug from her system.

It also gave him time to double-check that the cabin was escape proof. Tess was a fighter. Once she got beyond the initial shock of the situation, her primary concern would be gaining her freedom. Which clashed with Dallas's primary concern of keeping her safe.

It pleased him to see some color returning to her cheeks. She had been too pale when he'd freed her from the pantry. In shock no doubt. He had sponged the grime off her face and hands as best he could and smoothed a salve on her dry lips before attending her other injuries.

The cut on her forehead didn't look as severe now that it was clean. He knew it would sting like hell later. At least it didn't require stitches, which he wouldn't have hesitated to administer and which wouldn't have endeared him any further.

And right now he needed to endear himself. Reassure and draw her out. Like it or not, he was stuck with her.

He thought over the plan he'd formulated. His part would be easy. He needed to gain Tess's trust and sympathy as quickly as possible, through whatever means necessary. Brainwashing. Emotional blackmail. Even seduction.

She was vulnerable right now. He had to push that advantage. Hard and fast. He needed to establish unequivocally their roles as captor and hostage and initiate *transference*.

He hated to use textbook head games to control her, but he had little choice at this point. Once transference was established, once he managed to brainwash her, as Patty Hearst's captors had, Tess would become an ally, a very strong one. Normally the process took weeks. He had days, hours. Which meant he would be pushing every button at his disposal.

There had been a strong physical attraction between them when they'd first met. He needed to purposely cultivate and exploit that. If it wasn't already too late. She had every reason to detest him. But whether she liked it or not, cooperated or not, his agenda *would* prevail.

He shook his head. He needed some sleep. He'd been awake over thirty-six hours and was starting to feel punchy.

Kneeling beside the couch, he bent over her. He brushed his fingers lightly against her neck, finding her pulse steady. "Tess, wake up."

Her eyes fluttered open with a sharp intake of breath. He nudged her chin up, carefully noting the reaction of her pupils. In spite of the drug still in her system, they contracted slightly in response to the light. A good sign. Though semi-dilated, her eyes were surprisingly focused. And filled with anguish.

"Dallas."

It wasn't a question. He knew by the look on her face that she remembered where she was and how she'd gotten there.

Another positive sign. She'd undergone a fair amount of trauma, and her head injury still concerned him.

She struggled to sit up, accepting his help briefly before pulling away.

Dallas squatted in front of her. "How are you feeling?"

She didn't answer right away. The events of the night spilled into her mind. "I've got a splitting headache. Which isn't bad given the circumstances. I suppose I should feel glad to be alive."

He ignored the jibe and held up two fingers. "How many?"

It took Tess a moment to realize he was concerned about her head, not testing her math ability. It was tempting to lie. If she said four, could she convince him she needed medical help?

Then she thought about Bogen's threat to take her back if she caused any problems. She wasn't eager to test the man. *And end up in the bottom of the lake beside Matt Michaels.*

"Two fingers," she whispered, tears welling in her eyes. "I don't think I've got a concussion."

Nodding, Dallas offered her a glass of water. She started to refuse, but caught the slight negative shake of his head.

"Refusing only makes you more miserable."

She hated that he was right. Her tongue felt parched, and her throat hurt. She took the glass, carefully avoiding his touch, and found the water sweet and cool.

He watched her, quietly. And instead of looking away she met his eyes, searching the silvery depths, wishing she could see inside and *know* him, truly know him. His motives, his intentions. Who he was.

He seemed different from Bogen and Snake. But was that because she needed to believe he *was* different? Because she sorely needed a ray of hope?

In a world gone crazy he was suddenly the only constant. The only thing familiar.

What she saw in his eyes reassured her. Regret, concern, and compassion. Emotions lacking in Snake and Bogen. While Dallas was guilty of criminal acts, she didn't believe his crimes included murder. Which relieved her, but didn't let him off the hook.

She glanced away, struggling to get her bearings. She remembered Dallas freeing her from the pantry, knew he'd carried her through some woods to this cabin. She remembered glimpsing a small log structure that had seen better days. The front porch sagged, and honeysuckle vines covered one whole side where nature fought to reclaim it.

Tess looked around the interior, finding it small, but in better shape than she had expected. The wide plank floor, though worn and uneven, was clean. She sat on an ancient avocado-colored couch. A matching chair sat off to the right, facing an oversize stone fireplace. Banked flames crackled from behind the wire screen, the only source of heat.

A small table and chairs took up another corner with a spartan kitchen tucked in an alcove. Two doors punctuated the wall on the opposite side of the room.

"Bathroom's on the left. Bedroom on the right." Dallas pointed to the doors.

She recalled how filthy the bathroom at Bogen's had been and decided she'd postpone going as long as she could.

"Where are we?" she asked.

"My cabin."

"Who else stays here?"

"No one. Bogen has the main house. The rest of us have cabins around the perimeter of the woods."

It sounded like a potentially large encampment, she thought, her mind already scanning for escape routes. But if there were woods nearby, she'd have plenty of hiding places.

"How many cabins like this are there?" The more she knew about the layout the better.

"Twenty. It was a Cub Scout camp back in the sixties."

The irony hit her. Cub Scouts. And Bogen was the den mother from hell.

"How many acres?" she pressed.

Dallas took the glass from her and stood. "The compound is huge, Tess. There's only one road in, and it's guarded. If you're thinking of making a run for it, I'd advise against it."

"Then can I have my own cabin?"

Dallas chortled at her audacity. "With or without room service?"

"Either."

He moved to the chair and began yanking off his boots. "Consider this home for now. Granted, it's not the Marsh Suite in New York, but it's got the basics, and it's private."

Tess's mouth opened. He knew her identity!

She thought back, remembering that he'd strapped both her backpack and duffel bag to his motorcycle. He had no doubt gone through her things and made the connection. Possibly even read her letters.

Maybe he planned to ransom her. She leaned forward. "My father will pay well for my safe return. My fiancé—"

"You and your fiancé broke up two months ago, much to your mother's chagrin."

"You—"

Dallas cut her off. "Look, Bogen doesn't do ransom notes. In fact you'd be wise to keep your identity a secret. It could backfire on you."

Dallas had indeed searched her bag, burning her identification and the letters from her mother—after reading them. Though he hadn't made the connection right off, he'd done so after searching her wallet. He knew the Marsh reputation, was familiar with their elite social status, the hotels and department stores that bore their name. Hell, Tess had been a news story at age ten when her parents fought a bitter custody battle in a very ugly, very public, divorce.

If Bogen got wind of her pedigree, he'd order her dumped. High-dollar names like Marsh attracted too much media attention. Bogen was already nervous.

"So what do you intend to do with me? Kill me?" Tess fought to keep her emotions under wrap.

"I told you before I wouldn't hurt you, Tess. You're safe with me."

"My family will miss me. They'll start a search."

"They won't find you. Besides, I doubt anyone misses you at this point. You were scheduled to be gone a couple more weeks."

Tess looked away, not wanting him to see that he was probably right. Like a fool she had told him her plans for the summer. Plus he'd read her mother's letters. "They'll still expect me to call."

Dallas tugged off his socks. "We'll talk later."

Tess shot up from the couch. A wave of dizziness caught her off guard. Her steps faltered. She closed her eyes. If she got sick, she'd be mortified.

"You're not feeling well." Dallas closed the small distance between them and pulled her into his arms.

She pushed at his chest, finding it solid. "Let me go!"

"And let you fall flat on your face? How long have you been dizzy?"

"Just that once. Don't worry, I'm not going to faint."

Dallas drew her closer, knowing she didn't want that, yet knowing he needed to establish who was in charge. "Is it so hard to believe I'm concerned? Or have you already written me off with Snake and Bogen?"

She tried to wriggle free. It *was* difficult to reconcile his soft-spoken worry with her image of him as a ruthless kidnapper.

And being held close to his broad chest, so intimately, proved even more disconcerting. Her head hurt terribly, and she felt fuzzy. A heavy ripple of fatigue washed through her once more. She fought it.

"You still need more sleep," he said. "So do I. It's been a long night."

"I'm not tired."

"Yes you are. You're running on pure nerves and fighting the effects of the tranquilizer. When that bottoms out you'll collapse. Is that what you want?"

He abruptly released her. "I'd been driving twelve hours straight before I came across you, and hadn't had any sleep before that. We both need some shut-eye."

Tess backed away slowly. "I'll sleep on the couch."

"You're sleeping in the bedroom, with me. And if you're concerned I have a hidden agenda, you can rest easy. Whether you choose to believe me or not is your prerogative."

He moved toward her, hand outstretched.

"Go to hell!" With the last of her energy, Tess headed for the front door. Only to find it locked.

She turned, dismayed to find Dallas right behind her. When he charged, she feinted left, but in the small confines of the cabin, he only had to take a few steps to catch her. Slinging her over his shoulder, he headed to the bedroom.

"Put me down!"

She bucked wildly, but he merely tightened his grip around her knees, cutting off movement. She pummeled at his back, hurting her hand.

He kicked the bedroom door closed with his heel and walked directly to the bed.

"We can do this the easy way or the hard way," he ground out between clenched teeth. "Your choice."

"I hate you," she hissed, renewing her attack with the little energy she had left. "Let me go!"

"The hard way it is." Dallas dumped her on the bed, rolling her onto her stomach and pinning her in place with a knee in her back.

The air *whooshed* from her lungs, startling her. It took a few moments for the bed to stop spinning. She heard the drawer of the bedside table slide open. She tried to squirm free but he captured first one hand, then the other, easily pulling both arms over her head. She felt cold metal press against her wrist, heard the telltale *snap* of handcuffs. As soon as her wrists were secure, Dallas lifted his weight from her.

She stared at her hands in horror. He'd chained her to the bed frame! She tugged uselessly at the restraints. The bed had an old iron-spindle headboard and footboard. Solid as a rock. She rolled onto her side, watching him warily.

Ignoring her, Dallas moved to the opposite side of the bed peeling off his T-shirt as he walked, revealing a wide-shouldered physique. A three-inch scar ran across his ribs. His skin was nut brown, as if he spent a lot of time outside, shirtless. A well-worn, gold, Saint Christopher medal hung around his neck, coming to rest in the hollow of his breastbone, right between his flat nipples.

She caught a glimpse of a tattoo as he raised his arms over his head. The small but elaborate Celtic cross was imprinted on the inside of his upper arm, making it invisible when his arms were lowered.

Emptying his pockets, he unfastened his belt, then tugged it free. As she watched, his hands loosened the top button of his jeans, then paused. She stared.

Until he winked.

Embarrassed, she quickly turned her head, closed her

eyes. She heard the zipper rasp down, heard the soft *thud* of denim hit the floor.

The reality of the situation suddenly seemed suffocating. Would Dallas force himself on her?

She trembled by the time the bed dipped with the weight of his body, struck mute with fear. She felt helpless, weak. Horrified. God, this couldn't be happening!

She held her breath waiting to feel his hands grab her.

Waiting . . .

Waiting . . .

And eventually had to take another breath.

She opened one eye, expecting to find him leering over her. He wasn't.

Cautiously she turned her head. Wearing only a pair of white briefs, Dallas stretched out beside her, eyes shut. His thick dark hair, freed from the ponytail, was even longer than she'd realized. She could see lines of weariness etched on the side of his face. The chain on the handcuffs jangled as she relaxed her arms a fraction.

Dallas's eyes opened. She tensed once again expecting the worst.

Rolling onto his side, facing her, he propped his head on one elbow and looked pointedly at the handcuffs. "I know they're not comfortable, but you should be able to find a decent position for sleep if you slide down a little and bend your arms."

"You certainly know all the ins and outs, don't you? How many women before me have been handcuffed to this bed?"

"The others asked to be."

Instantly he regretted the sharp retort. He knew her biggest concern. *Rape.* It was written all over her face in spite of her barbed words.

Not that he didn't want her. Christ, she was lovelier than any woman he'd ever met. And sexy as hell in a naive sort of

fashion. Her response to his kiss had seemed downright innocent. Which intrigued him. But her fear of him was as effective as a cold shower.

He purposely lowered his voice. "You can relax, Tess. If
it means anything, I've never made love to a woman who
didn't want me to. And I don't intend to change now." He
grabbed the blanket from the foot of the bed. She shook her
head at his offer to cover her. "Suit yourself."

Turning his back to her, he moved to the opposite side of
the bed leaving a good two feet of space between them. He
wanted her to know she was safe, in that regard, with him. He
also didn't want to alarm her with the erection he knew
would *happen* if he kept looking at her.

Tension drained from Tess like air from a balloon, leaving
her depleted. Relieved.

Exhausted.

She stole another glance at his back. He hadn't moved.

Did she trust him? Oddly enough she wanted to. It was his
damn eyes again. How convenient to be a criminal with honest eyes.

She relaxed slightly, stretching her legs. Her own eyes felt
scratchy, tired. The remnants of the tranquilizer suddenly
seemed to conspire against her.

Following Dallas's cue, Tess rolled away, drawing her
knees up slightly. The digital clock beside the bed read 8:00
A.M. An early riser, she'd normally have been up four hours
by now.

A yawn escaped her, followed by another. The last thing
she wanted to do was sleep. She needed to concentrate on
planning her escape. . . .

Tess snuggled deeper beneath the blankets, tucking her nose under the sheet to scratch it. Groggy, she looked at the clock. It read 4:17. In the afternoon? The hand cupping her breast twitched, squeezing lightly, then relaxing.

Immediately her eyes widened with recall. She'd been on top of the blankets—handcuffed—when she'd fallen asleep. When had that changed?

She moved experimentally, confirming that her hands were indeed free and discovering yet another shocking surprise. She didn't have any pants on! Underwear, yes. Jeans, no. And her jewelry had disappeared.

A gentle snoring sounded in her ears. *Dallas!*

They were curled together, under the blanket, spoon fashion, her rear end fitted tightly against his groin and held firmly in place by a well-muscled leg cast over hers. His arm was slung over her, too, his hand anchored squarely between her breasts.

Sometime during the night—no day—he must have unfastened the handcuffs. And removed her jeans. And she hadn't even noticed! What else had he done?

She inventoried her body parts. She didn't feel violated. Surely she wouldn't have slept through *that*.

The drug! Though she felt fine now, she'd no doubt still been under its effects earlier.

Hardly daring to breathe, she debated her next move. Judging by the pattern of his breathing, she knew he slept. The question was, how deeply?

She must have been totally out of it for him to undress her and put her beneath the covers without her knowledge. But now he seemed deeply asleep himself. Could she slip out of bed, out of the cabin, while he slept?

As if warning against it, he clutched her closer, pressing himself directly against her buttocks, making her acutely aware of just how thin cotton underwear was. *And how thick he was.* She quickly thrust the sensation from her mind. She had to stay focused.

She eyed the door, mentally gauging the distance. Slipping out of bed wouldn't be easy. But she had to try.

Very slowly, very carefully, she tentatively eased her shoulder away from him. His breathing didn't change.

She waited a few seconds, then inched her butt forward. He reacted swiftly to that move, pulling her beneath him in a smooth roll and settling himself intimately between her legs.

She felt smothered, completely covered by his long body. His warm breath tickled her ear, followed by a soft snore. So much for her idea of getting *out* of bed. For now she'd be satisfied with getting *out* from *under*.

Chewing her lip, she debated waking him. How would he react? Would he try to take advantage of the situation?

Unbidden, thoughts of kissing him sprang to mind. Tess had done her share of dating and experimenting—mostly in college—but half of the guys she met left her cold. The other half were candidates her mother introduced. All were enamored by her family's wealth.

No one had ever moved her with just a kiss. Left her wanting more.

So why did it have to be *him*? And why now?

His face was turned toward her, and in sleep he looked irresistible. She studied the planes of his cheeks, the shadow of whiskers. She thought about the scar she had spotted on his side earlier, doubting it had its origins in medicine. An altercation, more likely.

A long strand of his dark hair lay across her cheek. Unbound, it fell thick and straight to his shoulders. His damp hair smelled of shampoo, soap. He must have showered while she slept.

It occurred to her that she really didn't feel overly threatened by Dallas. Yes, he was bigger and stronger and could physically overpower her. But she didn't feel *personally* endangered in his presence. Quite the opposite, she'd felt safe with him, especially when Snake and the others were around.

She sighed. Of course none of that took away from the fact she was being held against her will.

Still, a part of her wondered what had driven Dallas to a life of crime? Was he the product of a broken home? Had one or both parents abandoned him at a young age?

What did it matter?

She closed her eyes, clearing those thoughts. The bottom line remained unchanged. She was his prisoner, and her biggest concerns with Dallas remained unanswered. *What did he intend to do with her and how would she get free?*

At that moment, Dallas coughed. Then he stretched. His medal, warm from his skin, fell forward against her. His ribs grazed hers, muscles taut. Then she felt the growing hardness—lower—and remembered he wore little. Very little. She struggled for air as his head raised.

"Good morning," he yawned.

"You're squishing me!"

Frowning, he pushed up on his elbows, allowing her to draw a deep breath. While he was in no hurry to move off her, he didn't want her to be uncomfortable. This new position brought his groin directly in contact with hers. The fit would be perfect.

"Sleep well?" he asked, dropping his head back down to nuzzle her neck, as if waking up on top of her was a normal, everyday occurrence. Gently he bit the sensitive skin below her ear, laving the injury with his tongue.

Totally unprepared for his action, Tess jerked at the erotic gesture, inadvertently rubbing her lower body along the entire length of him. He hardened instantly, fully.

Dallas drew a sharp breath, his teeth clenched as he struggled for control. "Don't move. We've got a problem."

There was no mistaking the *problem*. She felt his erection burning against her abdomen, the length and breadth alarming her. He couldn't really be that big, could he? She froze for what seemed like an eternity. When it became apparent he wasn't moving, she spoke. "Let me up!"

"Say please."

"Go to hell."

"Tsk. Tsk. Are you always this grumpy when you wake up, or is it just me?" He rubbed his nose against hers, Eskimo style, inhaling the delicate rose scent he adored. "Is that why you and Geoffrey broke up?"

She huffed, twisting her face away. She and Geoffrey had been ill matched from the beginning, but it had suited Tess to maintain the relationship to keep her mother from interfering in her life. Madeline Marsh fancied herself a matchmaker, and when she wasn't busy finding herself a husband, she was looking for one for her daughter.

Geoffrey was the last person Tess would discuss with Dallas . . . though she didn't want him to know that. "Geoffrey and I are still very close."

"The man must be an idiot to have let you get away."

"He didn't *let* me . . . oh! Quit trying to change the subject. I demand you let me up," she began. "And you had no right to remove my clothes."

He stared down at her, brows raised. He found her defense of Geoffrey irritating. "Right now I have every right. Remember that. Besides, you slept better without them. The handcuffs, too. Though I know you won't admit it." He traced a finger lightly over her collarbone. "Holding on to you was the only way I could remove the cuffs and know you couldn't get free."

She stared at him, wanting to disagree. "Let me go, Dallas. *Please*." Placing her hands on his shoulders, she shoved but couldn't budge him.

He knew she asked for more than her freedom from the bed, from his embrace. A question he needed to deal with— but not with her. He caught her hands, stretching them over her head and lowering his mouth to within inches of hers. He wanted to grind his hips against her again. Bury himself in her. Instead he grunted.

"I can't release you, Tess. You have to know that and accept it. But I promise no harm will come to you while you're in my care." Once more he felt torn. God he wanted her, he'd go crazy sharing a bed with her, holding her, touching her. But *not* taking her.

Unable to withstand another minute of torture, he moved to get up. "You can have the bathroom first." Bracing his hands on either side of her, he hovered above her.

For a moment their eyes met, and she thought he would kiss her. And for a moment she wanted it.

In the space of a heartbeat, he lowered his mouth to hers, brushing her lips in a soft whisper. Her hands pressed against his chest. Pushing him away . . . or drawing him closer?

Then just that quickly he jumped free of the bed. Tess struggled to sit up, grabbing for the sheet. "Go ahead and get up," he said gruffly.

Stung by his sudden brusqueness, Tess snapped. "Am I allowed to use the bathroom in private? Or are you a pervert who likes to watch?"

Too late, she bit her tongue. No sense antagonizing the man. She needed to stay calm and maintain control. She waited for him to retaliate, wondering if the wiser move might be to apologize.

To her surprise Dallas ignored the remark, slipping a shirt over his head. She caught a brief glimpse of the bulge tenting his briefs before he turned away. "Help yourself," he said.

Snagging her jeans from the floor, she slid them on and hurried into the bathroom.

The first thing she noticed, besides the fact that it was infinitely cleaner than the one at the main house, was no lock on the door. Then she noticed the small window. Her spirits soared. Yes! It would be a tight fit, but she could squeeze through. And then . . .

Then she'd get as far away from the cabin as possible. She knew she wouldn't get much of a head start so every second would have to count. Starting now.

Moving quietly, she attacked the window pushing determinedly on the wooden sill. It didn't budge. Damn! She shoved again, then looked closer, spotting the bent nail hammered into the frame. She tugged at it, barely able to grasp it with her fingers, finding it immovable.

She needed something to pry the nail out. Scrambling back to the sink and turning on the water to cover the noise, she opened the mirrored medicine cabinet.

To her surprise the cabinet contained her toiletries. He'd undoubtedly unpacked her bag. Shampoo, deodorant, cosmetics. Her razor was conspicuously missing. So were her tweezers. She was disappointed, yet it didn't surprise her. Dallas struck her as a thorough man. He'd never have let her in the bathroom alone otherwise.

A knock sounded on the door.

"Just a minute!" she yelled, quickly splashing water on her face. With no lock he could have simply walked in. She supposed she should have felt grateful, but she didn't. Opening the door, she found Dallas holding a neat stack of her clothes.

"Any more dizziness?" he asked.

"No."

He thrust the clothes at her. "Then go ahead and take a shower. The water's good and hot, but it won't last long."

Her first instinct was to refuse. Except what did that gain her? A shower and clean clothes would feel heavenly. Still she hesitated.

"There's no lock on this door," she pointed out. *What's to stop him from barging in?*

Dallas shifted, leaning comfortably against the doorjamb. "After that pervert remark I ought to make you leave the door open. However, I'm a reasonable guy, and I'll give you the privacy you need. As long as it's not abused. Just remember that if I want to come in, nothing can stop me. Besides, if you got dizzy and fell—"

She snatched her clothes from him. "I won't!"

He glanced at his watch. "Good. Then you've got ten minutes. Take it or leave it."

Chapter Four

*E*ven though Dallas allotted her ten minutes for a shower, Tess only spent half that time beneath the water. First she tried again to pry the nail free with her fingertips. Unsuccessfully.

Damn, what she wouldn't give for a claw hammer. Or a telephone. *And a gun.* Frustrated, she threw open the bathroom door.

A delicious aroma greeted her. *Food.* Her stomach growled, reminding her of exactly how long it had been since her last meal. She turned toward the kitchen, frowning at the man who controlled too much of her life.

Dallas looked up, noting her scowl. Most people would have already buckled under the strain. Not Tess. Her moxie pleased him. And challenged him.

His glance swept to her sock-covered feet then slowly traveled up as he recalled his plan. Exploitation. *Seduction.* The assignment wouldn't be a problem on his part. He was keenly aware of her. Could still taste her. And fair or unfair, her survival hinged on his gaining her confidence, making her dependent.

"Feel better?" he asked.

She nodded.

His eyes held hers. "Head still hurt?"

"A little."

He grabbed a bottle of aspirin from a shelf and tossed it to her. "Take two. It'll help."

She started to toss the bottle back, then stopped. Her head *did* hurt. Bad. Moving past him to the sink, she ran a glass of water.

"Chow's almost ready. Sit there." Dallas pointed to a chair, then turned back to the stove. "Eggs, bacon, toast. Nothing fancy."

She ignored the chair, leaning instead against the counter. The shower had revived her, left her in the mood to pick a fight. "You cook for your prisoners? How quaint."

"Only the skinny ones." He gave her a quick once-over then looked away again. "Personally, I prefer a woman with a little more cush on her tush."

Tess opened her mouth, then closed it, glad to know she didn't fit his image of an ideal woman. Ignoring his back, she surveyed the cabin, the urge to escape stronger than ever. She studied the brand new dead bolt on the front door. On the off chance it was unlocked, she doubted she'd make it far without a better head start. Besides, where would she go?

The last thing she wanted was to get away from Dallas only to run into Snake. Or Bogen. For now she needed to be patient and learn the lay of the land. She also needed to make sure no one was around when she made her break.

"Hello?" Dallas stood right beside her, skillet in hand. "Scrambled okay?"

She jumped, flustered that he'd caught her lost in thoughts of escape. Needing distance, she took the chair farthest from him. "Yes."

Her eyes widened when Dallas set a plate in front of her and slid into the chair next to her. She stared at the plate.

There was enough bacon to clog an elephant's arteries. And it was extra crispy—just the way she liked it.

She pushed the plate away. "I'm not hungry."

Dallas's hand closed over hers, stilling the motion. "Starving yourself won't change the situation."

Tears stung her eyes at his unnecessary reminder. She glowered at him. His tendency to be thoughtful confused her. And infuriated her. "What *will* change it?"

"For now, nothing."

"Don't say that!" She snatched her hand away. "You had no right to bring me here. If you've got a shred of decency left in you, you'll let me go." Her voice lowered in desperation. "Please. I'll do anything."

"Anything?" Dallas looked at her. Fueled by the memory of her beneath him in the bed, his imagination supplied searing images laden with hot potential. *Anything . . .* What would she look like wearing only willingness and all that long golden hair?

He shook himself mentally, yanking hard on his control. Not for the first time he felt the sting of regret over his actions. But that didn't alter a thing. His path was carved in stone, and now she was part of it. A complicated part. And it was going to get personal.

Bogen had been right. She'd definitely gotten under his skin. Scrubbed free of dirt and makeup, she was, he found, even more attractive, her skin flawless, her cheeks delicate. And as he'd originally thought, she did have blue eyes. Dark blue, with long spiky lashes.

And right now those lashes were trembling as she attempted to hold back tears. She was angry and frightened. He didn't blame her. She had to be bordering on a breakdown. She needed food. She needed comfort.

He needed to comfort her.

"Come here."

The silky undertone of his voice caught Tess by surprise. She opened her mouth to refuse, then stopped. Exactly *what* was she willing to do to gain her freedom? How far would she go? Was she willing to barter her body?

She swallowed, remembering the kiss he'd given her earlier. A part of her had been gratified by it. Without a doubt the man was accustomed to pleasure. Giving and taking.

And there was nothing to stop Dallas from taking. As if that wasn't enough to cope with, Bogen's threat came back to taunt her. *I can take you back if you're a problem.* What would happen if she didn't please Dallas? Would he hand her over to Bogen? Could she survive that?

Under the circumstances, she'd do whatever it took to remain with Dallas. To stay alive. To stay alert for an opportunity to escape.

She peeked at Dallas from beneath her lashes. She didn't sense the same violence in him that she did in Snake and the others. Perhaps she could even appeal to him without . . . going all the way. He stared at her openly, his silvery eyes giving away nothing of his thoughts. Or his intentions. He was seated to the right of her, close enough to touch if she stretched out her hand.

"Come here." The order was repeated. Softly.

Swallowing nervously, she climbed to her feet. In two faltering steps she stood directly in front of him. Dallas took her hand, tugging her closer till she stood between his spread legs.

"Sit."

He indicated that he expected her to sit on his lap. She lowered her bottom until it made contact with his muscled thigh. She kept her eyes locked on his, wary, recalling the first time she saw him, when she'd been struck by what a handsome man he was. Potent. Sensual. Dangerous.

Dallas's body responded to her nearness, his jeans growing increasingly uncomfortable. She held herself as far away from him as possible, sitting as stiff and rigid as certain parts of his body. He knew she couldn't be comfortable. And it reminded him that she didn't want to be there. That he shouldn't be doing this . . .

But he needed for her to get used to him. He needed to establish a strong bond between them, and quickly. Her survival depended upon it. The fact that he wanted her was secondary.

Yeah, right.

"Relax." She couldn't weigh more than his bed pillow. Reaching forward, he tugged her legs over his, drawing her tightly into his lap. She struggled, accidentally rubbing her palm against his groin. When she recognized the hardness, she stilled, snatching her hand away as if it burned.

Under different circumstances, Dallas would have taken her hand in his and stroked it up the entire length of him, in an intimate introduction. *Did she like it fast or slow?* Instead he reached for a piece of bacon.

"Open," he commanded.

Caught off guard, Tess obeyed, automatically biting when he stuck the food in her mouth. It could have tasted like tree bark for all she knew. Her awareness was focused on the ridge pressed against her thigh. It felt hard and hot. Could she really go through with it? Use sex in exchange for freedom? And live with herself afterward?

"Chew." Dallas watched her, knew she felt his erection and wished he could read her mind. *Did she moan or scream?* He'd bet he could make her scream. . . .

She chewed mechanically, then swallowed. Dallas held up a mug of coffee. "Hot," he warned, watching as she took a cautious sip. Blistering hot. *Would he melt inside her?*

He offered the mug again. "More?"

When she shook her head, he set the coffee aside, shifting

his position slightly. Pushing her *away*. He couldn't take much more of this himself.

As soon as Tess swallowed the coffee a forkful of eggs appeared. "Open for me," Dallas quietly urged.

"You don't need to feed me," she whispered, and drew her legs closed.

"You said you'd do anything. Right now I want you to eat."

Right now, her mind echoed. The *what about later* hung between them. "I can feed myself."

"Humor me."

Whether she wanted to admit it or not, the food did taste wonderful. And so far his requests had been reasonable. With little choice anyway, she opened her mouth, content for the moment to eat.

When she'd gone through half the eggs, Dallas grabbed a triangle of toast. She was about to tell him she was full when he put the toast to his own mouth and bit off a corner. Silver eyes held blue ones captive as the piece of toast turned, the already bitten end offered to her. She knew exactly what he was doing. Teasing. Testing.

The vague sense of well-being vanished. Cold reality set in once more. She would do this. She could do anything necessary to survive. She stared at his lips. He had a perfect mouth. A perfect kiss.

The toast shifted closer.

Very slowly she nibbled one edge, in her mind tasting him again.

The toast dropped, forgotten, as Dallas drew her close. In the space of a heartbeat, he lowered his mouth to hers, brushing her lips in a soft whisper. He kissed her, drawing his tongue lazily, reverently, across her bottom lip.

She pretended to enjoy the kiss. Or at least that was her intent.

Her lips throbbed under the tenderest of assaults as his fingers slowly threaded through her hair. He turned her head slightly, positioning her expertly, then drawing her closer. As he deepened the kiss, his teeth gently caught her lip, tugging, demanding entry, his rogue tongue delving deeply into her mouth when she finally opened to him.

She closed her eyes in an effort to hold back the small moan building at the back of her throat. Her hands pressed against his chest. Pushing him away . . . or urging him closer?

Dallas wrapped his arms tighter around her, letting sensations bombard him. The scent of her, fresh from the shower. The creamy softness of her skin. And her magnificent breasts, tips pearl-hard, pressed against him, testing his sanity.

Suddenly the pressure grew too great. He had to stop this now. *Or go forward.* And considering the circumstances, he knew the former choice to be the right one . . . his turgid flesh be damned.

He pulled back, tucking her head beneath his chin, exhaling sharply as he fought for control.

Tess clamped her eyes shut, wishing she could disappear. How could she have allowed herself to lose track of her intentions? Her lips felt raw where he'd plundered, her pulse raced. And low, very low, a treacherous warmth blossomed, budding moisture. Desire?

It couldn't be.

Yes, they'd shared a kiss. But it didn't mean—She couldn't do it. She couldn't close her eyes and pretend they were lovers, that he hadn't kidnapped her. And what must Dallas be thinking now? *That she'd do anything?* She almost had.

But one thing puzzled her. He had been as affected by their momentary intimacy as she. And it bothered him. Why?

She would have expected him to act on his animal instincts, not struggle *against* them. Unless . . .

Did he feel guilty? Maybe she did have more of a chance with him then she realized.

When a knock sounded at the front door, she started. Dallas swore, setting her on her feet.

"Just a minute," he yelled out. Signaling to Tess, he lowered his voice. "Get in the bathroom and stay there."

Thankful for the interruption, she didn't argue, hurrying into the bathroom as Dallas strode to the front door. Once inside, Tess eavesdropped. At first she heard nothing. Then she recognized Duke's voice.

"Bogen's called a meeting," Duke said. "Thirty minutes, at the barn. You and Eddie are making a beer run afterward."

Knowing Tess probably listened, Dallas stepped outside, onto the porch and shut the door. He pierced Duke with a cold stare.

"You wouldn't know anything about the cut the woman's got on her head, would you?"

Duke's chest puffed belligerently, then just as quickly deflated when Dallas's hands fisted at the collar of his shirt.

"Hey, man, she fell. It was an accident. If that bitch told you anything else, she's lying."

"She's mine, Duke, and I'll kill anyone who lays a finger on her while she's in my possession. *No excuses*. Spread the word."

Tripping over his own feet, Duke nearly fell down the steps in a hurry to get away.

It would have been a lot more satisfying to deck the little prick, Dallas thought. Except right now Duke was scared—far more useful. He'd keep a healthy distance from Tess and warn the others as well. Oh sure, there'd be a few who wouldn't listen. Like Snake. But Dallas knew who they were, knew to keep an eye out for them.

Turning, he went back inside.

Tess had listened, disappointed when the men stepped outside to talk. What were they discussing? *And what would Dallas expect when he returned?*

She grew warm, remembering. She had never thought of sharing food as a sensual act until Dallas offered her that piece of toast. The food had served as foreplay, the prelude to his kiss. Then she lost control. How could she respond that way toward a man she should despise?

She didn't despise the man. She despised the situation.

In fact the man was attractive to her in more ways than one. He was different from the others. The round peg amidst square holes—he didn't quite fit. And, perhaps most importantly, if she appeared to cooperate, he might free her.

When she heard the outside door, she quickly turned the faucet on and grabbed her toothbrush.

When she entered the kitchen a few minutes later, she smelled coffee. Dallas handed her a mug.

"We need to talk," he began. "About your role here."

Tess frowned setting the coffee aside. "Do I have any say in the matter?"

"No." Dallas didn't like it any more than she did. Their options were limited. "We both know you'd prefer your freedom. That's not in my power to grant. Bogen runs this camp with a tight fist. He considers everyone here to be under his domain. You will be allowed to stay in my keeping as long as I take proper precautions. One is to assure you can't escape."

She bristled. "I'm surprised you allow a man like Bogen to exercise so much control over your life. What happens when you want one thing and Bogen wants another? Does Bogen *always* win?"

Not if he could help it. Dallas realized Tess baited him. The residual tension from their kiss crackled in the air.

Whether she wanted to admit it or not, she'd been affected by it. He liked that.

"I knew the rules when I signed up," he said.

"Well I didn't!" Her mounting frustration cracked. "You're nothing but a bunch of kidnapping murderers! Do you think I don't know what's going to happen to me? Do you think I want to end up like—" Realizing she'd said too much, she turned away.

Dallas was beside her before she could blink. The man moved faster than light. She tensed as he grabbed her, pulling her close. Unwilling to back down, she stared at him coldly.

"Murderers?" he repeated. "An interesting choice of words. What makes you say that?"

When she didn't respond, Dallas exhaled sharply. Something had happened. He could see it in her eyes. *Horror.* The question was what. He knew when. She'd only been out of his sight for those few hours she'd spent locked in the pantry. Snake had returned to the big house during that time. Had he or Bogen threatened her?

"You don't want to end up like whom?" he prompted once more.

She swallowed, suddenly unsure of how much she should tell him. She hadn't missed the brief look of surprise that flashed across his face. Shock. Disbelief. In other words, *Dallas still didn't know about the man Snake had murdered.*

Was it a secret between Snake and Bogen? If she let on that she knew, would Dallas tell Bogen? Would it make her position in camp even more precarious? She recalled Bogen's threats. He'd take her from Dallas and do God knows what. Blinking, she looked away.

"You're hiding something," Dallas said, relaxing the grip on her arms. "While I can't blame you for not trusting me, there's a few things you should know. If Bogen starts to feel like you're a threat to him or his operation, he'll get rid of you. And I don't mean kill you. There's a huge demand outside this country for women like you. Your stay here will seem like a week on a luxury cruiser."

She paused, absorbing his words. He was trying to frighten her into submissiveness. Like Bogen had. Except he didn't frighten her nearly as much as Bogen.

Feeling bold, she called his bluff. "I'd welcome the change! Nothing can be worse than this! Nothing."

The fingers gripping her arms instantly tightened, snatching her up against his chest, leaving her feet dangling inches off the floor. His hold constricted unmercifully as he spoke.

"Are you familiar with the term 'white slavery,' Tess? You're shipped out of the country and sold to the highest bidder. Don't look so stunned. There's a part of the world where that type of thing happens with alarming regularity. In fact, demand exceeds supply. And with your looks and body, guess what commodity you'd be expected to provide? For perhaps a houseful of guests. You'd be abused mentally, physically, and sexually."

He shook her, his eyes raking her body, lingering on her heaving breasts, purposely violating her, his voice cruel. "Yeah, you'd be stupid enough to fight. Until they whipped off a layer of skin. Or had you addicted. Have you ever seen what an addict will do for a fix, Tess?"

She shook her head, too aghast to speak.

"Then think twice before you open your mouth around here. I know this isn't nice. I know you think it's unfair. But it can be a hell of a lot worse." Relaxing his fingers, he set her down, keeping a grip on her when she faltered. Damn, he hadn't meant to lose his temper.

Stunned, Tess stared at him. She'd touched a nerve. Dallas *was* different. She'd seen it in the boiling disgust he kept carefully hidden below the surface. A small thread of hope flickered inside her.

"You don't condone something like that, do you?" She could barely speak.

Dallas wrestled with his conscience. "Whether I do or don't is immaterial. The point is that the consequences of breaking Bogen's rules are bad."

She drew a deep breath. Whether she liked it or not, she needed to play the game to stay alive. "And what are these rules?"

"Anytime you're not with me, you've got to be secured."

"You mean handcuffed?"

He nodded. "When the two of us are here alone, I'll give you free run of the cabin. That changes if someone else is around. You've probably figured out that Bogen and his cronies consider women chattels. Right now you're considered mine. Everyone will respect that as long as I maintain control."

Tess paced across the room toward the couch, not liking what she heard. She turned, pinning him with a cold stare. "How long do you honestly expect to keep me like this? My family and friends *will* miss me. They'll notify the police."

"They won't find us, Tess."

The conviction in his voice shook her. "You're just saying that so I'll go along willingly with whatever you say. Like I have a choice!"

Dallas shrugged. "Would you prefer Snake's company over mine?"

"That's not a choice, and you know it." Tess suppressed a shudder of revulsion. If she had to stay in Bogen's camp, she'd choose Dallas. He'd already proved to be far more considerate than expected.

And he *was* different. In ways she couldn't yet define. She'd seen glimpses of it, sensed it. Yes, the man was a devil. But a chivalrous devil. He hadn't taken advantage of the situation. The question was why? She was his prisoner. He could easily overpower her.

Yet he didn't. And something deep inside her said he wouldn't. A small bubble of hope surfaced.

"You're not like the others," she whispered drawing close once again, seeking his eyes. "Who are you?"

"I'm more like them than you know. Don't push it."

He wasn't being honest. Confused, she changed subjects. "Exactly how many other people live here?"

He moved away to refill his coffee cup. "Exactly? Still planning an escape?"

She rubbed her upper arms where he'd held her, certain she'd have more bruises. "Just curious. Are there other women in camp?"

"Three or four. But they're here by choice. You won't be allowed any contact with them. Which is probably for your own good. They're a jealous bunch. Snake's girlfriend, Liz, is the worst. She'd just as soon cut your heart out as look at you."

"Sounds perfect for Snake."

He glanced at his watch and set his cup aside. "I've got to go out. I don't know how long I'll be, so I suggest you finish eating and use the bathroom."

"Are you going to handcuff me again?"

"Yes."

"For how long?"

"As long as it takes."

Tess reached out, stopping him when he would have turned away. "Can I go with you?"

"No."

She saw him glance at his watch yet again and knew time was running short. "Can we compromise and just cuff one hand?"

He shook his head, playing his trump. "The only alternative is to leave you locked in the pantry at the big house."

Her shoulders fell. She'd rather stay here, chained to Dallas's bed, than step foot back inside Bogen's house. She'd even abandoned her idea of getting to Bogen's telephone and calling for help, not wanting to risk getting caught by Bogen himself.

After using the bathroom, Tess refused his offer to eat, and this time he didn't push it. She followed him into the bedroom and sat meekly on the bed.

"Lie down. Hands over your head." At first he thought she was going to fight him. Then she lay down.

Her acquiescence left a bitter taste in his mouth. He grasped her hands easing them up. He felt her resistance, knew what it cost her to obey. "I'll be in town. Do you need anything?"

"The police."

He snapped the cuffs in place. Gently. Then he trailed the tip of his finger down the inside of her arm. "My thoughts ran more along the lines of chewing gum or a magazine."

She shook her head. He stood.

"Dallas?" She stopped him before he left the room.

He turned, expecting her to ask for something from town. Her troubled visage tore at him, reminding him how unfair the situation was to her. He came back and sat on the bed.

"What . . . what happens to me if you don't return?"

The knife in his gut twisted. That was something he didn't want to think about. Leaning forward, he traced the fine lines in her forehead, trying to erase them.

"I promise I'll return."

Chapter Five

The barn was in better shape than most other structures on the property. Originally built to house horses, most of the stalls had been ripped down, leaving plenty of space for Bogen's clan and their motorcycles.

Dallas arrived last. Frankie tossed him a beer and made room at one of the dilapidated picnic tables.

Preferring to stand, Dallas downed half the beer and leaned against the fender of Bogen's brand-new pickup. All the cars and motorcycles the gang drove were legally owned and registered. Another one of the rules. No one drove hot vehicles.

Dallas scanned the small crowd. Fourteen handpicked men, not counting himself. Snake, Duke, and Eddie were part of Bogen's original gang. They had started out twelve years ago in Southern California dealing in stolen property. Since then they'd tried their hand at almost every other crime. Drugs proved most lucrative, and they had built up a profitable trade between Mexico and Los Angeles.

Then Bogen hooked up with Sanchez's organization. The Big Boys. The South American Source. Bogen's operation rapidly increased to include the entire West Coast. About nine months ago, when the heat got too hot in California,

Bogen packed up and moved operations to a deserted corner of Montana, where he was preparing to expand into another profitable joint venture with the South American cartel: white slavery.

Dallas had been with the gang eighteen months. Bogen himself had recruited Dallas after a fight in a sleazy Sacramento bar where Dallas inadvertently saved Bogen's life. A knife meant for Bogen's heart had deflected neatly off Dallas's rib cage. It had taken over sixty stitches to close the gash but had earned him something beyond measure: Bogen's trust.

For the first few months after joining, Dallas handled petty stuff: stolen cars and truckloads of stolen cigarettes. Bogen immediately recognized Dallas's shrewd ability to turn a higher profit, and he quickly moved up the ranks.

At that moment Bogen stood, clearing his throat. The barn grew quiet.

"Everyone knows the people we work for have been nervous the past several months. They've had a few close calls."

"They've always been nervous," Duke shouted. "Afraid we'll take over."

Bogen waited until most of the laughter subsided. "The bottom line is, we've got orders to shut down temporarily. Normally I wouldn't comply, but this time my gut tells me to listen. And everyone here knows I've got pretty good instincts."

The decision to comply with Sanchez's order surprised Dallas. It wasn't like Bogen to back down in a situation like this. Dallas had expected a confrontation between Sanchez and Bogen—a token act of defiance if nothing else. But to roll over and play dead? Why the sudden change of heart? Several of the men grumbled, urging Bogen to reconsider.

Dallas noticed that Snake remained uncharacteristically quiet. That was odd, too. Snake never kept his opinions to

himself. Dallas's senses went on alert. What was going on?
Something had happened between the time Bogen and Dallas had discussed Sanchez last night and now. The question
was what?

He thought back to his suspicions that Tess hid something.
Either he was growing paranoid, or everyone else knew
something he didn't. And if not everyone, then certainly
Bogen, Snake, and Tess.

"I suggest you stick close to camp for the next week or so,
until this blows over. I'm sending Haynes and Eddie to stock
up on supplies. If anyone needs something, see them."

Bogen looked briefly at Dallas, then continued. "Everyone's curious to see Haynes's new acquisition. Too bad. He's
not sharing." With Bogen's word it was official. Tess was his.

Several men hooted lewd encouragements, which Dallas
ignored. Snake dropped his beer can and strode off. But not
before shooting Dallas a venomous look.

The exchange left Dallas feeling uneasy. Snake would
cause trouble the first chance he got. Dallas needed to get
Tess out of the way, as soon as possible, but without casting
suspicion on himself.

The problem was *how*.

⌐⌐

"Her name is Tess Marsh, age twenty-six. She's one of
the Marsh heirs."

The man on the other end of the phone, Dallas's FBI supervisor, Barry Neilson, whistled. "How the hell did they get
her?"

Dallas was parked near the drugstore, talking on his cellular phone. Eddie had made a beeline for the local pool hall
when Dallas mentioned stopping to pick up supplies for Tess.
Dallas figured he had fifteen minutes at the most.

He quickly explained the circumstances leading to Tess's abduction. "Bogen doesn't realize who he's got. And I think I've convinced her to keep her identity secret. But if Bogen finds out, her life won't mean squat. He'll bury her rather than take risks with a high-profile name. I want her out, Barry. Now."

Barry grunted. "That'll be tricky, especially since she's in your care. She disappears; all eyes turn to you. And we're close, buddy. The signal's coming in strong."

The signal was one of several homing devices Dallas had planted on Sanchez's beloved pet greyhounds. The animals went everywhere Sanchez went. If Sanchez were going into hiding at the cartel's headquarters, the dogs would accompany him.

"Sanchez is waiting to complete one more shipment," Barry continued. "It should go down within the next two or three weeks. He's got at least ten women ready to move. And get this: At least two of them are under eighteen. Unfortunately, he's got them well hidden. He's already nervous—if we put the squeeze on him too soon, he'll take off like a skyrocket. And we could lose the girls. We've got to let this deal go down as planned."

Dallas frowned, scanning the streets. Barry had a point. There were other considerations besides freeing Tess. The cartel had to be stopped before one more innocent young woman was snatched.

This wasn't what Dallas had originally signed on for—not that he'd have backed down. What was supposed to have been a routine FBI undercover drug operation for Dallas and his partner had quickly expanded once they learned Bogen had connections with Sanchez. Hector Sanchez's elusive association to the cartel's white slavery operation had been a bane to international authorities, who wanted Sanchez's boss. The head honcho, Quito Ramon.

Dallas's connection to Sanchez through Bogen was the first time anyone had ever gotten so close. Consequently, the scope and duration of Dallas's assignment changed drastically. He'd been undercover almost two years on a job that had initially been expected to last about three months. And they were too close to turn back now. No matter how tired of it he was.

"I don't want to take unnecessary risks with the Marsh woman's life," Dallas reiterated.

"Agreed. But we don't want to put *both* of you at risk by acting at the wrong time." Barry sighed. "Let me check on a few things. Like making sure we can squelch any news stories that surface if she's reported missing. I'll leave word with Michaels—as soon as I catch the bastard. He was taking a day off to go fly fishing, and I haven't heard from him yet."

Matt Michaels was another undercover FBI agent posing as a local mechanic in nearby Jordan. He was Dallas's partner and intermediary. Dallas had worked with Matt on several other cases. The men worked well together.

"In the meantime," Barry continued, "keep the woman as close to you as possible. And stay in touch."

After hanging up, Dallas punched in a seventeen-digit code. The cellular phone was one Bogen furnished to all his men. An additional computer chip in Dallas's phone scrambled his transmissions and allowed only the Bureau to eavesdrop on his conversations.

The code changed the billing records to show Dallas had indeed placed a call—to his bookie. The same bookie Bogen occasionally used. In fact, while Dallas spoke with Barry, someone masquerading as Dallas made a simultaneous call of the same duration to the bookie.

Climbing out of the truck, Dallas hurried into the drugstore. He'd grab a few things for Tess, then pick up Eddie and get back to camp. He didn't want to leave her alone any longer than necessary.

━━━

Tess stared at the ceiling, blinking back tears, disoriented. *Count to ten.* She'd once been told that you couldn't count in your dreams. One, two, three . . .

And that's all it had been: a bad dream. She stared at the clock. Two hours had passed. She must have dozed off only to awaken back in the nightmare that had become her life: being chained to Dallas's bed.

She shivered, unable to shake the final remnants of the grisly dream in which Snake had dumped her concrete-weighted body into Lake Summer. She'd floated downward in slow motion, sinking in terror to land amidst a watery graveyard of decomposing bodies with fish-eaten eyes. Her lungs ached as she held that final breath, refusing to relinquish her life.

Seven, eight, nine . . . She struggled to sit up.

How would she get out of this mess—alive and unharmed?

Dallas's harrowing description of her potential fate had left her numb. *White slavery.* Could she survive being sold, being raped, or being made a drug addict?

A sob broke free. How many women had met fates like this, were victims of such a grossly offensive crime? Did anyone suspect that such a thing had occurred, or were the women assumed to be victims of some other atrocity? What must their families be going through?

For the millionth time she thought about her own family. In her case, it could be another four weeks before her family even missed her or suspected something was wrong. Her shop was closed for the summer, which gave the two college

kids that worked for her a chance to go home until the fall se-
mester. Her mother was husband hunting on the French Riv-
iera. That left her father and brother, who had an empire to
run. If Tess remained incommunicado all summer, they'd
hardly notice.

The only other person who might notice her absence was
her ex-fiancé, Geoffrey. She knew from her mother's letters
that Madeline was encouraging Geoffrey to "try again." But
Tess had her doubts. Geoffrey had wasted little time finding
a suitable replacement.

The sad truth was no one would miss her on a day-to-day
basis. Tess had planned on following the summer craft show
circuit across the Midwest, interviewing potential designers
for her shop. Because she had wanted to leave room in her
schedule for spontaneous forays, she hadn't left an itinerary
with anyone. And she had used cash the last two times she
purchased gas and food, leaving no credit-card trail. Once
they discovered her missing, how would they find her?

Unless someone fortuitously pulled her car up from the
lake, it could be a long while before anyone suspected foul
play.

She closed her eyes, thinking about the man Snake had
killed, and once again saw the knife plunge, blood spill
across the floor. The man hadn't even cried out. Didn't beg
for mercy. And she'd never felt so helpless and frightened in
her life. Matt Michaels. Who would miss him? Family?
Friends?

Bogen seemed to think Michaels was working with someone else. If that someone connected Snake to Michaels,
would they come around asking questions? That had seemed
to be Bogen's primary concern. He wasn't concerned over
the fact Snake had murdered a man. He'd been worried it
would draw attention to their operation.

What had she gotten into? Snake was a murderer, but

clearly Bogen authorized it. How many cars and bodies lined the bottom of Lake Summer?

Would Dallas learn about Michaels's death at this meeting? How would he react? She felt certain Dallas wouldn't sanction murder. That didn't necessarily mean he'd turn against Bogen and Snake though. *Or did it?*

She recalled Dallas's warning against letting anyone know her secrets. The more she thought about it, the more it seemed that Dallas, for whatever reason, was indeed trying to protect her. But just how far would he go for her? And how far was she willing to go to test it?

She shifted positions, recoiling when one of the cuffs chafed against a sore spot on her wrist. She grimaced, seeing the raw skin. After Dallas left, she'd tried in earnest to break free. She had pulled and tugged, determined to squeeze one of her hands through the opening. It had proved futile. Her flesh gave way more readily than stainless steel.

She tensed when she heard a noise at the front door. Someone was entering the cabin. Please, if it wasn't the sheriff, let it be Dallas. Pure, choking dread rose in her throat at the thought of Snake or Duke finding her like this.

Chained.

Helpless.

She held her breath as the bedroom door opened slowly.

"Miss me?" The quip died on his lips as Dallas took in her obvious distress.

Moving to the bed he unshackled her. Her wrist bled where she'd tried to escape the cuff. Damn it, didn't she know she couldn't force them open?

But could he blame her for trying?

He tossed the cuffs on the floor, silently cursing the circumstances that required their use. Sitting beside her, he gently pulled her arm forward to examine it.

She reacted violently, swinging her other arm. "Let me

go!" she shrieked, launching herself at him, raking his cheek with her nails. "You have no right—"

Dallas responded without thought, flipping her onto her back and quickly pinning her to the bed, allowing her to vent her frustrations by struggling uselessly beneath him.

Within moments she settled, turning her face away, eyes closed. He could feel her tremble as she wept.

For the first time since getting involved with Bogen, Dallas questioned his course of action. God, he didn't want to be a hero. This slip of a woman had cracked his tough façade, made him want to forget about the others and focus only on her and her needs. Which he couldn't allow himself to do. Not now, anyway.

The temptation to put her on his motorcycle and drive as fast and as far as he could was strong. But where would that leave the ten women Sanchez held captive? They deserved their freedom every bit as much as Tess. And if the cartel wasn't stopped, how many others would be victimized?

"You can let me up." Tess's voice sounded hoarse, but steady. "I won't fight you again."

Dallas studied her, took in her puffy eyes and red-tipped nose. Her bottom lip quivered. The urge to kiss her was strong—to kiss, to console. To hold her and make things right again. Instead he brushed his fingers lightly against her tear-stained cheek. She shivered with cold.

"Would you believe I'm more concerned that you don't hurt yourself?" In one smooth move he rolled onto his feet, leaving her alone in the bedroom.

Tess sat up, straightening her clothes. Before she could stand, Dallas returned carrying a first-aid kit and a wet towel. Kneeling before her, he took one wrist. When she offered no resistance he gently bathed the abraded skin.

Tess recoiled, but not from his ministrations. His cheek sported two bloody welts where she'd scratched him. The sight appalled her. What had come over her? She'd never been violent a day in her life, had never physically hurt another person for any reason.

Until now.

Was this how it started? How violence begets more violence?

She reached out and gently touched his cheek, her hand shaking.

"I'm sorry I scratched you," she whispered.

He stared at her a long moment, wishing he could kiss away the hurt, the anguish he saw in her eyes. Instead he looked away.

"I'm sorry for a lot of things, Tess. Most of which I don't know how to fix right now."

An awkward silence ensued as Dallas smeared antiseptic cream on her wrist. When he finished, Tess picked up the foil tube, weighing it in her palm.

When Dallas started to stand, she stopped him. Very deliberately she smoothed a small amount of the antiseptic over his scraped cheeks. "If we're both sorry, that's a start."

For a moment she thought she saw remorse race across his eyes. But just as quickly it disappeared, replaced by that odd, unreadable look she was coming to recognize.

Dallas tugged her to her feet. "Come on, I'll take you for a walk outside."

~

The days settled into a routine, one indistinguishable from the next. Dallas fixed breakfast, then handcuffed her to the bed—a stark reminder she was his prisoner. He stayed gone most of the day, never mentioning what he did nor where he went. After the first week she quit asking. The second week was harder.

The notebook Dallas gave her was filled with half-finished jewelry sketches. Uncertainty prevented her from completing most of them, but that didn't stop her from picking up the notebook daily to battle the nerve-wracking boredom.

Her thoughts remained a perpetual loop of brooding over the future and reliving the past. Did her family realize she'd been abducted yet? Did anyone even suspect she was missing?

She thought over Dallas's warning about keeping her identity secret. Once the press learned that John Marsh's daughter had been kidnapped it would make headlines, and Bogen would know who she was. In spite of his promises to protect her, could Dallas really keep her safe if Bogen ordered her killed?

Thankfully, she hadn't had contact with any of the other gang members since that first day. Except in her recurring nightmares. Still, she worried every time Dallas left that he might not return. And what would happen to her then?

Every day that he handcuffed her to the bed was one more day she stayed alive. Had she been in anyone else's keeping, she didn't believe that would be true. And he went out of his way to see to her comfort. Left her extra pillows, wrapped cloth around her wrists to avoid chafing. Too bad he didn't leave the key.

More and more she wondered what kind of person Dallas really was, how he came to be involved with Bogen. She found him an enigma. He didn't seem to fit the mold of outlaw.

He hadn't kissed her since that first day, though there had been several occasions when she thought he would. And more than once when she had wanted him to. He rose before she did every morning, but not in time to keep her from being aware of him.

There was no denying the physical attraction that existed

between them, an attraction that seemed to flourish with the closeness of her captivity. He was her sole contact with the outside world, and she was dependent on him for virtually everything.

One night after supper, when she thought she would go crazy from not knowing about her family, Tess brought up the subject. The sun was fading, and she and Dallas were sitting outside on the porch steps.

"Do you know if my family is looking for me?"

The forlorn note in her voice tore at Dallas's gut. He'd talked with Barry two days ago. The Marsh family had not filed a missing person report and was not expected to. Even though she'd been with him two weeks now, her family wouldn't expect her back for several more. Barry decided not to jeopardize the situation by contacting her family and risking a leak to the press.

With Matt Michaels's disappearance, the situation had grown even more volatile. Foul play was strongly suspected, and Dallas could not risk exposing himself by asking questions about Matt in Jordan or the other surrounding towns.

To do nothing frustrated him. Every day the trail of clues surrounding Matt's disappearance grew colder. And Dallas knew Barry was every bit as exasperated.

The only good news was that Sanchez seemed ready to leave his Canadian stronghold. Barry anticipated making arrests soon, and then this house of cards would fall. In the meantime, Dallas's primary objective was making sure Tess remained safe.

"I haven't heard anything," Dallas finally replied. "But news travels slow in this part of the country."

Tess's shoulders fell as she struggled against tears of self-pity. She supposed she should be grateful her situation hadn't been jeopardized by public knowledge of her abduction. But that wasn't much comfort. She wanted to be free. *Now.*

"I wonder if I'll ever see them again," she whispered.

Not for the first time he wished he could tell her everything. Except that changed nothing. The cold, hard fact remained that if Bogen learned Dallas's true identity, Dallas was a dead man. He'd known that from the start. And Tess would end up in a shallow grave beside him. After Bogen did God-knows-what to her. Bogen had a cruel streak as wide as his ass.

He stood, gruffly pulling her to her feet, eager to change the subject, hoping to lighten the mood. "If you want to take a walk, let's go."

Dusk yielded slowly to darkness as Dallas and Tess walked in silence. She was still no closer to knowing that much about Bogen's compound. On previous nights they'd walked the different paths through the woods, all of which seemed to circle back on each other and lead right back to his cabin. She suspected the camp had originally been designed that way to prevent little Scouts from getting lost. She also suspected Dallas purposely selected this time of day to take her outside. In the growing darkness the paths appeared similar, which made it even more difficult to memorize their course.

Still, it felt good to be out and moving. A breeze rustled through the leaves causing her to wrap her arms around herself.

She walked without watching her surroundings and was startled when Dallas suddenly pulled her off the path and under the spreading branches of a weeping willow. Sliding a hand gently across her mouth, he whispered, "*ssshhhhhh*," and pointed over her shoulder.

A short distance ahead, a doe and her twin fawns meandered along the path, spending the last quiet minutes of dusk foraging. Dipping its head beneath its mother's belly, one fawn nursed, oblivious to the audience. Tess held her breath, enthralled by the sight. By the time the animals wandered off, she had a cramp in her neck from holding still.

Encircled by his arms, she turned, looking up at him. "They were so beautiful. And so close."

Her words echoed his thoughts. *She was so beautiful.* And so close. Time and circumstance ceased to exist as he lightly drew her against his chest.

If it was a sin to want someone this bad, then he was damned. He ached with the rawness of desire, searching her eyes for a reason to stop . . . and finding none.

His mouth closed over hers, tentative at first, growing bolder when he met no resistance. He whispered her name, drawing her completely into his embrace. His fingers slid into her hair, pressing her scalp, holding her still as his tongue delved deeper.

Tess's arms found their way around his neck, her hands tugging at the thick silk of his long hair as she pushed up on tiptoes, opening to his kiss, lowering her guard. She felt his hands move down, inching slowly beneath her jacket. His fingers skimmed her ribs.

With exquisite tenderness he grazed the undersides of her breasts through her clothes, his knuckles sensitizing the skin. For a moment she imagined his hands on her bare flesh, his fingers on her breasts. Her nipples hardened. Breathing was suddenly difficult. She flexed her hands, rubbing his neck.

"I want you, Tess." He groaned, pressing forward, letting her feel the proof of his arousal, desperately wishing she'd caress him *there*.

Waves of uncertain delight battered her, making it hard to think. His low growl sent goose bumps zinging up her spine. She had already tugged his T-shirt free—when?—and edged her fingers into the waistband of his jeans, fidgeting with the top button. Seeking.

The thought that she wanted to touch him intimately

shocked Tess. She couldn't deny that his kiss was exciting. That she craved his touch. *That she wanted more . . .*

Dear God, what was she doing? She pushed away, confused by her reaction, afraid of how he'd interpret her response. She felt her face flame with embarrassment, glad for the cover of darkness. Why had she let him kiss her, touch her? Why had she touched him?

And worse, how could she enjoy it?

For a long moment the only sound she heard was their breathing. Heavy. Hot. Unsatisfied. Then Dallas reached for her hand, drawing it to his mouth. Ever so gently he pressed a kiss to her open palm and closed her fingers over it.

"There's no denying that something lies between us, Tess. But I want you to know you're still safe with me."

Tess snapped her hand back, grasping for anger to conceal the raw ache. "Safe? You expect me to believe that? There's nothing between us, Dallas. I'm your prisoner. Period."

He watched her stalk away, toward the cabin, and gave her space. She was lying. She wanted him. He knew it just as surely as he knew he wanted her. The problem was she knew *he knew* now. And under the circumstances that bothered her.

Dallas took another sip of warm beer. The ancient clock above the bar threatened to strike midnight. Behind him pool balls *clacked* and sank into worn pockets. Last time he checked, Snake had been down twenty bucks and was in a foul temper.

Dallas's mood wasn't any better. He wanted to get on the road and get back to camp. They'd been gone all day transacting business for Bogen, which was bad enough. Then Snake suggested they stop for a beer, which typically wouldn't have been an issue.

Dallas had never liked Snake, but he'd always been careful to give him his due as one of the brethren. And he'd gleaned a lot of vital information from Snake over the course of his investigation. Drunk, Snake tended to talk too much.

Tonight, though, Dallas wasn't in the mood. They should have been back hours ago. Tess was most likely miserable. Snake knew it, too. This was just another way to get back at Dallas for keeping her.

Once more Dallas's thoughts strayed to the woman who was chained to his bed. They had barely spoken since he kissed her two nights ago. The sexual tension between them was tangible, a seething caldron on the verge of boiling over. God, he wanted her, needed her even, the same way he physically needed his next breath.

He glanced at the clock once more, mind made up. He was leaving, with or without Snake.

Snake's voice, from the back of the bar, broke into his thoughts. "You ain't quitting till I get my dough back."

Dallas turned, cursing as he caught sight of Snake threatening his opponent with a cue stick. And sneaking up behind Snake was a man with a chair.

"Look out!" Too late, Dallas yelled a warning. The chair crashed across Snake's lower back, wood splintering.

Snake doubled over and shook his head, then let out a yell before charging the dumbfounded man who'd hit him. The man hadn't moved, clearly expecting Snake to go down.

Dallas shoved his way into the melee, intent on dragging Snake away even if it meant knocking him out cold. The bartender was already on the phone calling the cops, which meant they probably had less then five minutes to get the hell out.

The wet floor glistened with shattered shards of a beer bottle. A fist glanced off Dallas's jaw. Dallas grabbed the man who'd thrown the punch, spinning him around and twisting his arm painfully behind him.

"Do that again, and I'll break it," Dallas hissed.

The front doors swung open and three deputies hurried in. "Freeze! Sheriff's department!"

"Jesus, he's breaking my arm." The man Dallas held started squealing in a high-pitched voice, switching easily from aggressor to victim. "Make him stop! Officer!"

Two of the deputies had weapons drawn. Simultaneously they pointed them at Dallas. "Hands on your head, scumbag."

Moving slowly, Dallas released the man and did exactly as the deputies instructed. In seconds he was flat on his stomach, his wrists cuffed behind him.

"You guys wanna help me with this one?" the third deputy asked.

Dallas twisted his head, catching sight of Snake standing in the corner, a broken cue stick held threateningly out in front of him.

"Drop the stick, now!" one of the officers commanded.

Snake smiled maliciously. "Why don't you try and take it?"

The question went unanswered as a fourth officer, who'd crept in the back door, hit Snake on the back of the head with his black baton. Snake crumpled, dropping in an unconscious heap on the floor.

One of the officers radioed for an ambulance while rough hands yanked Dallas to his feet. Shoving him forward against the pool table, another deputy patted him down searching for weapons. They confiscated his knife.

"You're under arrest, pal." The deputy grinned, clearly enjoying the feeling of power his badge inferred. "Disorderly conduct. Assault and battery. You have the right to remain silent . . ."

Dallas knew they were going to jail, knew there was nothing he could do about it. The best he could do was cooperate, act drunk, in hopes they'd get him processed into the local jail as soon as possible. He had a phone call coming, and the sooner he made it the better.

～

Tess shifted on the bed, the handcuff chains clanking. This tactic was new. Abandonment? It was nearly two in the morning.

Dallas had never left her this long before. She shifted her arms, trying to burrow further beneath the tangled blankets.

Things had been more stilted than usual between her and Dallas the last few days. He had avoided her since the other night, when they'd watched the deer. He'd even spent the past two nights on the couch, though she knew he wasn't sleeping. She heard him pace, no more able to sleep than he was. It bothered her more than she cared to admit, for in the final analysis he was her only affirmation that life existed outside her immediate surroundings.

When he *was* around he barely spoke to her. Of course, she'd started that. She had been mad at him for kissing her. For making her feel things for him that she shouldn't. But what had made her think the silent treatment would gain her anything?

Dallas held all the cards in this game. More and more it felt as if he held all her emotions as well. Yeah, it wasn't fair. It wasn't right. But that didn't change the situation.

Right now she desperately wanted, needed, to see Dallas. And not just for food, or to get up. She needed to know he was coming back.

She heard a noise at the door and strained to listen. Unbidden, tears sprang to her eyes. Dallas! Thank God! She struggled to sit up, determined to do whatever it took to make things right between them again. She never wanted to be left alone like this again.

Her apology died on her lips when the door was flung open and the overhead light cruelly snapped on, temporarily blinding her.

"Boo! Bet you thought you'd seen the last of us." Eddie stood in the doorway, then strolled over to the bed. Duke followed, looking distinctly uncomfortable.

Tess cringed, moving back against the headboard, her range of movement severely limited. "Get out of here!"

"Miss High-and-Mighty thinks she can tell us what to do." Eddie sneered, his eyes raking slowly over her. "I bet Haynes had fun taking you down a peg or two. Fucked you silly, huh?"

Had? Her mind seized ruthlessly on the word. Past tense. Tess's heart bumped painfully against her throat. "Where's Dallas?"

Ignoring her question, Eddie swaggered closer holding out a handcuff key. "I'd love it if you gave us some trouble." He winked lewdly.

The bubble of raw dread that had been building inside her burst as Eddie freed her hands.

"Stand up," he ordered, grabbing her harshly by the shoulder and jerking her to her feet. "Put your hands behind your back."

Duke surged forward, shoving Eddie's hand away. "He said to let her use the john."

Tess's hope soared then just as quickly plummeted. These two men were most likely acting on Bogen's order. "Please, tell me where Dallas is."

Eddie's hand bit into the soft flesh of her upper arm as he propelled her, urgently, toward the door. "All you need to know is he ain't here, lady." His lips stretched into a depraved smile. "And we are."

~~~

When Eddie and Duke took her from the cabin she'd had no idea where they were taking her, or worse, what their intentions were. And her mind readily supplied all the worst-case scenarios.

To her dismay, they locked her in the dark pantry at Bogen's house. She'd fought and lost. And this time, besides leaving her hands cuffed, they gagged her and bound her ankles with heavy rope.

Perspiration soaked the thin shirt she wore. She had been surprised when they left her untouched.

It seemed she had escaped rape . . . for the moment at least. But who knew what lay ahead. Thankfully, she hadn't been drugged, though depending on what happened next, she might wish she had been. She recalled Dallas's description of enforced servitude, wanting to vomit at the thought of the pain, the abuse that awaited her. *White slavery.* She wouldn't be able to withstand it.

She no longer tried to stop the tears from tracking down her cheeks. She felt miserable and frightened, scared of what was to come. *And she knew it would be awful.* With Dallas she had maintained hope, maintained a belief that in some crazy way it would all work out. Now that hope was gone.

Ignoring the roiling of her stomach, she tried to breathe deeply, fighting the distressing blackness simmering at the edge of her mind. As much as she hated her present predicament, the thought of passing out and waking up in a worse scenario was beyond imagining.

She huddled in the corner, listening for what seemed like hours, but the house remained quiet. Her scattered thoughts turned to Dallas again and again. Why hadn't he returned? She couldn't believe he had turned her over to Bogen.

Unless . . . something had happened to him. Her chest squeezed painfully at the thought. Was he injured, hurt?

Or had he simply tired of her and wanted her out of his life?

No. She refused to believe that. Dallas had been right. There was something between them, a bond, a link. Something more than the ever-present, physical attraction. As much as she tried to deny it or ignore it, it was there.

And only now did she realize how fully she'd come to depend on him for her mental well-being. He'd protected her, nurtured her.

Dallas. He had to be all right. And he had to return for her. For sanity's sake she held on to that thought.

She felt thirsty and tired, but didn't dare close her eyes. In the short time she'd been locked up she'd realized a surprising thing about herself: She was a fighter. She'd do whatever it took to survive.

She shifted, trying to find a comfortable position. The pantry was not only unheated, there were several holes in the wooden floor that allowed cold, damp air to waft in from what she assumed was a basement below the house.

A faint noise caught her ear. Holding her breath, she listened. There it was again. A slight scraping sound. Followed by a faint squeak.

God, what if Bogen or one of the others was coming for her? How could she possibly stop them?

The noise repeated itself, and this time she frowned. It almost sounded as if it came from within the pantry. She peered around in the darkness, unable to see much.

Then it moved. And squeaked again.

A rat.

She tried to scream, scrambling backwards toward the

door. The creature stopped, seemingly frozen in its tracks as it assessed her. She banged her feet on the floor, making as much noise as she could.

The rat retreated and for a moment she thought she'd frightened it off. Until she heard it squeak again.

And heard an answering squeak from its mate.

Chapter Six

$\mathcal{B}$y midmorning Dallas and Snake exited the county jail. They were arraigned promptly at nine o'clock and as soon as the judge set bail, Duke posted it.

Getting their motorcycles out of impound, however, wasn't as straightforward.

First they had to wait for the sheriff's department to approve the release, in triplicate, on the proper form. Then someone had to radio the tow-truck operator to find what he had done with the keys.

What little patience Dallas had rapidly disintegrated. For the thousandth time he cursed Snake for his boneheadedness in starting the fight in the first place. And Bogen for insisting that Dallas accompany Snake to oversee a routine money drop. In hindsight, Dallas questioned Bogen's motives for sending him. It almost seemed Bogen hadn't trusted Snake. Which was odd.

Thrusting on a pair of sunglasses, Dallas silently scrutinized Snake. Snake's mood had not improved with their incarceration. Dallas knew he was hung over, knew he probably had a good size knot on his head from where the deputy had coldcocked him with his baton.

But he didn't feel sorry for him. In fact, he felt like

punching him. If it weren't for Snake, he wouldn't have been up all night worrying about Tess.

Duke confirmed that she was at the big house, in the pantry. Dallas's conscience spasmed painfully. Spending the night in jail had been a stinging reminder of what life must be like for Tess. Except his loss of freedom had lasted less then twelve hours. And his captors, while they clearly hadn't liked Dallas and Snake, had acted professionally, observing Dallas's and Snake's rights.

How many times had he heard it said that criminals had more rights than their victims? Hell, he'd said it himself on numerous occasions. It was an awful truth.

He scowled, thinking of Tess, what she was going through now, what she'd been through these past two weeks.

And how easy it would be to free her when he got back.

He could wait until dark and leave the compound with her. No one would question him. They could be across the state line in two hours. Or in Canada.

But could he throw it all away for her? God, he wanted to. He had the power to make it happen, knew she deserved it.

But so did the others. And his honor—damn it—wouldn't let the story unfold any differently.

Dallas opened the pantry door, his eyes taking in the entire scene.

Tess was huddled next to the door, her legs bound and curled up close to her body. She'd drawn back at first, her face wild with panic. Recognizing him, she'd started crying hysterically, a pathetic, strangled sound coming from behind the gag.

He stepped over her, kneeling directly in front of her, purposely blocking her view of the dead rat in the opposite corner. The rat's head was bashed; there was blood on the heel of her shoe. He could imagine what had transpired. He tugged the gag away and enfolded her in his arms. She buried her head in his shoulder, against his neck, pressing herself as close to him as she could, the force of her sobs shaking her.

There were no words to make it right, but he said them anyway. Hushed promises, quiet assurances. Soothing sounds.

He hugged her, held her, rocked her, until at last her sobs softened to a low keening. In spite of her disjointed words, he was able to confirm that she hadn't been physically harmed by Duke or Eddie; nor bitten or scratched by the rat before she killed it.

After removing the cuffs and freeing her ankles, he massaged her shoulders and arms for a few minutes, restoring blood flow, before pulling her to her feet.

"Can you make it to the cabin?" It was tempting just to pick her up and carry her back, but the slight exercise of walking would probably be good for her.

She nodded, then raised her head, searching his eyes. "I'm sorry for whatever I did," she croaked, voice hoarse. "Don't ever leave me like that again."

He brushed a finger over her lips, then rested his hands on her shoulders wrestling against the urge to swallow her slight frame in a crushing bear hug, to beg forgiveness. "You have nothing to apologize for."

"Then what did I do to end up here?" A single tear escaped and ran down her cheek. "Is it because—"

"It's nothing you did or didn't do. I got tied up." He looked away briefly not wanting to tell her the truth, afraid that if she knew he'd just gotten out of jail, she'd be even more frightened. "I was worried about you being chained to the bed all night and thought—mistakenly, perhaps—that you'd be better off up here."

His low, caring tone was her undoing. Right now, she'd grant him any wish, forgive him any sin. He'd come back for her, and that was as much as she could focus on for the moment.

Leaning forward, she buried her face in the front of his shirt. Her arms threaded tightly around his waist. "Take me home. Please."

Her surrender almost undid Dallas. Her words echoed in his mind. *Home.* It was a place he desperately wanted to return to himself.

But after the last eighteen months, he wondered if he even knew the way.

~

While Tess showered, Dallas changed clothes. He'd taken a shower before leaving jail, and while he wouldn't have minded taking another, he wasn't about to cuff her again.

Instead he made hot cocoa and filled two mugs. He would have preferred to fix her a hearty breakfast, but knew she was too upset to eat. And he wasn't going to push her. They'd eat later.

Right now he was more worried about her frame of mind. Last night's experience must have been horrendous. Duke and Eddie coming for her. What had she expected? Rape? Torture? Murder?

Then she'd been locked in that rat-infested pantry. Dallas had hoped Bogen would have the decency to lock her in one of the upstairs bedrooms. Lousy bastard.

When the bathroom door opened, he saw her poke her head out cautiously, as if checking to see that he was still there. She stepped out, her relief tangible.

"Better?" he asked, crossing to offer her a mug.

She nodded, but remained quiet. Didn't seem to understand that he meant for her to take the cocoa.

"Let's get you to bed, then. I know you're exhausted."

She shook her head. "No. I'm—" Unshed tears glistened in her eyes, making them appear impossibly bluer. "I don't want to be alone right now."

"Come on." He led the way to the couch, unsure of how to proceed. He didn't know what she needed right now.

But he knew what would make him feel better. He sat down and held out his hand.

"I'd like to hold you, but I'll respect a no."

Tess hesitated only a second, unable to think of one good reason she should refuse the consolation he offered.

Normal reasoning simply did not apply to this situation. She felt as if her psyche had been ripped, battered. As if she'd been cast into a dark pit, and Dallas was the only one who shined light her way.

Taking his hand, she let him pull her onto his lap. His strong arms surrounded her, hugging her, making her feel safe. His large hands cradled her head, tucking her neatly against his shoulder as if the spot were made for her alone.

The walls she'd managed to erect around her emotions while in the shower crumbled under his gentle ministrations. In spite of her prior resolve not to speak of it, she found herself telling him about her awful night in the pantry. How afraid she'd been that he wouldn't return.

And once the words started flowing it seemed impossible to stop them. How long they stayed on the couch, she didn't know. Nor did she care. The only thing that seemed to matter in the moment was the fact that she felt safe.

When she quieted, Dallas pressed yet another kiss to the top of her head, wondering if she was even aware that he'd done so. Hesitant to break the spell, he broke another rule and asked about her personal life.

"Tell me about your life in Boston."

For a moment he thought she'd drifted off. Then she sighed. "I have a town house downtown that I'm trying to sell. I've decided condo life is not for me."

"You want a yard?"

"A farm. With an old barn I can convert into a studio."

Dallas was finger-combing her hair, torturing himself by separating the thick, damp, strands. "Will you have animals?"

"Dogs and cats. Mostly dogs probably. To keep my mother away."

Dallas chuckled. "You'd sic dogs on your own mother?"

Tears stung her eyes. She hadn't meant that the way it sounded. "She's allergic. Or at least that was her excuse when I was a child and wanted one."

"You don't get along with your mother. What about your father and brother?"

She shrugged, uncertain how to describe her family relationships, puzzled that she even wanted to. "My father's whole life is business. My brother learned early on that following in his footsteps was the best way to keep his attention."

"Weren't you tempted to join the family business, too?"

"My father comes from a long line of sexists. He doesn't believe in working women."

Dallas shifted her slightly, massaging her scalp, wanting her to stay relaxed enough to keep talking. "How did he react to you opening your own shop?"

"He nearly had a stroke. When he realized I was serious, and discovered that I actually had some talent, he insisted I showcase my designs exclusively through the Marsh stores."

"And you said no? How did he take that?"

She made a strangled sound. "Not well. My father is accustomed to getting his way no matter how many vice presidents, managers, secretaries, or wives he has to fire. He didn't like the fact his own daughter opened a shop in downtown Boston. We get along fine, now. In spite of his idiosyncrasies, I love him. And miss him. Especially now. My mother, too."

For a few moments the silence hung heavy between them, then Tess spoke again. "Tell me about your life, Dallas. Where did you grow up?"

He intended to lie, but when he opened his mouth, the truth dropped out.

"Pennsylvania." He skipped over his years in college and offered another half-truth. "I moved around a lot as a kid, then eventually joined the Army."

He started rattling off the places he'd been stationed. When she didn't respond, Dallas glanced down. She'd fallen asleep in his arms, as trusting as a baby.

He pressed a kiss to her forehead and settled back, satisfied to watch the flames in the fireplace die down. He didn't care if she slept for hours. For now he was content just to hold her.

⌁

Tess woke up in his arms, like she did every morning now, her bottom spooned low against his abdomen, his leg pressed possessively between hers. She slept in one of his T-shirts and a pair of her own underwear.

He'd given her an ultimatum on sleepwear. She could either wear the silky nightgown he'd found in her bag or a T-shirt. She'd picked one of his T-shirts because they were longer then hers.

For a few moments she lay still, savoring the closeness, relishing the odd security she felt at being wrapped tightly in his arms. In the days since freeing her from the pantry, Dallas had only left her twice. Both times he'd kept his word and been back within an hour.

Outside of kissing her, which, if she was honest, she'd

admit she enjoyed, he hadn't made any untoward advances. Just as he promised.

Maybe it was that integrity that made her wonder what an intimate relationship with him would be like. After these weeks of waking up in his arms, his body was familiar to her. She knew the contours of his wide shoulders, knew the ripple of his abdomen pressed against her back. He was much taller, yet she didn't feel threatened by his size.

In fact she grew increasingly . . . curious. In the nights they'd spent together, she'd felt his rock-hard erection pressed against her on more than one occasion, felt it rub against her buttocks. It wasn't unpleasant.

It was odd, but during the time she'd spent with Dallas she realized how superficial her relationship with Geoffrey had been. They'd had no physical connection; both of them had been too wrapped up in their different careers. Geoffrey, in fact, spent the majority of his time in the London offices of his father's export company while Tess built her business in Boston.

One day, when Tess realized Geoffrey had been gone two months and she didn't miss him, she broke the engagement. It had all been terribly civilized. Madeline, her mother, had been more distraught by the news than either she or Geoffrey had been.

Tess sighed. Had Dallas ever been engaged? Married? Had there been one special woman he adored above all others?

She could readily imagine him in a relationship. She'd bet he'd be solicitous. Slightly jealous. Wondrously attentive. And sexually demanding. Exactly what would it be like to be made love to by Dallas Haynes? Hot? Sinful?

Illicit.

And something she didn't need to think about experiencing with this man. Not now. Not here. Not ever.

Closing her eyes, she forced her thoughts to clear. Here she was dreaming about making love with a man she should still be trying to escape. And it wasn't just about sex. She was falling for Dallas, which made it even more critical than ever that she get away.

Not caring if she woke him, she moved. "I'm going to take a shower."

Dallas yawned and rolled away. "I'll make coffee."

Alone in the bathroom, Tess turned on the faucet, then started tugging at the nail in the window. Every day she tried to loosen the nail, to no avail. Until yesterday. She thought she'd felt it turn.

To her amazement the nail popped free as soon as she grabbed it, pinging noisily against the tile floor before skidding and ricocheting off the tub.

She almost squealed.

Pressing her fingers against the sash, she pushed, but still the window wouldn't budge. Applying pressure at a different angle, she pushed again, using every bit of strength she possessed, but with no success.

Damn! What was wrong? She'd already checked the edges to be certain they hadn't been painted shut. She frowned. At least not from the *inside*.

Glancing back briefly to check the door, she pressed her nose against the glass, peering down toward the outside sash. That's when she saw the line of nails. Five of them.

Dallas had nailed the window shut from the outside, too.

Her heart pounded dully in her ears, disappointment bringing tears to her eyes. She had been so focused on getting the single nail out that it hadn't even dawned on her the window might refuse to open for other reasons.

Turning the shower on full blast, she stepped under the spray. She would have to find another way to escape.

They had just finished breakfast when someone banged on the door.

Tess looked expectantly at Dallas. To her surprise, he didn't order her to hide in another room. Nervous, she started clearing the table. When she finished that, she peeked around the door, wondering who Dallas talked to.

Immediately she regretted her impulsiveness as Snake leered at her over Dallas's shoulder, his black eye patch making him look even more evil. Her stomach tightened as she remembered the last time she'd seen Snake . . . when he'd murdered Matt Michaels. Her hands started shaking.

"Bogen said you've got extra coolers," Snake said, looking directly at her. "He needs one."

She backed up until the kitchen counter pressed into her spine, struck anew by the physical prowess of these two men. They were huge. She wouldn't stand a chance against either of them.

For a long moment Dallas blocked the doorway. Finally, he stepped aside, allowing Snake to enter. Crossing to where Tess stood, Dallas reached over her head and grabbed one of the battered ice chests stacked on top of the refrigerator.

Turning, he tossed the chest at Snake. Remaining in front of Tess, Dallas reached around and possessively tugged her up against his back, out of Snake's view. "You got what you came for."

"Yep. I'm looking forward to the cookout, *amigo*." Snake laughed. "She'll make an interesting main course."

As soon as he was gone, Tess yanked her arm free and stepped away. "What was he talking about?"

"Bogen's having a party tonight. A cookout. We're invited." Dallas had known this moment would come sooner or later.

"I'll stay here."

"It's not optional," he said. It was obvious that Snake's

visit had upset her. He noticed that her hands were trembling. "But you'll be with me every moment."

"Who will be there?"

He caught the edge in her voice. "The entire camp. They're curious to see you, Tess. I told you before there are several women here at the camp. I've never been with any of them, nor have I ever brought a woman here, so you're somewhat of a novelty."

He paused, waiting for her to look at him. "I'll be frank. They will assume we've had an intimate relationship. Don't try to correct them. They won't care whether it's a consensual arrangement or not. In fact they'll assume it wasn't. As you know, they'll be crude. Ignore them, and I'll get us out of there as soon as I can."

Once again she saw a flicker—compassion?—behind those silver eyes just before he turned and walked away, leaving her alone in the kitchen. He wasn't as indifferent to her situation as he'd have her believe.

Perhaps she did have a chance at convincing him to let her skip Bogen's little soiree. She followed him quietly, intent on asking again if she could stay behind.

Dallas was in the bedroom, rummaging through the boots he stowed in the back of the closet. "Damn Snake," he muttered. "I'm sure that bastard had something to do with Michaels's disappearance."

His words surprised Tess. "Matt Michaels?"

Dallas spun around, irritated that he hadn't heard her approach, shocked by her question. "How did you know that was his first name?"

She felt her face redden. "I . . . I . . . guessed it. I'll go finish the dishes."

Dumbfounded, Dallas watched her hurry away. *Damn.* She knew. He had suspected all along she was hiding something.

He just hadn't thought it pertained to Matt. Jesus, how stupid could he be?

Sitting back on his heels, he forced his temper to cool. He needed to know exactly *what* she knew about Matt. And how she'd found out. The problem would be convincing her to tell him about it without raising suspicion that might imperil his assignment or endanger her.

A few minutes later he walked out to the kitchen where she stood with her back to him, furiously washing dishes. Moving closer he grabbed a towel and started wiping a plate.

The tension between them stretched, as brittle as spun glass, until finally he spoke. "Tess, I know you don't deserve anything that's happened to you. But I hope you recognize that I've gone out of my way to protect you and will continue to do so. If you know anything about Matt Michaels, you need to tell me."

Tess looked at him squarely. "No. The only thing I *need* to do is stay alive and get back to my family."

He tossed the towel down. "I knew Matt Michaels from town. He worked on my bike a few times. In fact he did work for several people here. Everyone liked him."

She opened her mouth, then just as quickly closed it and tried to move past him.

Silver eyes pinned her in place. "Everyone except Snake."

"I don't know anything," she blurted.

"I think you do, but you just don't want to tell me." He reached out, wrapping a golden strand of hair around his finger and tugged it lightly, urging her closer. "Why?"

Tess scowled, resisting, pulling away. "You warned me against letting anyone know my secrets. You said it could put me in even more danger here. So to be perfectly honest, I'm scared. Of Snake. Of Bogen. Of you."

Dallas eyed the clock, wishing they had more time to discuss this. Unfortunately he had a meeting scheduled with

Bogen. They were going to call Sanchez. For now he had to leave.

"I've asked you several times to trust me, Tess. Have I betrayed you yet?"

Angry tears glittered in her eyes. "You're holding me prisoner!"

"Funny. I thought I was keeping you safe from the others."

Moving away, Dallas started preparing for his meeting, but his mind was still on Tess. She knew something about Michaels's disappearance, of that he was sure. But she didn't believe in him enough to tell him what it was.

Well, tonight Dallas was going to change that. He'd lay on the charm as soon as they returned from Bogen's party. Hell, maybe sooner. He wanted Tess's trust, needed it. And tonight he'd do whatever it took to win her confidence.

They rode Dallas's motorcycle to the cookout, which was held a couple of miles from the main house, on the shore of a lake. He assured her it wasn't Lake Summer—which didn't make her feel any less uncomfortable.

In the dark it was impossible to see the water, but Dallas said it was only a short distance away. "I'll take you for a walk along the shore later," he offered.

Tess shook her head. Her fear of water had seemed to magnify with each passing nightmare of Matt Michaels's lifeless, concrete-weighted body. Being anywhere near water held little appeal for her.

Besides, she was still furious with Dallas for marking her neck. Just before they had left the cabin, he pulled her into his arms and started kissing her. Tender, maddening kisses, as if she were the most precious thing on earth.

Tess had melted on the spot, powerless against his touch,

the feel of his lips nuzzling her throat. Then she'd felt a slight sting, felt his teeth graze and nip. Twice.

One look in the bathroom mirror confirmed her suspicions. He'd given her two unsightly love bites, right in the middle of her neck. "How dare you!" she accused, embarrassed to have once again lost her reasoning while in his embrace.

"It's insurance, Tess. Everyone will look for signs of my ownership. They'll challenge any perceived weakness. I don't intend to show any."

Well she didn't either. Self-conscious, Tess fought the urge to put her hand on her neck as they walked through the woods toward the party. Light from a fire flickered through the trees.

Dallas looked at her. "You okay?"

She nodded. No, she wasn't *okay*, but she didn't feel like discussing it.

"You're awful quiet," he said.

"So was Daniel when they led him to the lions."

He chuckled. "I'll keep you safe. Trust me."

Trust him? After the little hickey episode? Right!

Actually, she was still trying to decide how to handle his questions about Matt Michaels. She'd spent the afternoon debating the pros and cons. One minute she would decide to confide in him. The next she worried it wasn't prudent, that it might jeopardize her own situation if word of it got back to Bogen.

Only one thing seemed clear: Dallas didn't know all the details about Michaels's disappearance, and he wanted her help in filling in the blanks. But why question her? Why not ask Bogen or Snake?

Unless Dallas didn't want them to know he knew.

Oddly enough she found she wanted to trust him, but for reasons she didn't want to examine too closely. The more she explored her feelings for Dallas, well, the less clear everything seemed. Too often lately she found herself wondering what it could have been like to meet him under different circumstances.

She shook her head. That train of thought was insane. And dangerous. Which only proved that now, more than ever, she needed to escape.

They had reached the perimeter of the fire. It was apparent the group used the spot regularly. Downed trees ringed one side of the blazing bonfire.

On the other side, two picnic tables were butted together near a row of rusted barbecue grills. Open bags of potato chips and several coolers filled one table.

It seemed everyone talked at once, yelling to be heard above the music blaring from a portable stereo. She recognized Eddie's voice when he yelled, "Look who's here."

All talk ceased. Tess became painfully aware of their stares, their blatant disregard for her person. To them she was an object. A sexual commodity.

She looked away. Several women hovered near the food. Judging by their scowls, she guessed these women to be the ones Dallas had mentioned previously. If they were here by choice, they certainly wouldn't feel any sympathy for Tess's plight.

One woman stepped free, yelling back at Eddie. "What's the matter? You never seen blond hair and big tits before?"

Another woman lifted her shirt, exposing her breasts briefly to a round of applause. Tess hunched her shoulders forward.

"Jealous, Liz?" someone shouted, touching off peals of laughter. The conversations picked back up, more frenzied than before.

Tess glanced away. So that was Liz. Snake's girlfriend. She had jet-black hair dyed the exact shade of her leather jacket and sported an equally dark bruise on her cheek. If that was a souvenir of life with Snake, Tess felt sorry for the woman.

Dallas led her to a secluded spot at the far side of the campfire keeping one arm slung casually around her neck. He ran a hand down her side, squeezed her bottom.

"Easy," he hissed when her eyes widened. "They're watching." He squeezed again, then patted possessively.

"Sit there." He pointed to one of the logs circling the fire, then leaned in close to whisper in her ear. "I'll be right back."

Whether he meant to reassure or warn, she wasn't certain. But with everyone watching she'd be a fool to attempt to leave.

The blaze generated welcome heat. She nervously scanned the crowd, recognizing several of the men from the night she'd been abducted. There were also a few new faces.

She noticed Snake was conspicuously absent. She looked away when she spotted Bogen huddled in a dark corner, hoping to avoid his attention.

A small group of men gathered on the far side of the fire, one of them pointing at her, another making an obscene gesture. She covered her neck with her hand, which only made them laugh. Growing increasingly uncomfortable with their attention, she tried to watch Dallas's broad shoulders as he circled the picnic table filling a plate, willing him to return.

Liz came up behind Dallas and wrapped her arms around his waist. The sudden flash of irritation Tess felt puzzled her. And pricked her temper. She didn't care what Dallas did or with whom. Or did she?

Unable to look away, Tess watched as Liz suggestively rubbed herself against Dallas's butt, crooning loudly. "How about sharing a tent with me tonight? Let Eddie and the boys have a go at her."

Several catcalls of encouragement arose from the crowd.

Dallas set his plate down long enough to unhook Liz's arms. "I don't think Snake would appreciate your offer."

Liz plainly took Dallas's refusal as an insult and turned to cast a malignant look at Tess. A look that spoke a thousand words—all of them bad.

To Tess the problem was instantly apparent. Did Dallas realize Liz had a thing for him? Did Snake? Tess stood as Dallas approached, taking the beers from his outstretched hand.

"I can't do this," she whispered. "Please get me out of here."

With one hand free, Dallas grasped her head and caught her lips in a lusty kiss. For show. Someone hooted in approval. "You're fine. And the worst is over."

Moving behind her, Dallas sat on the log. Grasping her hand, he pulled her down between his legs, giving her no choice but to sit on the ground, subservient, at his feet. Yet another part of the show.

"This way," he said, indicating she should sit facing him. "Then you don't have to watch them." He winked.

Dallas handed her a fork, indicating they'd share the plate. "Stew and beans." He took a bite of the stew, then lowered the plate to her. "This stuff will make you appreciate my cooking."

Tess started to decline, when she caught Dallas's gaze. *Eat or be fed.*

"Trust me, you don't want to piss off the cooks around here," he murmured.

She took a small forkful, quickly followed by a swallow of beer. The spiciness burned her tongue.

Dallas nodded. "There's plenty more beer."

By the time she'd finished her second beer, she'd eaten enough to satisfy Dallas. She sat forward once again, watching the flames. The fire burned brightly, tucking everyone in the shadows. Tess drew her knees up and huddled closer between Dallas's legs.

"Cold?" Without waiting for her response he began rubbing her upper arms.

She nodded, suppressing a yawn. Beer made her sleepy. And worse, made a trip to the bathroom a necessity.

Which perhaps presented an opportunity for escape. She had watched several of the men disappear into the woods, no doubt relieving themselves. If she could just get enough head start and find a good hiding place until morning . . . Tonight's full moon would serve her well, but it would also help her captors.

"Dallas, um, I need to use the ladies' room."

"Come on, we'll head back." Pulling her to her feet, he led the way toward the picnic tables.

She tugged his arm to get his attention. "I don't think I can wait."

Dallas frowned. "That only leaves the woods. And I'll have to go with you."

Liz appeared out of nowhere, resting a hand on Dallas's shoulder. "I can take her. Besides, Bogen wants to see you."

Dallas shook his head and was about to say something, when Tess interrupted. "Actually, I'd be more comfortable with a woman."

And her chances of escaping Liz in the woods were probably better than getting away from Dallas. It could gain her several precious minutes.

For a moment she thought Dallas would refuse. Then he nodded, turning to Liz. "I'll meet you back here in five minutes. Don't let her out of your sight."

Chapter Seven

*H*urrying after Liz, Tess stepped into the dark woods, silently cursing Dallas for reminding Liz to watch her. The path narrowed, wending up a steep incline. Liz carried a flashlight but it cast little light in Tess's direction, making it difficult to distinguish the terrain.

"The women use the top of the hill," Liz said when they finally stopped in a small clearing. Tess squinted, trying to get her bearings. She needed to make her break quickly. Each second counted.

When she looked back at Liz to ask for privacy, she was alarmed to see the dull glint of metal. Liz sliced the air between them with a knife. A vision of Matt Michaels, pooled in blood, flashed through Tess's mind. She eased backward.

"I could easily slit your throat," Liz hissed. "And throw you over that cliff into the lake."

Only then did Tess realize Liz had backed her in a corner. She peered warily over her shoulder. Just a few paces behind her was a drop-off overhanging the lake.

The lake.

Tess's fear of water weakened her knees. Dizziness rang in her ears as bursts of bright colors swam before her eyes.

She felt herself grow faint and despised her own cowardice. "Don't do this."

A hand clamped over her mouth as someone grabbed her around the waist, from behind.

"Hello, darlin'. Told you we weren't through."

Tess recognized Snake's voice and immediately began to struggle.

Snake shifted his grip, placing a hand over her breast and squeezing. "Hold still, damn it. I don't want anything you ain't already given Haynes. And who knows?" He smacked his lips noisily in her ear. "You might like me better than pretty boy. I guarantee it'll be different."

Tess knew she was going to be sick. Snake's hand continued to grope coarsely across her chest, even as Liz watched.

Bitter, regretful tears stung Tess's cheeks. She never should have left Dallas's side. Belatedly she realized that only with him was she safe.

"Let's go." Snake tugged her backward, toward the trees. *Toward rape. Toward death.*

Frantic to break free, Tess renewed her struggle. Forcing her mouth open, she bit Snake's hand, simultaneously stomping on his foot. He howled, loosening his grip. She dashed forward, but didn't get away.

"Damn you!" he snarled. Catching a handful of her hair he yanked her to the ground, slapping her viciously. "You'll pay for that."

Dallas stepped out of the shadows. "Let her go, Snake!"

Snake's grip unexpectedly relaxed as he shoved her aside and charged Dallas.

Rolling to her feet, Tess shot away. She cast a glance backwards and saw that Dallas had Snake's head vised in the crook of his arm. Blood poured from Snake's nose.

At that moment Liz stepped forward, blocking the path, knife flashing. She grabbed Tess's forearm, catching her off guard and spun her backwards, in a semicircle. Toward the cliff.

The knife rested dangerously close to Tess's throat, but it was the sight below that made her heart beat erratically.

The lake.

Liz had her perched on the very edge of the precipice. Moonlight reflected on the water below. The soft dirt crumbled, giving way beneath her foot.

Tess shrieked.

Dallas looked up and immediately released Snake. "Drop the knife, Liz. Now!"

At first it seemed Liz wouldn't comply. She stared at where Snake lay sprawled in the dirt, then shrugged. "Guess you win this round."

Throwing the blade at Dallas's feet, Liz stepped away. But not before shoving Tess harshly between the shoulders, sending her over the side of the cliff.

It seemed to take an eternity for Tess to hit the water. *An eternity suspended in hell.* She sank immediately. The water's numbing coldness shocked her, breaking her stupor.

Arms and legs flailing wildly, she broke the water's surface, desperate for air, but unable to keep herself afloat.

Her cries were cut off as water filled her mouth, choking her. *"Dallas!"*

The water felt heavy, tugging on her, pulling her down. Every bad dream Tess ever had about drowning crowded into her brain, horrifying her. She sank deeper.

Thoughts of her family flashed through her mind. The last words she'd had with her mother. So many regrets, so many things she had yet to experience. She thought of Dallas. Damn it, she didn't want it to end like this. She didn't want to die.

She wanted to live.

She felt a hand close over her shoulder and began struggling. Frequently, in nightmares, there had been hands holding her under, not letting her up. Death. She had to battle it.

To her amazement, she broke the surface once more. Gasping for breath she renewed her attack.

"Tess! I've got you. Don't fight me."

She surged forward, pushing uselessly, trying to find Dallas in the eerie darkness. "Can't swim." The dream closed in. She coughed, taking in more water. "Drowning."

His voice came from behind her. "I won't let you. Just relax."

Relax? She choked. Water burned her nose. An agonizing cry of panic broke free as she fought her fears. He didn't understand. Nobody understood the abject terror that water represented.

"Tess, I have you. Reach up and feel my arm around your shoulders."

With jerky motions, she did as he asked. "I feel you, but I can't see you. Where—"

Dallas heard the rising panic in her voice and sought to calm her. "Trust me. We're almost there. Focus on my voice. Picture me in your mind."

Closing her eyes, Tess tried to call his image to mind. His long dark hair. Broad shoulders. Silver eyes. The eyes that didn't lie. *Dallas.* It took every bit of courage she had to take that blind leap of faith and force her legs to stop flailing.

Immediately she sensed movement. Dallas was swimming, towing her. *Saving her.*

Exhausted, she quit struggling. Trusting . . .

As soon as Dallas felt mud scrape his foot, he stood, sweeping Tess into his arms. She huddled close, clawing, weeping, clutching frantically at his shirt. Several of the men lined the shore, having heard the commotion. Dallas yelled for a blanket, fearful of hypothermia.

When Frankie tossed him a blanket, Dallas bundled Tess

in it. He would have preferred to strip the wet clothes from her first, but he wasn't going to subject her to that, not with everyone standing around. He needed to get her back to the cabin. Picking her up, he headed for his motorcycle. "Just a few more minutes, Tess."

When they reached the cabin Dallas carried her straight to the bathroom. Sitting her on the commode, he turned on the shower, full force. He looked at her.

She hadn't said a word since he had dragged her out of the lake. Her eyes were closed, and she trembled violently. He yanked off her wet sneakers, then pulled her to her feet. Clearly in shock, she offered no resistance as he stripped off her sodden jacket and clothes.

Damn both Snake and Liz! If Dallas hadn't been there, she would have drowned. The thought made the blood harden in his veins.

Steam started rising above the shower curtain. "This will warm you up." He pulled her to her feet. "Keep it as hot as you can stand it and shut it off as soon as it starts turning cool."

She nodded, then swayed. He caught her shoulders, shaking her slightly. "Stay with me, Tess."

This wouldn't work. She had nearly fainted. Quickly stripping off his own wet clothes, Dallas picked her up once more and stepped into the shower with her.

She cried out as needles of hot water stung her frozen skin. He grimaced, sorry to cause her further discomfort. "Give it a minute, and it'll feel better."

The water stung his own skin, making Dallas aware for the first time of how cold he was. He and Tess had only been in the lake a few minutes, but it was enough for the icy water to leach the core warmth from their bodies.

Pulling her close, he held her beneath the spray, rocking

her gently. She buried her face against his chest, tears falling freely. Dallas let her cry as he fought his own demons.

Damn it, he should have been more careful. It had been pure dumb luck that while he was talking with Bogen, he saw Snake slip along the path after Liz and Tess. If anything had happened to her . . .

He tightened his grip, drawing her infinitesimally closer. Her arms were wrapped tightly around his waist, hugging him, her head tucked beneath his chin. He was acutely aware of her bare skin pressed against him.

Gradually she quieted, her trembling subsiding somewhat. When the water cooled, Dallas shut it off. With quick efficient movements he wrapped her hair turban-style. Grabbing another towel, he swiped her dry, then wrapped yet another dry towel around her, swaddling her in terry cloth before wrapping a towel around his own waist.

She looked dazed, her cheek red where Snake had struck her. He promised himself that at the right moment, Snake would pay.

She whimpered. Dallas pressed a finger to her lips. "We'll talk in a minute. Stay here while I build a fire."

Leaving her in the steamy warmth of the bathroom, Dallas started a fire, then piled all the blankets and pillows he could find in front of the hearth. He stoked the growing blaze, adding as many logs as the grate would hold, before carrying her to the soft nest he'd thrown together in front of the fire.

Setting her down, he grasped her hands between his. She felt cold as ice, but it was her demeanor that concerned him most. She still hadn't spoken.

He started rubbing his hands briskly down her arms. "I'm sorry, Tess."

Those were the wrong words.

Snapping out of her trance, she screamed like a wounded

animal, then launched herself at him, knocking him backwards. She sprawled across him, pounding her fists on his chest.

"You're sorry? You think that makes it all better? You promised to keep me safe, yet look what happened," she cried. "You never should have stopped that night. Damn you! I would have been better off if you had left me on the side of the road."

Careful only that she didn't hurt herself, Dallas let her expend her energy, not saying anything until she lowered her head to his chest, sobbing once more.

"If I hadn't stopped, Snake and the others would have found you." They were honest words, but that didn't make it any easier to explain. He stroked a hand down her bare back. Her towels had scattered when she attacked. "I thought I did you a favor keeping you here with me."

His words undid her. Though Tess didn't want to admit it, she had thought of that before. But tonight the message really hit home. He was right; there were a lot worse things than being held captive by Dallas Haynes. And more: When the world had turned against her, he had fought back. For her. In a life gone chaotic he suddenly seemed the only tangible force, the only person she could count on.

The hand stroking beneath her hair was oddly hypnotic. Slowly she relaxed, letting go of her anger, drawing comfort from his touch. She shivered, suddenly realizing she was lying on top of him, naked and cold.

Embarrassed, she moved to grab a towel.

"Easy. I got it." Dallas moved, wrapping her in a sheet instead, drawing her fully into his lap as he sat up.

It was just as well they'd changed positions. He didn't know how much longer he could have held her like that, nude. Lush.

For a long time they sat quietly, Tess cradled in his arms, watching the fire, savoring its warmth.

She was the first to speak. "Did I thank you for saving my life?"

Dallas pressed a kiss to the top of her head, battling dark emotions, unwilling to accept gratitude for something that shouldn't have happened in the first place.

"Tell me how it is that you don't know how to swim," he asked.

At first he thought she wouldn't respond. Then she started talking, her voice a dull monotone.

"When I was four we were boating with friends. I climbed up on a rail and fell overboard. The life preserver I wore was too large, and I slipped out of it."

She shuddered, remembering the dark, the cold. The dying. "They revived me on the boat, and I spent a few days in the hospital. I was never able to get near the water afterward. I realize it's stupid, but it's my earliest childhood memory."

His grip intensified. It maddened him to know such tragic memories lurked in her mind. "Is that what you dream about?"

She looked up at him. "How—"

"Did I know? You've had nightmares almost every night since being here. At first I figured it was the circumstances, but then you kept talking about the lake and saying *no*. Maybe if we talk about it, I can help you get over your fears."

She realized he thought the wrong thing about her nightmares. Tears too long held in check slid down Tess's cheeks, the weight of her horrible secret suddenly unbearable.

"Snake killed Matt Michaels and dumped his body in Lake Summer. In my nightmares, Snake does the same with me. I keep seeing Michaels's face, his wide staring eyes. His mouth is open as if he's trying to tell me something."

Her words stunned Dallas. Matt was dead. Murdered. It felt as if the flesh was being peeled from his body. Slowly. Painfully. In long, agonizing, strips.

He caught her chin, noting her distress, regretting that he had to push. Had to know the details. "Tell me what happened. Everything."

She looked at him sadly, tears pooling in her eyes. "That first night, when I was in the pantry. Snake brought Michaels into the kitchen. He, he had been badly beaten. Bogen questioned him ... and when he refused to answer ... Snake stabbed him. In the back. I watched through the door."

"Jesus." Closing his eyes, Dallas held her as she wept, the entire story spilling out in bits and pieces.

In silence Dallas grieved for his friend, angered by the cruelty, stunned by Tess's horrific chronology. By the time she finished, she was spent. Still he embraced her, drawing strength from her as well as giving it, amazed once more by her fortitude.

Even though he and Barry expected the worst with Matt's disappearance, it was still a blow to learn the truth. His friend was dead. By Snake's hand. Dallas looked up at the rafters, offering a silent prayer. Remembering. Regretting. *Promising.*

He'd notify Barry first thing in the morning, though he knew they wouldn't be able to search for Matt's body yet. Lake Summer, particularly Scab Point, was a popular spot with the gang. Any suspicious activity would be noticed right away and could imperil the carefully laid snare. And it wouldn't bring his friend back to life.

The fire had died down, and he got up, cinching the towel tighter at his waist.

"Don't leave," she implored.

"I'm just adding more wood." When he returned he pulled her close, pressing a kiss to her temple. "Thank you for telling me." He picked up one of her hands, alarmed to find it felt lifeless. "You're still freezing. We've got to get you warm."

Dallas grabbed the oversize quilt and shook it open. Piling the pillows behind him, he motioned for Tess to move closer.

"Sharing body heat is the quickest way to warm up," he explained.

For a moment, she debated getting up, getting dressed. Except . . . she didn't want to leave his side, afraid the fragile peace would flee. And she desperately wanted, needed to be held. *By him.*

Holding on to her sheet for modesty, Tess moved up beside him and was instantly drawn into his arms as Dallas wrapped them into a quilt cocoon.

"Better?" he asked.

She nodded. It felt safe to be in his arms. Familiar. She thought back to her ordeal in the lake, how she thought her life would end. How she'd thought of Dallas. He'd saved her.

She had nearly died tonight, only to realize she'd scarcely lived. Too much of her life had been spent being the ideal daughter, the model student. Pleasing others.

No more. It was time to please herself.

She was tired of contemplating her every thought, questioning each emotion. She didn't want to think about right or wrong. For now, she just wanted to be with Dallas. To feel alive.

Only one thing seemed certain. She wanted this man in ways she'd never desired anyone before.

"Dallas?"

"Hmmm?"

"Kiss me."

Her words surprised him. For a moment he hesitated. There were a hundred reasons why he shouldn't kiss her. It was one thing when he'd been playing a part, with a specific goal in mind. Seduction in the line of duty.

Burning, blinding desire was another thing. It was personal. Unstoppable. And he could no more deny her request then he could deny breath to his own body. He captured her lips in a hungry kiss.

She opened to him, drawing him in. Ready and willing. The cravings she'd been fighting since they met flared to life, burning away her misgivings, her fears. Her inhibitions.

Dallas pulled her close, allowing her to fill his senses. "Tess."

He sucked in a breath as her hand gingerly slid up his side to caress his chest. He moaned, encouraging her, his own hands tightening on her waist.

Dallas lowered his mouth to the side of her neck, tasting her, knowing he'd never get enough. His lips traveled lower still, trailing kisses down her throat, eliciting faint sounds from her.

He pulled back, looking at her in the dusky glow of firelight. Her long hair tumbled across the pillows like liquid gold. The two love bites on her neck looked erotic, primitive, reminding him how he'd marked her, claimed her. A savage, animal act. She was breathing heavily, the sheet barely clinging to her breasts, hiding the treasures he longed for. He ached with wanting her. Yet he held back.

Something had changed tonight. At other times she had been slow to respond to his kisses, always pulling back when things started to heat up.

And they were way past that point tonight. While part of him was elated, the other part recognized why she was suddenly without inhibitions. She'd been through a terrible shock tonight, and, as much as he wanted her, he couldn't take advantage of her.

"Tess, think about this. Where this is heading."

She closed her eyes, gulping in air. She had thought about it. Every time Dallas kissed her. Or touched her. And even when he didn't. On some level he cared for her.

For now that was enough. The encounter with Liz and Snake had made her realize one thing: She didn't know what would happen next. She could have been killed tonight, and only one thought kept her from hysteria. *Dallas had saved her.*

She wanted him with a rawness that overwhelmed her. The circumstances be damned.

She looked at him, saw the uncertainty in his eyes. Those sexy, sinful, silver eyes. In that moment she knew they were going to make love. "I have thought about it, Dallas. Often. Don't make me beg."

Her words pushed him over the edge. "I should be the one to beg." He caught her mouth in his, kissing her soundly as he pressed her back down, tugging the blankets free. He had never wanted a woman this badly in his life.

The sensation of bare skin on bare skin shook Tess. His masculine strength complemented her feminine softness, her feminine strength. She moved, enjoying the rasp of his coarse chest hair against her hardened nipples.

Dallas's hands traced the outline of her breast, teasing, circling, driving her wild before capturing the tip between his finger and thumb. She moaned when he tugged, rolling the sensitive peak between two fingers. Her nipple elongated, responding to his touch.

"Touch me." Dallas's voice was low and commanding. Hypnotic.

"Where?" Hands shaking, Tess eased her fingers past his ribs, pausing at the towel tucked in at his waist, afraid to loosen it.

"Lower," he urged.

Her hand skimmed downward, nervously testing the

length of him through the terry cloth. He felt impossibly large against her hand, and with increasing curiosity she ran her hand up and down his complete length, measuring.

She knew the basics of what happened between a man and woman. She'd heard talk about size not being important. But this? Inside her? Would it hurt?

For the first time in her life she felt inept because of her . . . lack of experience.

She felt Dallas's fingers trail across her abdomen to the juncture of her thighs. Heat flashed along her nerves. His hand slipped down, sure and confident, cupping her, caressing her intimately. His mouth suckled her breast, a heavenly feeling directly connected with the growing pressure between her legs. The sensation seemed wildly taboo. And arousing beyond belief.

"Open for me," he commanded, finding her hot and wet when his fingers parted her.

"Damn, you're tight." He kissed her tenderly sliding his finger in slightly before stopping completely. He knew immediately. "Tess?"

She was on fire now. More than anything she wanted to go forward, follow this wondrous feeling to the end. She heard the question in his voice, sensed his slight withdrawal. If she said "no," it would end. She knew that, and was grateful.

But it was too late to turn back.

"I haven't done this before," she confirmed, voice shaky. "Please . . ."

Clamping an iron band on his thundering passion, Dallas closed his eyes. Never in his life had it been a struggle to take the high road. To be a gentlemen. It took every ounce of willpower he possessed to remove his hands from her. And push away.

Tess didn't reciprocate, tightening her hold on his hardened flesh where she'd been stroking him through the towel.

Dallas groaned and she immediately relaxed her grip. "Did I hurt you?"

Unable to resist, Dallas leaned forward and brushed her lips with his. He would love to be the one to teach this woman. To give and receive. But . . .

"I won't take advantage of you," he whispered hoarsely. *Damn ethics.* "And I can't take any more of this."

He thought about getting up, going to the bathroom. The need for release was crippling. Two strokes, maybe three and he'd come. Unsatisfying, but necessary. He captured her wrist, pulling it away from him.

She searched his face in the flickering firelight, seeing the struggle reflected in his silver eyes. She'd always been right about him. He wasn't like the rest.

And with that realization came the admission she trusted him. *And she wanted him more than ever.*

As he moved away, Tess reached beneath the towel, taking him in her bare hand. She gasped at the unexpected sensation of heat and strength, felt his penis pulse in her hand.

"You're right. You're not taking advantage. I am." By backing away, he'd given her the gift of choice. It was her choice to do this. *With him.*

Surging up, seeking his mouth, she sweetly pulled him down. "I want you, Dallas, and I want this."

She wanted him. The last of his reservations crumbled with her words. With her bold touch. He would be her first. The thought echoed in his mind and made him feel oddly possessive. *Powerful.*

Stripping away his towel, he closed his hand over hers, marveling that her small fingers could scarcely span his width, teaching her what he liked, how he wanted to be handled. Her feather-light touches weren't enough, drove him mad for more. He liked a firm grip. *Like that*.

"Good girl," he praised, voice tightening.

He lowered his mouth, capturing a taut nipple gently between his teeth. He heard her sharp intake of air and tugged lightly, knowing she had yet to learn what she liked. The possibilities were endless. And he planned to take all night showing her.

As he suckled, his hand moved down, trailing to the damp tangle of curls. Gently he parted her, patiently stroking.

"Spread your legs," he urged.

She did and immediately felt the heated sweep of his fingers invading her flesh. His thumb flicked over her swollen nub, causing her to grow wetter, easing his way, causing delicious tremors of pleasure to wash over her.

Tess trembled at the sensations, cried out at the pressure building inside her. "I can't take this."

Her grip had tightened on his manhood, stroking up, up, faster, harder. Dallas yanked her hand away, desperately close to losing control. He had never known a *need* this fierce. "Easy, sweet. I'll explode."

"No!" As if to deny his words, she touched him once more, pushing him dangerously near the edge. "Please!"

Grasping her hands, Dallas eased her onto her back, then levered his weight on top of her. He held himself propped on his elbows, letting her get used to the feel of him.

Her eyes widened with comprehension. Apprehension. He was big all over. He could crush her. But she knew he wouldn't. The momentary panic fled on the heels of wonder as she acquiesced to his dominance.

Dallas watched her eyes as he slowly slid his shaft against her. Unable to stop himself, he groaned, and repeated the motion. Sweet Jesus. She was heaven.

Tess bucked beneath him, grinding her hips against his, shuddering at the sensation.

"Tell me what you need," he rasped.

She pressed her lips against the base of his throat, shuddering. "You. Inside me. Now."

Her confession slashed the last of his restraint. He ran a hand down her side, to her hip, positioning her, holding her. "Raise your knees," he instructed.

He drew back, his blunt tip poised at her slick opening. Slowly, he let some weight ease forward, watching her face for signs that he was going too fast.

He pressed deeper, feeling her body's resistance. At her soft moan he hesitated, wishing he could make this first time easier for her. Wished he could make it last forever. Her eyes fluttered shut.

"Look at me, Tess. I want to watch you." He kissed the tip of her nose. "I want to be the only thing you think about. The only thing you feel."

Tess wrapped her arms around his neck, locking her eyes onto his. She gasped at the sensation of him parting her, entering her, knowing this was only the beginning.

He lowered his mouth and started tugging at her nipple. She felt the heat increase and moved against him slightly. Experimentally. She wanted more of him. *All of him.* The pain . . . The pleasure . . .

The pressure between her legs grew, invading, cleaving, until it felt as if she might split in two. For a wild moment she wanted him to stop, the pain too great. She cried out, unable to stop the tears. Then there was a sharp tearing, a burning sting.

And he was in. Deep. Filling her like nothing ever had. Hurt gave way to marvel at the feeling of being joined, of being one.

He rained kisses across her face reassuring her with soft words. "Talk to me, sweetheart. Tell me you're okay."

"I'm okay."

"Sure?"

She caught his mouth, wanting his lips on hers. "Positive."

He withdrew slightly, then slid back in, deeper, saw her eyes widen. "What are you thinking?" He wanted it all; her thoughts, her feelings, her physical response, wanted nothing held back.

"I didn't think you'd fit . . . this well."

Dallas grinned. The fit was perfect. Cupping her bottom, he drew her closer, moving in and out with longer strokes, watching her reaction, enchanted.

Tess bolted as if hit by lightning. The slight change in positions brought him in direct contact with her center. The sensations he caused were building, growing.

"Dallas." She felt painfully short of breath. "More."

Her simple plea nearly made him lose it. He fought for control and found it. "Wrap your legs around my waist."

She did, moaning as Dallas buried himself to the hilt— then pulled back. Only to do it again and again and again, raising her slightly with each stroke.

She felt him intimately, buried inside of her. Fanning the flame. Now she understood where the feeling was leading. If he kept this up, she would burst into a thousand pieces.

Dallas had no choice but to continue. She was too tight, too hot. He pumped faster, deeper. Harder. Showing her the rhythm.

Tess squirmed beneath him, panting, crying. Within seconds she screamed.

Dallas sealed her mouth with his, absorbing her cries. When she raked her nails down his back, he felt his control slip, on the verge of snapping.

Time to stop.

But when he moved to pull back, Tess suddenly tightened her legs, grasping his buttocks to hold him in place as she scraped her teeth against his shoulder, nipping him, lost in her own vortex of shimmering passion.

Dallas felt her womb clench tightly, milking him. Unable to stop, he exploded in a powerful climax, claiming her.

Cursing, he stiffened as he felt himself pouring into her, too late to withdraw.

Too late to use protection.

Chapter Eight

Two days later, in the middle of the night, Dallas hurried along the dark path toward his cabin.

The air was oppressive, charged with static from the approaching storm. Behind him the wind kicked up, blowing dirt and grit. It was going to be one helluva storm. Long overdue.

The path turned sharply, the ground inclining as the cabin's outline finally appeared around the bend. Against the black horizon the small structure appeared even darker. No light shone from within.

He scowled. Friggin' electricity was probably out again. If she was awake, she was probably terrified.

He took the porch stairs two at a time. Unlocking the door, he slipped inside and paused, allowing his eyes to adjust to the much darker interior. He listened carefully for a noise to confirm his worry. All he heard was his own harsh breathing.

You promised never to leave her again, like this, at night. Cursing himself and the circumstances that required his absence, he eased from the doorway, silently picking his way across the room to the bedroom door.

He entered quietly, grateful for the hazy moonlight filtering through the window. The slight form on the bed didn't move. Dallas released a pent-up breath as he stepped closer and confirmed—thankfully—that she was sleeping soundly. She wouldn't ask questions about how long he'd been gone.

He felt the stab of conscience. She was probably exhausted. She'd slept little the night before, and they'd made love twice before he'd left.

He watched her, his eyes skimming over her from top to bottom. She was lying on her left side, in the middle of the bed, her head half on his pillow, half on her own, arms extended over her head.

His hostage.

The quilt covering her rose and fell slowly, following the rhythm of her deep, even breaths.

Shifting back, Dallas shrugged out of his leather jacket and silently pulled off his boots, his eyes never leaving her. A thousand weights seemed to drop from his shoulders knowing she was safe—asleep—just as he'd left her.

He removed the nine-millimeter semiautomatic he had tucked at his back, securing it within easy reach, before he peeled off his shirt. In the distance a low roll of thunder rumbled. The storm was moving in.

Tess stretched slightly, drawing his attention once more to the bed. Damn, she was beautiful. He felt himself harden and enjoyed the uniquely male sensation. Did she know she had the power to arouse him so instantly, so innocently?

The top button of his worn jeans gave way. She'd entered his life a little over three weeks ago, captured his heart and nearly destroyed the master scheme he and his partner had been working on the past two years.

He kicked aside his jeans, brooding.

Every thought, every move had been meticulously calculated. Nothing had been left to chance. Every option had been preplanned, every action purposeful. Except for *her*. Except for *his* reaction to her.

And his partner's untimely death.

Dallas recalled his movements of the past few hours. Soon it would end. Or just begin.

He was ready for it to be over. He had literally put his entire life on hold to take on this assignment, immersing himself so deeply in the game that at times it had been hard to remember his life before.

He hadn't seen his father or sisters in nearly two years. From what Barry reported, he had a new niece, courtesy of his sister, Beth Ann. His family knew, of course, had always known that Dallas's job required him to disappear for long stretches of time. They didn't like it, but they also knew not to ask questions.

This particular assignment, though, had proved longer and tougher than anyone had imagined. Sometimes the only thing that kept him going was knowing it would be his last undercover job. He had decided months ago he'd had enough of covert operations, that he was no longer willing to pay the price.

Watching Tess, he realized that, now more than ever, he wanted his life back, his freedom. His integrity. All the things he'd sacrificed to take on this role.

Soon, he promised. Very soon. The end had already begun.

Sanchez had made his move, had left his Canadian headquarters. The women he was transporting in a private jet would be free by morning. That was the good news.

The bad news was that divers searching Lake Summer tonight had located Matt's body. Just as Tess had described. Stabbed in the back. Dallas's gut tightened.

The noose around Snake's neck was tightening. Soon the ax would fall on Bogen and Sanchez as well. With any luck, Snake and Bogen would receive the death penalty for Matt's murder. Plus there were a host of other charges to be levied, from kidnapping to drug trafficking.

And how Tess would react was the only answer that still eluded him. How would she feel about him when she learned the truth? *How did he want her to feel?*

Would she understand why he couldn't tell her? Would she forgive him? *Could he forgive himself?*

Oh, yes.

In fact he'd do it all over again if it was the only way to have her in his life.

He didn't regret what he'd done to her, to her life. Nor did he regret the passion they'd shared. The past was immutable. The future . . .

His flesh throbbed, pulling him away from the abyss of dark thoughts, but still he made no attempt to enter his bed, content to watch, finding satisfaction in the steady rise and fall of her covered breasts. Guilt cooled his ardor. She was sleeping so peacefully he'd not awaken her.

Above him, he heard the persistent drum of raindrops hitting the roof. He started to leave the room when a different noise stopped him.

In a heartbeat Dallas was on the bed, beside her, reaching to where her arms were still outstretched above her head. *I should have freed her first thing, instead of watching her,* he berated himself.

She whimpered, rolling and twisting, tangling in the sheets as she fought the unseen terror in her nightmare, sought to be free of the bed and the bonds that held her arms immobile.

"Tess," Dallas whispered fiercely.

He released her and yanked back the confining weight of the quilt before gathering her close. "Tess, wake up. You're dreaming, sweetheart."

She pushed against him, her eyes fluttering open in confusion. "Dallas." She buried her face in his chest, seeking sanctuary from the spinning remains of her desolate dream. "It was awful."

"I know."

"I keep thinking it will go away."

"It will." He shifted, easing farther down on the bed, wrapping her more tightly in his arms. She shivered. The rain picked up, the thunder lower, closer.

"How long has it been raining?"

"It just started," he whispered.

"I can't see the clock."

"Power's out. It's gonna be a bad storm." He kissed the top of her head. "Go back to sleep."

"I'm cold."

Keeping one arm around her shoulders, Dallas grabbed the quilt and pulled it back up, bundling them both in warmth.

"Better?" he asked.

She nodded, pressing her nose against his shoulder as she burrowed against him. "I wonder if I'll have nightmares the rest of my life."

Tell her the truth. End it here and now, while she's in your arms. What difference would a few hours make?

Dallas rejected the thought, pulling her closer, hugging tightly as if to squeeze out the night terrors that tormented her. Keenly aware this was his last time to offer consolation in the dark. *Soon . . .*

Slowly her trembling subsided beneath whispered comforts and reassuring strokes. The room was alive with the sounds of the storm.

Eyes shut, Dallas allowed his hands to sweep over her, imprinting her curves into his memory. The thought of not seeing her again was painful, foreign. But what kind of relationship could they have after this? The odds were against him.

And more, it had to be by her choice. A choice made in complete freedom. From captivity. *From him.* Christ! Could he let her go if it meant not seeing her again? Not touching her again?

His fingers slowed, grazing the perfect swell of her hip.

He'd sworn to himself that earlier tonight was their finale. His physical and emotional good-bye to her. Already his body forgot the pledge.

Tess wriggled, boldly peeling off the shirt she wore, then wrapping her arms about his neck. Her cold-roughened nipples stabbed against his chest as she started to nibble the sensitive skin below his ear. Her passion amazed him, the knowledge that he'd been her only lover enflamed him.

Dallas pressed her close, knowing full well that he should discourage her. Instead he welcomed her, tangling his hands in her long, silky hair, his knee sliding intimately between hers, holding her still as his mouth sought hers. It was wrong, but the line between right and wrong had wavered a long time ago. So had he.

He caught her bottom lip tenderly between his teeth, loving it gently, then releasing it as his tongue swept deeply into her mouth. Her breath came out on a sigh as his mouth traveled lower, caressing first one breast, then the other. She arched against his leg, rubbing, seeking friction.

His hands teased, dropping to her abdomen, then trailing down to find her most tender place. Her hips undulated slightly as his thumb stroked the hot little nub, coaxing a shudder from her. A low, deep moan escaped her throat. Encouraging. Gratifying. Confirming he knew exactly how much pressure to exert to drive her wild. And exactly when to stop to keep her from going over the edge without him.

He recalled his promise, tamping down control over his

rising passion. For the rest of the night, he'd only pleasure her. He watched as she writhed with delight in his arms. *So damn beautiful . . .*

He thought about how she'd changed, evolving from innocent to seductress over the past days, changing him as well. Three mere weeks. Once in a lifetime. How could he ever let her go?

She had entered his dark world like a bright promise, reminding him of the life beyond this assignment. A life he had started to think would never be his own again.

Then her fingers dipped low, encasing his steel with a velvet grip. With practiced hands, she measured the length of him, tightly, without reserve. She'd learned quickly what he'd liked and hadn't hesitated to please him, tease him. Torment him. Her hand slid slowly, firmly down his shaft.

"I want you, Dallas," she whispered. "Please."

He gave up, slamming away all recriminations, yet acutely aware time was running out. Fumbling in the drawer beside the bed, he snagged a foil packet, ripping the edge with his teeth and quickly, efficiently, protecting her.

Not for the first time, the thought came that she could already be pregnant. His fault if she was. Except for that first night, he'd taken responsibility for birth control. She obviously hadn't had to worry about it before he came along.

Tess's impatient hands hovered over his, helping, tugging. She cupped his sac, weighing, squeezing lightly. It was more than he could bear.

With a growl, he rolled, taking her beneath him and burying himself completely with a swiftness that shocked them both. The slight resistance of her body, the excruciating tightness of her sheath was an exquisite, nearly painful, sensation.

At his urging, Tess wrapped one leg around his hip, taking him even deeper. She moaned. Expectant. Begging. Waves of extreme pleasure rocketed through his veins as deep thrust followed deep thrust. She was ablaze with desire, all wet, all heat. Her nails bit into the flesh of his shoulder as Dallas plunged into her yet again, demanding more. Demanding everything.

In a thousand years, he knew he'd never get enough of this woman. He had conquered her body as surely as she'd conquered his. And still he wanted more.

"I want you, Tess. All of you." He hadn't meant to speak. But set free, the words seemed to resound about them, a deafening sound that triggered an avalanche of raw passion.

Outside the storm raged. A brilliant burst of lightning flashed, illuminating the room for seconds, capturing their movements in pulses of strobe.

Tess let out a cry, taking them both over the brink. Dallas collapsed over her, his mind reeling as his body pumped on without conscious effort, draining him, cleansing him.

The sound of a lone gunshot shattered what should have been their lovers' afterglow, followed by the rapid-fire chatter of a machine gun.

"Stay down," Dallas ordered, swiftly rolling off the bed, dragging her with him to the safety of the floor.

"What's going on?"

"I'm not sure." It was an honest answer. He grabbed his jeans. The shots had definitely been fired somewhere on the grounds. But by whom?

Another burst of gunfire punctuated the charged silence. Echoing, then fading.

The raid wasn't supposed to start until morning. Damn it. Had something gone wrong? Had some idiot pushed forward the time schedule? Or had someone settled a personal problem?

He checked his watch, listening for more shots, but the night remained eerily quiet. He debated staying put, but knew Bogen would expect him at the main house. Without Tess.

Dallas thrust clothes at her. "Put these on, quickly. And keep down."

With shaking fingers, Tess slid into the sweatshirt and pants. Reaching under the bed, she found a pair of sneakers and quietly slid them on. She watched Dallas creep back to the window and peer cautiously beneath the curtains. Muffled shouts drifted in from outside.

"Promise you won't leave me," she whispered, hearing the quake of trepidation in her own voice.

Dallas merely nodded, motioning for her to be silent. Tess didn't know what to think other than she was scared. Did the gunshots mean law enforcement had finally arrived? Was she going to be rescued?

She glanced at Dallas, wondering not for the first time how her ultimate rescue would affect him. Questioning if she still wanted to be rescued. Whether she wanted to be free.

When had things stopped making sense, stopped appearing in black-and-white? The shades of gray were hard to judge, even tougher to decipher.

In the past few days she'd tried not to look too closely at her feelings for Dallas, tried not to read too much into their lovemaking. Into the fact that she craved the one-to-one, personal contact of their physical relationship.

She knew she cared for him. Knew she shouldn't. At what point had she become unable to distinguish whether he was a bad guy or a good guy? He'd saved her . . .

Her heart constricted painfully at the thought of anything happening to him. He was her rock, the solid foundation she'd clung to. Without him, she wouldn't have endured this ordeal. Because of Dallas, she'd maintained a grasp on reality, held back the hounds of hell nipping at her sanity over the past weeks. She wasn't ready to lose him now.

But lose him she would . . . eventually. It was inevitable.

Dallas moved to the footlocker at the end of the bed, where he stored his reserve of ammunition and firearms. He crammed extra clips in his pocket.

He looked at her for a moment, wondering what she was thinking, torn between wanting to explain and thankful there was no time for explanations.

"Come here." Holding up his leather jacket, he helped her slide her arms into it, yanked the collar up. "I want you to stay right behind me," he instructed. He didn't know if taking her along would place her in more peril. But he couldn't protect her if he left her behind. "Make as little noise as possible."

"Where are we going?"

"To the main house." He had to find out what was happening, who had fired the shots. He didn't dare try to make it off the grounds with her until he knew who the players were. Bogen's men would shoot to kill. His own men might also.

"But people are shooting out there. I'm scared, Dallas." *For you.*

He tugged her against his chest, crushing her close to his heart. He brought his mouth down on hers, the kiss deep but quick. "Just stay by me."

They avoided the main path in favor of one of the lesser-used trails through the woods. Rain came down in sheets, blinding and cold, turning the paths into small, muddy rivers. She was soaked to the skin in no time.

Tree branches and brambles scraped at her, catching strands of hair and clothes, tearing at her externally just as her thoughts tore away at her insides. She had a million questions she knew not to voice.

She kept her eyes on Dallas, remembering his fierce love-making of moments before, knowing he had forever changed her. Did she want it to end now, tonight, if it meant never seeing him again?

Would things have been different if they had met under other circumstances?

Extremely different circumstances, she amended, thinking about her life back in Boston. They were worlds apart. Tears rolled down her cheek and were quickly washed away in the rain. She'd been robbed of autonomy. Her life had become a blur of uncertainty and fear. Except for Dallas.

Without him, she would have been dead. She owed him her life. But not her heart.

Lightning flashed, the main house revealed clearly for just a moment. He tugged her close as thunder boomed, the ground beneath them trembling. "Remember. Do everything I say."

The house was once more shrouded in darkness. A shadowy figure emerged from the bushes as they approached.

"That you, Haynes?" The guard nodded when Dallas replied. "They're in the basement."

Dallas pulled her to the back of the house, urging care as he lifted the cellar door and descended into the basement. Bogen, Snake, and Eddie were crowded at a table, arguing loudly. A single propane lamp sitting in the table's center cast eerie shadows on their faces.

Thrusting her into the safest corner, Dallas strode to the center of the room and slammed his fist on the table. "What's going on, Bogen?"

"Feds. They're moving in, getting ready to storm the front gate. Duke's dead, but Snake got away."

Dallas whirled, pinning Snake with an accusing glare. "Feds? What the hell are they after?"

"I was going to ask you the same thing." Snake looked derisively at Tess. "Perhaps their bloodhounds smell a bitch in heat."

"I oughta—" Dallas lunged forward

"Enough," Bogen yelled, as he stepped between the two men. "It's a valid question. One that doesn't matter right now."

"I heard shots. Who got trigger-happy?" Dallas asked, looking pointedly at Snake. "Feds would have to have a search warrant to come knocking on our door. And right now there's nothing here they can bust us for."

"What about her?" Snake pointed an accusing finger at Tess.

Dallas grabbed the other man's finger, wanting to break it. Just for starters. "I can handle her."

Bogen jabbed Dallas's forearm, breaking the two men apart. "You can settle this later. For now—"

An urgent pounding on the door interrupted. The guard burst through the doors, soaking wet. "Jesus, you should see them. Fucking hundreds of 'em. And they're closing in fast."

Bogen opened a metal locker and started handing out machine guns identical to the one the guard carried. And extra ammo clips. "Upstairs," he ordered.

Everyone moved at once, hurrying up the far set of stairs to the main floor of the house. Dallas pulled Tess along. "Stay behind me," he ordered.

Tess had never been so terrified in her life. The array of firepower the men carried was frightening. Even more alarming was the realization that both she and Dallas could be killed.

"Dallas, please—"

"Ssshhh."

They were in the living room now. The sound of a single, wailing, siren pierced the night.

"This is the FBI," an electronically amplified voice announced. "Surrender your weapons and come out with your hands up."

"Shit," Snake yelled, releasing the safety on his gun. "They won't take me alive."

"Nobody fires unless I give the word," Bogen said, peering cautiously out a window. "How many do you see, Haynes?"

"Stay here," Dallas ordered, tucking Tess beside the desk. Crouching low to the floor, he moved to huddle with Bogen and the others.

Tess couldn't hear what was said because they were again being addressed over the scratchy microphone. "You've got five seconds to acknowledge this warning. Then we're moving in."

Dallas was back at her side, watching over his shoulder as Bogen and the others crawled toward the back of the house.

Grabbing a heavy glass ashtray, Dallas flung it through one of the front windows. The pane shattered noisily.

"We've got hostages," Dallas shouted.

Seconds ticked by, the wind howling. "Release your hostages."

"Back your men up a hundred feet and we'll send one of them out."

Tess started at Dallas's words. He meant to free her. End it. She shook her head. This was all so crazy, so impossible.

Three weeks ago she'd have given anything for this moment. Three weeks. A lifetime ago. She looked at him, staring at his profile, the long wet queue of dark hair.

She leaned forward, tugging at his arm, unashamed of the tears. "I won't go without you. It can't end like this. We'll find a way—"

From outside the voice cracked through the night. "It's done. Release a hostage, and nobody will get hurt."

"Haynes," Bogen hissed from behind them. "Get her out now! We're leaving."

Tess searched his eyes, disbelieving. Dallas wasn't really

considering leaving her. She'd seen the torment in his eyes earlier, knew he cared.

"Don't leave me," she pleaded. "Please."

His response shocked her. He grabbed her arms, pinching the tender flesh. Gasping in pain she looked up, appalled by the uncompromising features on the face she adored. Contempt glittered from the silvery eyes she'd come to know intimately.

"Little fool," Dallas shook her roughly. "You mean nothing to me. You were a convenience, a way to pass time. Now you're a bargaining chip. Get out."

He shoved her away, toward the door, then hurried off to follow Bogen. Her wet shoes skidded across the floor nearly causing her to lose her balance. God, what was happening? What had she done?

"We've kept our end of the deal," the voice outside warned. "Send out a hostage or we move in."

It was over.

Trembling, Tess walked toward the door, opening it without looking back and stepping onto the porch. The rain fell in torrents, pushed by the wind. Blinding lights greeted her, forcing her to shield her eyes.

She heard a sharp metallic *clack* as someone chambered a round. Her knees buckled. What if they shot her? How could Dallas do this to her?

She started to turn away, to run back in the house when a voice called out. "It's okay, ma'am. Just walk straight ahead."

She was crying now, frightened. When she cleared the steps the man rushed forward, throwing a heavy vest over her.

"FBI, ma'am. It's bulletproof." She didn't catch his name. He tugged the vest in place, shoving her head down as he hurried her away from the house. "Don't let it worry you."

The night came alive with activity. Grim-looking men and women—some uniformed, some not—swarmed over the clearing and the surrounding woods. All carried shotguns. Two officers hustled her into a waiting car, well away from the house.

One of them ducked his head into the car, oblivious to the water pouring in with him, peppering her with questions. "How many other hostages are inside? How many men are guarding them? Did you see what kind of weapons they have?"

Tess blinked. "I, I was the only hostage. I saw four men in the house, but . . . there could be more." *Dallas, forgive me.* "And they all have machine guns."

Before she finished gunshots echoed through the night.

"Stay down," the man yelled, shoving her onto the floorboard. She buried her head on her knees as the gunfire escalated and grew deafening, covering her cries.

Just as quickly as it had begun, it was over. Someone yelled, headlights came on, people rushed about. "We'll get you out of here soon, ma'am," the man promised before hurrying away. "I'll be right back."

A loud rumble of thunder boomed, echoing like a cannon shot. Deadly.

"We need an ambulance at the back of the house." A voice came across the two-way radio in the front seat, causing her to stiffen.

Dallas.

A vision of him lying on the ground, covered in blood, flashed through her mind, quickly followed by the picture of him yelling at her. *You mean nothing to me.*

She looked down at the leather jacket she wore, remembered how he'd wrapped her in it before leaving the house, assuring her comfort over his. Or so she'd thought. She hid her face in her hands, felt bile burn her throat. Sobs wracked her body. *This couldn't be happening.*

The car door was wrenched open startling Tess. A tall, middle-aged man in a dark trench coat smiled at her, his kind eyes staring out from behind rain spattered glasses.

"I'm Barry Neilson, FBI, Washington." He reached down, squeezing her cold hand. "Are you okay, Miss Marsh?"

Tess shook her head, moving to get out of the close confines of the car in spite of the rain. Standing, she gulped in the night air, resting her head on the metal doorframe. Nothing made sense.

"I keep thinking this is a dream." She was crying again, tears slipping free even though she kept her eyes tightly clenched. "That I'll wake up and none of this will be true."

"It's not a dream, Tess."

The sound of Dallas's voice brought her head snapping up. She blinked in disbelief as she saw him move in beside Neilson, calmly offering her a white foam cup of coffee, rain sheeting off the dark slicker he wore. Her mouth opened and closed soundlessly.

She launched herself into his arms, weeping. "You're alive! I was so afraid . . ."

Behind her she heard Barry cough. "Tess Marsh, may I introduce a colleague, Grey Thomas."

Colleague?

Removing her hands from Dallas, Tess backed away looking from Barry to Dallas.

Wait a moment . . .

How did Barry know her name? And why *was* Dallas here? Why wasn't he with Bogen and the others? A prisoner . . .

She stared at the badge hanging around Barry's neck identifying him as FBI. Dallas wore an identical one. Her pulse pounded loudly in her ears. She shook her head trying to clear the mist of denial.

"I can see you two need to talk. Excuse me." Barry backed away, blending into the crush of people.

But his words came back to her. He called Dallas . . . *Grey.* Grey Thomas. Something was terribly wrong here. "Dallas? I don't—"

Ignoring the rain, he pulled her through the mud toward the rear of the squad car, trying to find a more private spot. "It's Grey, sweetheart, and I'm sorry to have duped you, Tess."

She stared at the badge hanging around his neck. "FBI?" she questioned, never taking her eyes off him. *Dallas was an FBI agent.* Dallas's name was Grey. Grey Thomas.

It felt like she'd been slapped. Rage exploded in her head as the implication dawned on her, crystalline clear, leaving her feeling betrayed. Violated.

Sweet Jesus. She'd slept with him—all the while thinking he was a gangster. *All the while thinking she cared for him?*

A part of her had nearly died at the thought he'd been injured earlier. And before that, when he'd forced her to leave the house, her heart had broke. She hadn't wanted freedom then. She'd wanted to stay with him, even when he'd pushed her away.

What was wrong with her?

They had made love. Again and again. She had begged him to take her. Gave up her will to escape. Believed she would die without his protection.

Grey moved closer, watching the confusion, the fury, play across her face. He knew the news was a terrible shock. He desperately needed to talk to her alone, to explain, to reassure. And to make sure she knew which parts had been real and which hadn't. Christ, he needed to figure that out himself. This was unfamiliar territory.

She shoved her hair from her eyes, her voice trembling. "You knew how frightened I was. And you had the power to take all that fear away—*at any time*."

He squeezed her shoulders lightly. "I was afraid you'd act differently if you knew the truth. If Bogen and Snake had even suspected you weren't afraid, you could have been in even more danger."

"So you used me?"

He couldn't deny it. "There were ten other women being held captive that we had to account for. Would you have sacrificed them for your own peace of mind?"

"Of course not." She stepped away, shrugging free of his touch. There had been other women being held? It would have been comforting to know she wasn't alone. "If you had given me a choice, I would have played along. Helped you."

"I didn't need help. I needed to keep you safe."

His statement appalled her with its sheer male arrogance.

"You didn't have to sleep with me to do that."

"You're right. I didn't have to. I *wanted* to. Just give me a chance to explain, and I think when you hear the whole story you'll understand."

"Understand?"

Oh, she understood perfectly.

Forgiving was another matter.

She turned away, unable to face him as every little nuance of her captivity replayed in her head. He had deliberately misled her. Used her fears against her. Manipulated her trust. He could have spared her a lot of distress, a load of angst when she believed herself to be infatuated with an outlaw. God, how foolish he must think her.

Once more his hand closed over her shoulder, turning her back to him.

"Tess, please say something, sweetheart."

Sweetheart? How dare he patronize her now?

Stepping back, she clenched her fist, hating what he'd done, the grief he'd caused. Worst, he'd stolen her heart, then trampled it. Just as he'd stolen her innocence. Her outrage swelled, exploded.

"Bastard," she hissed. Then she slugged him in the face with every bit of strength she possessed, sending him sprawling backward into the mud.

Chapter Nine

Grey's jaw smarted.

He levered himself off the ground as Tess backed away, obviously shocked by what she'd done.

"Oh, God, I—" She whirled, disappearing into the edgy chaos surrounding them.

"Tess, wait."

A car barreled past Grey, its tires spinning in the mud, the trampled vegetation offering scarce traction. He shot the driver a look, then tore after Tess, almost catching her before he realized his intent.

He slowed. Damn it, he couldn't just run up and overpower her. Force her to listen.

Or handcuff her to the nearest bed and make love to her until the anger passed and there was only pure, honest sensation.

Dallas would have done that.

Grey couldn't.

His temper sparked, wanting to flare as he struggled to contain his frustration, reluctant to give her space. He couldn't. Not yet. Not until they'd talked.

Actually, he just wanted her to listen. He wanted to do all

the talking. Unfair as hell, he knew, but he wanted it just the same.

He scowled at his own narrow-mindedness. Tess had a perfect right to be mad, she had a right to demand answers. To scream . . . to cry . . . to rail against the injustices she'd been forced to endure.

Instead she'd sucker-punched him and fled.

Of all the outcomes he'd imagined this hadn't been one.

Peeling off his muddy jacket, he stepped around the open door of the patrol car and into the noisy clearing beside the house. The yellow glare of headlights artificially illuminated the night, giving everything a surreal appearance. The rain had picked up again, in earnest, soaking him anew.

He noticed several officers huddled near a battered trailer, talking on two-way radios, an impromptu command center. The raid was multijurisdictional and included officers from FBI, ATF, the county sheriff, and the state police. Even though everyone would have been briefed before the raid that Grey was an undercover agent, he got more than one second glance, more than one inquisitive stare. So had Tess. Which bothered him.

He knew how the grapevine worked at a major crime scene, knew many of them had already put two and two together. They knew Tess had been Grey's hostage.

His feelings of protectiveness ballooned as he watched Tess's blond head weave through the commotion. For a moment he debated getting Barry Neilson to go after her. Maybe for her sake, Grey needed to back away, give her time.

But when he saw the direction she was headed, he started swearing again. Quickening his pace, he ran, hoping to cut her off.

Tess didn't care where she went. The need to get away, to be alone, drove her blindly. Had everyone but her known Dallas was an undercover FBI agent? That *Dallas* wasn't even his real name?

She ducked around vehicles, avoiding stares, hating the pity she glimpsed in more than one face. A large van emblazoned STATE POLICE loomed directly in her path. A uniformed officer headed toward her, hand raised. "Stop, ma'am."

Tess stepped sideways, intent only on bypassing the officer. To her horror, she came face-to-face with Bogen.

His hands were cuffed behind his back, and officers flanked either side. His trademark sunglasses were gone, his scarred face more frightening than ever. Bogen snarled when he saw her.

"Well, if it ain't Haynes's whore! I should have taken care of you that first night. I still might."

Even as he spoke the officers shoved Bogen into the van and out of sight. Though the confrontation lasted only seconds, Tess felt herself start to shake. She turned, struggling to retrace her steps, unsure of where to go. She felt sick, scared, humiliated. Utterly helpless.

A hand gently grasped her shoulder. Strong, familiar arms embraced her. Even now she didn't think, didn't hesitate to turn to Grey.

"Tess."

"Make it go away," she wept. "Tell me it's not really happening."

He saw the depth of her torment, knew it was something he couldn't fix. "I'm sorry."

She lowered her head against his chest, giving in to the nearly debilitating need for comfort, not caring who watched or what they thought.

Behind them, ATF agents and SWAT team members filed in and out of the basement, carrying confiscated weaponry.

Grey tugged her away, into the darkness, shielding her from prying eyes.

When they were alone he smoothed the wet hair from her forehead, pressed his lips to her temple as he enfolded her against his body, offering warmth. Her clothes were soaked. Her skin felt clammy and she was trembling. Shell shock.

He held her tightly, letting her cry, wishing he had the words to heal her anguish. But no words were adequate. There wasn't a damn thing he could do to make it better. He wanted to pick her up and kiss her until neither of them remembered the pain, the problems. The mess that was their life, their relationship. And they did have a relationship— good or bad—whether either of them wanted to admit it or not.

When she quieted, Grey pulled a bandanna from his pocket and pressed it into her hand. The muffled sounds and shouts coming from the compound intruded, shattering the fragile moment.

She straightened, wiping her eyes.

"Grey . . . Dallas. I don't even know what to call you." She stepped away, crossing her arms to ward off the chill.

He knew there were a lot of things she could call him, was grateful she didn't. He stepped closer but kept his hands at his sides. She had to be freezing, but he sensed she'd resist any attempt to draw her back in his arms.

"We need to get you someplace warm. I'll have Barry take you—"

"Are you coming, too?" She pinned him with eyes that were huge, sad; her voice low, anxious. "I . . . I don't want to go anywhere without you."

He knew what that admission cost her, could sense her inner turmoil. He wished he could promise to stay at her side, to fight all the battles for her. But he couldn't. Besides, once she regained her bearings, she wouldn't want him to. *Once she regained her bearings, she might hate him.*

As if on cue, Barry stepped out of the shadows. He exchanged a knowing glance with Grey. Both men had dealt with hostage situations, knew the tumult of emotion experienced upon release. Barry, however, definitely had the advantage of professional distance in this case.

"Grey needs to stay here a while longer," Barry interjected smoothly. "I'll take you somewhere quiet. You can contact your family. Then we'll need to get a statement."

Tess cast a wary look in Grey's direction, her uncertainty plain.

"You can trust Barry," Grey said. "He'll take care of you, keep you safe."

Safe? Tears stung her eyes. For the past three weeks, the only time she'd felt safe had been with Dallas. The need to stay close to him battled with her desire to retreat. "When will I see you again?"

"Soon."

She noticed the slight flattening of his lips, the evasive shift of his eyes. *Soon?* It felt like a brush-off.

She stiffened. Why had she expected more? He had a job to do . . . had been doing his job all along.

She moved toward Barry, taking yet another step away from Grey. From Dallas.

"Do you want me to get your personal belongings from the cabin?" Grey offered.

"No." She suddenly felt exhausted. Befuddled. More than anything she simply wanted to be alone. To try and make sense of what had happened. "I don't want anything that will remind me of the time I spent here."

The next eighteen hours were long and arduous. First Tess went to the local hospital for a physical. She lay on the table, silently counting tiles overhead, trying not to think about being poked and prodded. A female agent remained during the exam, taking notes. One more humiliation. The questions were as cold and sterile as the small exam room. Had she been raped? Physically abused? Drugged?

She shook her head each time, then remembered the pills Dallas gave her the first night.

"Did you suffer any long-term effect from taking them?" the doctor asked, scribbling on her chart.

"No."

"Is there a possibility you were sexually abused during the time you were drugged?"

Tess closed her eyes, recalling that awful night in the pantry. She shook her head again. "No."

"You understand, we have to ask—to assess whether you were exposed to any sexually transmitted diseases," the doctor explained with polite frankness. "Or at risk for pregnancy."

Heat crept into her cheeks.

At risk for pregnancy.

The doctor moved on to other questions, his assumption plain: She hadn't been raped; therefore, she couldn't be pregnant.

Oh, but she could.

Dallas had not used a condom that first time.

Automatically her mind tried calculating days. Exactly when was her last period?

Right before she was captured—three weeks ago. She wasn't even due to start yet.

She clung to the slight feeling of relief. She was probably safe, though it was too soon to know.

After the doctor finished his exam, an older woman came

into the room. She introduced herself as a psychologist and talked briefly about post-traumatic stress, recommending that Tess consider counseling upon her return home. Tess was grateful the woman didn't push. The last thing she wanted to discuss was how she felt. She honestly didn't know. At this moment she felt detached. Five minutes ago she'd wanted to cry.

Barry Neilson waited for her at the hospital, ready to transport her to a nearby motel.

"You might want to contact your family first thing," he suggested as they drove. "News of the arrests will be made public later today. I can keep your name away from the press for a day, perhaps two, but that's it."

Tess looked out the car window watching but not seeing the scenery. *Her family.*

"They never knew I was missing, did they?"

Her thoughts went back to the beginning of the summer. Tess had been eager to head west. Her father and brother had just kicked off a huge hotel expansion project. And her mother was spending the summer in Europe. Normal stuff.

"I've sent a liaison officer to speak with your father personally, to explain what happened. I'm sure your family's main concern will be that you're unharmed."

Barry's words reminded her that, thanks to Dallas, she hadn't been hurt. If Snake had been the one to find her that night, the liaison officer could have been delivering very different news. Tess shivered.

"Would you have preferred to tell them yourself?" Barry asked.

"No." The thought of answering fifty questions right now was overwhelming. Letting someone else rehash the story bought her a little more time to herself. A little more distance.

At the motel she showered and was provided with clean clothes. The tags were still on the clothes, indicating a recent purchase. The sizes were correct. A lucky guess or had Dallas picked them out? Told someone her size?

A meal was sent to her room, but she couldn't eat. The female agent who stayed with her was solicitous but professional, asking no questions. The questions, Tess discovered, came later. Giving her statement took over six hours.

She gave a chronological description of her captivity, squirming when the queries turned personal. When pressed, she acknowledged her physical relationship with Grey and was grateful the subject was dropped soon after establishing mutual consent. She didn't, however, believe it would be the last she heard on the subject. She wondered if Grey was facing the same questions, wondered at his responses. Did he offer excuses for their lovemaking? Cast the blame on her?

The questions intensified, the toughest ones centering on that first night, the night she was abducted. How many men had ridden up with Snake? Could she identify them if she saw them again? What exactly had been said? She told her story, hearing the words as if spoken by another.

Some of her recollections seemed hazy, while others were eerily detailed. Like how the red plaid shirt Snake wore that night had two patches on the left elbow, one blue, one black. How Matt Michaels had been wearing a faded green T-shirt with a beer logo. And how his blood had swirled in Technicolor beneath him, as his body convulsed. She wept as she described Matt's death, breaking down completely at the end.

By the time Barry escorted her back to her motel room it was evening. "I know this hasn't been easy," he said. "Unfortunately, we'll need to go over it again in the morning. See if you recall any other pertinent details. In the meantime, if anything comes to you, write it down, no matter how insignificant. I've seen entire cases broken on small, seemingly irrelevant, facts."

Tess nodded halfheartedly. Earlier Barry had outlined the next steps. She would fly home tomorrow afternoon. The FBI would have additional questions, then someone from the U.S. Attorney's Office would contact her. After charges were pressed, there would be depositions. And ultimately the trials.

Barry had also explained that the case was federal in scope. A government agent had been murdered; a federal capital crime. The list of other federal violations was lengthy. Drug trafficking and kidnapping were only the tip of the iceberg.

Right now the processes seemed daunting. Once again her thoughts wandered to Dallas. She hadn't seen him since leaving the compound early that morning. She wanted to talk to him, see him.

"Is Dallas staying at this motel?"

"Grey. Grey Thomas," Barry corrected gently. "I know you only knew him by his undercover name."

And only by his undercover persona, Tess recalled. Her chest tightened. Did the man she knew—or thought she knew—even exist?

"Grey will probably be busy most of the night," Barry continued. "Would you like Franklin to stay with you?"

Franklin was the female agent who'd been with her most of the day. Tess shook her head. "No, thanks."

"I'll post a guard outside your door in case you need anything." Barry removed his glasses, his own exhaustion evident by the circles beneath his eyes. "Look, if it's any consolation, I've known Grey Thomas for years. He's a great guy. A great cop. Anything he did, he did for your protection or for the well-being of the other women involved. Now . . . well, now it's probably best if he stays away."

Tess didn't miss the subtle note of censure. Was Barry discouraging her against seeing Dallas . . . *Grey*? Or simply trying to reinforce that Grey had been doing his job?

She slipped into her room, shut and locked the door, alone for the first time all day.

Alone and free.

She'd been a captive for over three weeks, had thought of this moment thousands of times. So why didn't it feel better than this?

In retrospect, she realized she'd thought in terms of her life picking up where it had left off. As if her kidnapping, Matt Michaels's murder, had never happened. But it had, and there was no going back.

She looked around the small room, at the bed made up with a faded turquoise spread that matched the faded turquoise drapes and knew she'd have a hard time sleeping tonight. *Without Dallas.*

She'd grown accustomed to sleeping in his arms. To making love with him before she slept. In the night, if she had bad dreams, he'd awaken her, comfort her. Then he'd make love to her, pushing in very, very, slowly as if she were more precious than life, until she thought she'd die from too much pleasure, too much sensation. *Too much hot, hard, flesh.*

Sometimes that was all he did. *Enter her.* The joining itself so phenomenal, so special, it required nothing else. Going so deep he touched her soul. When he was inside her there was room for little else. Only him. It was a total possession of body and mind.

She closed her eyes recalling his touch, his heat, his strength. God, how could she miss him?

The phone rang, the shrill, unfamiliar, ring startling her. She hesitated a moment, uncertain if she should answer it, worried that if by answering it she would only find herself subjected to more questions, more mental poking and prodding.

She stood there for several more rings before realizing that for the first time in weeks she needed to make *a decision*. That she had a choice.

She crossed the room.

"Hello?"

"It's Grey." The connection crackled, indicating he was on a cellular phone.

Tess sank down on the bed, the sound of his voice softening her knees. "Where are you?"

The melancholy note in her voice tore at him. "I'm on my way to Billings." Matt's autopsy was scheduled for late that evening, and Grey couldn't let his friend suffer that final indignity alone. "I just wanted to make sure you were okay."

Okay? She looked around the austere room. She'd be better if he were there with her.

Then she recalled Barry's words. *It's best if Grey stays away.*

"Tess? Is something wrong?"

"I'm tired," she hedged. "It's . . . been a long day."

Grey frowned, trying to imagine what it had been like for her, cursing the state of affairs that kept them apart.

He'd spent most of the morning at the compound with a small army of crime-scene technicians, helping tag and ID evidence. Then he'd started the tedious debriefing process. Though most of the criminal acts he'd witnessed had already been meticulously documented through another field agent, Grey had over eighteen months to cover.

He didn't want to think about what lay ahead. The mountains of paperwork, the interviews, the depositions. There would be multiple charges. A case of this size, with international scope, would take months to build. The trials could stretch interminably. Then there'd be appeals. It was far from over. For him. Or for Tess.

While part of him knew he had to leave her alone, bow out

of the picture—he couldn't. She'd become an integral part of his existence these past weeks. She'd come into his world and breathed life back into what little humanity he'd had left.

Leading a double life, going that deep undercover for so long extracted a heavy toll. She'd saved him even before he'd realized he'd needed saving. And she reminded him of why he'd taken on this assignment in the first place. To uphold justice. To serve.

To protect the innocent.

He winced, recalling Tess's innocence. Even now he wanted her, missed her presence. He'd been questioned extensively over the issue of whether their physical relationship had been truly consensual. Tess had, after all, been held against her will. Whether he could have been stronger, resisted a little bit longer was a moot point.

He also knew it wouldn't be the last he heard on the matter, knew he was expected to keep a professional distance from her. But he couldn't simply forget and walk away.

She had affected him deeply. Was different from anyone he'd ever met. And it bothered him that the *why* was so elusive. Had it truly just been the heat of the moment? The life-or-death intensity of their circumstances? Would he feel different if they hadn't made love?

He thought back to his prior relationships. He'd managed okay with casual affairs—the ones where sex was the glue. But the most important ones he'd screwed up.

So where did Tess fit in?

He didn't know. And right now, he didn't have time to give it more thought. Right now he needed to put her mind at rest about another matter.

"I spoke with Barry earlier. He said you'd seen a doctor. I know that wasn't pleasant. I know the questions they asked weren't easy." Hell, none of this was easy, so he waded right in. "I wanted to assure you I'm in perfect health, Tess."

She knew immediately what he was referring to. *Sexually transmitted diseases.* She flushed, glad now for her solitude.

"Thanks," she stammered, her mind fumbling for a different topic.

But Grey wasn't finished. "And if you're pregnant—"

"No!" The word escaped unbidden, the denial too sharp. "I mean, I can't be."

Her tone told him two things: She wasn't certain, and the subject upset her. Hell, the subject unsettled him, but it didn't relieve him of responsibility. He tried to pick his next words carefully. The last thing he wanted to do was cause this woman more anguish.

"I just want you to know I'm here for you if you are pregnant and—" The hiss of static cut him off.

The next word she heard was "shit." More static. "I'm losing my signal," he said. "Can we talk about this tomorrow?"

The last thing she wanted to think about or discuss was a possible pregnancy. However, she did want to see him. Talk about other things.

"Tomorrow," she confirmed.

But the line had already gone dead.

❦

Tess didn't see Grey again.

By morning, the story of her kidnapping and rescue had hit the wire services. Reporters, eager to capitalize on the Marsh name and the sensational aspects of the story, descended on the motel. With so many different agencies involved in the arrests, it was impossible to determine who leaked the information of where Tess was staying. Under Barry Neilson's watchful eye, she was hustled out under heavy security and flown back to New York on a private jet.

The reunion with her family was not without some tension. Their initial relief at Tess's safe return soon gave way to a more predictable course of action. Her father and brother alternated between heated debates of whether the FBI should have contacted them sooner, and recriminations over their own failure to keep closer tabs on Tess.

Her mother, who was still in France, lamented that the story, with all its lurid conjecture, had made headlines overseas. Tess was grateful when her brother suggested their mother remain in Europe until the publicity died down in the States. Though she knew her mother cared, there were certain things Madeline Marsh did not deal with well.

At her father's urging, Tess took up temporary residence at the Marsh mansion in the Hamptons, a walled estate that now had twenty-four-hour, private, security.

Tess's first weeks home passed quickly as she was interviewed several more times by the FBI. None of the agents she met were familiar. And while part of her longed to inquire about Grey, she couldn't bring herself to ask. She longed for him to the point it hurt, which she didn't quite understand. How could she have fallen so hard, so fast for him?

The question of whether the person she had fallen for even existed weighed heavily on her, and the fact that he didn't make contact with her added to the confusion.

Dallas Haynes was a myth.

Grey Thomas was a stranger.

She started seeing a counselor. While part of her resented the fact that she needed help to readjust, part of her rejoiced at being able to unburden herself to someone nonjudgmental. She learned about Stockholm Syndrome and how to deal effectively with the nightmares of Matt Michaels's murder. She was also working through the shock, denial, and anger associated with traumatic events.

Only one subject remained taboo: the lingering, wavering feelings she had for Grey. They seemed too personal . . . too private . . . and she wasn't ready to have them wiped away with a term like *white-knight complex*.

Not when she suspected she was pregnant with his child.

Tess looked out the bedroom window at the neat expanse of lawn. It was the end of August, and she was still in the Hamptons.

She should have been in Boston, getting her store ready for its fall opening. Instead she'd been forced to close her shop temporarily after it and her town house were vandalized. The break-ins occurred shortly after her return from Montana. While the police had no leads, they felt both acts were random, crimes of opportunity fueled by newspaper reports that she was staying out of town. As much as she'd hated closing her shop it was one less thing to deal with. And right now she had all she could possibly handle.

She stared at the box in her hand. *A pregnancy test kit.* In mere minutes, she might know the answer to a question that had been bothering her since the first day she'd been freed.

Was she pregnant?

She sighed. She couldn't put off knowing any longer. According to her calculations she should have had her period in early August. In the beginning she'd tried to convince herself she was late due to stress, kept thinking she felt the onset of cramps, but denial wore thin after the first week, replaced by a single, burning, question:

What would she do if she were pregnant?

She dismissed the idea of abortion immediately, knowing she'd keep the child in spite of the repercussions. There would be fallout. She'd be ostracized. Her family would oppose her decision, as would her friends. They would view pregnancy as an unwanted, unwelcome side effect of her captivity. Because none of them knew the truth of her relationship with Grey.

A lump formed in her throat. She didn't even know the

truth of it. In reality Grey was probably no more prepared to deal with an unplanned pregnancy than she was. She thought back to their last night together. She'd already been carrying his child then—

A knock sounded at her door.

Flustered, Tess slid the box into a drawer and quickly shut it.

"You have a call from a Mr. Barry Neilson with the FBI," the maid said. "Do you want to take it?"

Tess nodded. She hadn't talked with Barry since she'd left Montana. *Maybe he had a message from Grey?*

"Hello, Barry." She knew she sounded breathless.

They exchanged pleasantries, then Barry cleared his throat. "I'm afraid I have some bad news."

Her stomach clenched. Had something happened to Grey?

"Hector Sanchez was freed from jail on a technicality," Barry continued.

Her relief was torpedoed by disbelief. Sanchez was free? "How could that happen?"

"The search warrant for his plane wasn't signed at the time it was searched. Evidently there was a miscommunication between a couple agencies."

"But what about the other charges?"

"He made bail and already skipped the country. We can't touch him."

Tess thought about the women who, following Sanchez's arrest, had been tracked down and freed from "private ownership." She'd read an article about them. Some had been abused. All had been raped. And now, like a cruel joke, Hector Sanchez was free. Where was the justice for them?

"Can he be extradited?"

"Doubtful, but we'll try. It makes me sick to think we were so close to nailing him, that one of my men literally gave up almost two years of his life to catch that man."

Barry was talking about Grey, of course. Before she could stop herself, she asked, "How is he?" Both of them knew who it was she asked about.

Silence preceded guarded words. "He's been busy, Tess. As you know, there's a lot to be done on this case. And he's trying to reclaim his personal life. He virtually walked away from everything he owned, his family—"

"Family?" She closed her eyes, tried to picture Grey rushing home to a loving wife. She couldn't. Not in his line of work.

Children, though, were another story. She could picture Grey as a father, just as easily as she could picture him as a lover. Boyfriend.

A new and sickening scenario presented itself. What if Grey had left a special *someone* behind? Perhaps he *had* only slept with her in the line of duty. A pregnancy would be unwelcome news indeed.

"Grey has a father and sisters," Barry continued. "They know he does undercover work, which doesn't make it easy when he disappears as he did."

A father and sisters. She recalled the things he'd told her in Montana, realizing he had never mentioned specific details, like family, hadn't really shared anything personal, which made her regret having told him the smallest detail about her life. The fact that she knew nothing about him sharpened the sense of deception.

He'd talked about living in Pennsylvania, being in the Army. Both were probably fabrications, part of his cover. She'd known *Dallas Haynes*. A fictional, undercover, caricature. When would she get it through her head that *Dallas* didn't exist. He was fantasy. Vapor. Smoke.

"I didn't mean to pry," she said finally.

Barry sighed. "You understand why he hasn't contacted you, don't you? It's not appropriate under the best of circumstances for two witnesses on the same case to spend time together."

The inference was clear. *Best of circumstances* didn't include witnesses who'd shared an intimate relationship.

Or witnesses who might be pregnant.

She thanked Barry for calling and hung up, her thoughts straying to the test kit she had stashed in the drawer.

She already knew the answer the kit would reveal. What she didn't know was how, or when—or if—she'd tell the father.

Chapter Ten

$\mathcal{T}$he next six weeks passed in a blur of legal maneuverings.

Tess told no one she was pregnant, deciding to wait until some of the hubbub died down before even seeing a doctor—which was probably just as well, considering.

She had made three trips to Washington, D.C., meeting with the federal prosecutor and testifying before a federal grand jury. As a result, Bogen and Snake were indicted on first-degree murder for Matt Michaels's death—the worst of a long line of charges being levied. Subsequently, Bogen's and Snake's attorneys deposed her several times.

Both sides agreed to a change of venue, to the Washington, D.C. area, after the defense claimed they would have difficulty seating an impartial jury in Montana. While much of it went over her head, Tess gathered that if all parties to the trial agreed to the shift in venue, there was no basis for a later appeal on those grounds.

She had expected the case to languish in the judicial system for months but to everyone's surprise, Bogen and Snake exercised their right to a speedy trial on the murder charges, demanding that the prosecution try them immediately. Their case was placed on what the prosecutor called "the rocket docket."

Apparently Snake and Bogen felt there was a possibility that, like Sanchez, they could get off on a technicality. If so, they could then get out on bail pending the other charges. Not that anyone expected them to stick around if they posted bond.

In an unusual move, they also chose to be tried together. Were they worried that if they were tried separately, one might strike a deal to testify against the other?

She'd returned to Montana briefly, helping investigators recreate the scene of Matt Michaels's death. The trip had been grueling and brought back a host of unsettling memories.

It also made her miss Dallas . . . Grey.

She knew her memories of him were romanticized. The fact that he'd been such a gentle, caring, guardian didn't make him any easier to forget. He'd protected her, nurtured her, cherished her. Had it really just been *in the line of duty?* How could someone be like that, play a part so convincingly yet remain untouched?

Nights were the worst. Some nights her dreams were erotic, fevered, sensual, and she'd wake up to an empty bed, with a heavy heart. If she could have just one more night, one last chance to talk, to be held in his arms, to make love . . .

Other nights she'd wake up to find her hand resting protectively against her abdomen, the sense of loneliness not quite so oppressive when she thought of the baby.

Slowly, surely, she grew accustomed to the idea of being pregnant. Taking it one day at a time helped. She also broke down and called her doctor's office a few days ago, talked with his nurse. She'd told the nurse she was out of the country—a little white lie—and that she believed she was pregnant. A whopper. She *knew* she was pregnant.

"Congratulations," the nurse said. Then she asked several questions, assuring Tess it should be fine if she waited a few more weeks to see an obstetrician. "A lot of women wait until their third or fourth month before making their first appointment. Unless something goes wrong, naturally."

The nurse gave Tess a list of things to watch for. "And contact us as soon as you're back in the States."

Talking with the nurse eased Tess's conscience about not going to a doctor right away. It did nothing for her sense of guilt over hiding her pregnancy from the prosecuting attorney.

And Grey.

She grew resigned to the fact she wouldn't see Grey again until the actual trial. She mulled over ways to tell him about the baby. *Whether* to tell him. Wondered how he'd react.

She thought back to her last conversation with him. He'd brought up the subject of pregnancy. He'd promised to be there for her. Had he meant it? Or were they just words? Maybe he'd meant something different. That he'd be there to hold her hand when she got rid of it . . .

While she resisted the thought, she had no reason to believe Grey *wanted* a child.

As the heat of late summer surrendered to shorter, cooler days, Tess grew weary of being confined to the Hamptons. She'd set up a makeshift studio, sketching and tinkering with new jewelry designs, but it wasn't the same. She missed Boston, her friends, her shop. Her freedom. The press had moved on to other stories, giving her a small measure of privacy though she knew interest would heighten again when the trial opened.

She woke up one morning having reached a critical decision. No more being passive, no more hiding. No more dreaming about what might have been and what could never be.

It was time to reclaim her life.

Or at least take the first step.

Tonight she would attend the private art auction sponsored by her father's charitable foundation. An exclusive event, the tickets sold out months ago. Tess knew most of the attendees, and the press wasn't invited, so it was a perfect opportunity to get out. A *safe* first outing.

She eyed the dress on her bed, then threw another change of clothes in her suitcase, in case she wanted to spend an extra day in the city. The Marsh Manhattan had a private suite she could use for the night. And if she decided to stay even longer, she could go to her mother's apartment. Madeline was still overseas, so Tess would have privacy.

A change of scenery sounded ideal. So did a day of shopping, a museum, a play. A bagel and a latte. All the little luxuries she'd taken for granted.

Heartened, she picked up the stack of new mail on her desk and shuffled through it, discarding magazines and junk advertisements. She read a letter from her mother, then opened a small white envelope.

She frowned at the lack of return address and pulled out a single sheet of paper.

Testify and you die, the typewritten note read. *We will find you—whether you're in Boston, the Hamptons, Aspen, or Montserrat.*

Her hand moved protectively to her abdomen as she reread the note. *Testify and you die.*

It was unsigned, but she knew who sent it.

Bogen and Snake were connected with an international crime lord. A crime lord who didn't want to be implicated.

In cryptic fashion they were letting her know they knew about the Marsh family homes in the Hamptons, Aspen, Montserrat and her own town house in Boston.

Tess looked around the room that had become her virtual

prison, realizing there was nowhere to run, nowhere to hide. She'd never felt more alone in her life. Her frenzied thoughts turned to Grey, wishing he were there.

But he wasn't.

She had to face this on her own. Again.

Testify and you die. The threat was simple and brutal. But effective.

Though they had no way of knowing it, they threatened her child when they threatened her. Which infuriated Tess. Her protective instincts kicked in, surprising her with their ferociousness, overriding all concern for herself. She wouldn't jeopardize her baby's well-being for anything.

She paced her room, weighing options, testing alternatives, tired of being pushed around. But one thought overwhelmed all else: defy the note and die. In the end only one choice made sense for her child's safety.

She wouldn't testify.

Picking up the phone, she dialed Barry Neilson's number.

Grey stuck a finger under the collar of his shirt. He hadn't worn a tux since he'd been best man in a wedding six years ago.

He was alone in the private elevator of the posh Marsh Manhattan, ascending to the ballroom on the top floor. He straightened his cuffs, then tugged at the collar once more, impatient.

It had been two months since his return to *civilization.* Two months since seeing Tess. He ached with the need he'd denied every day they'd been apart.

He'd kept tabs on her through Barry, but that didn't satisfy Grey's desire to talk with her, be with her. Hear her voice. He regretted not seeing her before she left Montana. There had been much left unresolved between them.

She haunted his sleep. In dreams he tasted her lips, felt her nails score his skin as her heat scorched his flesh. He'd awaken, throbbing hard, on the edge of agony. He'd hear his own words: *Little fool. You mean nothing to me.* He felt the crack of her fist again and again.

He sighed. It had been tough. He'd known from the beginning that he was expected to turn and walk away. But it was the staying away, not even making casual contact with her, that had been excruciating. Their involvement had become a tricky issue, one which, if not handled properly, could jeopardize the case. And this case was tricky enough without the personal nuances.

He thought back over the past few months, the questions he'd faced. *Had his involvement with Tess been appropriate? Was his behavior befitting an officer of the law? Were his loyalties compromised?* A case could, and would, be made for and against. Both sides of the fence would be played.

He knew the questions hadn't been any easier for Tess. He also knew that despite the censure he'd received, the prejudices in a situation like this were still tipped in his favor. Too often men weren't expected to rise above their animal instincts, while women were held to a stricter, more unforgiving standard. There were different levels of disapproval based on sex. Unfair as hell, but reality all the same.

Out of respect for her, Grey played by the rules and kept away, even though it damn near killed him.

Until today.

In a surprising phone call, Barry reversed his position and asked Grey to contact her immediately.

Tess, Barry explained, had suddenly decided she didn't want to testify. Barry's first concern was she'd been threatened. That wasn't uncommon in a case of this scope. A second possibility was her family pressuring her. The Marshes were scions of society. The notoriety surrounding the case would be anathema.

Of course Tess could be forced to testify, but an unwilling witness usually did more damage than good. Barry wanted Grey to talk with her, see if he could get her to open up. Find out what prompted the switch, then get her to change her mind without official action.

Grey had jumped at the opportunity to see her. Yeah, he was worried about why she'd changed her mind. He didn't like the idea she might have been threatened. But he also didn't like the thought of her being forced to testify if she honestly didn't want to—a direct conflict with his desire to see justice meted out. His jaw tightened recalling Matt Michaels's fate.

He didn't want to think about where his loyalties were right now. His family, those closest to his heart, had always come first. And Tess was definitely close to his heart. Maybe too close.

The elevator doors slid open with a subtle *bing*. Grey stepped out, looked around. Crashing the party had been easy. The hotel's chief of security had taken one look at Grey's tux and ID, allowing him to pass without question.

A waiter glided up, offering wine. Accepting a glass, Grey backed into the closest corner, feigning interest in a watercolor while he oriented himself within the room.

The Marsh Manhattan was New York's newest high-rise. The ballroom was done in an elaborate, gold-leaf baroque and featured an intricate glass spire that soared nearly three stories at its peak. A balcony provided an unparalleled view of the city that never slept.

"She's going home with me."

Grey turned to the older woman who had insinuated herself between him and the watercolor.

Diamonds flashed on her wrists and fingers as she gestured dismissively, trying to hide the piece with her scrawny arms. "The painting. You don't fool me. I can tell you're interested. But don't even think about bidding against me. I want her, and I'll have her."

He chuckled at the woman's veracity. The term *dowager* came to mind. She looked harmless, but he bet she had a nasty-tempered, ruthless, Pomeranian at home that bit on command. He inclined his head, signifying acquiescence.

"She's a beauty." *But not the one he had in mind.*

Pleased with her imagined triumph, the woman launched into a monologue of the artist's biography. Grey's gaze drifted imperceptibly as he systematically checked out the crowd.

He noticed more than one person watching him—he was the newcomer; the unknown face. He avoided more than brief eye contact. There was only one person he was interested in.

And there she was. On the dance floor.

Tess.

He lurched, unprepared for the punch of reaction the sight of her wrought. Seeing her again was painful. Like having nails hammered into his solar plexus.

Christ, she was beautiful. She was wearing a sparkly gown the same shade of blue as her eyes, her hair neatly piled atop her head in a chic "do" he could wreck in seconds. She looked spectacular.

His eyes dropped, then drifted upward, taking in her sexy heels, the long, shapely legs. *Legs he remembered wrapping around his waist.*

Her partner laughed at something she'd said. Grey narrowed his eyes, watching the man squeeze Tess's waist.

"That frown is back," his matronly friend observed. "You're not having second thoughts about bidding, are you?"

"No, ma'am. But I see another work I might be interested in. Will you excuse me?"

~

"Have you heard a word I've said?"

Embarrassed, Tess stared at her partner. She and Jack had gone to school together. Their families had been close. A successful stockbroker, he had recently joined a prestigious Wall Street firm.

"Bear market. Bull market." She'd caught a word here and there. "The semantics go over my head. I tend to look at the bottom line. You've done well with the portfolio you're handling. I trust your judgment."

Jack preened. "You still need to understand the logic," he said, diving right back into a dissertation on market trends.

Tess's attention drifted immediately. Perhaps after this dance she'd leave.

She was definitely preoccupied, *and with good reason*, she thought, recalling the note.

Her conversation with Barry Neilson had not been good. She knew he wasn't buying her *I-just-don't-want-to* excuse. He'd asked point-blank whether she'd been warned against testifying.

Lying had made her feel awful. While much of what she told Barry was true—that she was tired of the questions, tired of the complete disruption of her life—the lie had wedged in her throat like a thin bone. Uncomfortable. Choking. In the end they'd agreed to discuss it later.

"Think about it over the weekend," Barry said finally. "Promise me you won't make any definite decision until we talk again Monday morning."

In the end those were the very words that goaded Tess toward action. She hadn't made a *definite decision* since her return from Montana. She'd reacted, not acted. She accepted the mantle of victim too willingly.

No more.

She'd gone ahead with her plans to attend the art auction, not wanting to stay in the Hamptons a day longer, but already she plotted a return to Boston. A return to the life she'd left behind.

"If you're in town for the weekend, perhaps we could have dinner tomorrow night." Jack's voice brought her back to the moment. "Catch up on old times. And no business. I promise."

Tess tilted her head, tempted. Jack was a trusted friend. Dinner meant dinner. Catching up meant being entertained with zany tales about mutual acquaintances.

He wouldn't pressure her for details on the trial or ask what her ordeal had been like. If she *wanted* to discuss it, of course, he'd listen. And offer sound advice. Jack was the type who'd offer to marry her if she told him she were pregnant. And he'd treat her and her child with loving respect.

She looked at him, tried to envision herself wedded to him. She couldn't. It would be like marrying her brother.

Grey had left a discomforting legacy. On one hand, she knew she'd never again settle for a passionless relationship. On the other, she knew no lover would ever compare. So was she doomed to a life of celibacy? Or a vibrator?

Someone had walked up behind Jack, tapped his shoulder. Startled, Jack broke off mid-sentence and turned, releasing her.

Grey stepped forward and took her hand. "Good evening, Tess."

Time snapped backward. "Dallas!"

"*Grey.*"

She shook her head in denial. Dismay. Disbelief.

He looked wonderful. Impossibly taller. Broader across the shoulders.

And totally different. She barely recognized him.

Gone were the long ponytail and mustache. In their place was a sleek, short haircut that accentuated his handsome, clean-shaven face, the strong jaw that she knew would have a five o'clock shadow by four.

That intimate memory gave her a chill, made her clench her fingers to keep from reaching out and stroking the smooth hollow beneath his cheek, the sexy cleft in his chin that had been hidden by the goatee he'd worn in Montana.

He looked . . . achingly gorgeous. Every bit the suave, handsome secret agent, a seducer of women in a black tux that fit him like a dream. *James Bond.* Her heart skipped a beat, then another, as time skidded to an uneven, unstable, stop.

Too late she realized she was gawking and struggled to withdraw her hand from his.

Grey tightened his grip, refusing to free her. Without taking his eyes from hers, he slowly brought her hand to his lips, brushing a kiss across her fingers. She looked elegant, ethereal. And more aloof by the moment. Had he imagined the flash of desire in her eyes?

No matter. He'd broken through her defenses before, he'd do it again. But this time he'd do it gently. . . .

He turned to Tess's dance partner. "May I cut in? We're old friends."

Jack looked deferentially at Tess. "You know him?"

She nodded. "I'll call you tomorrow, Jack. About dinner," she promised, as Grey tugged her away.

"Dinner?" Grey arched an eyebrow.

She ignored his tone and his question, careful to keep her own voice low, modulated. "What are you doing here? This is a closed function."

"I needed to see you."

A lump formed in her throat. God, what she would have given to hear those words weeks ago. On those nights when the grief and loneliness felt unbearable. When doubt threatened to drown her.

She blinked back tears, leaning heavily on her pride. She knew exactly what prompted Grey's visit. And it hurt.

"Barry sent you, didn't he?" she asked.

"Does it matter? I should have been here a long time ago."

The floor was crowded, the music just loud enough to mute their words. Tucking her hand near his heart, he let his thighs brush hers. "You look lovely, Tess." Too lovely, he thought. There wasn't a man in the room who hadn't looked at her without lustful thoughts. Or wishful thoughts.

Grey drew her closer still, a predator openly marking territory. *She was his.* The soft scent of roses teased his senses, as potent as an ancient aphrodisiac.

A glutton for punishment he pressed his mouth close to her ear. She jumped slightly.

"Relax," he murmured. "I won't bite."

Relax? Impossible. She felt his breath on her neck, remembered the feel of his lips there. Heat radiated from his body, causing every cell in hers to tremble in response. Her hypersensitive breasts felt even heavier, her nipples tightening almost painfully. Something inside melted, low. *Dangerous.*

She noticed the looks they were starting to receive, knew Grey held her too tight. She tried to pull back. "This isn't the place," she began.

Damn straight, he thought. The only place for her was his bed. A hundred shimmering images of her flashed through his mind, some memory, some illusion. In fantasies he'd explored all the territory they'd yet to chart.

He released a low growl. "We need a private place to talk."

She misstepped, her hip bumping his as she struggled to keep her voice from fracturing. "I was told not to discuss the case."

"I don't mean the case. I mean us."

Us? Tess's heart squeezed as she let her guard down. Did he mean it?

Seeing him again, being held in his arms, the solid, easy way he moved, evoked a host of sensual, uneasy, memories. Lust struck like lightning. Brilliant. Hot. Luring her with flashes of selective recall. Grey had been a magnificent lover, seeing to her pleasure before his own. He'd taught her what he liked; had encouraged her boldness in discovering her own preferences.

Her hand drifted across his chest, edging beneath his jacket, her greedy fingers tracing the strong line of muscle, remembering. She wanted to believe . . .

Then her knuckles brushed his shoulder holster. Bitter reality washed over her, blotting out hope. Reminding her that Grey could wield seduction like a deadly weapon; that she was merely a target being sighted in the crosshairs.

"You're wearing a gun." She tried to back away.

His fingers tightened at her waist, keeping her tethered. Captive. "I'm always armed, Tess. It's part of the job."

Get used to it, he wanted to say. He glanced around the room, spotted the door leading to the balcony. "Let's go outside."

Not wanting to draw more attention to them, Tess nodded.

The balcony was deserted, but Grey sought out the darkest corner anyway. "About us," he started.

"There is no 'us.' "

He drew close, cupping her face in his hands. She was wrong and he wanted to prove it. To her. To him.

She made a noise, a tiny intake of air as he lowered his mouth to hers. Desire shuddered through him as he held her immobile, his lips dancing lightly across hers, tasting, teasing. This thing that was between them hit a flash point. He could feel it in the uneven tempo of his pulse. In the yearning that raked his skin.

She drew another breath and Grey's tongue swept hotly into her mouth. She opened fully, her hands encircling his neck, her fingers spearing through his hair. Just like before . . .

But different. *A point he wanted to drive home.*

Grey's mouth left hers, trailing down her neck. "Say my name," he commanded in a throaty whisper. He wanted no ghosts between them, no memory of another touching her, kissing her . . . even if that other was him. *Dallas.*

She whimpered, resisting.

"*My* name, damn it." His teeth grazed the sensitive skin at the crook of her neck.

"Grey." The word was an anguished cry.

He sealed his lips over hers, claiming victory. He had her pinned against the railing, knew she could feel his heavy arousal.

The memory of making love to her made him grow even harder. He wanted to feel her hands grip him tightly before he buried himself deep inside her—

The doors behind them opened.

Grey abruptly stepped away, keeping a hand on her arm to steady her.

"Easy, I got you," he soothed. "Pretend we're discussing the auction."

Tess blinked, reaching for the railing, trying to calm her breathing. The auction?

How could he go from kissing like that to pretending they were discussing art?

The same way he'd chameleoned from Grey to Dallas. He was doing a job. He was still doing a job. Today's assignment was convincing her to testify.

She was a colossal fool. She'd spent the last weeks trying to bury her memories, forget what passed between them. And in the space of fifteen minutes he'd brought it all back.

Her eyes swept over him. All the things she'd struggled to forget—that dimple, those quicksilver eyes, the way he kissed—rushed forward, leaving her aching and unsure. Her pulse thudded low in her abdomen, reminding her of something else.

She was pregnant with this man's child.

Dizziness assailed her.

She'd been sick enough the past week to recognize the symptoms. She was going to be ill. She panicked, moving away.

"Excuse me," Tess said. "There's someone . . . I need . . ."

She was shaking. Grey grew concerned. He knew his presence here tonight had surprised her. He also knew the kiss they'd just shared had affected her. But this? She'd lost color, as if she'd seen a ghost.

Or been frightened.

His eyes quickly scanned the ballroom, senses alert, but he spotted nothing unusual. He focused on her again.

"Are you okay?" he asked.

"I'll be back in a minute."

Nodding to the other couple on the balcony, Tess headed toward the relative safety of the ballroom, praying no one approached her, knowing Grey couldn't stop her once she was lost in the crush of the people.

Grey watched her work her way across the crowded room. Her *I'll be back* rang false. He knew why. Christ, he'd practically attacked her out here. *Smooth move.* He'd give her a few moments to pull herself together, then he'd go after her. Apologize. Again.

But Tess didn't stop in the ballroom. She made a beeline for the door. *She was leaving.*

Swearing, Grey hurried after her.

Tess slipped into the private suite that was adjacent to the ballroom.

Feeling too warm, she quickly peeled off her beaded jacket, dropping it on the floor as she rushed toward the wet bar in the center of the room. She turned on the tap, slid her wrists beneath the cold water.

She heard the door open and close. Glancing back, she saw Grey striding toward her. "How did you get in here?"

He picked up her jacket, tossed it aside. "You left the door unlocked. Why didn't you tell me you felt ill?"

Moving deliberately, he wet some towels, wringing them out before placing them on the back of her neck. She looked ready to faint.

The cold compress felt divine against her flushed skin. "It's nothing. Please leave."

"And let you hit the floor?" He watched her intently.

Tess squirmed, feeling more awful by the second. "You don't need to do this."

"I want to help."

Help? *Then go away. Let her protect their child.*

A child he had the right to know about . . .

The thought made her stomach lurch even worse.

Oh God . . . She was going to throw up. *Right now.*

She scrambled to push past him, frantic to make it to the bathroom in time.

"Hold on." Two steps ahead of her, Grey shoved open the door and helped her inside.

Wrenching free, she shut the door in his face just before growing violently ill. She wept with embarrassment, knowing Grey was right outside.

He knocked on the door. "Tess, let me help you."

"Go away. I don't need—" Another bout of sickness interrupted her.

Grey pressed against the door, finding it locked. *Now she decides to lock doors.*

He rapped on the door, harder this time. "You okay in there?"

Tess drew a deep breath, no longer feeling as if she'd vomit from merely breathing. She turned on the water, rinsed her mouth. "Yes, I'm fine."

A heavy sigh preceded his words. "I'm not leaving, so you might as well come out. Like it or not, you're going to have to face me."

She wanted to scream with frustration but didn't have the energy. Straightening her clothes, she opened the door. But her light-headedness had settled in her knees. When she swooned, Grey caught her, carrying her to the couch.

She was too woozy to protest. And humiliated. Tears prickled the back of her eyes. She blinked rapidly, holding them back. She'd gotten sick—practically right in front of him—then she'd nearly fainted. The last thing she wanted to do was start crying.

She had her eyes closed when Grey returned with more wet paper towels. Very gently he draped them across her forehead, inspecting her closely. Her pallor concerned him. Pressing two fingers to her wrist, he found her pulse to be practically nonexistent.

He expected her to be stressed and nervous over the upcoming trial. And it was obvious that seeing him again upset her. But to be sick? Faint? Something about this episode didn't make sense.

"How long have you been feeling like this?"

"Since you showed up." *On a star-studded Montana night . . .*

Because there was no putting off the inevitable, and because it was easier to face *Grey* than to face the memories of *Dallas,* she opened her eyes and struggled to sit up.

He caught her by the shoulders keenly aware of her evasiveness. "Stay down. You still look green."

"Thank you, Dr. Haynes. Or Dr. Thomas." She scrambled to cover her vulnerability with sarcasm.

Grey knelt directly in front of her, picked up her hands. "I'm not trying to upset you, Tess. I just want to talk. Not about the case," he clarified. "Though at some time we do need to—in context to us and what happened in Montana."

His words tempted, until she remembered he was only here because Barry Neilson had sent him.

"I know what happened in Montana. *Stockholm Syndrome.* My reaction to you was classic. Hostage grows fond of and sympathizes with her captors. I'm told ours is a textbook example." She softened her tone. "I'm also aware you were doing a job. Playing a role. You still are."

Grey pressed a kiss to her hand. What transpired between them was more than hostage/captor syndrome. He knew it. And judging by the torment in her eyes, she knew it, too. The problem was determining what, if anything, they could do about it.

"This hasn't been easy for either one of us, Tess. Yes, I'm here at Barry's request, but with a very selfish hidden agenda." He pressed yet another kiss to her hand.

The feel of his lips on her palm rocked Tess, confirming a truth she'd tried hard to deny. *She still wanted this man.*

She tried to move away, to get some distance as twin bolts

of pain collided in her temple. She pressed two fingers to her forehead and started rubbing. "I'm scared of testifying," she blurted.

Grey straightened, gently easing her back against the slanted arm of the couch. When she didn't resist, he slid onto the opposite end of the couch and pulled her feet across his lap. Tugging off her shoes, he started rubbing the ball of her foot.

"Do you realize if you refuse to testify or deny the statements you made under oath in your deposition are true, you can be prosecuted for perjury?" He kept his voice low, his eyes diverted as he stroked the knotted muscles of her foot. He pressed his thumbs expertly along the inside edge of her instep. "Or possibly jailed for contempt of court?"

Tess peered at him in disbelief. She hadn't considered either possibility. "Isn't there enough evidence to put them away without me? What about the other women they kidnapped?"

"This is the murder trial. They're not involved. You're the only eyewitness who can tie Bogen and Snake to Matt Michaels's death."

She knew that. Someone else did, too.

She shivered, recalling the letter she'd received. *Testify and you die.*

If she told Grey about the note, would he help her? Would he go to the prosecutor and explain, intercede on her behalf?

She hated her own fearfulness in this situation. Especially since her decision not to testify ran contrary to her deepest, inner convictions. Damn it, she did want to see Bogen and Snake punished. But not at the expense of her child's safety.

She watched Grey from beneath lowered lashes, debating. Did she dare trust this man again?

"I got something in the mail," she began.

Grey's hand stopped. "What?"

She told him about the note. "Now do you see why I can't testify?"

Grey's blood pressure raised. He had received a similar threat, which wasn't unusual in his line of work. Tess receiving one was another matter. He knew how to take care of himself. She didn't. And Bogen had a lot of friends in subterranean places who owed him favors.

"When did the letter arrive? Did you keep the envelope?"

She nodded. Grey caught her chin, held her eyes. "This is serious, Tess. I have to tell Barry."

"Why? What can he do? It was anonymous."

"For starters, he'll arrange protective custody."

"No!" The last thing she wanted was to have her freedom curtailed again. She looked pleadingly at Grey. "If I agree to testify, will you forget I told you about the letter?"

"I can't look the other way. The risk these men pose is real. You can't imagine what they're capable of, Tess. They're dangerous and desperate. A lethal combination. And they don't make idle threats."

"I'll be careful."

Grey sighed. This was exactly why a cop wasn't supposed to get personally involved with a case. Objectivity.

He looked away, torn between his personal feelings for her and his professional instincts. Why did it seem that all the right choices put him at odds with her?

Like it or not, he had to do what was right, even if it ran counter to her wishes. Damn, he didn't want to be cast in that position again.

"I'm sorry, Tess . . . "

Grey made contact with Barry Neilson, who started the arrangements for Tess to enter protective custody.

Within the hour two more FBI agents arrived, and she was taken to another hotel, checked in under an assumed name. A temporary move.

She noticed that Grey hadn't left her side since calling Barry. Was his increased attentiveness due to guilt? Or a misplaced sense of responsibility?

He struck her as the responsible type, which reinforced her decision to keep the news of her pregnancy secret. She didn't want to add to his sense of *obligation*, didn't want her baby to be a burden to anyone.

He remained close while she gave a statement regarding the threat she'd received. Someone was dispatched to retrieve the actual letter though no one expected it to yield clues.

"What happens now?" she asked when they were finally alone.

"You'll be taken to a safe house until the trial." Maybe longer, Grey thought, knowing they would reassess the threat after she testified. "You'll be kept under guard twenty-four, seven."

Tess shut her eyes, thinking back to her plans of that morning, her intention to spend a few days in the city.

The trial wasn't even scheduled for another couple weeks. She was once more a hostage. Of the system. "It feels like I'm a prisoner. Like I'm being punished when I've done nothing wrong."

He took her hand. It was an awful truth, and platitudes wouldn't help. But he found himself offering them just the same. "Try not to look at it that way. Granted, you won't be able to come and go as you please, but you'll have access to movies, books, TV. Maybe the Internet. And they'll make arrangements to collect a few of your personal belongings from your house."

Tess looked around the hotel room. It reminded her that

she hadn't been *home*—her home—since before her abduction. As much as she'd felt stifled at the Hamptons, at least it had been familiar. The thought of going somewhere unfamiliar and being surrounded by more strangers was unsettling.

She looked at Grey. "Will you be close by?"

The disconsolation in her eyes tore at him. "No. But I'll keep in touch this time, I promise. Once you're settled you'll be able to make and receive certain calls. You'll be briefed on security protocols."

A knock sounded on the door. Grey and the other agents had their guns drawn before the echo faded. Once again Tess noticed that Grey positioned himself between her and the door. Shielding her.

Shielding their child.

Grey huddled with the others near the door, before coming back to where she sat. She knew by the look on his face that her time with him had ended.

"The U.S. Marshal's Service will take over from here, Tess. I know these men. They'll protect you."

A lump lodged in her throat at the thought of leaving Grey yet again, reminding her anew of how secure she felt with him. How badly she wished things were different between them.

Not trusting herself to speak, she nodded and stood.

"Come here." He tugged her into his arms, squeezing her as he pressed a kiss to the top of her head. "I know this is hard, but it'll work out," he whispered. "I promise."

Chapter Eleven

Tess was flown to a private airstrip near Washington, D.C., before being moved to a nondescript safe house outside of Baltimore.

It was roomier than she'd expected; three bedrooms, a living room, and a kitchen. At first she felt extremely self-conscious with the marshals, but after a few days she developed a rapport, got used to their schedules. And recognized that this type of detail was as boring for them as it was for her.

Security, however, was tight. Tess couldn't leave the house without an escort. The blinds were kept drawn, and she was instructed to stay away from the windows.

A box with her personal belongings arrived the second day. Inside was a card from Grey. *Thinking of you,* it read. *I'll be in touch soon.*

She reread the card, recalling his promise to maintain contact. It made her acutely aware that once more she had no easy way to get in touch with him. Any contact was totally up to him.

It also triggered an avalanche of indecision over whether keeping her pregnancy to herself was indeed the right choice.

Besides the perpetual loop of *should-she-or-shouldn't-she* tell Grey, she worried about the question coming up in court.

The prosecutor had warned her that the cross-examination regarding her sexual liaison with Grey would be riddled with thinly veiled accusations, designed in part to embarrass her—to tempt her to prevaricate and thereby damage her credibility with the jury. As much as she wanted it over, she dreaded the trial's approach.

By the end of the first week, the computer in her room was hooked up to the Internet. She was assigned a bland, numeric screen name.

"This puppy is encrypted with all the latest security, but you've still got to be cautious. No e-mail to family or friends, no shopping with credit cards." The marshal showed her how to log on. "Double click here and *voilà*. Welcome to the World Wide Web."

Glad for a new diversion, Tess spent most of the afternoon checking out jewelry-design web sites. Just as she got ready to log off, a small message flashed on the screen.

Mail waiting.

Curious, she clicked the icon.

The sender's name was as nondescript as hers. Tess's first thought was *spam*. Then she spotted the subject line.

From G.T.

Grey Thomas? She clicked READ.

The note was short. *Hope you're feeling okay. Are they treating you well? Yours, G.*

Tess traced a finger across the screen. *Hope you're feeling okay.* Such an innocuous statement. Would he have written that if he knew about the baby? Would he have even written at all?

She scanned Grey's e-mail again, wishing she could read something between the lines. All two of them.

She eyed the REPLY icon, recalling the marshal's warning against e-mail. *To family and friends.* Grey definitely wasn't family. Technically, he wasn't a friend. The term *sperm donor* popped into mind, leaving her scowling.

She tapped out a short, equally cryptic, reply.

Feeling fine. Wish you were here. T.

She frowned at the screen again. Did *wish you were here* sound too . . . personal?

She went to hit DELETE, intent on rewording the entire message. Instead she hit SEND. The screen went blank, then a little box appeared, confirming her mail had been sent.

"Guess that problem resolved itself," she muttered.

A knock sounded at her door. She snapped off the computer. It was one of the marshals, reminding her of an outside meeting scheduled with the federal prosecutor.

Tess gathered her stuff and glanced at the computer one last time. At least now she had something to look forward to.

At the meeting she learned the threatening note had been mailed from Canada but yielded no tangible clues to identify the sender. Hence no charges could be filed.

❧

When Tess returned to the safe house, there were no new e-mail messages. Masking her disappointment, she ate a light meal and retired early.

But sleep eluded her, and a book failed to hold her interest.

At a little after ten, one of the marshals rapped at her door. He looked hesitant when she answered.

"Uh, sorry to wake you, but Special Agent Thomas is on the phone. Said he had a few questions if you were still awake."

Tess's heart flittered as she picked up the phone beside her bed. "Grey? Where are you?"

"I'm at a conference in L.A. Hope I'm not calling too late. Were you in bed?"

"Yes, but I couldn't sleep."

He grunted. He hadn't had a decent night's sleep in months. "I got your e-mail."

Silence swelled.

Then Grey spoke again. "Did you mean it?"

Wish you were here.

She sighed, curling and uncurling the cord around her finger, tired of weighing every little nuance of every word and action. "Yes."

The tightness in his chest eased. "I'm glad."

Grey checked the time. He had a dinner meeting scheduled in twenty minutes. The time difference meant it was nearly ten-thirty on the East Coast. It would be too late to call again when he got back. For a moment he considered canceling his meeting, wanting to spend the evening on the phone with her. Why did talking to her make him miss her even more?

"What kind of conference are you attending?" she asked.

"A drug symposium. Boring."

"Oh yeah? I'll trade places with you."

He knew time in protective custody was tedious and monotonous at the same time. God, he'd make it all go away if he could. "I know it's bad, but what's the worst part? Lack of privacy? Microwave meals?"

"Trying to sleep, I guess," she said. "I don't get enough physical activity during the day to really get tired, so I toss and turn most of the night. Which gives me a backache."

"I know what would fix that."

"The insomnia?" A vision of Dallas, naked, flashed through her mind. *Wish you were here.* "Or the backache?"

"Both."

"What?"

He chuckled at her impatience. "Feel like playing a game?"

"What kind of game?"

"A mind game." Grey walked over and closed the drapes, darkening his room, wanting to concentrate solely on the sound of her voice. He sat on the edge of his bed, checked his watch again, knew he'd run late for his meeting. "I want you to get comfy."

"Comfy?" She stared at the small double bed that wasn't hers.

"Yeah. *Comfy*. Turn off the lights."

Intrigued, Tess snapped off the bedside lamp. Immediately the room was plunged into a thick, inky darkness.

"Still there?" Grey asked.

"Yes." She gripped the phone tighter, focusing on his voice. The house, the room, everything was still unfamiliar to her.

"Don't be scared. I'm right here," he whispered. "Your eyes will adjust to the dark in a minute. Are you *in* bed or *on* it?"

The husky timbre in his voice had her hand fisting in the spread. There was something calming and erotic about whispering in the dark. But only with this man . . ."I'm sitting on the bed."

"I want you to lie down. Under the covers."

Careful to keep the phone pressed to her ear, Tess slipped beneath the sheets, drawing a sharp breath as her bare feet slid along the chilly fabric.

"Sheets cold?" he asked.

"Very."

Grey lowered his voice to a raspy, seductive whisper. "If I was there, they'd already be warm."

The memory of lying in bed, beside him, on him, shook her. The tiny shivers of awareness she'd had since turning off the light suddenly morphed into waves of desire.

"If you ever get tired of playing secret agent, you could probably make a fortune doing phone sex." She regretted the remark as soon as she made it. She didn't want to think of him talking like this to anyone but her.

"Why?" He paused. "Is this turning you on?"

She shuddered, not wanting to admit it, yet not really wanting to change the subject. She answered back with his same question. "Is it turning *you* on?"

Grey groaned. If she could see him the answer would be obvious. He was hard as a rock. He adjusted himself, but got little relief. He had a psychic flash—saw a cold shower in his immediate future.

"Hell yes, I'm turned on," he answered bluntly. "You have a way of drawing in a little breath that drives me crazy. Makes me hard instantly."

Tess gasped, envisioning him. Long. Hot. *Hard.*

"See what I mean?" Grey said. "The next sound you'll hear will be the snap and crackle of fiber-optic line melting."

Tess shifted, growing warm. Wet. *Daring.* "So . . . if we *were* having phone sex . . . what would happen next?"

The connection grew quiet, and for a moment she worried he'd been cut off.

"I'd ask what you were wearing," Grey said finally. "Then I'd tell you to take it off. You'd have to be totally naked."

"You too?"

"Mmm-hmm."

"And then?" she pressed.

Grey shut his eyes, savoring the image in his head. He knew this dream by heart.

"Then I'd have you lie flat on your back with your hands clasped behind your neck. I'd tell you to spread your legs. You'd have to lie there, like that, while I told you in graphic detail what I would do to you if I were there."

Again silence stretched, hummed like taut wire. Then Grey's voice dipped low, almost gruff. "I'd start with your nipples."

Hers peaked painfully. Tess groaned, remembering the feel of his mouth. On her breast. On her belly. "Grey . . . I . . ."

"I know." Grey knew they were both close to the edge. He purposely backed away. When it came to physical reactions they were like flame and jet fuel. He could combust just thinking about her. And, damn it, that wasn't enough. He wanted more . . .

"But we're not playing *that* kind of mind game," he said finally. "At least not tonight. What I had in mind initially was a massage."

"A massage?" She stuttered, struggling for control. "Over the phone?"

"A verbal massage," he continued. "Roll onto your side. Use a pillow if that's more comfortable."

Tess obeyed, hugging the spare pillow. "So how does a verbal massage work?"

"I'll tell you what I'm doing. You imagine it and tell me how it feels."

That sounded like phone sex again.

"Think you can get into it?" he asked. "Play along?"

She closed her eyes, thought of Grey. Yes, she could get into it.

"Are you using oil?" she asked.

Grey made a choking sound. "Oil?"

"Massage oil." She felt her cheeks grow warm.

"You're a quick study. Yes, I've got massage oil. And it's heated." In spite of his earlier resolve, Grey touched himself, rubbed the fierce erection straining against his zipper. "Now, I'm going to slide your hair over one shoulder. The feel of my hands on your bare skin the first time might make you jump a little."

Bare skin.

Tess did lurch, clutching her pillow tighter as she imagined Grey's hands on her shoulders.

"How does that feel?" he asked.

"Good."

"It'll get better once you relax. You're tense as hell. That blocks pleasure. Take a deep breath and imagine my finger running down your spine. Tell me when to stop and rub."

"There," she said after a moment. "The small of my back."

"I'm going to start off lightly, get the muscles warm. Tell me when you're ready for more."

Tess kept her eyes closed, imagining the rhythmic stroking of Grey's hands on her body. Except in her mind his hands were all over, touching her breasts, cupping her buttocks, sliding up between her thighs, slipping inside her, while his lips grazed her nape, his teeth nipping . . .

She reached for the lamp, flicked it on. The light, while it hurt her eyes, broke the spell.

"I think that's enough," she said. A dishonest answer. *It wasn't nearly enough.*

"You're right." Grey's voice was tight. His own vision had been totally uncontrolled. He wanted to make love to her. Long and slow. Again and again. In person—not on the phone.

He glanced at his watch. He was out of time.

"You okay?" he asked.

No. "I'll be fine." *Once I see you again.*

"I need to go. I'll talk to you soon."

Tess stared up at the ceiling after they hung up, blinking back frustration. That had been erotic and unsatisfying at the same time. It also made her realize she could no longer deny the powerful physical bond that existed between them. That had always existed between them.

Too bad they couldn't build a life on lustful cravings. They'd have it made. . . .

An early winter teased the Baltimore area. It was barely the end of October and already they'd had frost, with more predicted that night.

By the time the trial got under way, Tess had been confined for almost a month. Jury selection seemed to drag on forever.

After that night on the phone, most of her communication with Grey had been through the computer. Short and impersonal, which fed her insecurities even though he explained he was on an assignment and had limited phone access.

She wondered what kind of assignment he was on. Undercover again? Knowing he faced danger daily in his job caused her to fret constantly. She didn't want to delve into what that meant. She didn't want to care about someone in his line of work. Wonder if they'd come home each night. The worry would eat her alive.

The trial had been under way for two days when word came that Tess needed to be present at the next day's proceedings.

The moment she'd been dreading had arrived. Could she sit in a courtroom full of people and recount everything that had happened?

Denny Bennett, the federal prosecutor handling the case, had warned her in a pretrial conference that he would reveal her intimate relationship with Grey, to present it in the best possible light. It also prevented the defense attorneys from springing it later as if it were a terrible secret the prosecution had tried to hide.

Tess had revealed her pregnancy to Denny, who asked point blank if Grey was the father.

She nodded, cringing when Denny noted it in his case file. "I'd prefer that wasn't brought out in open court," she said. "I haven't told anyone yet."

Denny grimaced. "Let me check with the higher-ups to see if we can keep it secret. Quite frankly, I expect the defense to raise the question, just to embarrass you and make you appear uncomfortable in front of the jury. It's a valid point to ask, given your physical association with Agent Thomas."

Tess prayed the question wouldn't come up. Denny also reminded her that Matt Michaels's parents would be at the trial. Tess hated they would have to hear her testimony on the awful sequence of events leading to their son's death.

Snake and Bogen would, of course, be present. More than anything she wished she didn't have to see them again. She recalled Bogen's parting remark at the camp. That he could still have her killed. The threatening note had underscored those words.

She barely slept that night and was awake and dressed an hour before the alarm went off. She had been advised what to wear. Subdued colors. Mid-height heels. Simple jewelry. She braided her hair, French style, down her back, and managed to choke down a slice of dry toast with tea before they left the safe house.

As she sat outside the courtroom, flanked by the two U.S. marshals, she caught a glimpse of Grey standing a little farther down the corridor, huddled with another man.

She hadn't seen him in weeks again, still hadn't adjusted to the physical differences between how Grey looked now—and how he'd looked as Dallas. He wore a sharp-looking suit, navy, double-breasted, that emphasized his tall, lean body.

Her throat felt as if it would swell shut at the sight of his strong profile. He was strikingly handsome. *Would their child look like him?*

Guilt deluged her as she realized how unfair it was to keep that news from him. By keeping her pregnancy concealed she had taken away his right to know. His right to decide.

God, she remembered how unjust that felt . . .

Should she walk over and ask to speak to Grey? Tell him now? She hadn't heard from Denny Bennett again, and assumed that Denny's silence meant he had no plans to disclose her pregnancy, leaving the decision up to her.

At that moment a bailiff summoned her into the courtroom.

Just before she looked away, Grey turned, catching her eye. Lowering his dark glasses, he winked. She felt herself grow warm, her face flush.

Standing, she smoothed her skirt, fidgeting with the single strand of pearls at her throat. She glanced at Grey one last time, determined to hold her head high and do what was right. In the courtroom and out. After testifying she'd tell him.

She made it through the morning without any problems. She kept her gaze focused on Denny Bennett as he asked questions, only occasionally glancing at the jury or the judge, thus avoiding any direct eye contact with Snake or Bogen, who were seated directly in front of the witness stand.

The defense made regular objections, but despite the interruptions, she recounted to the court everything from the night she'd run out of gas, to the moment she'd walked out into the glaring lights and rain three weeks later.

It wasn't easy. She felt like she spoke with a catch in her throat. Several times she dissolved into tears, especially when asked about the murder.

"What happened after Agent Michaels refused to name his accomplice?" Denny asked.

"Bogen nodded."

"Nodded? What did that mean?"

"Objection." The defense attorney stood.

Denny withdrew the question. "What happened after Bogen nodded?"

"Snake pulled a knife and stabbed Matt in the back. He . . . he fell to the floor."

Denny gave her a moment to compose herself before pushing on. "Did you see Agent Michaels once he fell?"

"Yes."

"What was he doing?"

Tess clenched her fists. "He was choking, his body jerking. Bleeding a lot. Then he . . . went limp. Stopped moving."

"What happened next?" Denny continued.

She looked down at her hands. "Bogen told Snake to dump the body in Lake Summer."

"Is that all he said?"

"No. He told Snake to use plenty of concrete."

From the back of the courtroom came a low, keening cry as Matt Michaels's mother dissolved into tears and was helped out of the courtroom. The judge pounded his gavel once, gaining everyone's attention.

Tess straightened. In that moment she knew that no matter how hard the trial seemed to her, for Matt's family it was a thousand times more difficult. Tess had lived through her ordeal. Matt Michaels had paid the ultimate price.

By noon, she felt battered, emotionally and physically. She spent the break alone, in a small anteroom, nibbling crackers and sipping water. The table was scratched, the chair ancient, uncomfortable. A stack of dog-eared magazines rested in the center of the table, but Tess ignored them.

Right after lunch the defense would question her, and in Denny's words, "It won't be pretty." Could she do it?

When they returned to the courtroom, she was immediately called to the stand. Averting her eyes, she walked toward the defense table. Snake and Bogen sat side by side. Malice radiated from them.

As she passed, she caught movement out of the corner of her eye. She heard the awful clinking of handcuff chains. Snake lunged, sending papers flying off the table.

She screamed, felt his hands dig into her shoulders, brutally yanking her backward. He slammed her down against the table. For a moment she thought her spine would snap. Her arm shot out, knocked a glass to the floor, shattering it.

Pain radiated down her back as Snake towered over her, his fingers pressed to her throat. "You were warned about testifying, bitch. They'll hack that baby out of you!"

Her baby. How did Snake know? His grip increased. She twisted, fighting back. Uselessly . . .

She caught a glimpse of the defense attorney jumping away. Heard a member of the jury gasp out loud, "She's pregnant?"

Then, finally, bailiffs and guards swept forward, overpowering Snake. She heard Bogen laugh as the judge pounded his gavel.

Rolling free, Tess fell to her knees on the floor, coughing, choking, finding it difficult to breathe.

Denny dropped beside her. "Easy. Are you all right?"

Dazed, Tess nodded, dragging in air. It hurt to swallow.

"Think you can stand up?"

Again she nodded, accepting Denny's help getting up.

Just as quickly as it all began, it was under control. Bailiffs escorted the jury from the room. Snake and Bogen disappeared amid a thick circle of officers. Reporters swarmed like flies. The judge barked commands, clearing the courtroom.

Tess searched the sea of retreating faces, looking for Grey, then remembered that since he was a witness, he wasn't allowed in the courtroom while she testified.

Dropping her head, she took a step backwards, feeling claustrophobic, afraid she'd get sick. Immediately she doubled over as searing pain tore through her abdomen.

Denny's arm looped around her shoulders, supporting her, preventing her from falling. Sharp cramps tore across her stomach in waves. She clutched his arm, terrified.

"My baby," she whispered. "Oh, God, *my baby*!"

The cramps stopped shortly after she arrived at the emergency room, but the physician insisted on keeping her overnight for observation. They placed her in a private room, with guards posted outside.

Lying in bed, unable to relax, she recalled how frightened she'd been. She stared at the IV drip line, tried not to feel sorry for herself. It would be so easy to break down, wallow in self-pity. She ran her hands across her middle. The baby was fine. That was all that mattered.

She turned her thoughts to another dilemma. Snake had known she was pregnant. That information could have only been leaked from Denny Bennett's office. While she wanted answers, it didn't change the fact that by tonight, her pregnancy would be all over the news. Her regret over not telling Grey, not telling her family, was sharp.

A knock sounded on the door. She turned, expecting a nurse. But when the door opened a huge bouquet of roses appeared, the arrangement so large it dwarfed the person carrying it.

"Set it here, please." She pointed to the table beside her bed, then struggled to sit up.

"Where?"

To her surprise Grey carried the flowers. She stared at him, inundated by raw emotion. She wondered at his thoughts, unable to read his face.

He selected one perfect red bud and pulled it free.

"Hello." Not bothering to ask permission, he sat on the edge of the bed, setting the fragrant rose on her chest.

She picked it up, nervous, brushed the petals to her cheek. "They told me I wasn't allowed any visitors."

"I got a special dispensation from my boss." He reached

forward and brushed a strand of hair from her face. For the first time all day he felt calm.

She looked tiny and helpless in the bed. He eyed the dark marks on her throat, felt his temper buckle beneath his iron control. Snake could have killed her. It had taken every bit of control Grey possessed not to pay Snake a visit in jail. The guards would have let him in. And turned their backs.

By the time word of the attack reached him she'd already been loaded into an ambulance. He died a thousand deaths waiting to hear that she was unharmed. *That their baby was safe.*

The news of her pregnancy flat out stunned him even though he had wondered about the possibility a hundred times. Hell, in the beginning, he'd even hoped she *was* pregnant, selfishly realizing that a child would forge a bond between them. But as the weeks passed and he heard nothing, well, he assumed she wasn't. Or if she was . . . that she'd had an abortion. She could have done so without his knowledge or consent.

He thought back to the night at the auction, when she'd been sick, kicking himself for not picking up on it then.

"When did you plan to let me know?" The words came out harsher than intended.

She burst into tears. "I'm sorry."

The guilt of knowing he'd caused her even more distress burned through Grey like a hot poker. *She was pregnant.* At another time in his life those words would have sent him running. Now . . .

"You have nothing to be sorry for. How long have you known?" he asked more calmly.

"I suspected it the first week I was home."

Relief speared through him. She'd known for nearly three months. Which only meant one thing. "You're keeping it."

Her eyes met his. "Yes!"

He grasped the sheet, tugged it down to her hips, exposing her. Very cautiously, his hand went to her stomach, low, pressing intimately. "You've lost weight, but your abdomen is definitely enlarged." He looked at the insubstantial hospital gown, noticing something else. "As are your breasts." They were *a lot* bigger.

He wanted to strip away her clothes, view the ripening of her body, then sweep her into his arms and tell her, show her, exactly how glad he was she was keeping the baby.

He tugged the sheet back over her, his chest tightening painfully at the realization he had no right to any of that.

"How are you feeling?"

"Better now that the cramps have stopped." Her hand went protectively to her midsection. "The doctor says everything's as it should be."

Grey placed his hand on top of hers, covering it completely. "Good."

Tess met his gaze again. "I *was* going to tell you. Today. Then—Snake knows I'm pregnant. How did he find out?" she blurted, unable to stop the words.

Grey wondered the same thing. Barry Neilson was already pushing for an internal investigation into how the news of her pregnancy had leaked. Unfortunately, it wasn't uncommon in high-profile cases like this one for someone to reveal details to the press. "Confidential sources" were routinely quoted in the paper.

Except in this case the reporters covering the trial had been as surprised as anyone to learn the news of her pregnancy. So had the defense attorneys. Which made Grey wonder at Snake and Bogen's connections. Did they have a mole in the U.S. Attorney's Office?

"I wish I had answers, Tess. Right now, I don't. But I swear nothing like this will happen again. I'll keep you safe."

She shook her head. "You can't be at my side every moment, Grey. And what about later? When the trial's over? I don't want to live like this, in constant fear, always hiding."

She put a finger to his lips, hushing him when he would have contradicted her. "I went along with you once. Now I'm following my own instincts. After I finish testifying tomorrow, I'm returning to Boston. Alone."

Grey grasped her hand, knowing she wouldn't like what he was about to tell her. "You won't be testifying tomorrow. The judge ordered a recess. The trial won't resume until next Monday."

"No! That's four days!"

"You can't expect to just walk away from this, Tess. There will be more trials on the other charges. Barry is already working on a plan to continue security. He feels you would be safe enough if you went back to your family's home in the Hamptons after you testify. Security there is top-notch, and we'll beef it up with federal support."

"You don't understand. I want to go home, Grey. *My home.*"

"I do understand." Very gently, Grey eased her chin up, holding her gaze. "When I was in Montana, I resented the circumstances that kept me from my house and family. I know it's hard."

A tear slid down Tess's cheek. Unable to stop himself, he leaned forward and gathered her into his arms. He shifted, looking down at her. The deep blue eyes that haunted his sleep looked troubled. With gentle fingers he traced the delicate lines of her brow, her cheek. When she didn't pull back, his thumb caressed the curve of her bottom lip. She was too soft, too sweet.

He was going to have to kiss her.

Lowering his head, he drew his tongue along the pink swell of her mouth, savoring her, capturing the tiny purr that escaped her throat. He kept the kiss tender, soft as thistledown, and was rewarded with a sigh of unmistakable abandonment.

Grey pulled back, pressing her head against his shoulder, rocking her slightly, unwilling to let her go. He was worried. The dark circles beneath her eyes spoke of too little sleep. And she had lost weight—which any idiot knew wasn't healthy for a pregnant woman.

He noticed the tray beside her. "You haven't touched your dinner."

Groaning she pushed away, plopping back against her pillows. "You might know the one night I feel like a cheeseburger, I'm on a liquid diet."

Grey moved off the bed and pushed the bedside table closer. If he had his way, she'd be eating steak and potatoes three times a day to gain weight. "If you eat this, I promise we'll find a cheeseburger tomorrow. With fries."

He removed the insulated cover. "Let's see. Mmmm. Chicken noodle soup, hold the noodles, hold the chicken. Apple juice. And red Jell-O."

She grimaced, reaching for the apple juice.

Grey tapped her hand, moving the juice out of reach. "Soup first."

She reached for the Jell-O, but wasn't quick enough. Grey snapped a napkin open and tucked it under her chin. Then he reached for the spoon. "Soup. Then Jell-O. Then juice. I'll even feed you."

Tess foiled him by picking up a straw. She stirred the pale-colored broth, before sipping it through the straw and making a face. "I hope someday when you're sick, someone bigger than you bullies you into eating something you don't want."

Her tone tore at him. "Real men don't bully." To prove his point, Grey leaned forward, kissed her cheek, and surrendered the Jell-O.

She fell asleep while he was still there. Actually, he refused to leave, stretching out in the recliner beside her bed, watching television.

When she woke in the morning, he was gone. Which left her feeling mildly depressed.

A feeling that mushroomed after she spoke with her mother.

The news of her pregnancy had greatly upset Madeline, who immediately pressed her to "get rid of it," then launched into a spiel about Tess's duty to the family name.

While it disappointed Tess, her mother's reaction didn't surprise her. She'd spent a good portion of her life trying to be a dutiful daughter, trying to live up to the Marsh name. Until one day she realized she could either live her own life or die trying to please her parents.

She'd never regretted striking out on her own, and she vowed that her child would have her support in whatever he or she chose to do.

"I have a duty to my child," Tess had said finally. If she was determined to keep the child, she had better get used to censure. Especially from her mother.

Though she knew her mother was concerned, the media attention generated by Tess's abduction and the subsequent trial clearly embarrassed Madeline. Madeline's life revolved around her social status. It was her religion.

In spite of her family's dysfunctional tendencies, Tess loved them. Still, her mother's response bothered her. Would Madeline ever accept the child?

She thought of Grey. What would he tell his family about her pregnancy? How would they react? Would this innocent child find resentment on both sides of its family tree?

As soon as the doctor made morning rounds she was dismissed from the hospital and whisked away in an unmarked patrol car.

Tess dreaded returning to the safe house. At least at the

hospital there had been other people. Doctors, nurses. Other women she could talk with about her pregnancy.

And while Grey had been there she'd been less lonely . . .

To her surprise, Grey was parked outside the safe house when Tess and her two guards arrived. She noticed he drove an oversize sport utility vehicle with deep tinted windows that he parked a short distance down the street, allowing the patrol car to slip into the driveway in front of the house.

Watching him approach, she wished she had time to escape inside the house before he saw her. She was still wearing her suit from yesterday. But he was beside the car before the engine even shut off.

"Good morning," he said, opening the back door and leaning in to brush a kiss on her cheek.

A cellular phone rang. All three men checked their pockets. Tess watched as one of the marshals nodded to Grey and stepped away, a phone pressed to his ear. The other climbed out of the car and headed toward the house.

It was obvious the two marshals knew about her and Grey and were trying to give them a private moment alone. Tess winced, wondering if the men thought she and Grey were an item. *A couple?* God, she was carrying his child, and she didn't even know *what* they were.

Grey took her hand, helping her out of the car. "How are you feeling this morning?"

Before she could answer, the marshal switched off his phone. "We got trouble."

Tess squirmed, trapped between the car and Grey. She peered around him, trying to catch the marshal's words.

"Bogen and Snake escaped this morning. We got orders to move her to another house. Pronto."

"No!" The words astonished Tess. "How could that happen?"

"They were being transferred to another facility, ma'am,"

the marshal said before turning to Grey. "I don't know all the details, but it sounds like they had help."

Grey pulled Tess into the protective circle of his arms, hugged her, then released her. "Get back in the car." He thrust her into the rear seat. "Watch your head."

"I'll call for backup," the marshal said. He stepped away, yelling for the other marshal to return to the car.

The other marshal was already unlocking the door of the safe house. He stepped back, looking puzzled. Then he started running.

At that moment an explosion split the air.

Grey yelled. "Get down!"

Instinctively, she dropped to the floorboards, huddling. Glass rained down on her as the car shook, the windows imploding.

Her first thought was worry for her unborn child. The second thought was for the child's father. Grey! Was he all right? What about the two marshals?

As quick as it happened, the awful noise ceased, leaving an ominous silence in its wake.

Tess raised her head cautiously, shaking off the shards of safety glass that covered her. She peered out the open car door.

The house was on fire, the front porch completely demolished by the blast. One of the marshals was crumpled on the lawn.

Twisting to get up, she caught sight of the second marshal lying on his side. Blood stained his shirt.

Bile rose in her throat. The glass cut her hands and knees as she climbed free of the car searching for one more person.

Grey.

Where was Grey?

Chapter Twelve

ess!"

Grey called her name, grabbing her.

"You're alive." She collapsed against him, aware he had his gun drawn. Aware they were still in danger.

He glanced down at her hands. "You're hurt."

She shook her head, oblivious of her own injuries, worried about the marshals. "We've got to help them. Call the police . . ." That's when she noticed blood seeping down the side of his neck. "Grey! You're bleeding."

He swiped the blood with one hand. The explosion had thrown him across the car's hood. He'd rolled, avoiding serious injury. "It's nothing."

Grasping her firmly by the shoulders, he eased her down to the ground. "Stay right here. Don't move. I'll see to the others."

Running to the front of the car, Grey checked the two marshals, glad to see both were moving, in spite of their injuries. One of the men was already on the phone, calling for assistance. Both had their weapons drawn as well.

"It was a delayed charge," the marshal who'd opened the door told Grey. The man winced, obviously in pain. "It triggered when the door opened. I spotted the wires right after you yelled."

Grey went cold at the man's word. *A delayed charge.*

Whoever rigged the bomb knew it would take a few moments for someone to unlock the door and get inside. He looked again at the blazing ruins, realizing no one inside would have survived.

A noise caught Grey's attention. He looked around, noticed a blue sedan driving slowly past the end of the street.

The first marshal started swearing. "I don't like this. Get the Marsh woman out of here. I'll stay with Roger."

Grey was already moving toward Tess. As much as he hated leaving the two men, he realized they were sitting ducks on the street. Especially Tess. *She* was their target. He had to get her out of there.

She struggled to stand as he approached. "Are they okay? Did you call for help?"

Grey carefully grasped her by the wrists, tugging her close while bustling her away from the house. The cuts on her hands and knees needed attention, but would have to wait.

His car was parked a short distance down the street and miraculously the windows were intact.

"We can't leave them," she protested. "They're hurt."

"Help is on the way."

"We can't leave," she repeated, pulling away.

Grey opened the door, forced her inside. He knew by the threadiness in her voice she was traumatized. "Neither of them was severely injured. But someone knows where you are, Tess. I have to get you away from here."

He climbed in the car. In seconds they were racing away from the house. Grey watched his rearview mirror for the blue sedan. Or any other suspicious vehicle.

Reaching across, he tugged Tess's seat belt over her torso, snapped it in place. Then he floored it, zigzagging across four lanes of interstate. He took an exit, slowing to *Mach 1* before climbing back on the interstate, two blocks west. No one followed. For now.

"You okay?" he asked.

"If you hadn't been there . . ." Tess shut her eyes, lowering her head, trying to block out the thought.

Grey grasped her shoulder, shaking her gently. "Stay with me, Tess. Just a little bit longer." He wanted her alert. Unconscious, she couldn't tell him if the cramping started again.

He pressed buttons on his cell phone, calling Barry Neilson. News of the explosion had already reached Barry. Grey gave a description of the blue car, and was relieved to hear backup officers had arrived on the scene.

"How in the hell did they know where to find her?" Grey demanded. This was the second time confidential information about Tess had been divulged. He didn't like it.

"I'm working on that," Barry said. "She's okay?"

Grey glanced at Tess. She was staring straight ahead, eyes glazed. "She's got some superficial cuts. Nothing life-threatening. Shock. I need to get her somewhere safe. Like—"

"Wait," Barry interrupted. "This isn't a secure line."

Grey grew silent. Barry was telling him something. Over the years, he and Barry had worked out a series of code words only the two of them knew. *Wait*, was an alert signal. Grey thought over what Barry had just said. *It wasn't a secure line.*

"We got a leak?"

"Looks that way."

That explained how they knew where Tess was staying. It also meant Grey couldn't take her to the next safe house as the marshals had planned. Hell, he probably couldn't take her to any of the Bureau's safe houses. If Barry was right and they did have a leak within the system, the wrong people would know their every move.

That left only one option. He would protect Tess himself, without letting anyone know their whereabouts.

"You know what I'm thinking?" Grey asked.

"I want contact every twenty-four hours," Barry said. "And I need a full report on what happened back there."

"Any word on Bogen and Snake?"

"Had a sighting north of here. They might be heading for the Canadian border, but we can't be certain."

After Grey hung up, he reached over and squeezed Tess's shoulder. She still looked pale but he knew that, unless it was an emergency, they couldn't stop.

"Can you make it a little farther?"

She looked wary. "Exactly where are we going? I don't think I trust your system anymore."

"Neither do I." Grey glanced away from the road. He promised to take care of her and look what had happened. "I know this is asking a lot, but can you trust me?"

When she didn't answer, Grey explained his suspicions that someone within the system had purposely given out information on her whereabouts, that possibly there was more than one leak.

"So what does that mean?" she asked. "I'm a walking target, aren't I? I'll be hunted the rest of my life. And the baby?"

Her voice was husky with distress. Grey wished he could pull over and take her in his arms. But right now he needed to concentrate on getting as far away from Baltimore as possible.

"You and I are the only ones who know where we are. No one knows where we're headed, not even Barry, and I intend to keep it that way until the situation's under control."

Tess contemplated his words. "What do you have in mind?"

"The latest reports indicate Bogen and Snake are heading north. I think we're wise to head south."

"Florida?"

"Not that far. I was thinking about North Carolina. I went to grad school at UNC-Chapel Hill, so I'm familiar with the area."

The irony struck her. She was having his baby, and she didn't even know his college alma mater.

"Where will we stay?"

"We'll find a quiet motel, somewhere we can lie low for a few days. We'll get some rest and talk."

She nodded. Talk. Rest. Hide. Would they ever have a chance to be normal?

Whatever normal was . . .

~

By the time they reached the outskirts of Richmond, Virginia, Tess felt a little more at ease. With the convoluted route Grey chose, she felt certain no one could possibly be following them.

And whether she wanted to admit it or not, she did feel safer alone with Grey. When she thought of what could have happened to her and the baby at the safe house . . . She offered yet another silent prayer of thanks that the explosion had not seriously injured either of the marshals.

She rubbed her forehead. "Will we be stopping soon?"

Her head hurt and her hands and knees stung where she'd picked out glass shards. The small first-aid kit Grey carried in his car proved woefully inadequate, but she didn't complain. Her physical discomfort was nothing compared to her fear of being caught by some of Bogen's friends.

From the way she massaged her temples, Grey knew she had a headache. He had pulled off the road briefly outside of D.C. to satisfy himself again that the cuts she'd received didn't require a doctor's care. And to assure her that the laceration on his neck was indeed minor. She promised to let him know if she felt the slightest abdominal twinge.

"We'll stop at the next exit."

Grey found a small drugstore right off the highway and picked up first-aid supplies, including nonaspirin painkillers.

"I'm sorry we couldn't stop earlier," he said when he returned to the car. He wrestled with the bottle's childproof cap, appreciating it through new eyes. "The pharmacist said these are safe for pregnant women."

Nodding gratefully, she swallowed the two tablets he offered. Then Grey parked in a secluded corner of the lot and focused on her injuries.

"This might burn," he warned, washing her abraded knees with peroxide. Next he smoothed on a cream that numbed the pain.

After he cleaned and treated all her cuts, he covered them with gauze. "You're awful quiet. Sure you're feeling okay? Any cramping or discomfort?"

She shook her head. "I keep thinking about what would have happened if you hadn't been there when we arrived. We would have gone straight into the house, and—"

"The point is, you didn't."

She looked at him, her eyes wide. "That's twice you've saved me. First from Snake and the others, now this."

He could have drowned in the blue vulnerability in her eyes. Except he didn't deserve her gratitude. She'd almost been killed. The Bureau had failed to protect her.

He'd failed to keep her safe.

Right now they needed to keep moving. That meant eating lunch in the car.

"Still feel like that cheeseburger?"

"No."

"You need to eat, Tess. You'll starve the baby." He hated using guilt, but if it got her to eat, he'd do it continually.

She shot him a look. "That's a low blow. But you're right."

A few minutes later they were headed south once more, eating cheeseburgers from a drive-through. Tess sipped a vanilla milk shake. When she finished she yawned, feeling groggy.

"That seat reclines. Why don't you lie back and try to relax," Grey urged.

"I don't know why I'm so tired all of a sudden."

"Traumatic let down." He frowned. "The last two days have been hell."

The painkiller she'd taken earlier was starting to work. Easing her seat back, she stifled another yawn. "Well, maybe a few minutes wouldn't hurt."

She didn't awaken for two hours.

~

"Tess, wake up."

She felt a hand gently squeeze her arm. Twisting, she saw Grey bent over her, concern in his eyes.

"How are you feeling?" His hand moved to cover her abdomen. "Any pain? Nausea?"

Tess sat up, shook her head. Nothing hurt. In fact, she felt decent. Rested. And the feel of his hand *there* sent frissons of awareness over her, left her feeling . . . alive. Grateful.

"How long before it's safe to return?" she asked.

He stretched his arm across the back of her seat, toying with her hair. "That depends on several factors, including how soon they recapture Snake and Bogen."

"What went wrong back there, Grey?"

He looked at her troubled face, tempted to kiss the frown wrinkling her forehead. His first instinct was to blow off her question with a trite answer. Except she deserved more than that. She deserved an honest answer. The most honest answer he could give anyway.

"I wish I knew. The more I've thought about it, the more other possibilities present themselves. Barry thinks we've got an internal leak. That could mean several things. Someone in the Bureau could be divulging confidential information. Which, by the way, would be the easiest scenario to resolve. But since the U.S. Attorney's and Marshals' Offices knew where you were staying, it could be someone there." And he couldn't forget that news of her pregnancy had been leaked as well.

He slid his hand under her hair to massage the tight muscles of her neck. "I'm certain we're not being followed now, Tess. I hope you believe that. I'll protect you and the baby with my life."

The baby. She touched her stomach. *His baby.*

Funny. Except for morning sickness, she didn't *feel* pregnant. Except when Grey touched her abdomen, something he seemed obsessed with of late.

He watched her hands move across her middle.

"Anything wrong?"

"I'm fine," she answered. "It's just that, well, sometimes I feel completely ignorant about pregnancy and motherhood. Should I have felt the baby move yet? Should I be showing by now? God, I don't even have a due date."

"Early April by my calculations. The first time we made love was July twenty-first. You had to conceive then."

Because it was the only time they didn't use protection, Tess recalled, blushing at the memory.

"Embarrassed?" Grey asked.

She looked away momentarily, unsure. To admit shame seemed to reflect wrongly on the baby.

She shook her head. "I'm not embarrassed. Insecure perhaps. I guess I'll feel better when I've seen an obstetrician."

"As soon as we're settled we'll get you in to see one," Grey promised.

"Now? While we're on the road?"

"Why not? I don't see any point in waiting. I realize it's probably one of those mystical female things to choose the proper obstetrician." He shrugged. "I've heard my sisters argue over it enough times."

She looked at him closely, his remark reminding her again of how little she knew of him personally. "Will you tell me about your family someday?"

He nodded. "What do you want to know? The basics? My dad's a retired railroad executive. He lives outside Harrisburg, Pennsylvania. Mom died seven years ago. I've got two younger sisters. Beth Ann and Brittany."

"How old are they?"

"They're both twenty-seven."

"Twins? Don't tell me they run in your family."

Grey chuckled. Okay, he wouldn't tell her. At least not now.

"Have you told them about the baby?" she asked.

"I told my dad last night. I didn't want him to read it in the newspaper. He sends his best."

She blinked. "Your father was happy?" *Was Grey?*

His heart constricted. "Of course. My sisters are probably fighting over a baby shower."

Tess squirmed, thinking about her mother's reaction. "I'm sorry they had to find out this way."

"Have you talked with your family?"

"I spoke with my mother this morning. She isn't . . . happy."

Grey sensed her distress over her mother's response, wondered if she had anyone in her family who'd welcome the news. Besides him. And he wasn't family. "She'll come around, sweetheart. I'm sure the news was a shock. Your family's had a lot to deal with lately."

His understanding almost undid her. So did the endearment. *Sweetheart.* She felt herself succumb to his dark looks. There was no denying it. She was definitely drawn to Grey for reasons that had nothing to do with lust. Or the baby.

She looked out the window, noticing for the first time where they were parked. Wal-Mart. Several smaller stores and restaurants flanked the giant department store.

"What are we doing here?"

"Neither of us has anything except the clothes on our backs," Grey pointed out. "I figure we can get everything from toothpaste to suitcases here."

Removing the key from the ignition, he reached beneath his seat and withdrew a large tattered envelope. Opening it he pulled out a large stack of bills.

Tess noticed most of the bills were hundreds and fifties. "What did you do? Rob a bank?"

Grey handed her several large bills, then crammed a large wad of cash into his pocket. "I learned long ago to be prepared for anything. Before we go in, we need to review a few things. We pay cash for everything. No credit-card purchases or bank withdrawals. Not even a telephone-card call. Second, we're married. I'm John Taylor; you're Jennifer Taylor. We're on vacation. Home is Boise, Idaho. The less said the better."

She watched him check his handgun, then return it to his shoulder holster. With his jacket zipped it didn't show. Knowing it was there made her shiver, reminding her this wasn't the everyday shopping trip.

He handed her a Cubs baseball cap. "Tuck your hair beneath this. I've got an overcoat in back you can wear, too. We don't want anything to call attention to us."

When she nodded, he continued. "You need to stay by me

at all times. And it's critical you do everything I say, without question."

She looked doubtful. "Are you sure we're safe here?"

"Positive." Needing to see her smile, he tweaked her nose. "But I'm still cautious."

~~

They hit the women's clothing department first. "Think warm," Grey advised. "They're predicting another cold front."

She selected a pair of jeans, holding them up to her waist to check the length. With her bandaged hands and knees, she didn't feel like trying them on.

Grey moved closer, wrapping an arm around her waist. "Don't flinch every time I touch you," he mouthed in her ear. "We're supposed to be married, remember?"

She suppressed a shiver. She had carnal knowledge of this man. She carried his child. And still his slightest touch nearly sent her through the roof.

"I'll be more careful, *John*," she whispered back.

Grey looked at the jeans she clutched. "Shouldn't we be looking at maternity clothes?"

Tess tossed the jeans into the shopping cart. *Maternity clothes.* She hadn't even thought of those. What would she look like nine months pregnant? Would Grey find her attractive then? Would he be around to see?

"Right now my normal size is still baggy."

"Which is something I intend to rectify. You're supposed to be eating for two, and you're barely feeding one." Grey reached forward and pulled several more pair of jeans in the same size off the rack. At her questioning look he shrugged. "Sorry. We're in a hurry and I don't want to shop more than once. What about those sweaters?"

When they moved to the lingerie section the cart was half-filled. Grey deftly fingered a silky bra. Tess flushed, recalling the feel of those long fingers on her breasts.

"What size are we looking for, darling? You're not going to tell me you can still fit them in a 36D?" His whisper was evil.

Tess shot him a quelling look. "*We* can find our own bras, thank you."

Turning away she rifled through another rack of bras. He did have a point. Unlike her stomach, her already ample bustline seemed to be increasing daily. Perhaps a maternity bra was in order.

Grey whistled softly, getting her attention. He held up a pair of deep blue bikini panties. "Size 5, right?" His not-so-subtle reminders that he remembered her underwear size from their time together rankled her. *And excited her.*

By the time she finished selecting bras, he had picked out socks and a few nightshirts. Plus a rainbow of silky panties. In the space of fifteen minutes she'd been outfitted.

They zoomed through men's wear, where Grey efficiently selected T-shirts, jeans, and flannel shirts, all in dark colors. She wondered what he'd look like wearing those black jeans and a black T-shirt. *Both tight.* With his dark hair and silver eyes . . .

She watched with curiosity as he selected prepackaged boxer shorts, threw them in the cart.

"This isn't nearly as much fun as picking out your underwear," he teased.

She shrugged. "It's educational. I thought you were a white-cotton briefs kind of guy."

He winked. "So you remember what I was wearing back then, too."

Tess felt her face flush as his meaning hit her. Actually

Dallas rarely wore underwear . . . how many times had she admired him naked?

She moved away, ducking around a display to avoid his eyes. "Uh . . . I think the last thing we need are shoes."

The first pair of sneakers she tried on fit perfectly. Unfortunately the sizes Grey needed were stacked beyond reach on overhead shelves. As he searched for a stepladder she wandered into the next department.

Immediately she froze, staring. *The infant department.*

She looked at the display of cribs, bassinets, and changing tables, her eyes wide. Suspended from the ceiling were hundreds of stuffed animals, forming a fuzzy canopy over another display of strollers, high chairs, and playpens.

To her right was a rack of tiny, frilly dresses. On her left were equally tiny suits for boys. She touched a miniature football jersey of soft terry cloth. Funny, she had a sudden feeling she carried a boy. Maternal instinct?

She sensed Grey behind her and didn't flinch this time when he placed an arm around her. "Anything in particular catch your eye?"

She shook her head. "I didn't realize they had so much . . . *stuff* for babies. How do you know where to start?"

"I take it you've never been around infants before."

She shook her head. "My brother's not married. All my cousins are younger. My best friend let me hold her baby once. It was so tiny, I was scared to death I'd drop it." She ran her fingers along the polished edge of a brass cradle, rocking it.

Grey squeezed her shoulders, thinking about the half dozen nieces and nephews he adored. "You'll do fine. It's not that hard, really."

She twisted free, staring at him before pointing toward a display. "It's not hard? Just look at all the different types of baby bottles. Every size, shape, and color. How in the world do you decide which one to use?"

He shrugged. "The first decision is whether to breast-feed or not. I think that's the healthiest choice for the baby, but it's not for everyone. Most of those decorated bottles are for older babies. The decisions for newborns are actually fairly simple."

"Is that the voice of experience?" She had never asked Grey point-blank if he had children.

"I've fathered no children," Grey interjected. "Except this one."

Light as air, his hand brushed intimately across her abdomen, causing her to draw a sharp breath. Flustered, she turned away, pushing the heavy shopping cart as far away from the baby department as she could get.

Grey caught up with her, slowing her flight by placing a hand on the cart. He drew her close, stroking her hair, calming her. Then he caught her head between his hands, forcing her to look at him.

The stark bewilderment in her eyes tugged at his heart. "I know that with everything else going on you've barely had time to adjust to the idea you're pregnant. But I'm here for you, and I hope you'll let me play an active part in your pregnancy."

Another couple drifted close, preventing Tess from responding. She stepped away, brooding, content to let Grey push the cart.

Just what did he mean by that? How much of a part did he plan to play? Daddy? Husband? How much did she want him to?

She glanced at his profile. Remembering . . . This was the man who'd taught her the physical pleasure unique to male and female. She'd almost fallen in love with him. Or thought she had, only to find out he wasn't at all what she thought. And now she carried his child.

While Grey was attentive and supportive, she still wasn't exactly sure whether he viewed the baby as anything more than *an obligation*. Her kettle of fish grew more perplexing by the day.

Grey stopped at a glass display counter containing jewelry. "We need wedding bands. What size ring do you wear?"

Wedding bands. Her heart lurched. She told him her size, thankful he didn't ask her to try on one of the simple gold bands he selected. It seemed too intimate all of a sudden. No longer a game.

By the time they made it through toiletries and cosmetics, Tess's stomach was growling again.

They hauled their purchases to the car and stowed them in the back. To her dismay, they drove another thirty minutes before stopping to eat. She knew by the randomness of their route that Grey was being cautious, still making certain they weren't being followed.

They finally stopped at a small café, dining on salads and fried chicken. Tess was relieved not to have to eat in the car again. Halfway through her meal, though, Tess pushed her salad away. The food didn't seem to agree with her.

Grey looked up from his plate. "What's wrong?"

The throbbing had started up again in her hands. In fact, she ached all over. "My hands are sore."

Reaching in his coat pocket, Grey retrieved the bottle of painkillers.

"I thought we'd stop for the night near Raleigh. It's not that far, maybe an hour from the North Carolina line. Can you make it?"

She shivered against a sudden chill. "When we get there I want to soak in a tub full of hot water. For three days."

The thought of her naked in a tub of bubbles made Grey want to leap over the table. Instead, he reached across, covering her hand with his.

"Let's go."

By the time they reached Raleigh it was dark. Grey stopped for gas at a small service station.

"I need to use the pay phone inside to check with Barry," he said.

Tess opted to stay in the car. Her headache had gotten worse in spite of the medicine she'd taken, and now her stomach lurched.

Afraid she was getting sick, she rolled down the window, hoping fresh air would help. Instead, she got a whiff of gas fumes. Instantly she grew nauseated.

Opening the car door, she raced toward the side of the building where the rest-room sign hung. She reached for the handle of the women's room door, only to find it locked.

Frustrated and miserably sick, she leaned forward, pressing her forehead against the cold metal door. The coolness felt good against her too warm face, and she gulped in a deep breath. In spite of the cool night air, she felt sticky beneath her clothes and realized she was perspiring.

She felt a hand tug on her purse. Turning, she opened her mouth to explain to Grey why she'd left the car.

To her horror a man in a hooded sweatshirt pushed her against the locked door. He pressed something against her ribs.

"Don't scream," the man hissed. "Just drop your bag."

Tess obeyed, unclasping her fist, praying that if she cooperated, the man would leave her unharmed. Then she heard Grey's voice.

"Step away from my *wife* before I kill you." Grey had his gun drawn and leveled at the man.

Releasing her, the mugger quickly threw his hands in the air. "Hey, man! I didn't hurt her!"

Tess stepped away as Grey roughly shoved the man against the wall. He kicked the man's feet apart in a spread-eagled stance and patted him down, withdrawing a knife from the man's pocket.

"I suggest you get as far from here as possible," Grey said pushing the man away. "The cops are on their way."

Moving slowly at first, as if not believing his good fortune at being set free, the man backed up. Then he took off running.

It infuriated Grey to release the mugger, knowing it would only be a short while before the man picked his next victim. He turned on her, fury flashing in his eyes. "I told you—"

"I'm sick," she wailed, waving him back.

Cursing, Grey forced the lock using the knife he'd taken from her assailant. She was adamant that he remain outside. Once inside, she locked the door and threw up.

After a few minutes, the queasiness passed, but her head hurt worse than ever.

No sooner had she turned on water to wash her face than the door opened and Grey stepped in. So much for a locked door when this man was around.

Grey looked at her closely. "Did he hurt you?"

"No. But he scared me."

She was still shaking when Grey drew her into his arms. "You're freezing." He started to peel his coat off but remembered his gun. "Come on. Let's get you back in the car."

It took a tremendous amount of self-control not to lecture her while they drove a little farther up the road to a well-lit motel. All he wanted to do was get her inside a room and let her get comfortable.

Then he'd lay into her. He had nearly died when he returned to the car and found her gone.

Once they were in a room, though, his resolve fled. He hadn't counted on her looking so fragile. And even bundled-up in his jacket she still trembled. She sat on the bed, hugging herself while he turned up the room's thermostat.

"There's only one bed," she pointed out.

"You can have it. I'll sleep on the couch."

Moving past her, he went into the bathroom and started filling the tub. He came back out and knelt in front of her, unfastening her shoes.

"I'll have you warm in a minute." He moved back to the bathroom, turning off the taps. Steam rose from the water, but he made sure it wasn't too hot.

She still had her arms wrapped around herself when he came back out. She offered no resistance when he tugged off the jacket. Pulling her to her feet, he began unfastening her blouse. That roused her.

"What are you doing?" She shoved his hands away.

"Sticking you in a warm tub." He pushed the edges of her blouse wide, hitching it off her shoulders.

She crossed her arms over her bra, hiding little. Grey felt himself harden at the sight of her.

"I can undress myself." She wasn't certain she wanted him to see her like this.

"Fine. I'll get the stuff from the car."

He welcomed the icy blast of air that hit him when he stepped out of their room, but it did little to relieve his suffering.

Not for the first time he wished things were different between them. What if they were really married and he could simply walk back inside and freely view his wife's ample charms? Play with them, for God's sake!

The feelings he had for her hadn't diminished over their months apart. If anything, they had grown sharper. But what about Tess's feelings? Did she care for him on a level beyond personal preservation?

He carried an armload of packages back to the room and dumped them on the bed. Striding to the bathroom door, he called her name. He heard water splash as if she'd sat up quickly.

"Yes?" she called through the door.

"Just checking. I'm going back down to get the rest of the stuff."

Tess relaxed, sinking back into the water as she heard his footsteps move away. The water felt heavenly, the warmth gradually seeping in to replace the bone-numbing cold. Thankfully, the nausea had left, and her aches and pains were slowly disappearing.

She yawned, slipping lower in the tub, submerging her shoulders. She should probably get out and help Grey. Another yawn bubbled up and she shut her eyes, giving in to the steamy warmth. Just a few more minutes, she decided, then she'd climb out.

After his final trip to the car, Grey turned on the news then began dumping the shopping bags out on the bed, methodically sorting and ripping off tags as he watched television.

His shirts. Her shirts. His underwear. Hers. And definitely more interesting than his.

He unwrapped the myriad of cosmetic products, opening the bottles and sniffing. No wonder men fell for women. They smelled so damn good. He twisted the cap off a pink bottle of lotion. The scent of roses filled the air. He felt his groin swell and quickly recapped the bottle. Why torment himself?

The last bag held a small white box. *Their wedding rings.* He cupped the rings in his palm. Side by side their differences were huge. Male. Female. His band was thicker and over an inch in diameter. Hers was tiny by comparison. Delicate. And not nearly good enough for her.

He closed his fist, pressed the metal against his skin, remembering how he'd found himself looking at diamonds in California. He'd found a monster solitaire that he liked. Had wanted something that said *she's taken*. A wedding band, though . . .

In the end he'd chickened out. "Scared?" the salesman had asked. *Damn straight*. Now more than ever. He'd told himself that when the time came, he'd go with the ring of his heart. His grandmother's engagement ring. A marquise-cut diamond surrounded by sapphires the exact deep blue of Tess's eyes.

He shook his head. That was the last thing he needed to be thinking about. Keeping her safe was all that mattered. There were two lives at stake in that one precious body.

He looked at the cheap, gold-filled bands, slid his on his left hand. Trying not to think of the significance, he set hers on the dresser.

The news report of this morning's bombing came on. Turning up the volume, Grey followed the brief story intently. They gave no new information on the morning's events, and most of what they recounted was inaccurate. Except the news of Tess's pregnancy, of course. Though no one would officially confirm it, the reporter quoted sources as saying FBI Special Agent Grey Thomas was the father.

He frowned, turning the set off. Barry had warned him earlier that this was happening. Barry also told him there was no new information on Snake and Bogen. Reports on sightings were trickling in, but unfortunately none had panned out.

In minutes Grey had all the clothes stowed in drawers. He gathered up the trash, amazed at the small mountain of boxes and wrapping he'd discarded. Then he slipped from the room one more time to fill the ice bucket and retrieve a few soft drinks from the vending machine.

When he returned, he locked the door and kicked off his shoes. Padding barefoot to the bathroom door, he listened. No sound came from within. He checked his watch, frowning. She had been in there nearly thirty minutes.

He called her name softly, not wanting to startle her like he had the last time. When she didn't respond he cracked the door and peeked in. As he suspected, she was sound asleep.

He fought with his conscience for all of five seconds. Yeah, he could call her name louder until she woke up. Or he could beat noisily on the door. And probably give her a heart attack in the process.

Or he could slip in and wake her gently.

Difficult choice.

Grabbing two towels, he eased the door open wide and knelt beside the tub. His eyes traveled the length of her, the sight robbing his lungs of oxygen. She was lovelier than he'd remembered.

And she was pregnant with his child.

Aside from being larger, her breasts had taken on a dusky hue, her nipples darker, swollen. Tender? he wondered.

Her waist was as narrow as ever, but the base of her abdomen rose sharply now as she slept, her body relaxed. It was apparent a babe slumbered there. *His.*

A fierce pride rose up in him, mingling with equally fierce possessiveness. He'd been the first man to know intimately this lush body, and if he had anything to do with it, he'd be the last.

His eyes were drawn once more to the slight mound below her stomach, to the tawny curls nested just below. He ached to touch, caress. Kiss. But he wouldn't take advantage while she slept.

Still, he wondered what she'd look like further along, heavy with child. He imagined a dark head, much like his own, suckling lustily upon her breast. He had to convince her to breast-feed.

Hell, first he had to convince her to let *him* stay around, be part of her life when there wasn't a death threat hanging over them.

Scowling, he trailed a finger in the water. Damn it! The water had lost all warmth. He touched her shoulder.

"Tess. You've got to get out, sweetheart. The water's too cold."

She didn't budge.

Leaning forward, he grasped her under the knees and behind the shoulders, lifting her out of the tub.

Water sluiced down her body, soaking him. She stirred, wriggling in his arms. "Grey, what—"

"Easy. I've got you." He snatched up a towel, holding her in one arm as he wrapped the towel about her torso. "You fell asleep in the tub."

Snagging extra towels, he moved to the bed. Sitting on the edge, he shifted her onto his lap, catching the long strands of wet hair and wrapping them in a towel.

"Now you're wet, too." Tess felt her teeth chatter. Her head pounded, and she felt sore all over.

Grey looked at her closely, concern darkening his eyes. "You don't feel well, do you?"

She shook her head. "I'm so cold."

Rubbing her briskly with the towel, Grey quickly dried her. Setting her on the bed, he moved to a drawer and retrieved one of her nightshirts. Ignoring her feeble protests, he stripped away the damp towel and slid the soft cotton over her head. Then he picked her up, pulled back the covers, and tucked her in the bed.

Grabbing the gauze he'd bought earlier, he rebandaged her hands.

"Better?" he asked.

"No." The sheets felt like ice on her skin. "Can you turn the heat up? Please."

Instead Grey unbuttoned his damp shirt and stripped it off, not trusting himself enough to remove his pants. He looked at her. "It's not what you think." He grabbed the cover she had knotted in her fists. "Move over and I'll share my body heat."

She looked ready to cry. "The last time we shared body heat I got pregnant."

"At least you don't have to worry about that this time."

Tess shoved his hand away. "Thanks, but no thanks."

Grey caught her wrists gently, feeling very much like the bull in a china shop. He apologized. "That's not what I meant. I promise to be a perfect gentleman. See? My jeans are staying on."

Scrunching the pillows behind him, Grey climbed onto the bed. She hesitated only a moment before snuggling as close to him as possible, too cold to argue.

Grey drew his arm around her, pressing her tightly to his side. She was his perfect fit. "Better?" he asked.

"Much," she whispered. She burrowed her cold nose into his side, willing the heat to leave his body and enter hers. "Thank you."

For someone shivering, Grey thought she felt too warm. He pressed his lips against her forehead, testing her skin temperature. She was burning up.

"Tess, I think you're running a fever. I need to call a doctor."

She moaned. "The last thing I want to do is go out again. I just need sleep. I'll be fine."

Grey hugged her close, rocking her gently, while he fought his own internal monsters. He didn't blame her for not wanting to go out. She didn't feel well.

But he didn't want to take any chances where she or the baby were concerned.

Besides, the doctor he was going to call was a person he trusted explicitly. In fact, she was the obstetrician Grey was going to recommend Tess see while they were in the Chapel Hill area.

His ex-wife.

Chapter Thirteen

*G*rey looked down at Tess, noticing she'd drifted off to sleep, which made his decision easier. He'd feel better if Elise saw Tess, but how would Tess feel about seeing the woman Grey had once been married to?

He thought about Geoffrey Hurst, Tess's ex-fiancé. Grey wouldn't want to see him, even if he were dying and Geoffrey held the cure. But that was him.

Right now, with her sick and them in hiding . . . well, calling Elise seemed the best option. Of course, that assumed Grey could reach her.

Slipping from the bed, he reached for his wallet and withdrew a creased business card.

Her answering service gave him the number of a local hospital, where Elise was on call. She sounded harried when she answered the page.

"Grey! Kevin and I watched the reports on the trial. Are you okay?"

"I'm fine Elise, but I've got a big favor to ask."

Briefly he explained the situation.

"So it's true," she said. "The Marsh woman is pregnant. There's speculation you're the father—"

"I am."

"Well, congratulations! Now tell me more of her symptoms. How high is her fever?"

"I don't have a thermometer, and I'm hesitant to leave her to go find one."

"I'm off duty in thirty minutes. I can come there."

Grey breathed a sigh of relief. "Thanks Elise."

"You can thank me when I get there. What's the address?"

Grey gave her directions and their room number. "We're registered under an alias, Elise, you—"

"Yeah, I know. It's top secret. You'd tell me more, but then you'd have to kill me. Blah, blah, blah. I remember the drill from when we were married."

"You probably got the same lines from Kevin." After he and Elise divorced she married his best friend, a fellow FBI agent. Kevin had only stayed with the Bureau a few months after that though. He'd been smart enough to realize undercover work didn't mix well with a marriage and family.

"There's not many people I can call right now." Grey admitted.

"Say no more. I figure if you didn't trust me, you wouldn't have called." Elise paused, but only to draw another breath. "And, by the way, those tired old lines about stuff being top secret don't work anymore, so be prepared to tell me *everything*, Grey."

～～

"Your *ex-wife* is an obstetrician?" Tess shoved her still-damp hair off her forehead. She was wide-awake. "And she's coming here? Now?"

Grey nodded. "You need a doctor, Tess. You're running a fever, and I know I can trust Elise."

Trust wasn't the issue. For now at least.

She was still reeling over the news Grey had been married

before. To a woman who was en route this instant to see Tess . . . who carried the woman's ex-husband's child.

She scrambled from the bed only to be caught—gently—around the waist by a strong arm.

"Let me go!" she demanded.

"What are you doing? You belong in bed."

"I'm going to get dressed and brush my hair."

"Why?"

"Because I probably look like something a cat tried to bury."

"So? You're sick. She knows that."

Tess smacked his hand, twice, miffed that he hadn't even tried to contradict her. She must look even worse then she felt. "I suppose she also knows I'm pregnant and you're the father."

Damn it, he wished she'd hold still. "The whole blasted country knows that. Remember?"

For a moment she looked stung, and Grey regretted his remark. He loosened his grip, instantly contrite.

"Tess . . ."

She moved away, ignoring him, pulling open drawers until she found her clothes. Grabbing a soft blue sweater and jeans, she stepped into the bathroom. But not before shooting Grey a wounded look. Then she slammed the door and crumpled to the floor, eyes blurry with unshed tears.

Why did the news of Grey's past seem so upsetting? Of course he'd had a life before meeting her, before the time they spent together. So had she. It was just . . .

What?

Why did it upset her so to think of Grey loving another? *It didn't.*

The thought that Grey *still* cared was what rankled.

They obviously still had a bond. Grey trusted her. In his hour of need he'd called his ex-wife.

And, quite simply, Tess was jealous.

Her head snapped up at the thought. She couldn't be jealous. That meant she had to care about him deeply. And she couldn't. She didn't know him well enough . . . in spite of all that had passed between them.

She thought back to her weeks in Montana. Of the time she'd spent with Grey as a hostage. She'd been a helpless pawn in a frightening game.

And she'd loved him even then.

No.

No.

No!

Grey knocked softly on the door. "Tess? Are you okay?"

Drying her eyes, she straightened and quickly pulled on her clothes. When she opened the door he was casually leaning against the jamb, blocking her way, his arms crossed over his bare chest.

She wished he'd put on a shirt. She stared at his chest, his small brown nipples. The medal that rested between them. She ached to touch him. Except she was still confused.

"I'm fine." She squeezed past him, avoiding physical contact as if he were covered with leprous sores. No small task considering the size of her breasts and the fact that he obviously wasn't budging. Picking up a hairbrush, she moved toward the couch.

"I owe you an apology." He followed her, snagging a dry shirt and jamming his arms into the sleeves. "Probably a dozen of them."

She remained silent.

He ran his hands through his hair, flexing muscles as he moved. "One, I shouldn't have snapped at you. Two, I should have checked with you before calling a doctor. And three, I need to respect your space and your feelings."

He knelt in front of her, mesmerized by the hairbrush

shimmering through her hair, knowing he'd be lost if he reached out and touched. When she still didn't speak, he sighed.

"Okay, I also should have told you sooner that I had an ex-wife."

The hairbrush stopped mid-stroke. His last remark made her realize she was behaving childishly. She looked at him, repentant. "You owe me no explanations on your personal life."

"I know I don't *owe* you one. I would, however, like to share with you." He reached out, taking the hairbrush from her hand.

When she didn't resist he eased up to sit beside her and began gently brushing the long golden strands.

"I'd also like it if you shared some of your life with me. I'm tired of the way we tiptoe around each other, like there's an invisible wall that can't be breached." He ran a finger down the hollow of her cheek, tracing the line of her jaw. "There's so much I don't know about you. It drives me crazy sometimes."

She looked away, not wanting him to see that she felt the same. Not until she understood it herself. That wall was there for a reason.

"Ours hasn't exactly been a normal relationship. We've been thrown together under extreme circumstances twice now. First in Montana, now this. My everyday life would probably bore you."

Tipping her chin back toward him, he pressed a kiss to the tip of her nose. She was still too warm, her eyes feverish. He hoped Elise would arrive soon.

"Funny, I've felt the same way about my life." His smile was bittersweet. "So does that mean you accept my apology?"

"For being overbearing? Yes."

He grunted. "What about my calling Elise?"

Tess looked at him squarely not wanting to delve too deeply into feelings that felt too tender right now. "I realize she's doing a tremendous favor coming here this late. And if you say she's a good doctor, I'll believe you."

At that moment a knock sounded at the door. Picking up his gun, Grey checked the peephole, then opened the door.

A petite redhead rushed into the room and launched herself at Grey. She kissed both his cheeks before stepping back and giving him the once-over. "Nice. The *GQ* look suits you. The last time I saw you, you had hair down to here."

She pointed to his gun and rolled her eyes, unimpressed. "Stow that and grab my bags. I set them down outside." She jabbed at his open shirt. "And button up. It's nippy."

Elise whirled around, pinning Tess with a friendly smile as she peeled off her coat. "You must be Tess Marsh. I'm Elise Barnes."

Tess nodded dumbly, unable to take her eyes off the other woman. Elise was stunning. A riot of rust-colored curls framed the woman's delicate face, complementing her emerald green eyes. But the most amazing thing to Tess was the woman's stomach.

Elise Barnes was pregnant.

"Number five and six," she announced proudly, patting her stomach. She winked at Grey. "Twins. Beat you to it!"

The room grew silent. Elise's head turned from Grey to Tess, then back to Grey. "Uh, you did tell her twins run rampant in your family, didn't you?"

Tess's mouth fell open. Rampant? "He mentioned twin sisters. Is there more?"

Elise laughed, clearly pleased to have gotten Grey in hot water. Until she looked at Tess. Then she started clucking like a mother hen. "Ignore me, hon. I'm just giving him a hard time."

Somehow Tess didn't think Elise was kidding about the possibility of twins. A subject she'd pursue with Grey later. "You're really having twins?"

Elise nodded. "Kevin, that's my husband, says we're naming them *The* and *End*. Of course, he said something similar after the last four, and look at me."

Elise sat next to Tess on the couch. "If you don't mind me saying so, you look awful, kiddo. May I?" She grasped Tess's wrist, checking her pulse.

"You look wonderful," Tess blurted. "I mean, pregnancy obviously agrees with you. It doesn't me."

Elise chuckled sympathetically. "We'll have to see if we can change that." She motioned for Grey to hand her the black medical bag. She withdrew a digital thermometer and stuck it in Tess's mouth.

"One-oh-one fever," she announced a moment later, grabbing a blood-pressure cuff.

The room was silent except for the steady hiss of air from the cuff. "And your blood pressure's low."

Removing her stethoscope, Elise started asking Tess questions about her general health while she checked the glands under her jaw.

Tess winced when she hit a tender spot.

"Sore?" Elise asked. "They're swollen. You've had a lot of stress the entire time you've been pregnant, haven't you?"

Grey, who'd been quietly pacing up till now, snorted. "That's an understatement considering that just today she survived an explosion and a mugging."

"A strong woman. My favorite kind." Elise hooked a thumb in his direction. "Bet you love being stuck with him, hmmm?"

Tess had to smile.

"Let me see your hands." Elise cut away the gauze and examined the cuts. "This might hurt but I need to check for glass and infection," she warned before pressing on the abrasions.

"Looks like you got it all," Elise said finally. "I'll leave an antiseptic ointment to put on that. It'll help relieve the pain, too."

Standing, Elise looked at Grey. "I need a few minutes alone to examine Tess."

Grey grabbed a jacket and the room key. "I'll go buy a newspaper."

When they were alone, Elise patted Tess's hand. "I'd like to check the baby, if that's okay with you. I just want to feel your tummy."

Nodding, Tess moved to the bed. Surprisingly, she felt very comfortable with Elise.

"Yes, there's definitely a baby in there," Elise remarked when she finished.

"And he's okay?" Tess asked anxiously.

"He?" Elise smiled. "I knew my first two were girls. *He* feels fine. However, there are some routine tests that need to be done, like a sonogram and blood work. You need to be taking prenatal vitamins, too. Maybe extra iron and folic acid if you're anemic."

Elise helped her sit up. Outside the door, they heard pacing footfalls. "Impatient as ever," Elise remarked, repacking her gear. "Shall we let him back in or make him suffer?"

"You can let him in. I know he's worried about the baby."

Elise winked. "I think he's worried about more than the baby."

Grey moved straight to Tess's side when Elise opened the door. Taking her hand, he sat on the bed. "So what's the prognosis, doc?"

Elise looked at Tess. "Educated guess? Exhaustion. Aggravated by stress. Which means, Tess, you're more susceptible to viruses. I suspect that's what's causing the fever, but

I really need to run some blood tests to confirm that. You're also slightly dehydrated, so I want you to increase your fluid intake immediately. That means drinking even when you don't feel thirsty. I'm going to leave you something to take tonight to ease the aches and pains. Don't worry, it's perfectly safe for a pregnant woman. And I'll call in the morning."

"I can't thank you enough," Tess said. She did feel better knowing the baby was fine.

Elise stood then turned to Grey. "You know, I thought about something on the way over. You obviously need a place to stay. And Tess needs prenatal care. A colleague of mine is teaching in Europe for a year. Kevin and I have free run of his vacation house in the mountains in exchange for me seeing some of his patients. You and Tess can stay there. It's only two hours from here, and it's very secluded, but has all the comforts of home."

Grey rubbed his chin. "I don't know."

Elise stuck both hands on her hips, offended. "What's not to know? It's a great idea. You'd be close enough I could see Tess myself."

"We have to keep a low profile, Elise."

"Fine. I'll see you after hours at my clinic. You can sneak in the back door after the staff's left. No one would know. And I've got a full lab and diagnostic center on the premises."

Tess shook her head. "I don't want to be a problem."

Elise gave her an understanding look. "That's a noble sentiment, Tess, but not the best choice for the baby. I don't want to alarm you, but under the present circumstances, I'd classify you as a high-risk pregnancy. You need rest, a better diet, and a more thorough physical examination than I can give you here."

Tess's hand instinctively went to her abdomen. Grey drew

her closer, one arm circling her shoulder, his other hand covering hers.

"Exactly who knows about this guy's place?" Grey asked. The last thing he wanted was to put Tess and the baby at additional risk. "What about other hospital staff?"

"Nobody knows. He just signed papers on the place. I think he's paranoid that everyone at the hospital will want to use it once they know he's got a mountain hideaway," Elise explained.

She reached in her pocket and handed Grey her cellular phone. "Call Kevin. You know he'll tell you straight." She winked at Tess. "My husband wouldn't hesitate to tell Grey to ignore me if he had the slightest doubt it wasn't perfectly safe."

Grey took the phone. Elise's proposition sounded perfect. He and Tess would have a private place to hide, and Tess could get proper obstetric care.

He looked at Tess, reluctant to give her a choice, but knowing it was the right thing to do. Under the circumstances, she might not want Elise to act as her obstetrician. "It sounds like a good solution, providing it's secure. How do you feel about it?"

The fact that he asked her opinion meant a lot to Tess. "I just want to be someplace I can feel safe. To sleep in peace. And while I hope this will all be over in a day or two, I would like to see Elise if we're going to be here a while." It was funny to realize she was thinking more and more of the baby.

After talking with Kevin, Grey promised to let them know something in the morning and walked Elise to her car. When he returned, Tess had changed and was snuggled beneath the blankets.

"Still cold?"

She nodded. "Thanks for calling Elise."

"She's a good woman."

His compliment prompted her next question, one she'd been thinking about since Elise arrived. "So why did you two divorce?"

Her blunt inquiry took Grey by surprise. He didn't think she'd like the answer.

He shook his head, pouring a glass of water and handing it to her along with the pills Elise left. "You're gonna get sick of me pressing you to drink more, but Elise said the dehydration thing's serious."

For a moment Tess thought he'd ignore her question. Then he moved to sit on the bed beside her, sprawling his legs out before easing her gently into his arms.

"We were college students when we married." he began. "I had just been discharged from the Army and was returning to finish my degree."

"So you really were in the Army?" His nod made her feel better. He *had* shared some personal information after all.

"Did you know Elise before your stint in the Army?" she continued.

"No. We met in Chapel Hill. Elise was a medical student. We were young and idealistically opposite, but madly in love. Then Elise started her residency. I was offered a job with the Bureau after I graduated from law school."

"Did you do undercover work back then?"

"No. But I worked a lot of overtime trying to make a name for myself. In the meantime Elise had started delivering babies and knew she wanted a couple of her own."

Grey tightened his grip on her shoulders, wishing there was another way to explain, to cast the blame somewhere other then on his shoulders. He pressed the gentlest of kisses to her temple.

"I didn't want children, Tess. It was selfish. I liked our lives just the way they were. I volunteered for an overseas assignment, thinking the distance would help bring our focus back on each other. It didn't. In her loneliness Elise grew even more desperate, begging me to come home and start a family. I refused, using every excuse in the book to avoid returning."

He pushed ahead with his story, knowing it was too late to turn back now. "Before I returned, I had a vasectomy. I don't think I could have come up with any worse way to hurt Elise. It destroyed our marriage, and drove Elise straight into the arms of another man, a man who'd been there for her when I was gone. My best friend, Kevin Barnes."

Stunned, Tess didn't move. "You, you had a vasectomy? But how?" Her hands went to her stomach.

He covered both her hands with one of his own. "As soon as I realized what an idiot I'd been, I had the surgery reversed. Obviously, it was successful, but unfortunately it was too late."

Grey hadn't wanted children. The knowledge tore through her. "Too late?"

"To save the marriage. We divorced, and she eventually married Kevin. Oddly enough, there's never been a moment's animosity between Kevin and me over their marriage. Kevin was there for Elise that whole time I was overseas, at first as a friend, then later . . . Well, the further apart we grew, the closer they became."

For a moment Grey wondered if Tess had drifted off to sleep. She didn't move or make any noise and briefly he regretted his honesty. When she finally spoke, her question surprised him.

"Do you still love her?"

Trick question.

He took a deep breath, wanting to answer honestly, praying he didn't stick his foot in his mouth. "Not in the sense you mean. We obviously care for each other, but on a platonic basis. And Kevin and I are as close as ever."

She grew quiet once more, and Grey couldn't stand it. He knew exactly what was bothering her. Shifting to his side, he nudged her chin up, forcing her to meet his gaze. Her eyes shimmered with unshed tears. He hated that he'd caused them.

"Would you believe me if I told you I'd changed my mind about wanting a family a long time ago?"

"How do I know you're not just saying that?" She shook her head. "This pregnancy wasn't planned by either one of us."

"Which doesn't mean the child's any less welcome."

Grey leaned down, tugged at the hem of her nightshirt, exposing her stomach. He brushed his fingers across her skin, reverent, then bent low and pressed a kiss to her abdomen, just below her navel. "There's a lot of things I wish I could change, Tess. But this isn't one of them. I want *this* child. Our child. How can I make you believe that?"

Tess searched his eyes, *eyes that didn't lie,* finding sincerity, assurance, in the silvery depths. A single tear ran down her cheek.

He *did* care about the baby.

He caught the tear on the tip of his finger. "I'd also like the chance to spend time with the baby's mother. It's no secret I'm attracted to you. That there's a certain magnetism between us."

She looked away, fumbling for the covers, feeling too . . . exposed. "That's what scares me most. From the very beginning we've either been operating on falsehoods or under duress. What happens when it's all said and done, and it's just you and me? Will we even like each other?" As much as she was attracted to Grey, she knew she'd never settle for only a physical relationship.

His heart squeezed at the uncertainty on her face. He knew he'd cared for her, had avoided trying to quantify it.

But the thought that she might not feel the same for him was sobering. Trying to imagine her *not* in his life was impossible.

"Look, if we take Elise up on her offer of staying at the cabin, we'll have a shot at some quiet time. Why don't we see how things go there?"

He placed a finger over her lips to prevent her from saying anything else. "Let's sleep on it. Fair enough?"

Tess blinked again, suddenly unable to hold her eyes open. The medicine she'd taken was starting to ease the pain in her hands, and tucked in beside Grey, she finally felt warm.

"But—"

"Shhhhh. Sleep. Remember?"

Suppressing a yawn, she bid him good night, and within minutes fell asleep.

Easing off the bed, Grey made sure the blankets were tucked securely around her, then kissed the top of her head. More than anything he wanted to keep this woman safe, to give her peace.

Spending time alone at a cabin did seem like an ideal solution. It would give him a chance to prove to her that he would be the perfect father. The perfect . . . what? Lover? Boyfriend? No commitments unless she wanted them? Was that what she wanted?

Mind restless, he moved to the couch, knowing it would be a while before he drifted off to sleep.

The cabin brought a smile to Tess's face. Snuggled in a hollow against a backdrop of the Blue Ridge Mountains, the cedar A-frame welcomed them.

"What do you think?" she asked anxiously. After getting

the keys and directions from Elise's husband, Kevin, Grey had once again take a roundabout way to their destination, driving an additional forty miles before he was completely satisfied they weren't being followed. She desperately needed a bathroom.

He peered at the cabin over the rim of his dark sunglasses. Secluded was an understatement. The long, private drive was only accessible via a locked gate. And the cabin itself, located in a valley, wasn't even visible from the highway.

The house was surrounded by twenty acres of wilderness. Kevin had done some discreet checking and learned that the nearest neighbor was five miles away. Most of the homes were used only in summer and again in January, when the ski resorts opened.

While the seclusion was perfect for hiding out, he was concerned about the distance to medical help. The closest hospital was thirty minutes in good weather, with no traffic. He'd feel better after Tess had a complete physical, which was scheduled for later that night at Elise's clinic.

He saw the concern in Tess's eyes, and was tempted to kiss her. Instead he smiled and stuffed his hands in his coat pockets. He had decided last night that he would give her some space while they were here. Let her be the one to make the first move. Already he doubted his ability to keep his hands off her, but how else could he convince her they had more than lust going for them?

"I think it will be perfect," he said finally. "Let's go inside and take a look."

The interior of the cabin was sumptuous. The soaring great room had a two-story glass wall split by a huge stone fireplace.

"Wow," she said gazing out on the view of the mountains.

"I'll bring in firewood later," Grey said. "Right after I bring in groceries."

"I'll help." Tess followed him out to the garage. "Do you really think we'll be here long enough to eat all this?"

"You're supposed to put on weight, remember? How can I get you to eat if I don't have choices to offer?"

She grabbed a paper sack, only to have it removed from her hand. "That's too heavy."

She reached for another one, only to have her hand lightly smacked. "So's that one."

She frowned. "Don't treat me like an invalid."

Grey handed her a bag with two loaves of bread. "You're confusing chivalry with chauvinism. I was trying to be polite."

As soon as the car was unloaded, they quickly stowed the groceries and supplies. Grey looked through the cabinets.

"The place is well equipped. Right down to crystal wineglasses."

"Too bad I can't have any wine," Tess murmured as she folded the last of the empty bags. "I'd love a glass of Chardonnay."

Grey came up behind her and placed his hands on her shoulders. "Tense?"

She nodded, clasping then unclasping her hands. "It feels like we've been on the run forever. I sometimes wonder if my life will ever be normal again."

He watched her fidget, wishing he could snap his fingers and make it all better. But as long as Bogen and Snake were on the loose she was in danger.

He'd checked with Barry that morning, but there'd been no news on the fugitives. They had arrested a man suspected of slipping a knife to Bogen during the courtroom melee, which Bogen then used in their escape. The man claimed to know nothing of Bogen and Snake's whereabouts.

"Change your shoes, and we'll explore outside. A little exercise will do us both good." He lowered his hand to cradle her abdomen. "Junior here could probably use a little fresh air, too."

She stepped away, still feeling his touch. It was odd, but for a moment she could have sworn she felt the baby move—respond to Grey's touch. But that was impossible—it was too soon. At least she thought it was. She needed to ask Elise about that. In fact she needed to start a list of things to ask about.

Grey was on the deck when she appeared a moment later. "We'll have a great view of the sunset," he said, casually reaching forward to zip her jacket.

At the edge of the lawn, a path disappeared into the woods, wide enough so they were able to walk abreast. Two squirrels scampered ahead, leapt to a tree, their tiny claws clattering against the bark. She took a deep breath, the air heavy with the scent of pine.

Grey's knowledge of the area amazed her. He told her some of the history, of how the Cherokee Indians had lived and hunted across the Carolinas.

"How long did you live here?" she asked.

"Four years, off and on, while Elise completed her residency in Chapel Hill."

"I visited Chapel Hill once, a few years ago. Shopped on Franklin Street. The stores there are fabulous. I remember having lunch at a grill in a quaint little drugstore."

"Sutton's Drug Store. It's been there forever and has the best french fries around." The connection, however slight, brought a smile to Grey's face.

"You liked living in North Carolina," she noted.

"Yes. Even after I transferred to Washington, D.C., I found myself coming down here every chance I got to camp or hike."

"Do you consider D.C. your home?"

He shook his head. "I have a condo there. My job is currently there. But home? Where my heart is? No, it's not that kind of home." Funny. He'd given that a lot of thought lately himself. Home would be wherever she was.

Tess nodded. "I guess that's how I feel about Boston."

"Do you plan to reopen your shop?"

"Yes. If only to prove that I can. I've got plenty of new ideas. I bet I filled ten notebooks with designs these past months."

"Have you given any thought to where you'll live after the baby comes?" With me, he wanted to say. But didn't.

She shrugged, a wistful look on her face. "Not really. I'm still considering a farm. The question is where. I mean, kids need space. A yard, a swing set. Maybe even a puppy. God, listen to me. I don't even know how I'll manage with a human baby, let alone a baby animal."

"I hear puppies are easier to housebreak."

Tess laughed. "Boston was a good choice for my business goals. I didn't exactly have a family in mind when I moved there."

So she wouldn't necessarily mind moving, Grey mused. Even at that Boston was only an hour from D.C. by plane. He could look into transferring to the Boston office. He definitely wanted to be close.

"So where else would you go?" he asked. "New York?"

She shook her head. "New York never felt right. I think because of my parents' divorce. My childhood was spent being shuttled between the two of them." She halted abruptly looking up at him. "I don't want that for my child, Grey."

"Our child," he corrected. "And don't borrow trouble. We're two sensible adults with the baby's best interests at heart. We'll do fine."

She looked unconvinced, but started walking along the path once more. "You still have me at a distinct disadvantage. You know a lot more about my family then I do yours."

"That's easy to remedy. The Thomases were one of the first families to settle in Pennsylvania. My ancestors fought in the American Revolution. They helped found the railroad and the steel mills."

"Wait a minute. Are you related to Thomas Steel Works?" Then she remembered his mentioning that his father had retired from a railroad company. "And Thomas & Stone Rail Lines?"

"They needed an efficient way to get ore to the mills."

Tess shook her head. Grey was a member of one of Pennsylvania's finest families. And one of the wealthiest. Yet he didn't act like . . .

She cut off that train of thought. There was no comparing Grey to anyone else she'd ever met.

"Will my family tree impress your mother?" he asked.

"Undoubtedly." But Tess had no intention of telling her. At least not right away. If she knew Grey's background, Madeline would switch from pressing for an abortion to demanding a marriage.

Grey tugged her to a stop. "You're the only one I care about impressing, Tess. I hope you know that."

He lifted her chin, forcing her to meet his gaze. The raw emotion she saw frightened her. And beckoned her.

For a sparkling second Tess wanted to throw caution to the wind, live for the moment. She'd been fighting a growing desire for Grey ever since seeing him again. And being this close made it worse, fanned the longing, the hunger. She wanted to feel his lips on hers, feel his hands on her bare skin. She wanted to see him naked again, feel him harden in her greedy hands. He was the only man who'd ever made love to her . . .

He was also the only man who'd ever seen her naked, though she wasn't so sure she wanted him to see her that way right now. The changes her body was going through, well . . .

she looked different. And she hadn't accepted those changes herself yet.

It was just one more reason to say no.

Grey saw the struggle in her eyes and secretly rejoiced. For a second she had looked ready to pounce on him. Then just as quickly she'd banked the passion, listening to her self-doubts.

It was all he needed to know. His hands were already on her shoulders and it was easy, natural, to pull her closer. When she didn't resist he lowered his mouth and captured her lips. Sliding his hands through her hair, he grasped her head, slanting it slightly as he deepened the kiss. His tongue delved into the sweetness of her mouth, stealing her breath, giving his own in its place.

She swayed in his arms, releasing the softest of moans. Small, hungry sounds that enflamed him.

She was standing between his spread legs, her body pressed fully against his. Her hands tightened at his waist, her fingers fidgeting, trying to loosen his shirt, then moving forward to tug at his belt. She made an impatient noise, her hand drifting lower.

He felt himself harden, knew that if she so much as touched him there, he'd shoot off like a firecracker with a short fuse. Grey pulled back first, stepping away from her.

"I promised myself I wouldn't push you," he whispered hoarsely. "But I can't take much more of this. I want you too damn bad."

He pressed a kiss to her forehead. "We need to head back. Don't forget we've got an appointment with Elise tonight."

Tess *had* forgotten. That's what his kisses did to her. It was darn right scary. She'd felt Grey's erection the moment he'd pressed against her and for a wild moment she'd wanted him right there, right then, in the pine needles on the forest floor in front of God and all the squirrels.

But what about later? When Snake and Bogen were recaptured and the trials were over? Would the passion burn as brightly without the fuel of constant excitement? She needed to know it would always be like this. She wanted guarantees.

Unfortunately, if she'd learned nothing else in this lifetime, it was that life offered no guarantees.

Even tomorrow wasn't guaranteed.

They walked back to the cabin in silence. "Go on in. I'll bring in some firewood for later."

Tess watched him saunter off, torn between wanting him and being afraid. Afraid she couldn't keep him.

Except . . .

They had just shared one hot kiss. And Grey had been as affected by it as she was. After leaving Montana she told herself that she'd imagined their affair being so sensational, so intense. It had been part and parcel of the overall drama. Nothing was that spectacular.

But it was.

She closed her eyes against the memory of his body over hers. Hot. Hard. Grinding. Grey was a demanding lover, greedy, but not selfish. Her nipples constricted at the thought.

Oh, it would be good. Damn good.

For a time.

Until the dawn, perhaps. And then?

Then . . . nothing.

The bottom line remained unchanged. She and Grey were once again drawn to each other in extreme circumstances. Circumstances where she was weak and he was strong. He rescued her, he slew dragons.

And once the dragons were dead, he'd move on. And take her heart with him.

Chapter Fourteen

*A*fter they ate, they headed to Chapel Hill. They were scheduled to meet Elise at seven. Grey arrived twenty minutes early and circled the entire town twice, or so it seemed, before finally parking in the alley behind Elise's clinic.

Elise was as vivacious as ever. "How did you like the cabin?" she asked. "Is it as nice as promised?"

Grey nodded. "Better. You and Kevin definitely need to plan on spending time there."

Elise tugged Tess down a corridor. "Come on, I'll show you to an exam room. While you get undressed, I'll show Grey the nervous daddy room."

When Elise joined Tess a few minutes later, Tess was bursting with curiosity. "What's the nervous daddy room?"

Elise grinned. "A room lined with a series of posters showing the various stages of pregnancy. Most men freak out their first time in. It's pretty cool. We have books and videos on every conceivable subject. Grey said he'll pick some for the two of you."

Tess nodded, unsure. Her knowledge of pregnancy and children was practically nonexistent. "Can nervous mommies go in the nervous daddy room?"

"Of course." Elise grew quiet as she checked Tess's vital

signs. "Good. Fever's gone. And your blood pressure's normal."

For the next few minutes Tess answered yes or no to questions regarding her and her family's health.

"Will you ask Grey the same questions?" Tess asked after they'd completed her medical questionnaire.

Grey's medical history was yet another part of the man she didn't know. He looked perfectly healthy, but were there any family predispositions to asthma? Heart disease? Allergies? Elise probably knew more about that stuff than Tess.

"Yes. In fact, I thought we'd do it right after the sonogram." Elise set her pen down and pushed back in her chair. "I don't mean to pry, but how much of a part do you plan to allow Grey to play in this?"

The question caught Tess off guard. "I haven't given it much thought. It's all so new and so much has been happening. Our circumstances—" Her voice faded as she searched for an explanation.

"I understand that the two of you did not plan for this to happen. And I applaud your decision to keep the baby." Elise leaned forward. "But still . . . I sense something between the two of you. A personal tie, besides the baby. He's a good man, Tess."

She nodded. Elise was right. Grey was a good man. And he'd probably be a great parent. Perhaps even better than she. He didn't seem nearly as insecure with the idea of a baby as she did. She hadn't even known about different baby bottles.

Elise patted her hand. "Of course, it's your choice, but most new fathers want to hear the baby's heartbeat and see the sonogram. It's their first contact with the little alien, and they usually fall hard. Although I suspect in Grey's case it will be a short trip."

Tess smiled, then immediately began crying. "I'm sorry. I

don't know what's wrong with me anymore. The tears always seem just below the, the . . . surface."

"It's not you. It's your hormones." Elise handed her a box of tissues. "Your system's overloaded with them right now, and even under ideal conditions they bring emotional ups and downs. The fact that you're also under a lot of external pressure doesn't help. My best advice is to take extra good care of yourself and just roll with it."

Tess blew her nose. "That's easier said than done."

"How is Grey dealing with this? Is he being supportive? Understanding? Men can be the most insensitive creatures."

Tess rushed to his defense. "I don't think he even realizes I'm having mood swings. He probably thinks I'm always like this." New tears filled her eyes. "I hope he doesn't think that. I try to keep it to myself. I don't want to be a bother."

"Honey, you're entitled to be a bother right now. You're pregnant." Elise looked at her closely. "And I think he's more aware than you give him credit for. I can tell Grey's crazy for you, and unless I've read you totally wrong, I'd say you feel the same way. Do you love him?"

The direct question surprised her. She knew the answer. And it wasn't admitting it that bothered her so much. The question was what good did it do to admit it? It changed nothing between them.

"I don't know that it's the right kind of love," Tess hedged.

"Love is love. I think you're overcomplicating the issue by trying to make it fit in a neat little square, which true love rarely does. Why not follow and see where it leads?" Elise squeezed Tess's hand. "You could do worse. And when you hit the horny part of pregnancy you might be glad to have him around."

Tess sniffed. "The horny part?"

"It's not real scientific, but I find most of my pregnant patients fall into two groups. The hungry ones and the horny ones. The first group can't get enough food. The second group thinks about sex constantly. Since you haven't gained a lot of weight, I'd guess you're one of the horny ones." Elise giggled. "Uh-oh. The look on your face confirms it."

The news relieved her. So it was the pregnancy making her crave Grey? Sex hormones? "I was beginning to think something was wrong with me."

"Nope. As you've probably already discovered it does no good to ignore it. There's only one cure. And as your doctor, I can assure you it's perfectly safe to have sex—even the hot, hard, kind—during pregnancy." Elise glanced at her watch. "Now let's get on with your exam so we can move on to the fun stuff."

"Fun stuff?"

"The sonogram. It'll blow you away."

Tess moved onto the examining table. "I think I would like Grey to be here for that part. If he wants to, that is."

Elise snapped on a pair of latex gloves and smiled broadly. "Oh I'm sure he'll want to."

Oddly, Tess did not feel self-conscious when Grey entered the examining room a short time later. Elise had already given her a thorough exam and declared her and the baby fit. Grey winked at her after hearing the news.

"Now let's see if we can find an itsy bitsy heartbeat." Elise pulled a stool close, motioning for Grey to sit beside the examining table on Tess's left side, while she moved to the opposite side. She held out a specially designed stethoscope with two sets of earpieces. "You can both listen at the same time."

Tess looked skeptically at the stethoscope. "Won't we hear my heartbeat?"

Elise shook her head. Earlier she had given Tess a modesty sheet to keep across her lap. Pulling up the gown slightly, she exposed the lower part of Tess's abdomen and pressed her own stethoscope there. "The baby's heartbeat is much, much faster than yours. You'll see."

Elise moved her stethoscope around, then nodded and grabbed the metal disk of the dual stethoscope, showing Grey the spot for him to listen. "There."

At first Grey heard nothing except a hollow noise. He frowned, shaking his head lightly. Tess's face reflected the same. His fingers grazed the skin of her abdomen as he moved the disk fractionally lower.

That's when he heard it. A fast, *zither, zither* of a heartbeat. He heard Tess's sharp intake of air and knew she'd heard it, too.

Their baby's heartbeat. Strong, steady, sure.

The sound of life shook Grey. Hard. Sweat dotted his forehead as his mouth dried.

Holy shit. Was he ready for this?

He'd always heard that being *a father* was more than the act of depositing a few million sperm in a fertile womb. The words slapped him with humility. He had helped to create a life. A new responsibility. Never again could he worry only about himself. There would always be another heartbeat he would worry about more than his own.

Their baby.

Elise excused herself to prepare the sonogram. "Listen as long as you like," she whispered before leaving the room.

But Grey barely heard her, his eyes locked on Tess's. For a moment time stopped, and they were the only people in the world, three lives united by one heartbeat. His hand reached up, grasping hers, squeezing it as they listened together to the sound they'd created.

The moment he'd heard the first stirrings of his child's heartbeat deep within her womb, he'd been lost. *Scared to death*. A bond that would never break had been forged with his child.

And now more than anything he wanted that same bonding with the child's mother.

Grey reached up and swiped at Tess's cheek. She was weeping; tears of joy. He knew he'd cared for her before. But it was an empty shell compared to what his heart felt now. "Pretty awesome, huh?"

Tess nodded, still so overwhelmed she could barely speak. Realizing on an intellectual plane that you were pregnant was quite different from *knowing*. Feeling. "I don't know if I'll be able to handle seeing it on the sonogram. This is so unbelievable, Grey. This is our baby we're listening to."

He leaned forward, the stethoscope forgotten as he sought her lips, wanting desperately to claim her heart.

She met him halfway, wrapping her arms around his neck and drawing him down. Her mouth slanted open, welcoming the onslaught, surrendering to the raw heat and stunning emotion of the moment.

Grey swept his tongue deeply into her mouth, claiming the lushness. He felt her hands fist in his hair, tugging him closer. With one hand cupped behind her neck he held her immobile beneath his mouth, while his other hand trailed lower quickly finding the front opening of her gown. Long fingers eased beneath the thin cotton, skimming upward along her ribs, his knuckles grazing the heavy undersides of her swollen breasts.

Tess's breathing had grown short, erratic. A small groan of pleasure escaped when his hand closed over one of her breasts, catching her hardened nipple between two fingers and tugging the oversensitized peak.

Tess felt a jolt of electricity run down her spine. Desire washed over her. She wanted Grey. And she wasn't going to deny herself, not this time.

Grey heard the footsteps before Tess and pulled back just as Elise rapped on the door and sailed back into the room.

"Okay, I'm ready with the sonogram." She looked from Tess to Grey, then smiled. "We can postpone it if you two want to continue—"

"We're finished," Tess stuttered. "Listening to the baby's heartbeat, I mean."

Grey stood, holding out a hand to help Tess up from the table.

He knew she was as shaken as he by the emotional moment of hearing the baby's heartbeat for the first time. But her reaction had been more than just that. She'd matched his passion; he'd tasted her desire.

Oh sure, she was probably trying desperately to convince herself otherwise right now. But it was too late. He knew that she wanted him every bit as much as he wanted her. And that was enough.

For now.

～❧～

It was late when they returned to the cabin. Tess woke up when she felt the car stop. Immediately she realized it had been a mistake to fall asleep in the car. Her back, already stiff from the night before, was a knot of pain. Moving slowly, she climbed out of the car.

Grey looked at her suspiciously. "What's wrong?" He could tell by the little furrows in her brow that she was feeling some discomfort.

She stretched carefully, trying to work out the kinks. "My back. Don't worry, it's been sore since this morning. The mattress at the motel was a lot softer than I'm accustomed to."

"Why didn't you mention it sooner?" Grey unlocked the

house and went in first, checking it out before letting her in. "The mattress in my room is pretty firm. You can sleep there tonight."

Unbidden, thoughts of sharing a bed with Grey sprang to mind. The steamy nights, the fevered touches. She turned away, grimacing. "Look—"

He mistook her grimace of frustration for pain. "You're hurting." Taking her elbow, he pulled her to the couch and handed her the remote control. "I'll go find some aspirin while you find something on television."

"Nonaspirin," she reminded him. Instead of turning on the TV Tess dug out the black-and-white sonogram picture Elise had given her of the baby. Actually, the photo looked more like a grainy, uneven blob, but it was *her* blob, and she felt a swell of maternal pride as her finger traced the image.

Grey returned a short time later carrying a tray with two mugs of hot cocoa. He offered her one, hesitating only a second before sitting next to her. "I still think he looks like me."

Tess accepted the mug and sipped gratefully. "What if he's a she?"

The thought rattled Grey. A girl? Jesus, he hadn't thought of that. Sugar and spice. And no dating. Ever. "Then I hope she looks like her mom and has her mother's disposition. Still . . ." He squinted at the photo shaking his head. "Call it silly, but I've got a feeling it's a boy."

"Me too." She pointed to the stack of books on the coffee table. "Don't tell me all those are from Elise?"

Grey nodded and leaned forward to grab a book. "The nervous daddy room has a lending library. This is for you. *What to Expect When You're Expecting*." He held up several other books. "There's *The Pregnant Father's Bible*, books on breast-feeding, Lamaze, baby names. And two videos on childbirth."

She inspected the book he handed her. By the time she fin-

ished skimming the table of contents she felt woefully ignorant about pregnancy. First, second, third trimesters. Home
births. Drugs or natural. This wasn't a simple matter.

Grey, on the other hand, was grinning from ear to ear as
he flipped through his *Father's Bible*. She glanced over his
shoulder at the picture he was studying.

She snorted. "Figures."

A nude and very pregnant woman was sitting in a lotus
position. The woman was obviously pleased and proud of her
state. Tess envied her self-assurance. And the fact that Grey
was clearly fascinated by the photograph.

He raised one condescending eyebrow. "I was admiring
her eyes. Look at them, the serenity. See how she radiates
confidence? I think she's lovely."

Tess felt her cheeks grow warm. Would Grey find her as
beautiful when she was that round with child?

She looked at him, suddenly wishing she could share in
his wonder, be a part of the awe. Instead of being so damned
afraid. "Doesn't any of this scare you?"

He looked at her, detecting the anxiety in her voice. Her
blue eyes were so wide with worry he could have fallen in
them. He reached over, skimmed the hair from her face, then
took her hand.

"The heartbeat threw me. That's when I realized what was
happening was beyond my control. I worry about you, what
you have to go through to carry this child for nine months
and then bring him into the world. I also worry about what
kind of father I'll be. If I'll be good enough."

"You? I've never even been around little children before.
What if I'm a horrible mother?"

Grey moved closer and pulled her into his arms. He knew
she was thinking about her own mother, and for a moment
he felt a burst of anger at Madeline Marsh for being so self-
centered. He pressed a kiss to her forehead.

"You're a wonderful person, Tess. You'll be a wonderful mother. And I think you'll find that taking care of your own child is easier then you think." *And I'll be there to help,* he promised quietly.

While his reassurance was comforting, Tess noticed that he still hadn't mentioned what part—if any—he planned to play in their child's life. Did he see them as two single parents? Separate units? Her heart turned over beneath her ribs.

She straightened, shuddering as a twinge of pain radiated up her back.

"That's it." Grey pushed off the couch. "I can't bear to see you hurting. Go change into something comfortable. You're getting a back rub. A *real* back rub."

Her thoughts flashed to that night on the phone. Verbal massage. Verbal sex. Both paled in comparison to the real thing.

"You don't need to—"

"I want to," he said. "Please?"

She headed to her room to change. The thought of someone rubbing her sore back was delightful. The knowledge that someone would be Grey caused tiny shivers to skim along her spine.

She kicked off her jeans, then caught a glimpse of herself in the full-length mirror, wearing only her bra and panties.

Maybe this wasn't such a good idea after all. She looked . . . funny. Her breasts were swollen and heavy, seeming to have enlarged into two obscenely huge pointy things that strained against the lacy fabric of her bra. Oddly enough her waist was as narrow as ever.

But just below her navel her abdomen protruded sharply, a warm nest for the babe. She slid her hands down, hugging her belly. Would Grey find her attractive now?

A floorboard squeaked.

She looked up and caught Grey's reflection in the mirror,

where he stood behind her in the open door. The look of raw hunger on his face answered her question. He was very, very attracted.

In a bold move, she turned, facing him, willing him to turn and run if he didn't like what he saw. Or didn't want what she was offering. The move left her feeling exposed. Open. Vulnerable.

The air left Grey's lungs in a rush and refused to reenter. He felt his heart pounding in his chest, seeking oxygen. He had come after her to suggest she bring some lotion and instead found her standing in front of the mirror nearly naked.

His eyes had slowly traversed her reflection from head to toe, then back, reveling in the glorious changes. And when she turned to him . . .

He stepped into the room, slowly, cautiously, giving her every chance to move, run, hide. Or stay.

"You're beautiful," he whispered.

The note of haunting sincerity in his voice weakened Tess's knees. The self-consciousness she'd felt over her changing body fled under his scorching appraisal, beneath the silver eyes that missed nothing.

He reached out, grasping a long strand of her hair and slowly winding it around his wrist, tugging her closer as he advanced. She came willingly into his arms, her blue eyes smoky and wide. Unafraid.

Tess expected a fierce kiss, was ready to return it, eager for him to shed some of his clothes before she chickened out.

But instead, Grey turned her back to face the mirror, catching and holding her eyes in the silvered surface. His hands swept lightly up her sides, causing gooseflesh to spread.

"You look like a goddess, the most incredible woman I've ever seen." His hands rubbed softly down her back then circled forward to cradle her abdomen. "It excites me beyond words to know that my child sleeps here."

He pressed forward against her, letting her feel the proof of his arousal. His hands swept upwards again, not stopping until he captured her breasts, lifting them in his hands. "And will seek nourishment here."

Tess's breath was ragged now, her legs shaky. His hands on her body fanned a raging desire. A desire she was tired of denying. He wanted her. She wanted him. It was that simple. That uncomplicated.

She turned, intent on kissing him. Instead, she found herself swept up in his arms. "I promised you a back rub," he said.

"It can wait."

He chuckled at her impatience, amazed he didn't take advantage of her blatant invitation and drop her on the bed and bury himself. No, he was going to take his time, savor her. Make her feel so wonderful she'd never doubt they were meant for each other. And damn it, they were meant to be together. He knew it as surely as he knew the child within her was his.

Since her room had twin beds, he carried her to his room, setting her on the bed as if she were sculpted of fragile porcelain. He moved away, turning on the bedside lamp, before slowly peeling off his shirt.

She admired the ripple of his abs, noticing once again the gold Saint Christopher medal. "Is that the same one you had in Montana?"

Grey picked up the medal, removed it. "It belonged to my mother. It reminded me that there was another world outside of Bogen's compound."

Tess nodded, eyes wide. She reached for him, but Grey shook his head.

"Back rub. Remember?" He handed her a pillow to hug,

afraid it would be uncomfortable to lie flat on her stomach. "Roll onto your side," he whispered.

Acutely aware that she was only wearing underwear, Tess did as he asked, holding her breath until she felt that first touch as his fingers slid down the center of her back. *Just like their phone call.* He gathered her hair, smoothing it before draping it across one shoulder, exposing her. Then he unclasped her bra and eased the straps away, baring her skin to his touch.

It was all she could do to hold still. He started massaging, with feather-soft touches that gradually grew firmer as he expertly kneaded the tense muscles in her back. Her skin grew warm, muscles relaxing as Grey worked magic on her flesh. It was heaven.

And just when she thought she'd flow onto the floor in a puddle, he pressed his lips to the base of her spine, his tongue lapping lightly at the twin dimples there.

Before she could react, he turned her, laying her flat on her back. With sure hands he swept away her bra, allowing his eyes to worship her.

In that moment Tess did feel like a goddess, her body ripe. She reached up, threading her arms around Grey's neck, pulling him down. Closer. To touch and be touched.

He wasn't prepared for the jolt that swept through him as her rock-hard nipples teased his chest. At the exact same moment she caught his lower lip between her teeth, gently nibbling. He felt captured. Willingly. He held himself still, letting her make the moves, reveling in the feeling of being suspended above her as she took her own sweet time and loved his mouth.

When she moaned softly, he moved to cover her, unable to stop himself from rubbing his erection against her mound. He gritted his teeth at the exquisite sensation.

"God, I want you," he whispered hoarsely. "I've wanted you forever."

Tess was lost. It felt as if he'd struck a match to her damp fuse and left it to burn slowly, steadily, toward the inevitable explosion. She arched slightly, enjoying the sensation of his body pressed against hers, the drag and friction of hard flesh on fabric. Knowing the feeling would only get better.

"I want you too, Grey. Please."

It was all he needed to hear. Taking extra care to keep most of his weight suspended from her, he lowered his mouth, searing the side of her neck with blistering kisses, working his way lower until he captured a pouty peak in his mouth. As he'd suspected, her nipples were ultrasensitive, making him wonder if he could bring her to orgasm just by sucking.

Tess writhed beneath him, her frantic hands moving to stroke the hard muscles of his back, as he suckled first one breast, then the other. And when she thought she couldn't take it anymore, he started again.

She squirmed, trying to work her hands around to the front of his pants. He still had his jeans on, which wasn't fair considering she was only wearing a very thin, very wet, pair of panties. And judging by the feel of him, it couldn't be very comfortable either.

"I want these off."

Grey raised his head, grinning wickedly. "Your wish . . ."

Pushing off the bed, he unbuttoned his jeans, then deliberately lowered the zipper, never taking his eyes from her as he shoved them down.

Tess drew in an audible breath at the sight of jutting male flesh that couldn't be contained by his underwear. Sitting up, she carefully tugged at his boxers, exposing him inch by glorious inch.

Reverently, she drew a finger along the swollen head,

smearing the single drop of fluid from the tip. He jerked violently, making her wonder what reaction she'd have gotten if she had used her tongue.

Grey caught her wrist, pulling her fingers away. "Touch me like that again, and I'll lose it."

Tempted to disobey, she hid a smile, desperately wanting to see him lose control for a change.

The mattress dipped as he leaned forward on one knee, then hesitated. "You're sure it won't hurt the baby for us to do this?"

This time she did smile, curving a hand around his neck to draw him closer. "Elise said it was okay."

"You asked?"

She felt her face grow warm. "It came up while she was explaining the horny part of pregnancy."

"The horny part?" He felt her hand dip low, grasp his erection. Cursing, he tried to breathe. "Christ!"

Just then a shrill beeping noise sounded. Grey groaned. Of all the lousy-ass timing . . .

"My pager." As bad as he wanted to ignore it, he knew who it was. "Barry's the only person who has the number."

Tess released him, but not before brushing a light kiss against his shoulder. "He wouldn't use it unless it was important."

Grey pushed away, to grab for his jeans. Let it be a wrong number, he prayed.

It wasn't: 9-1-1. Twice. That meant big emergency. He pulled on his jeans, leaving the waist unfastened—out of necessity. "I'll be right back. I've got to use the telephone."

Barry answered on the first ring.

"What's up?" Grey asked, pacing, his mind elsewhere.

"Bogen and Snake were just arrested in Vancouver."

A weight lifted from Grey's shoulders. "What? Were they

with Sanchez?" Maybe they could bust Sanchez for harboring fugitives. Or aiding and abetting.

"No. They were alone."

Grey was eager to share the news with Tess. Eager to get back to her. "It's still good news. How long before the trial's rescheduled?"

Barry sighed. "I don't think all those details have been ironed out. News of the arrest hasn't even been made public yet. I'd like to bring Tess back right away."

Barry's request caught Grey off guard. He pinched the bridge of his nose. While he was glad Bogen and Snake were once again behind bars, he wasn't ready to let Tess go.

Especially right now.

They'd been on the verge of making love. If he could have just one more night with her . . .

"Give me another twenty-four hours, Barry. I'll return to D.C. tomorrow night."

A tense silence crackled across the connection.

"There's no reason to wait, and I don't want aspersions cast on my department again. I backed you once. Now tell me where you are and I'll send marshals to pick her up."

Grey knew his next words would probably cost him his job. "I can't tell you, Barry. Just trust me. I'll have Tess back in D.C. tomorrow night."

And with that he switched off his phone.

Chapter Fifteen

Without Grey in bed with her, Tess quickly grew cold. She scooted off the mattress and hurried to her room, where she pulled on some clothes. Then she went downstairs.

She found him pacing the living room, a frown marring his forehead.

"What's wrong?"

"Snake and Bogen were recaptured."

A chill flashed up her spine. "Isn't that good?"

Grey nodded. "Barry wants you back in D.C. right away."

Her relief crumbled. She reached out, stopping his frenetic motion. "Tonight?" She thought of their near lovemaking that Barry's call had interrupted. "Can't it wait till morning?"

The plaintive note in her voice tore at him. "Is that what you want?"

Tess closed her eyes as her emotions suddenly crystallized. This would be their only night alone in this cabin. She wanted to be with him. *All night long.*

"I want you, Grey. Make love to me."

His heart soared at her words. He tugged her into his arms and kissed her. The fire that burned between them burst into greedy flames of passion. He trailed his lips down the side of her neck, rough, eager. His unshaved chin rasped harshly against her skin.

Tess drew back. He grimaced at the marks the coarse stubble of his beard left on her tender skin. "I need to shave. And shower."

"Me, too."

"Come on."

He tugged her down the hall to his bedroom. Then he pressed her against the wall and kissed her deeply once more, taking extra care not to chafe her. He felt the earth move. His balls tightened as anticipation licked his skin.

"I'll use the other bathroom," he whispered hoarsely, stepping away.

"Wait."

The word hung in the air, stretching between them.

Tess met his gaze and knew she held the moment. He would do whatever she asked. Give her whatever she wanted.

And God, she wanted.

She put her hand on his chest, stopping him from leaving. "I need you," she whispered boldly, going up on tiptoe to press a kiss to his mouth. "To wash my back."

Her invitation undid Grey. He growled, pulling her closer, pressing her against his arousal. "Is that all you need?"

Her eyes grew dark, dilated. "No." Her hands dropped to his jeans, fondling him through the coarse denim. "I need this."

Grey groaned, then caught her wrists. "Let me shave. *First.*" He brushed a kiss to her lips, then released her, and disappeared into the bathroom.

Tess took advantage of the moment to catch her breath. She wanted Grey so bad it was frightening. No second thoughts. No regrets. Just pure, raw, desire. There would be no turning back.

She stripped off her clothes and stood outside the bathroom door. She thought back to the first time she and Grey had made love. It had been extraordinary. He'd been such a tender, giving lover. And each time they'd made love after that had simply been better and better.

She heard the water running in the shower, knew Grey had finished shaving. She thought of him naked and ready. Waiting. For her.

It was time.

She stepped inside the steamy bathroom and saw his muted outline behind the glass shower door.

Grasping her courage in hand, she opened the door slightly and drew in a sharp breath. Grey stood under the spray, eyes closed, water sluicing down his sharp cheekbones, dripping off the sexy cleft of his chin. His arms were raised, the muscles bunched as he rinsed shampoo from his hair.

She spied the Celtic cross tattoo, a reminder that Grey and Dallas were one and the same. She loved both.

Her eyes drifted down, admiring his well-muscled chest, the dark hair that arrowed down toward his trim waist to his erection. His engorged shaft sprang upward, curving heavily from a nest of dark curls. Huge. Thick. Throbbing. And hers for the taking.

Grey stepped forward, shaking the water from his eyes. He'd known the minute she'd entered. He'd watched her through slitted eyes as she admired his body, her glance lingering, shifting slowly lower.

Yeah, he'd enjoyed watching her look, liked the way her eyes had widened slightly when she saw how ready he was. He'd let her look her fill, gave her time to change her mind. *But not much . . .*

When she stepped into the shower he opened his arms. She moved into his embrace, let him shift her around so she was under the spray. Her hands went up, smoothing back her hair, wetting it completely.

He groaned. "You look sexy as hell." His hands crept up, catching her breasts, weighing them and reveling in their new fullness. She'd been more than a handful before getting pregnant. Now she burgeoned. *And they'd only get bigger?* He'd surely die. . . .

He captured her nipples between his thumbs and index fingers, rolling the twin peaks, testing their sensitivity. Tess moaned, biting her lip.

"Feel good?" he asked, tugging lightly. Testing. Watching pleasure slacken her features.

"It feels divine." She reached down, wanting to stroke Grey.

He sidestepped her, reaching for shampoo. "Shower, first. Remember? Turn around."

Reluctantly, Tess obliged, turning her back to Grey. He purposely pressed his erection against her back as he soaped her hair. Tess responded, rubbing her fanny against him.

"So finish telling me about the horny part."

Tess glanced over her shoulder, confused.

"Before we got interrupted," he reminded her, "you were just starting to explain the horny part of pregnancy."

She closed her eyes, enjoying the feel of his fingers as they massaged shampoo into her scalp, recalling the feel of his fingers, elsewhere. "Elise says pregnancy heightens the sex drive of certain women. They think about it constantly."

"Do you?"

Loaded question, she thought. "I don't think all of it's the pregnancy. I've thought about it constantly. Since meeting you." The words came out a tortured whisper.

Her admission nearly undid him. He had her back pressed fully against him now, his shaft sliding sinuously along the cleft of her bottom, the warm spray of water gilding their flesh. His hands drifted forward, lightly teasing her nipples.

Then he turned her in his arms and caught her lips in a demanding kiss. "You're all I've thought about for months. Come here."

She stepped closer and ran her hands down his chest, exulting in the feel of hard muscle beneath wet soapy skin. His arousal burned against her abdomen begging for her touch. Unable to resist, her fist closed around him, stroking firmly, the way he liked.

He seemed to grow impossibly harder, longer, in her grasp. Her hand slipped up and down his throbbing flesh, fascinated by this part of him.

Grey deepened the kiss, his tongue sweeping fully into her mouth. *Sweet Jesus!* She'd make him come if she kept up *that* motion much longer. Unable to stop himself, he pumped against her fist. Hard. Once, twice. Then pulled away.

"Let's rinse your hair," he growled.

Tess ducked back under the spray, as eager as he was to reach the bed. She felt very close to the edge, knew he was too. She rinsed the soap clean, then moved to let Grey under the water.

But he had other ideas. He'd used those few seconds to regain an iron control. He looked at her, eyes glinting with new determination. And held up a bottle of conditioner.

She shook her head. "Takes too long."

He grinned, opening the cap. "Three to five minutes." He squirted a generous dollop of creamy conditioner into his hand, the sound oddly erotic. "I can keep you busy three to five minutes."

He pulled her away from the water and quickly slathered her long locks with the cream. Then he kissed her again. Fierce. Demanding.

"Don't move," he whispered, running kisses down her

neck. His mouth moved lower, capturing first one pouty nipple, then the other. He touched her with only his mouth, elongating the nipple by sucking, then grazing his teeth against the sensitized nub.

Tess groaned, especially when his mouth clamped tightly over her, sucking hard. She could feel the first tingling of orgasm ripple over her and Grey wasn't touching her anywhere below the waist. He didn't even have a hand on her. Only his mouth. And tongue. And teeth.

She panted, fighting the sensation. Until he sucked even harder. She screamed, writhing frantically, grabbing for him as her first orgasm hit. But he stayed out of reach, pulling back just slightly, before switching to her other breast and wringing yet another orgasm from her.

Not stopping, he dropped to his knees spreading wildfire kisses across her swollen abdomen, and lower. His fingers parted her, exposing delicate flesh.

"Spread your legs," he bid.

Helpless, she complied. Taking his time, he inserted a long, thick finger inside her, probing, teasing, gradually slipping past her body's resistance. "You're wet. Dripping. And your clit's hard."

He flicked his thumb over it, then drew her to his mouth. His tongue traced her, licking and sucking, while his hands curved around her hips, holding her immobile as he focused fully on that one, single spot.

Electricity jolted down her spine, all feeling centered on the exact place Grey's mouth loved her.

"No," she cried. But her fingers were already tangled in his hair, holding him in place. Afraid, yet trusting, having never experienced this degree of sensual gratification.

Her hips bucked forward, urging him on. She rocked up on her toes and back, again and again, defenseless against the onslaught, unable to stop the waves of pleasure that were rapidly building.

She screamed his name, but Grey didn't remove his mouth until the last tremor of orgasm waned. He stood, pulling her gently forward, holding her briefly before turning her back under the water. "To rinse out the conditioner," he reminded her.

Tess stared at him, astounded by what he'd done to her. For her. And he hadn't even entered her yet, hadn't experienced his own release, while she'd orgasmed at least three times.

She glanced down at his erection. It was enormous now. The head was deep red, nearly crimson and looked painfully swollen, ready to burst.

"Come on," he urged.

Shaking her head, Tess grabbed the bar of soap from the ceramic holder and held it up.

"I'm not finished." And very deliberately she dropped the soap.

His sharp intake of air sounded agonizing.

Moving slowly, Tess lowered to her knees in front of him. She looked up, catching his gaze, holding it. The thought of him in her mouth made her shake with hot anticipation. But first . . .

She shifted her focus, reaching for his rigid penis. He was as stiff as he looked. Enthralled, she ran her hand down the length of him. And back. Measuring. He shuddered, groaning, the sound alluring, inviting.

She closed her hand around him, fascinated by the failure of her fingers to span his circumference, and his reaction as she tried. The skin here was incredibly soft, stretched over heated steel. So hot it burned. Would it scald her?

She shivered, eager to try . . . yet dubious. "Will it fit in my mouth?"

Grey hissed, could barely speak. "Try."

Growing bold, she held him firmly at the base and kissed only the tip. Then she ran her tongue along the flanged edge. Grey bucked, a violent, controlled surge of power.

"You like?" she asked.

"I like," he growled.

"Good," She felt his hands move to grasp her head as her mouth closed fully over the head. Instinctively, she drew him in farther, then withdrew, boring down, drawing back, mimicking the dance of life.

He swore. Wicked, nasty words. *Erotic*. The guttural tones excited her.

"I assume I'm doing this part right." She repeated the motion.

He sucked air between clenched teeth not certain whether he wished to live or die. "Baby, you're doing just fine."

She ran a hand across his tight buttocks, let her fingers edge downward along the cleft. "Put your hands behind your neck," she whispered. "And spread *your* legs."

She reached up, cupping his heavy sac, experimenting, fondling his swollen testicles before closing her mouth over his hot penis yet again. He heaved forward slightly, once, as if unable to stop himself.

Encouraged, she took him deeper, tracing her tongue along the veined underside. Allowing herself to explore the delicious sensation fully. He groaned in approval as her busy hands clenched him *there* yet again.

Already on tenterhooks, Grey looked down, unprepared for the sight of his cock disappearing in and out of her mouth. She glanced up, boldly staring. And held his gaze as she started sucking. *Hard*. Grey locked his knees and threw back his head as his universe buckled with sensation.

That was it! He pulled away, hauling her abruptly to her feet.

"But I wasn't finished." Her breathing was uneven.

"We'll finish together." His hands shook as he fumbled to shut off the water. He picked her up, carrying her to the bed, oblivious of the water dripping everywhere. "After that little trick, I won't last long. I want you too damn bad."

His mouth descended roughly on hers as he took her down onto the bed, his hands and mouth everywhere, teasing, plucking, fanning her desire to a raging inferno. She started begging.

"Please, Grey."

Splaying her legs, he surged into her, burying himself all the way in one incredible plunge that lifted them both off the bed. Her fingers dug into his shoulders at the swiftness of his invasion. She whimpered at the sensation of him filling her, stretching her. *Completing her.*

She wrapped her legs around his waist, clinging to him, taking him deeper. And bringing him in contact with her most sensitive spot.

Grey withdrew, his distended shaft dragging against her inner flesh, the hindrance almost painful, tormenting him before he surged forward yet again. She was hot and wet and impossibly tight.

He shuddered, recalling the sight of her mouth on his penis, sucking frantically, trying to take all of him. The strength it had taken not to shoot off . . .

He flexed deeper, the world seeming to grow smaller and smaller, until it was only the two of them and their frantic, grinding rhythm.

He watched ecstasy play across her face as he buried himself again and again in her slick, welcoming heat. *Coming home.*

She met him thrust for thrust, opening her mouth willingly, sweetly, to receive his tongue. And gave herself fully.

He branded hot kisses down her neck, not wanting it to

end. He rubbed his face in her cleavage before trailing more kisses across to capture a sulky nipple. His mouth clamped over her, his tongue pressing the elongated tip against the roof of his mouth, milking sensation from her.

His tough/tender suckling pushed Tess to the brink. Helpless, she screamed. And when she would have hurtled over the edge he caught her, kissing her deeply, before bringing them to a simultaneous climax.

Tess felt him stiffen before he began pumping furiously. Hot seed exploded in her, bathing her womb in wet, pulsating, heat. She heard her name leave his lips in a rush.

And in that one glorious second before she shattered, she knew that right or wrong, good or bad, *she loved him*.

The doorbell ringing in the middle on the night woke them both. Tess clamored for the sheet, disoriented as Grey slid from the bed.

"What—"

"Ssshhh."

Grey tugged on his jeans, then grabbed his gun. "Get dressed."

Tess scrambled from the bed. "Who can it be?"

The doorbell rang a second time. Whoever it was, was impatient. "It's probably nothing."

"Then why take your gun?"

Grey didn't answer. He moved to the door. "Lock this." He tossed her his cell phone. "If I'm not back in five minutes, call the police."

"But . . ."

He had already slipped out the door. Tess's first thought was to disobey and follow him anyway. Except . . . Grey was armed. If she startled him, she could accidentally be shot. Her hand slid to her stomach. The baby . . .

She locked the door, then stared at the cell phone, tempted to call the police immediately. Her heart pounded in her ears. This was the first time since the explosion in D.C. that she'd felt frightened. These last two days with Grey . . . she'd felt safe.

She pressed her ear to the door listening, hearing nothing.

Perhaps it was simply a stranded motorist seeking help for a disabled vehicle. They were out in the middle of nowhere. If you broke down out here, where would you go except to the closest house?

Besides, someone who meant them harm wouldn't come up and ring the doorbell. Right?

Grey cautiously made his way to the front door. The outside spotlight, triggered by motion detectors, shone through the front glass panels. Whoever it was didn't seem overly concerned by it.

Moving without noise, he pressed up to the front door and peeked out the glass.

Barry Neilson stood on the porch. Grey lowered his gun and moved to release the security chain.

"Sorry for waking you." Barry shifted his weight from one foot to the other.

Grey held the door open. "Come on in."

Tension bristled between the two men. For the first time he could ever remember, Grey felt awkward with his boss. Of course tonight had been the first time Grey had ever directly defied Barry. Or a direct order.

Barry could have sent marshals. The fact that he came himself meant Barry was under pressure. Everyone had a boss. And now that Snake and Bogen were back in custody the Bureau would want to keep tabs on Tess through normal channels.

"I needed time alone with her, Barry."

The other man nodded, stepping into the foyer. "Believe it or not, I understand. You love her. We all do things we normally wouldn't, to protect those we love."

Grey motioned toward the living room. "Have a seat. I'll get Tess."

He wanted to let her know it was only Barry. She'd been scared when he left and now he was eager to reassure her.

Grey started down the hall, then slowed as another thought occurred to him. *How did Barry know where to find them?*

Before he could turn, an excruciating pain exploded in his head. And everything went black.

~~

Tess stood beside the door, listening. From down the hall she could hear muffled voices. They weren't raised in anger. That had to be a good sign. If Grey were talking to someone . . .

She looked at the clock. He'd said five minutes and it had been four.

Just then a knock sounded on the door, a single rap that make her jump since she was pressed against it. The doorknob jiggled slightly.

"Tess? Open up. It's Barry Neilson."

Relief poured over her as she recognized his voice. She jammed Grey's cell phone in her pocket and unlocked the door.

Barry stood in the doorway, wearing a rumpled trench

coat that looked as if he'd slept in it. Tess motioned awkwardly toward the door. "Grey told me to lock it."

And not open it for anyone but him. Gooseflesh spread up her spine.

"Where's Grey?"

"He's in the living room. He said you'd be worried and asked me to get you."

She stepped through the door, preceding Barry. Before she made it halfway down the hall, he stopped her.

"Tess, there's something you need to know."

She turned.

And nearly ran into him. Barry reached out, a hand on either side, steadying her.

"It's about Grey," he began.

Tess leaned closer, her senses on alert. Something was wrong, she could feel it in the way her heart lurched.

That's when Barry's hands slid down her arms, bracketing her wrists. She felt cold metal press to her skin. Immediately she began struggling. Handcuffs. A creepy sense of déjà vu swamped her. *Bogen's camp. The pantry. The rats . . .*

She shuddered in revulsion. "Take these off! Now!"

"I can't, Tess." Regret shone from Barry's eyes. "Please understand."

"Grey!" Tugging her hands free, she began backing down the hallway. "Grey!"

The house remained ominously quiet. Her fears escalated. Something had to be wrong for him not to respond. Something bad.

"Where is he?" she demanded, never taking her eyes off Barry as she continued backing down the hall.

Her heel hit something solid, nearly causing her to topple. Stopping, she glanced down. Grey was crumpled facedown on the floor.

She screamed and dropped beside him. The back of his

head was covered with blood. She reached forward, gingerly grasping his shoulder thankful Barry hadn't cuffed her hands behind her.

Was he breathing?

She moved to check his pulse, but Barry tugged her back, his hands on her forearms as he forced her to her feet.

Tess fought. "What did you do? Let me help him!"

Barry shoved her against the wall. She hit with a painful thud. Her hands crossed over her midsection.

Barry stepped closer to Grey's body, his gun drawn. "That's right. Think of your child." He waved his gun toward the door. "Let's go."

"I won't leave him."

Barry pointed the gun toward Grey. "You will."

"Why are you doing this? You were his friend. He trusted you."

For a moment Tess thought she had touched a nerve. Barry seemed to waiver . . . then just as quickly shook it off.

"Why doesn't matter. But I'll make a deal with you. Come along peacefully, and I'll let you call 9-1-1 when we get to our destination."

"Let me call now. He could be dying!"

Barry shook his head.

Tess knew her options were limited. Barry was armed and obviously desperate. He could easily knock her out like he had Grey. She was better off cooperating. With Grey injured *she* was their only chance. Grey's cell phone was still in her pocket. If she got half a chance she'd use it.

"Where are you taking me?"

"No questions."

"But—"

Barry held his gun up, right in her face, his voice raised on a note of impatience. "No buts. No more waiting. Let's go."

Hostage.

Tess's feet suddenly refused to move. The thought that this could be happening to her yet again was paralyzing.

She looked at Grey, remembering their fierce lovemaking of mere hours ago. She loved him. She'd always loved him. And she'd never told him.

Barry's hand closed over her forearm. Tears blurred her vision but still she stared at Grey's unmoving form, willing him to live.

Willing him to find her.

~

It was still dark when they reached their destination. *Pirate's Cove Marina*, Wrightsville Beach, North Carolina.

Tess looked out the car window. At first glance she thought the place looked deserted due to off-season. A second glance told her the marina was abandoned.

Barry helped her out of the car. "You promised if I cooperated I could call for help, for Grey," she reminded him.

She'd kept her end of the bargain.

"In a minute," he stalled.

"Where are we going?" She couldn't keep the catch from her voice.

"You'll see."

They walked past a boarded-up shack advertising live bait. Empty beer bottles littered the ground. A single lightbulb burned dimly on one side of the building, attracting moths. The cool air was tangy with the brackish scent of salt water.

Involuntarily she pulled back as Barry headed toward the deserted pier.

Water . . .

She recalled the night Liz had shoved her into the lake. How Dallas . . . *Grey* had rescued her.

Tonight there'd be no rescue. Grey was over a hundred miles away. He could even be dead. Her knees buckled.

"Come on." Barry tugged her arm.

"I . . . I can't."

Barry looked nervously at the end of the pier. "Then we'll wait here."

"Wait?" At that moment a faint sound caught her ear. A boat engine. Heading this way.

The sound grew louder. A few seconds later Tess saw the small green starboard light as a craft headed directly for them.

Sweat beaded on her forehead. "Damn you, Barry! Tell me what's going on!"

He ignored her. The boat slowed, waves breaking against the dock and seawall as it pulled up at the very end.

Tess strained to see who was in the boat. She heard muffled sounds, felt the dock rock slightly as the boat bounced against it. Heavy footsteps approached, boards creaking.

"Stop right there," Barry said, his gun drawn. "I've kept my end of the bargain. What about you?"

A man stepped forward into the small pool of light. Dressed in an Armani suit with a flower in his lapel, he looked out of place in the shabby setting. Foreign. Behind him, tucked in the shadows, were three or four other people. How many she couldn't be certain.

"Greetings, Ms. Marsh." The man spoke with a pronounced Hispanic accent. "We haven't met formally, but I've heard a lot about you."

Barry held his ground. "Our deal, Sanchez."

Sanchez.

Tess's stomach sank as she realized who it was. Hector

Sanchez. The cartel's number one henchman. *Free on a technicality to commit more crimes at will.*

Sanchez made an annoyed sound, then snapped his fingers.

Two figures from behind him started moving. When they got a little closer, Tess noticed that one was a female in her mid-twenties.

"Daddy!" the woman cried.

Barry lurched, visibly shaken. Now Tess knew why Barry had double-crossed them. Sanchez had his daughter.

Barry's next words confirmed her worst fear. "I've brought the Marsh woman."

"She doesn't look pregnant." Sanchez stepped closer. He was tall and surprisingly good-looking, proving evil came in all shapes and sizes. His dark hair was slicked back and clubbed in a short ponytail. He had a thin, black mustache.

Tess glanced at Barry. "Please don't—"

She choked on her remaining words, knowing that he wouldn't betray his own daughter for her. Tess was a bargaining chip. His daughter's ticket to freedom.

Barry pointed his gun directly at Sanchez. "Release my daughter. Now."

Sanchez started laughing, an oddly melodic sound that echoed across the water.

"You are a fool," Sanchez said.

A gun fired.

Tess flinched. The sound came from behind them. Her first instinct was to run except Barry still held her by the arm. For a moment his grip tightened, then it relaxed.

"No!" From the shadows Barry's daughter started crying hysterically.

Barry fell to his knees. With an awful horror, Tess realized he'd been shot. As if confirming her thought, a man strolled out from the shadows behind them, his gun still drawn.

"You double-crossing bastard." Barry was breathing heavy.

Tess dropped beside him, but could do little with her hands cuffed together. A dark stain spread across the front and back of Barry's shirt. The bullet had passed all the way through his body, at his shoulder.

Barry still clenched his gun, but the shooter was right beside him now. "Drop it," the man ordered.

When Barry hesitated, the man kicked his hand, sending the gun sailing into the water and snapping Barry's wrist in the process. Tess cringed at the awful sound of bone shattering.

Barry moaned, the pain obviously intense. "My daughter, Sanchez! Don't kill me in front of her."

Barry's daughter was beyond hysteria now, sobbing uncontrollably.

Sanchez laughed. "We're not going to kill you, my friend. I need you alive to deliver a message to Special Agent Grey Thomas."

"I could have brought you Thomas!" Barry rasped.

"No need. He'll come. And she's the insurance that he'll come alone."

"Grey won't fall for it."

"Sure he will. You did. Love makes monkeys of us all."

The man who shot Barry moved closer and yanked Tess to her feet, tugging her away.

"No," she resisted. "He needs a doctor!"

Sanchez interrupted. "You're a smart woman, Ms. Marsh. Don't make us use force. Think of your child."

Her child. Tears blinded her as she was dragged forward.

When they reached Sanchez, the gunman released her. From behind them, in the shadows, she heard Barry's daughter weeping.

Sanchez nodded to the gunman. "Finish up. Just remember he needs to live long enough to make a phone call."

Tess flinched when Sanchez ran his hand down her cheek. "You are a beautiful woman. And strong. This will be . . . interesting."

Turning away, Sanchez gave an order to one of the other men behind him.

"Bring the Marsh woman."

The man nodded and stepped forward. "Hello, darlin'. Long time, no see."

Tess's knees buckled as Snake stepped up and grabbed her.

Chapter Sixteen

Grey's head felt like someone had tried to dynamite it off his shoulders. His heart hurt even worse.

"If you won't go to the hospital, at least let me take you back to Chapel Hill, where Elise can check you." Kevin Barnes, Elise's husband, squatted in front of Grey. "I'm no doctor, but I'm sure you have a concussion—"

"Tell me again what Barry said."

Kevin sighed. "Sanchez has Tess and Barry's daughter. He claims he'll release both women in exchange for you. Unarmed and alone."

"When and where?"

"Tonight—9 P.M. off the coast. The GPS coordinates Sanchez gave Barry are about twelve miles offshore from Wrightsville Beach."

"In international waters." Grey grimaced, attempting to stand. "Then I better get moving. That's twelve hours from now. And I've got to procure a boat."

Kevin straightened, reaching out to help his friend. "You're not really going through with this, are you? Sanchez will double-cross you, like he did Barry. Let the Bureau handle it."

"I can't risk Tess and the baby. I know Sanchez plans to

kill me. But if I can just live long enough to get close to her, I have a chance at helping her."

"You can help her more going through proper channels."

"I can't."

"You have to."

"I doubt Barry is the only inside contact Sanchez has. If word of a rescue is leaked—" Grey cut the thought short. "I thought you of all people would understand."

"Damn it! I do understand. And right now I'm thinking more clearly than you."

Grey hated that his friend was right. The thought of Tess in Sanchez's hands made him crazy. Knowing Snake and Bogen were with Sanchez was worse. "I have to go, Kevin. I'm her only hope. It's my fault they've got her to begin with."

Grey had committed the unpardonable sin of heading to familiar ground. That was the first place cops checked. It made Barry's job of finding them that much easier. He had failed Tess and their child once. He wouldn't fail them again.

"I'm going with you. We'll figure out some way to hide me."

While Grey knew that Kevin was sincere in his offer, he also knew Kevin felt guilty. Kevin had disclosed the cabin's location to Barry after Barry told him the fictitious story about Snake and Bogen being recaptured.

Grey didn't blame Kevin in the least. Barry's defection stunned them all.

Barry had been able to reach Kevin by phone again, explaining the situation and delivering Sanchez's message before lapsing into unconsciousness. Besides suffering a gunshot, Barry had been badly beaten and was currently undergoing surgery. From what Kevin said his chances at recovery weren't all that great.

"Sanchez will have spies posted all over Wrightsville Beach. He'll know if I arrive in town with someone."

"Who says you gotta go out of Wrightsville? Your only stipulation is to be at the GPS coordinates at nine."

"Alone."

Kevin ignored the word. "We can go farther south, to Long Beach. I know a guy who owns a marina near there."

Grey's head throbbed. "I don't like it. I need to go by myself."

Kevin shrugged. "You're walking into a trap."

"That doesn't change a thing."

"Then at least let me help. You're in no shape to drive right now. And you need someone on the outside to know what's going on—in case you don't return."

Both men knew he really meant *when you don't return.*

Grey closed his eyes. Kevin did have one valid point. Grey couldn't drive right now. He had double vision, a sure sign of a concussion.

"Then let's get going. We don't have much time, and I want to make a few stops on the way."

The skiff ride to Sanchez's yacht was blessedly short. Tess tried to comfort Barry's daughter, Nancy, which helped keep her own mind off the fact they were on *water.*

Several times she caught Hector Sanchez staring, which unnerved her. Was he sizing her up for punishment? Or the auction block? With increasing dread, she remembered that Sanchez had personally raped every woman he'd taken captive. Had Nancy already been victimized?

Once they reached the larger craft Nancy was taken below deck by one of the men on board. A pair of greyhounds danced excitedly at Sanchez's feet. She counted seven men including Snake and Bogen, who both glared at her.

The men gathered close, forming a semicircle around Tess. Snake stepped forward, flashing a knife. She backed away, but another man shoved her forward, back toward Snake.

Snake clearly relished her fear. "Gotta strip-search you, darlin'. Same shit they did to me in jail." One of the other men laughed. "Drop your jeans."

Tess shook her head, unable to speak, more afraid than she'd ever been in her life. They had patted her down before leaving the dock, finding and confiscating the cell phone. This would be far worse.

"Fine. I'll do it myself." Snake took a step forward.

Sobbing, Tess held out her still-cuffed hands. "No!" With shaking fingers she unbuttoned her jeans, shoving them down as best she could before kicking free of them. *The baby.* She thought of Grey's child, knew she was willing to suffer anything to keep it safe.

Cold air stung her bare legs.

"Watch this." With that Snake moved up, grabbing the end of her T-shirt. She pulled back, inadvertently assisting him as he ripped her shirt open clear to the neck.

Flashing his knife yet again, Snake easily slit the shoulder seams. The shredded cotton fell to her feet, leaving her standing in nothing but her bra and panties. She was shaking violently. From cold. *From fear.*

Snake yanked her bra up, exposing her, before cruelly twisting one of her nipples. She cried out in pain and swung her arms out.

Snake roared, lunging for her.

"Enough!" Hector Sanchez broke through the crowd and stood in front of her. "We've got work to do."

As the men sauntered off, Sanchez turned and slowly rearranged her bra. Tess turned her face, recoiling in revulsion at the feel of his hands on her. While she was grateful for his intervention, she harbored no illusions that Sanchez had a soft spot. She knew by the look on his face that he was merely saving her for himself.

Sanchez caught her chin, forced her gaze back to his. "It will be good. You'll see."

He crooned something in Spanish, his tone low, his hands brushing down her sides. She cringed.

Sanchez laughed. "I find your fear *arousing*. Take her below," he ordered.

To Tess's relief, she was taken to the same room as Barry's daughter. Nancy had also been stripped down to her underwear. She sat huddled on the floor, crying softly. The guard unfastened her handcuffs then chained Tess to the leg of a table and left.

"Did they hurt you?" Tess asked.

Nancy shook her head. "This is all my fault. My dad's probably dead, and it's all because of me."

"You can't blame yourself for what these men are doing."

"Oh, but I can!" Nancy's voice broke. "Sanchez and I go way back."

Through fits and starts, Tess pieced together the story. When Nancy's mother died six years ago, Nancy started using drugs to deal with her loss. She'd turned to prostitution to support her habit.

She was living in a cartel compound in Mexico when her father finally located her. But she didn't want to leave or give up her drug habit. Her father formed a brief alliance with Hector Sanchez, which allowed Barry to come in and snatch his daughter and return to the States. Nancy spent a year in a private clinic overcoming her problems.

What kind of price had Sanchez demanded of Barry over the years in exchange for that favor?

Tess closed her eyes, thinking of Grey. Was he okay? Had someone found him yet? Looking back, she realized Barry never intended to let her call for help. He'd merely held out that hope to force her cooperation.

And while she knew Sanchez had left instructions for Grey with Barry, there was no guarantee that Barry had indeed conveyed the message. Barry had not only been shot, but was being beaten when they'd been escorted off the dock.

The penalty for being a cop, Snake said. Tess knew the penalty for being a cop who sold them out would be even worse. Sanchez wanted personal revenge on Grey for infiltrating his operation.

Nancy was crying again, and Tess wished she could hold the girl. "You've got to think positive," Tess whispered. "That your father's alive and that help will come."

That was the only thing keeping Tess from losing it.

That Grey was alive and could somehow free them.

Kevin and Grey reached Long Beach without problem. Since Kevin knew the marina's owner, he was able to procure a fast, late-model powerboat without question. The price for doing so was Grey's promise that Kevin would accompany him. "I won't let you go alone."

Night was falling. They were sitting in Kevin's car, studying nautical charts by flashlight. "I wouldn't worry too much about these. The boat's got a state-of-the-art autopilot. Once we're out of the intracoastal waterway we can plug in the GPS coordinates and let her do the hard work."

Grey checked his vision. An ice pack had helped ease the swelling on the back of his head, and, in turn, the double vision and nausea had subsided. At least for now.

Looking at his watch, Grey started rolling up the charts. "You've got the guns? Ammo?"

Kevin nodded. Between the two of them they were carrying four handguns. Plus they had a small arsenal hidden on the boat. Both would likely be searched. Hiding Kevin was the trickiest part. They had finally agreed Kevin would go over the side in a heavy wet suit with dive equipment.

Or so Kevin believed.

Grey picked up the metal handcuffs lying on the seat between them. Moving swiftly he snapped one cuff on Kevin's wrist, simultaneously snapping the other to the steering wheel.

Kevin started swearing. "Don't be an ass, Grey! Unlock these! This is a suicide mission."

Grey shook his head and climbed out of the car. "I hope you're wrong. But if you're not, you've got four kids with two more on the way. They need you. So does Elise."

Kevin tugged uselessly on the cuff. "As soon as I'm free, I'm calling it in, Grey. The Coast Guard will stop you before you even make it to international waters."

"No you won't." Grey met his friend's eyes. "You've got to give me a chance to save Tess. And if the worst happens, you'll see that somebody goes after her."

~~~

Grey reached the designated spot thirty minutes early and shut off his engine. The ocean was calm even though he could see nothing in the dark. Stars twinkled overhead, reminding him of another starry night, when he'd first met Tess.

God, let her and the baby be safe.

For the millionth time he wondered how she fared. Who knew what they'd done to her. Or what they had planned.

He checked his watch, then began double-checking his cache of firearms. There was a strong possibility Tess and Nancy wouldn't even be on the boat meeting him. But if they were, their safety was paramount in Grey's mind.

Damn, he wished he had a plan. But until he knew where she was and how many people he was up against, he couldn't even hypothesize.

Waves lapped gently against the hull as he listened for an approaching boat. But the night remained quiet.

At nine-fifteen he started pacing. In all likelihood Sanchez was toying with him. But what if Barry, in his injured state, had gotten the coordinates wrong . . .

It was nearly midnight when Grey heard a motor. On the water it was difficult to tell which direction it came from.

Moving swiftly, he turned on his running lights. The noise grew steadier until Grey finally saw lights off the port side. When the craft got close enough he studied it through night-vision binoculars. His concern that it might be another boat other than Sanchez's evaporated instantly.

As befitted the cartel, the boat was a sixty-foot cabin cruiser. Armed men stood on either end of the boat, machine guns drawn and ready. Grey spotted Sanchez, Snake, and Bogen on the deck, along with at least two other men. So far he'd counted eight people including the pilot. Bad odds.

He swept the approaching boat one last time, searching for a sign of Tess or Nancy, finding none. He'd already accepted the possibility that he'd be killed without ever seeing her again. *Without ever telling her he loved her.*

The yacht slowed as it drew near. Grey was temporarily blinded as the yacht turned on its searchlights and swept his boat before spotlighting him.

The beam was so powerful Grey could feel its heat. He held up his hands, indicating falsely that he was unarmed.

When the yacht pulled up a mooring line was tossed over. "Tie it off and step back," the man in front yelled.

Grey did as he was told. The man then jumped from the larger boat onto Grey's. A second man followed.

"Hands on your head," the man shouted.

When Grey complied the man stepped forward and patted Grey down. They found his knife and three guns. After they finished their search, the guard slammed Grey in the jaw with the butt of his rifle. Grey fell backward, pain radiating through his whole body.

While one man held him at gunpoint the other searched the boat, tossing weapons to the deck as he found them. "All clear," the man finally shouted.

"Greetings, *amigo*." Sanchez ambled over to the railing and looked down. "Long time, no squeal."

No sooner had Grey pushed to his feet than the guard delivered a second blow, in the stomach this time, causing Grey to drop to his knees. He fought the spinning dizziness that made him want to vomit, knowing he had to be strong for Tess's sake. And the worst was yet to come. Sanchez was merely fucking with him right now. Cat and mouse.

The real pain would come later. The cartel dealt harshly with traitors. And Grey's defection would merit the fiercest of punishments. He would die at their hands. Eventually.

But first he had to get word to Tess, let her know that others would be searching for her. That no matter what happened, she had to go on—for him. *For their child.*

"Where is she?" Grey yelled. "I want to see her."

Sanchez and the others began laughing. "That's what I liked best about you. Your colossal arrogance. Even now you think you can give orders."

Snake stepped up beside Sanchez. "It's gonna be fun

watching you beg us to kill you. We're taking bets on how long you live once we start. The minimum is three days. Winner gets a wallet made from your hide."

Grey knew Snake was serious. The cartel was capable of the most inhumane of tortures. But he couldn't let himself think of that right now.

"I can still be of use to you, Sanchez," Grey shouted. "I've got a lot of Bureau secrets I'd be willing to share. You need me." It would all be lies, but it might buy him time.

"The only thing I need you for is this." Sanchez nodded, and Grey received another resounding blow with a rifle stock. This time on his knee, shattering bone. Blinding spots of color shot across Grey's field of vision as he fought to control the pain.

"Now pay attention," Sanchez said. "You wanted to see your girlfriend. Here she is."

Grey watched as a guard brought Tess up to the rail. His heart lurched at the sight of her. She was wearing nothing more than her bra and panties, her hands cuffed behind her. She dragged her feet, pulling away.

Then she spied him. "Grey!" she sobbed.

His adrenaline spiked at seeing her. As best he could tell she was unharmed.

"You're okay?" he called.

She nodded.

"No matter what, remember I love you always," he shouted. "The baby, too."

Sanchez made as if to wipe a tear from his cheek. "So touching. I'm sure your words will comfort her after you're gone." He moved up to Tess, trailing a hand across her stomach. "And after the baby is gone as well."

"No!" Tess struggled uselessly as the guard pressed her forward against the rail.

"I'm sorry my dear," Sanchez lamented. "But your body

is a commodity. Having a child will lower its value." His hand drifted upward, reaching into her bra and fondling one breast. "Let's give your lover one last look."

"You're dead, Sanchez!" Grey lunged forward just as all hell broke loose.

Shots rang out from either end of the boats. Two of the guards on Sanchez's boat fell. The man beside Grey screamed, then dropped.

Moving quickly, Grey swung round, catching the other guard's gun and shoving it hard into the man's chest. The man lost balance and fell. Grey dived for the gun just as a dark-clad figure sprung over the end of the boat.

Divers. Coast Guard and FBI.

Grey spun back toward Sanchez's boat. Four armed divers were on that boat, one with a gun on Snake, another with a gun on Bogen. The other two had their weapons trained on Sanchez . . . who held Tess, a gun pressed to her temple.

Grey's heart lodged in his throat. He limped forward.

"Give it up, Sanchez. You're outnumbered and outgunned."

"Ahh . . . but look who I've got? *Mamacita.* Tell them to back off, or she gets it."

"You won't get away."

"That's not the question. Whether your girlfriend survives or not is. I beat your system once on a technicality. I can do it again. But can your girlfriend and her child survive a bullet to the head, at close range?" Sanchez cocked the gun.

Tess felt the cold metal press into her temple, heard the awful *click* as the gun's cylinder advanced.

She looked at Grey, remembering his words. *I love you always.* If her life was to end, there was something she had to say.

"I love you always, too."

Sanchez started laughing behind her, his voice loud in her

ear. He shook with his mirth. "You two make me sick, with all your talk of love. You're *loco*."

When Sanchez dissolved in another fit of laughter, he loosened his grip slightly.

Without a second thought, Tess took advantage of the movement, unlocking her knees and dropping straight down. Catching Sanchez off guard for mere seconds, giving the FBI a clear target, was her only chance. She had to take it; prayed it was enough.

Two shots rang out in the night.

Grey watched in horror as Tess crumpled to the deck, Sanchez on top of her. Ignoring his own injuries he clambered onto the larger boat.

"Tess!" he called, as one of the divers cautiously pulled Sanchez off her.

Her sobs told him she was alive. Grey tugged her into his arms, frantically checking her for a bullet wound.

"I'm fine," she wept.

Grey kept her face averted as he looked down at Sanchez's body. Twin bullet holes—one on either side of his temple—punctured Sanchez's skull.

Grey saluted the two divers. Then he pointed to Bogen and Snake. "These two men are fugitives."

One of the divers tossed a blanket to Grey, which he promptly wrapped around Tess.

The diver, an FBI agent Grey had worked with before, nodded toward Tess. "She's okay?"

Grey nodded. "Barnes tip you off?"

"Yeah. You owe him your ass."

Kevin had obviously escaped the handcuffs. Kevin knew the GPS coordinates, the players involved and the back story. He also knew exactly who to call at the Bureau to make things happen fast. Thank God . . .

"Any word on Barry?" Grey had to ask.

"Died in surgery."

Another diver accompanied Barry's daughter to the deck. "Don't tell her now," Grey said. "Not out here."

The night came alive with noise as the *whap-whap-whap* of an approaching helicopter filled the air. Lights from approaching boats dotted the horizon.

"You're hurt," Tess looked at Grey.

"It's nothing. Is the baby okay?"

She nodded shifting. "He's pretty tough. Like his dad."

Grey pressed a kiss to her temple. "Will you marry me, Tess?"

"Yes."

He tugged her close as the helicopter swept low over the boat, "I'll propose properly later," he yelled.

"In that case I take back my yes—until later." She looked cautiously at the activity around them. "It it really over?"

"The bad part. The good is just beginning."

His lips swept down, capturing hers as his hand brushed protectively against her abdomen. Abruptly, he broke off the kiss.

"Was that what I think it was?"

Tess smiled, tears glistening in her eyes. She covered his hand with her own and nodded.

"Our baby's first kick."

Epilogue

Five Months Later—New York City

promise to love—*oowww*—honor and cherish you all the days of my life." Tess was breathing heavy now, wanting to kick the minister. If he didn't hurry . . .

Grey looked suspiciously at Tess, noting the fine sheen of perspiration on her forehead. He turned to the dumbstruck minister, prompting him.

"I think now might be a good time to pronounce us man and wife."

Tess nodded, unable to hold back another groan.

The red-faced minister hurriedly muttered the words, his voice squeaking. "You may kiss the bride."

Grey ignored the man, prying the bouquet of roses from Tess's grip and thrusting them at his new mother-in-law. "How long have you been having contractions?" he asked quietly.

Madeline Marsh lost all color. "Oh my God! She's having the baby," she shrieked. "Get a doctor! Call an ambulance! We need pain medication!"

Tess squeezed Grey's hand, closing her eyes against the rising pain. "They started this morning, then stopped."

"Why didn't you tell me?" He held up a hand, cutting her

off. "Don't tell me. You wanted to be married before the baby came."

Tess nodded, miserable. She had also insisted they wait to marry until the trials were over. After numerous postponements, Bogen and Snake were finally convicted on first-degree murder last week.

Grey brushed a kiss to her cheek. "Don't you think this is pushing it?"

"Push, yes." Her face grew flushed as another contraction wracked her. "I thought I had plenty of time. They say the first baby takes forever."

Grey checked his watch. "How close are your contractions?"

"I . . . don't . . . know . . ."

Too close. Grey was already moving her toward the elevator, praying they had enough time to make it to the hospital. He looked around at the startled guests, not surprised to find a hundred pairs of eyes watching.

What was supposed to be a small family wedding in the ballroom at the top of the Marsh Manhattan had quickly mushroomed once Madeline had become involved. But at least she'd been more supportive.

Grey nodded at Madeline. "I think now is a good time to break out the champagne. Just save us a bottle."

Kevin Barnes pushed through the crowd, gently taking Tess's other arm. "Elise just stepped out to pump some breast milk."

Tess squealed. Kevin grew pale, and backed away. "I'll go find her."

"We'll meet you downstairs," Grey called as the elevator doors opened. He helped Tess inside, then punched the button for the lobby, thankful they were in a private elevator.

He looked at his wife. *His wife.* After all these months,

Tess was his. He didn't deserve her. Didn't deserve this precious gift of life her body was prepared to give.

She wore a full-length, off-the-shoulder white gown, with a long beaded veil that trailed behind her. He touched her protruding stomach reverently, knew he'd never get tired of seeing her like this . . . already thinking about getting her pregnant again. And again. And again.

"Did I tell you how beautiful you look? How happy you've made me?"

She shook her head. "We didn't even get pictures. Ohhh!"

Grey touched her shoulder, taking in her obvious discomfort, wishing he could do more. "Want to start the breathing exercises?"

"No . . . my water just broke."

Grey felt a moment's panic as he glanced up and saw that they still had twentysomething floors to go. He needed to distract her. "Pant, sweetheart!"

They were both thrown off-balance when the elevator suddenly jolted and started to slow. Grey's arms shot out, catching her, holding her.

The lights flickered twice then went out. The elevator lurched to a stop and immediately a yellow glow lit the cubicle as the emergency battery-powered lights came on.

"What happened?" Tess demanded.

"Power failure." Grey depressed the emergency button twice, then turned just as Tess started sinking toward the floor.

"I can't hold it." She grimaced, then screamed. "Oh, God!"

Grey whipped off his coat and dropped down beside her, grasping her hand. A strong contraction shook her, causing her to raise up.

"Squeeze my arm," he encouraged. "We'll be out of here before you know it."

Her nails dug into him as a second contraction gripped her. "Too late. It's coming. Now," she panted.

"Now?"

Disbelieving, Grey peeked under her frothy wedding dress surprised to find the baby's head cresting.

Just like in the video he'd watched a thousand times.

He'd never felt so inadequate in his entire life.

Shoving her gown out of the way, he yanked off her shoes and quickly peeled off her nylons. *Not a moment too soon.*

"Push," he ordered.

Tess screamed, bearing down.

"Again," he said.

Tess screamed once more, straining.

"Good girl. Once more."

Tess fell back, sobbing. "I can't."

Another contraction overtook her. Grey moved behind her, holding her, urging her. "We'll do it together. Push!"

Buoyed by her husband's strength, Tess pushed. And panted. And pushed yet again.

Ten minutes later, Chelsea Marsh Thomas drew her first breath, in her father's hands, and began crying right along with both of her parents.

More
Lauren Bach!

Please turn this page
for a
sneak peek
at

SLOW HANDS

Available Summer 2002
from Warner Books.

Alec Dempsey preferred to stay north of the Mason-Dixon Line. Way north. Like Seattle.

He wasn't happy to be in Tennessee, in a suit and tie, in the stuffy conference room of the Memphis FBI field office.

He also preferred to work with his own kind. ATF. Alcohol, Tobacco, and Firearms.

FBI agents hogged the spotlight in joint ventures. They had huge egos, big superiority complexes. *Little dicks.*

The two FBI agents sequestered with him were prime examples. Condescending, but polite. After all, they wanted something from him.

His boss said he'd been specifically requested for this assignment. His gut told him that wasn't a good sign. He'd just been cleared for active duty after two months warming a desk. He didn't want to play second string.

Special Agent Horace Phelps, balding and overweight, sat directly across the table. He bared his teeth in what Alec presumed was a smile.

"I'll cut to the chase, Dempsey. We want you for an undercover job in Freedom, Arkansas."

The tightness in Alec's middle increased. "You're joking." He looked from Phelps to the second agent leaning silently against the wall. Neither man laughed. "Undercover? In my hometown?"

"Yeah. You'll go in as yourself," Phelps went on. "The prodigal son."

From what Alec recalled, the prodigal son was welcomed home with open arms. He doubted many people in Freedom even remembered him. And the one person who knew him best would probably prefer to see him crucified.

Though he already knew he'd refuse the assignment, he feigned interest, more than a little curious. "What does the FBI want in Freedom?"

Phelps slid a mug shot across the table. "This guy

look familiar? Ian Griggs. AKA inmate number 84736. You went to school with one of his younger brothers."

Alec looked at the photo, eyes narrowed. He remembered the brothers Griggs. They'd been the town scourge. Bad seeds, all three of them. And they'd come to an even worse end.

"I think half the country remembers those boys," Alec drawled.

Five years ago, Ian Griggs and his two brothers hijacked an armored truck outside Little Rock and made off with two million in cash. The money was never recovered. Alec recalled the story. Or at least the sensational headlines the media frenzy garnered. As rumor spread that the pilfered cash was stashed in the Ozarks, treasure hunters descended in droves, clashing frequently with private landowners, and even forced the closing of several state parks.

The news coverage had also brought to light another, lesser-known, story that Alec had followed with far more interest. His unease grew.

"The men were subsequently arrested, but two of the brothers died from wounds received during a shoot-out with police," Phelps continued. "Ian Griggs went to prison, refusing to plea-bargain the location of the money in exchange for a reduced sentence."

Alec frowned. "Don't tell me Griggs wants to strike a deal now?"

Phelps shook his head. "He doesn't need to. His sentence got commuted. Which means he qualifies for parole at the end of this month. He's been a model prisoner, and we believe the request will be granted."

"You're not opposing it?"

"We're pressing for supervised probation in a halfway house in Freedom." Phelps leaned forward. "He's got two million reasons to return, and we want someone there to watch him."

While the news of Griggs's likely parole surprised Alec, it didn't shock him. He'd been with ATF five years. Army Special Forces before that. He knew justice wasn't always served and he accepted that. Except in this instance. Ian Griggs had never even been tried for the worst of his crimes. *Assault and battery. Attempted rape.*

"You're perfect for this job," Phelps pressed.

Alec shoved the photo away. He'd heard enough. He'd left Freedom ten years ago, sworn he'd never return. It had been the right choice then. It was the right choice now.

Pushing his chair back, Alec stood. "Find someone else."

Phelps's fake smile evaporated as he scrambled to his feet. "There is no one else, and time is short. You know yourself how tight-knit those people are. Fucking clannish. And they can spot a fed a mile away."

Meaning the FBI had already tried and failed. Alec could imagine the problems they'd encountered trying to plant an agent in town. Ignorant people, like Phelps, thought of Freedom in terms of Dogpatch. Thought everyone there was a hillbilly relative of Snuffy Smith. A little condescension went a long way in Freedom.

"An ATF agent would be particularly unwelcome," Alec pointed out. Besides being the hometown of the state's most notorious criminals, Freedom, Arkansas had a pre–Civil War history of producing the finest moonshine in the South. Thanks largely to ATF anti-crime initiatives, few people actually made a living making 'shine anymore, though lots of old-timers kept stills. *And believed the only good revenue agent was a dead one.*

"So we fudge that part." Phelps had an answer for everything. "You've been undercover since joining ATF. Outside of your immediate supervisor, who knows your real employer?"

"My mortgage company. American Express."

Phelps snorted. "I'm serious."

"So am I." Alec took a step toward the door. "I'm not interested in this job."

"Keira Morgan is in danger." The second agent, Miles Ostman, who'd been quiet up to now, moved forward. *Mr. Nice Guy*

Alec turned. He recognized the ploy. Good cop, asshole cop. Agent Phelps cleared his throat and sat back down, grinning, arms tucked behind his neck, his part of the job complete.

Alec closed the door and leaned against it, legs spread slightly. "What about Keira?"

"Ian Griggs blames her for the death of his brothers," Ostman said. "Word is he's going back to Freedom to claim his cash *and* to settle the score with Miss Morgan."

"Take her into protective custody. Now."

"The request got denied."

"By whom? Did they know what Griggs did to her before the robbery?"

"Officially, charges were dropped." Ostman shrugged, noncommittal. "It's probably just talk. Griggs would be a fool to jeopardize his parole for the sake of vengeance. We figure he'll grab the loot and run."

Alec's jaw tensed. He was being manipulated, didn't like it. He knew Griggs's history, knew the man posed a very real danger to Keira. And they knew he knew. "If you know about my past with Keira Morgan, then you know I'm the last person she'd want to see."

"We'll handle that," Ostman countered smoothly. "Before you go in."

"Using what cover?" *Prodigal SOB?*

"We'll play it like you've just been discharged from the Army, following an injury from an explosion. You've completed physical therapy and are looking for a quieter, safer line of work."

Alec *had* just completed physical therapy. "And why would I look in Freedom?"

"You used to be fairly close to Keira Morgan."

Fairly close was the mother of all understatements. At one time, Alec couldn't envision life without her.

"She's still attractive as hell, currently unattached . . ." Ostman let the sentence hang. "In fact, you used to work construction with her, didn't you? Electrical contracting? She owns her own business now, and we hear she's hiring."

Ostman's innuendo didn't faze Alec. Exploitation— or sexploitation—was the chief weapon in an undercover arsenal. The FBI wouldn't think twice about asking him to seduce his way back into town. What bothered him was the underlying note of desperation in Ostman's voice.

"You're blowing smoke," Alec said. "What are you really after?"

The two agents exchanged glances. Phelps shrugged.

Alec turned away.

"Wait. You win. But this doesn't leave the room." Ostman pulled out a crushed box of Marlboros. "The truck Griggs knocked off that night was one of old man Ciccone's. Used to transport his freshly laundered money."

Alec recognized the name. Joseph Ciccone headed up the south-central mob. Had his fingers in everything illegal from Memphis to New Orleans, then ran legitimate businesses, like the armored truck service, to cover.

"You want to protect Griggs from Ciccone?"

Ostman shook his head. "Don't need to. They're practically in bed together."

"You're kidding?" Most people who crossed Ciccone ended up dead. Hell, Ciccone could have had Griggs executed in prison.

"Griggs has something Ciccone wants," Ostman continued.

"The two million?" Alec raised an eyebrow. "I guess that's a lot of dough to lose even if you are Joseph Ciccone."

Ignoring the NO SMOKING placard, Ostman lit up a cigarette. "Believe it or not, Ciccone's not out a dime. Insurance ate the loss. Ciccone's real good at covering his tracks, so on paper it all looks legit. He's greedy, though. Wants it all. We believe Ciccone's offered Griggs a deal. Ciccone bribes a judge or two, calls in a favor from someone on the parole board. Griggs gets out, recovers the money, and gives most of it back to Ciccone, who makes out like a bandit. Until we bust him with stolen property."

Bingo, Alec thought. The FBI didn't care about Ian Griggs or the money. *Or Keira.* They wanted a mob bust. They wanted Joseph Ciccone. He'd be a huge feather in someone's cap. Which meant this case had a wider scope than these two clowns let on. He made a mental note to check on a few things.

"My sudden reappearance in Freedom, right on the heels of Griggs's return, would still raise questions," Alec pointed out. Coincidence only stretched so far.

"Not with the right romantic spin, it wouldn't,"

Ostman said. "We've done our homework. You'll go in right away, before news of Griggs's release is made public. We'll let it slip that you and Miss Morgan have been corresponding on-line for a while. Worked out your differences. Then we'll cement it with rumors of an impending engagement."

Alec almost laughed. No wonder the FBI had been so unsuccessful in planting their own agent. *Homework?* They didn't know jack. "I can tell you right now Keira Morgan won't buy into that one."

Phelps guffawed, then tried to cover with a cough. Ostman shot him a quick look.

Alec didn't miss the exchange. "You've already talked to her, haven't you? And she turned you down. Probably told you where to stick it."

Ostman sighed. "She'll come around."

No, she wouldn't. Not where Alec was concerned. Though they didn't realize it, he was off the hook. "I'll tell you what. You get Keira Morgan to agree up front to hire me on *those* terms, I'll do it." He opened the door, confident he'd heard the last of the subject. "Good-bye, gentlemen."

As soon as Alec left, Ostman turned to the other man and started swearing. "You almost blew it!"

"Sorry." Phelps didn't look apologetic.

"Have you talked with the Morgan woman again?"

Phelps shook his head. "She won't return my calls. And her secretary's a real snot. Want me to fly down and see her in person?"

"No. It'll raise more flags. I'll try her at her home tonight myself," Ostman said.

"So what's this big fucking secret you promised to let me in on?"

For a moment Ostman remained quiet, debating the wisdom of showing his hand. But he needed help to pull this off, help from someone who'd follow orders with a minimum of questions.

He inhaled, blew out a stream of smoke. "You know all that shit about angels looking out for fools? It's true. Besides the cash, that truck was transporting a cache of stolen, rare gold coins, scheduled to be fenced in Miami."

Phelps laughed. "Where the hell did you hear that one? Two million plus a bonus in gold. Right! Bullshit stories always pop up after sensational crimes."

Ostman waited until Phelps quieted before continuing. "We recently busted a guy in New Orleans for running prostitutes on the riverboats. He started talking to me in hopes of cutting a deal. The guy gave the gold to Ciccone to have it fenced in lieu of protection money. But get this: he didn't trust Ciccone to give him credit for the full value, so he had the coins privately appraised and photographed. Gave me a copy of the report."

Phelps nearly fell out of his chair. "Jesus H. Christ! We recover those coins, we can tie Ciccone to money laundering, racketeering. It will be the bust of the century."

Ostman nodded. Possession of stolen property was an easy rap to beat. RICO violations were a different ballgame. "Yeah, but we have to make certain Ciccone gets the gold first."

"I don't follow."

"We have to let Griggs recover the loot and actually turn it over to Ciccone. Then we move in." Ostman exhaled, stubbed out his cigarette. "I figure Ciccone will keep a finger on this personally. So while Alec Dempsey does the grunt work on the inside and follows Griggs, we'll keep an eye on Ciccone. It should be a cakewalk."

"Cakewalk my ass," Phelps winced. "You haven't talked to the Morgan woman yet."

The inside of Ian Griggs's prison cell was dank. He paced the short distance to the calendar he had scratched in the wall, marked an X through another day.

The line from an old Janis Joplin tune rolled through his mind. *Freedom's just another word for nothing left to lose.*

Griggs had nothing left to lose in Freedom. And everything to gain.

He thought over his plan, reviewed the steps. One, two, three.

Money.

Revenge.

Whiskey.

Not necessarily in that order. Five years behind bars had taught him the virtue of patience. Of restraint. Of moderation. And of keeping a few cards up his sleeve.

"Soon, Keira," he rasped to his empty cell. "Soon."

LAUREN BACH loves to write almost as much as she loves to read. A member of Romance Writers of America and Heart of Carolina Romance Writers, Lauren writes contemporary romantic fiction with a definite sensual slant. A Maggie and Emily finalist, Lauren's writing has garnered numerous awards, including the RWA's prestigious Gold.

Her favorite endeavors include being outdoors, traveling, gardening, and spending time with family. Her favorite places include malls, bookstores, and libraries. She laughs a lot and is delightfully curious—which is a nice way of saying she can be loud and nosy. She doesn't like chocolate.

Lauren's love of writing can be traced back to her childhood. One of seven children, she was born in Iowa, but raised in Florida. She currently resides in North Carolina and is busy working on her next book. For an excerpt, visit her Web site at www.LaurenBach.com.